George Gilfillan

Specimens

with memoirs of the less-known British poets - With an introductory essay - Vol. 2

George Gilfillan

Specimens
with memoirs of the less-known British poets - With an introductory essay - Vol. 2

ISBN/EAN: 9783337093297

Printed in Europe, USA, Canada, Australia, Japan

Cover: Foto ©Andreas Hilbeck / pixelio.de

More available books at **www.hansebooks.com**

SPECIMENS

WITH MEMOIRS OF THE

LESS-KNOWN BRITISH POETS.

With an Introductory Essay,

BY THE

REV. GEORGE GILFILLAN.

IN THREE VOLS.

VOL. II.

EDINBURGH: JAMES NICHOL.
LONDON: JAMES NISBET & CO. DUBLIN: W. ROBERTSON.
M.DCCC.LX.

CONTENTS.

CONTENTS.

vi

CONTENTS.

CONTENTS.

SPECIMENS, WITH MEMOIRS,
OF THE LESS-KNOWN BRITISH POETS.

SECOND PERIOD—FROM SPENSER TO DRYDEN.
(CONTINUED.)

WILLIAM HABINGTON.

THIS poet might have been expected to have belonged to the 'Spasmodic school,' judging by his parental antecedents. His father was accused of having a share in Babington's conspiracy, but was released because he was godson to Queen Elizabeth. Soon after, however, he was imprisoned a second time, and condemned to death on the charge of having concealed some of the Gunpowder-plot conspirators; but was pardoned through the interest of Lord Morley. His uncle, however, was less fortunate, suffering death for his complicity with Babington. The poet's mother, the daughter of Lord Morley, was more loyal than her husband or his brother, and is said to have written the celebrated letter to Lord Monteagle, in consequence of which the execution of the Gunpowder-plot was arrested.

Our poet was born at Hindlip, Worcestershire, on the very day of the discovery of the plot, 5th November 1605. The family were Papists, and William was sent to St Omers to be educated. He was pressed to become a Jesuit, but declined. On his return to England, his father became preceptor to the poet. As he grew up, instead of displaying any taste for 'treasons, stratagems, and spoils,' he chose the better part, and lived a private and happy life. He fell in love with Lucia, daughter of William Herbert, the first Lord Powis, and cele-brated her in his long and curious poem entitled ' Castara.' This lady he afterwards married, and from her society appears to have derived much happiness. In 1634, he published 'Castara.' He also, at different times, produced 'The Queen of Arragon,' a tragedy; a History of Edward IV.; and 'Observations upon History.' He died in 1654, (not as Southey, by a strange oversight, says, 'when he had just completed his fortieth year,') forty-nine years of age, and was buried in the family vault at Hindlip.

'Castara' is not a consecutive poem, but consists of a great variety of small pieces, in all sorts of style and rhythm, and of all varieties of merit; many of them addressed to his mistress under the name of Castara, and many to his friends; with reflective poems, elegies, and panegyrics, intermingled with verses sacred to love. Habington is distinguished by purity of tone if not of taste. He has many conceits, but no obscenities. His love is as holy as it is ardent. He has, besides, a vein of sentiment which sometimes approaches the moral sublime. To prove this, in addition to the ' Selections ' below, we copy some verses entitled—

'NOX NOCTI INDICAT SCIENTIAM.'—*David.*

When I survey the bright
  Celestial sphere,
So rich with jewels hung, that Night
Doth like an Ethiop bride appear,

My soul her wings doth spread,
  And heavenward flies, ·
The Almighty's mysteries to read
In the large volume of the skies;

For the bright firmament
  Shoots forth no flame
So silent, but is eloquent
In speaking the Creator's name.

No unregarded star
  Contracts its light
Into so small a character,
Removed far from our human sight,

But if we steadfast look,
        We shall discern
In it, as in some holy book,
How man may heavenly knowledge learn.

It tells the conqueror
        That far-stretch'd power,
Which his proud dangers traffic for,
Is but the triumph of an hour;

That, from the furthest North,
        Some nation may,
Yet undiscover'd, issue forth,
And o'er his new-got conquest sway,—

Some nation, yet shut in
        With hills of ice,
May be let out to scourge his sin
Till they shall equal him in vice;

And then they likewise shall
        Their ruin brave;
For, as yourselves, your empires fall,
And every kingdom hath a grave.

Thus those celestial fires,
        Though seeming mute,
The fallacy of our desires,
And all the pride of life, confute;

For they have watch'd since first
        The world had birth,
And found sin in itself accurst,
And nothing permanent on earth.

There is something to us particularly interesting in the history of this poet. Even as it is pleasant to see the sides of a volcano covered with verdure, and its mouth filled with flowers, so we like to find the fierce elements, which were inherited by Habington from his fathers, softened and subdued in him,—the blood of the conspirator mellowed into that of the gentle bard, who derived all his inspiration from a pure love and a mild and thoughtful religion.

EPISTLE ADDRESSED TO THE HONOURABLE W. E.

He who is good is happy.   Let the loud
Artillery of heaven break through a cloud,
And dart its thunder at him, he 'll remain
Unmoved, and nobler comfort entertain,
In welcoming the approach of death, than Vice
E'er found in her fictitious paradise.
Time mocks our youth, and (while we number past
Delights, and raise our appetite to taste
Ensuing) brings us to unflatter'd age,
Where we are left to satisfy the rage
Of threat'ning death : pomp, beauty, wealth, and all
Our friendships, shrinking from the funeral.
The thought of this begets that brave disdain
With which thou view'st the world, and makes those vain
Treasures of fancy, serious fools so court,
And sweat to purchase, thy contempt or sport.
What should we covet here ?   Why interpose
A cloud 'twixt us and heaven?   Kind Nature chose
Man's soul the exchequer where to hoard her wealth,
And lodge all her rich secrets; but by the stealth
Of her own vanity, we 're left so poor,
The creature merely sensual knows more.
The learned halcyon, by her wisdom, finds
A gentle season, when the seas and winds
Are silenced by a calm, and then brings forth
The happy miracle of her rare birth,
Leaving with wonder all our arts possess'd,
That view the architecture of her nest.
Pride raiseth us 'bove justice.   We bestow
Increase of knowledge on old minds, which grow
By age to dotage ; while the sensitive
Part of the world in its first strength doth live.

4

Folly! what dost thou in thy power contain
Deserves our study?   Merchants plough the main
And bring home th' Indies, yet aspire to more,
By avarice in the possession poor.
And yet that idol wealth we all admit ·
Into the soul's great temple; busy wit
Invents new orgies, fancy frames new rites
To shew its superstition; anxious nights
Are watch'd to win its favour : while the beast
Content with nature's courtesy doth rest.
Let man then boast no more a soul, since he
Hath lost that great prerogative.   But thee,
Whom fortune hath exempted from the herd
Of vulgar men, whom virtue hath preferr'd
Far higher than thy birth, I must commend,
Rich in the purchase of so sweet a friend.
And though my fate conducts me to the shade
Of humble quiet, my ambition paid
With safe content, while a pure virgin fame
Doth raise me trophies in Castara's name ;
No thought of glory swelling me above
The hope of being famed for virtuous love ;
Yet wish I thee, guided by the better stars,
To purchase unsafe honour in the wars,
Or envied smiles at court; for thy great race,
And merits, well may challenge the highest place.
Yet know, what busy path soe'er you tread
To greatness, you must sleep among the dead.

TO HIS NOBLEST FRIEND, J. C., ESQ.

I hate the country's dirt and manners, yet
I love the silence; I embrace the wit
And courtship, flowing here in a full tide,
But loathe the expense, the vanity, and pride.

No place each way is happy.   Here I hold
Commerce with some, who to my care unfold
(After a due oath minister'd) the height
And greatness of each star shines in the state,
The brightness, the eclipse, the influence.
With others I commune, who tell me whence
The torrent doth of foreign discord flow;
Relate each skirmish, battle, overthrow,
Soon as they happen; and by rote can tell
Those German towns, even puzzle me to spell.
The cross or prosperous fate of princes they
Ascribe to rashness, cunning, or delay;
And on each action comment, with more skill
Than upon Livy did old Machiavel.
O busy folly! why do I my brain
Perplex with the dull policies of Spain,
Or quick designs of France?   Why not repair
To the pure innocence o' the country air,
And neighbour thee, dear friend?   Who so dost give
Thy thoughts to worth and virtue, that to live
Blest, is to trace thy ways.   There might not we
Arm against passion with philosophy;
And, by the aid of leisure, so control
Whate'er is earth in us, to grow all soul?
Knowledge doth ignorance engender, when
We study mysteries of other men,
And foreign plots.   Do but in thy own shad
(Thy head upon some flow'ry pillow laid,
Kind Nature's housewifery,) contemplate all
His stratagems, who labours to enthrall
The world to his great master, and you 'll find
Ambition mocks itself, and grasps the wind.
Not conquest makes us great.   Blood is too dear
A price for glory.   Honour doth appear

6

To statesmen like a vision in the night;
And, juggler-like, works o' the deluded sight.
The unbusied only wise: for no respect
Endangers them to error; they affect
Truth in her naked beauty, and behold
Man with an equal eye, not bright in gold,
Or tall in little; so much him they weigh
As virtue raiseth him above his clay.
Thus let us value things: and since we find
Time bend us toward death, let 's in our mind
Create new youth, and arm against the rude
Assaults of age; that no dull solitude
O' the country dead our thoughts, nor busy care
O' the town make us to think, where now we are,
And whither we are bound.   Time ne'er forgot
His journey, though his steps we number'd not.

A DESCRIPTION OF CASTARA.

1 Like the violet which, alone,
      Prospers in some happy shade,
  My Castara lives unknown,
      To no looser's eye betray'd,
        For she 's to herself untrue,
        Who delights i' the public view.

2 Such is her beauty, as no arts
      Have enrich'd with borrow'd grace;
  Her high birth no pride imparts,
      For she blushes in her place.
        Folly boasts a glorious blood,
        She is noblest, being good.

3 Cautious, she knew never yet
    What a wanton courtship meant;
Nor speaks loud, to boast her wit;
    In her silence eloquent:
        Of herself survey she takes,
        But 'tween men no difference makes.

4 She obeys with speedy will
    Her grave parents' wise commands;
And so innocent, that ill
    She nor acts, nor understands:
        Women's feet run still astray,
        If once to ill they know the way.

5 She sails by that rock, the court,
    Where oft Honour splits her mast:
And retiredness thinks the port
    Where her fame may anchor cast:
        Virtue safely cannot sit,
        Where vice is enthroned for wit.

6 She holds that day's pleasure best,
    Where sin waits not on delight;
Without mask, or ball, or feast,
    Sweetly spends a winter's night:
        O'er that darkness, whence is thrust
        Prayer and sleep, oft governs lust.

7 She her throne makes reason climb;
    While wild passions captive lie:
And, each article of time,
    Her pure thoughts to heaven fly:
        All her vows religious be,
        And her love she vows to me.

8

JOSEPH HALL, BISHOP OF NORWICH.

THIS distinguished man must not be confounded with John Hall, of whom all we know is, that he was born at Durham in 1627,—that he was educated at Cambridge, where he published a volume of poems,—that he practised at the bar, and that he died in 1656, in his twenty-ninth year. One specimen of John's verses we shall quote:—

THE MORNING STAR.

> Still herald of the morn: whose ray
> Being page and usher to the day,
> Doth mourn behind the sun, before him play;
> Who sett'st a golden signal ere
> The dark retire, the lark appear;
> The early cocks cry comfort, screech-owls fear;
> Who wink'st while lovers plight their troth,
> Then falls asleep, while they are loth
> To part without a more engaging oath:
> > Steal in a message to the eyes
> > Of Julia; tell her that she lies
> Too long; thy lord, the Sun, will quickly rise.
> Yet it is midnight still with me;
> Nay, worse, unless that kinder she
> Smile day, and in my zenith seated be,
> I needs a calenture must shun,
> And, like an Ethiopian, hate my sun.

John's more celebrated namesake, Joseph, was born at Bristowe Park, parish of Ashby-de-la-Zouch, Leicestershire, in 1574. He studied and took orders at Cambridge. He acted for some time as master of the school of Tiverton, in Devonshire. It is said that the accidental preaching of a sermon before Prince Henry first attracted attention to this eminent divine. Promotion followed with a sure and steady course. He was chosen to accompany King James to Scotland as one of his chaplains, and subsequently attended the famous Synod of Dort as a representative of the English Church. He had before this, while quite a young man, (in 1597,) published, under the title of ' Virgidemiarum,' his Satires. In the year 1600 he produced a satirical fiction, entitled, ' Mundus alter et idem;' in which, while pretending to describe a certain *terra australis incognita*, he hits hard at the existent evils of the actual world. Hall was subsequently created Bishop of Exeter, where he exposed himself to obloquy by his mildness to the Puritans. ' Had,' Campbell justly remarked, ' such conduct been, at this critical period, pursued by the High Churchmen in general, the history of a bloody age might have been changed into that of peace ; but the violence of Laud prevailed over the milder counsels of a Hall, an Usher, and a Corbet.' Yet Hall was a zealous Episcopalian, and defended that form of government in a variety of pamphlets. In the course of this controversy he came in collision with the mighty Milton himself, who, unable to deny the ability and learning of his opponent, tried to cover him with a deluge of derision.

Besides these pamphlets, the Bishop produced a number of Epistles in prose, of Sermons, of Paraphrases, and a remarkable series of ' Occasional Meditations,' which became soon, and continue to be, popular.

Hall, who had in his early days struggled hard with narrow circumstances and neglect, seemed to reach the climax of prosperity when he was, in 1641, created by the King Bishop of Norwich. But having, soon after, unfortunately added his name to the Protest of the twelve prelates against the authority of any laws which should be passed during their compulsory absence from Parliament, he was thrown into the Tower, and subsequently threatened with sequestration. After enduring great privations, he at last was permitted to retire to Higham, near Norwich, where, reduced to a very miserable allowance, he continued to labour as a pastor, with unwearied assiduity, till, in 1656, death closed his eyes, at the advanced age of eighty-two.

Bishop Hall, if not fully competent to mate with Milton, was nevertheless a giant, conspicuous even in an age when giants were rife. He has been called the Christian Seneca, from the pith and clear sententiousness of his prose style. His ' Meditations,' ranging over almost the whole compass of Scripture, as well as an incredible variety of ordinary topics, are distinguished by their fertile fancy, their glowing language, and by thought which, if seldom profound, is never commonplace, and seems

10

always the spontaneous and easy outcome of the author's mind. In no form of composition does excellence depend more on spontaneity than in the meditation. The ruin of such writers as Hervey, and, to some extent, Boyle, has been, that they seem to have set themselves elaborately and convulsively to extract sentiment out of every object which met their eye. They seem to say, 'We will, and we must meditate, whether the objects be interesting or not, and whether our own moods be propitious to the exercise, or the reverse.' Hence have come exaggeration, extravagance, and that shape of the ridiculous which mimics the sublime, and has been so admirably exposed in Swift's 'Meditation on a Broomstick.' Hall's method is, in general, the opposite of this. The objects on which he muses seem to have sought him, and not he them. He surrounds himself with his thoughts unconsciously, as one gathers burs and other herbage about him by the mere act of walking in the woods. Sometimes, indeed, he is quaint and fantastic, as in his meditation

'UPON THE SIGHT OF TWO SNAILS.'

'There is much variety even in creatures of the same kind. See these two snails: one hath a house, the other wants it; yet both are snails, and it is a question whether case is the better; that which hath a house hath more shelter, but that which wants it hath more freedom; the privilege of that cover is but a burden—you see if it hath but a stone to climb over with what stress it draws up that artificial load, and if the passage proves strait finds no entrance, whereas the empty snail makes no difference of way. Surely it is always an ease and sometimes a happiness to have nothing. No man is so worthy of envy as he that can be cheerful in want.'

In a very different style he discourses

'UPON HEARING OF MUSIC BY NIGHT.'

'How sweetly doth this music sound in this dead season! In the day-time it would not, it could not so much affect the ear. All harmonious sounds are advanced by a silent darkness: thus it is with the glad tidings of salvation. The gospel never sounds so sweet as in the night of preservation or of our own private affliction—it is ever the same, the difference is in our disposition to receive it. O God, whose praise it is to give songs in the night, make my prosperity conscionable and my crosses cheerful!'

Hall fulfilled one test of lofty genius: he was in several

11

departments an originator. He first gave an example of epistolary composition in prose,—an example the imitation of which has produced many of the most interesting, instructive, and beautiful writings in the language. He is our first popular author of Meditations and Contemplations, and a large school has followed in his path—too often, in truth, *passibus iniquis.* And he is unquestionably the father of British satire. It is remarkable that all his satires were written in youth. Too often the satirical spirit grows in authors with the advance of life; and it is a pitiful sight, that of those who have passed the meridian of years and reputation, grinning back in helpless mockery and toothless laughter upon the brilliant way they have traversed, but to which they can return no more. Hall, on the other hand, exhausted long ere he was thirty the sarcastic material that was in him; and during the rest of his career, wielded his powers with as much lenity as strength.

Perhaps no satirist had a more thorough conception than our author of what is the real mission of satire in the moral history of mankind;—*that* is, to shew vice its own image—to scourge impudent imposture—to expose hypocrisy—to laugh down solemn quackery of every kind—to create blushes on brazen brows and fears of scorn in hollow hearts—to make iniquity, as ashamed, hide its face—to apply caustic, nay cautery, to the sores of society—and to destroy sin by shewing both the ridicule which attaches to its progress and the wretched consequences which are its end. But various causes prevented him from fully realising his own ideal, and thus becoming the best as well as the first of our satirical poets. His style—imitated from Persius and Juvenal—is too elliptical, and it becomes true of him as well as of Persius that his points are often sheathed through the remoteness of his allusions and the perplexity of his diction. He is very recondite in his images, and you are sometimes reminded of one storming in English at a Hindoo—it is pointless fury, boltless thunder. At other times the stream of his satiric vein flows on with a blended clearness and energy, which has commanded the warm encomium of Campbell, and which prompted the diligent study of Pope. There is more courage required in attacking the follies than the vices of an age, and Hall shews

12

a peculiar daring when he derides the vulgar forms of astrology and alchymy which were then prevalent, and the wretched fustian which infected the language both of literature and the stage.

Whatever be the merits or defects of Hall's satires, the world is indebted to him as the founder of a school which were itself sufficient to cover British literature with glory, and which, in the course of ages, has included such writers as Samuel Butler, with his keen sense of the grotesque and ridiculous—his wit, unequalled in its abundance and point—his vast assortment of ludicrous fancies and language—and his form of versification, seemingly shaped by the Genius of Satire for his own purposes, and resembling heroic rhyme broken off in the middle by shouts of laughter;—Dryden, with the ease, the *animus*, and the masterly force of his satirical dissections—the vein of humour which is stealthily visible at times in the intervals of his wrathful mood—and the occasional passing and profound touches, worthy of Juvenal, and reminding one of the fires of Egypt, which ran along the ground, scorching all things while they pursued their unabated speed;—the spirit of satire, strong as death, and cruel as the grave, which became incarnate in Swift;— Pope, with his minute and microscopic vision of human infirmities, his polish, delicate strokes, damning hints, and annihilating whispers, where 'more is meant than meets the ear;'—Johnson, with his crushing contempt and sacrificial dignity of scorn;— Cowper, with the tenderness of a lover combined in his verse with the terrible indignation of an ancient prophet;—Wolcot, with his infinite fund of coarse wit and humour;—Burns, with that strange mixture of jaw and genius—the spirit of a *caird* with that of a poet—which marked all his satirical pieces; —Crabbe, with his caustic vein and sternly-literal descriptions, behind which are seen, half-skulking from view, kindness, pity, and love;—Byron, with the clever Billingsgate of his earlier, and the more than Swiftian ferocity of his later satires;—and Moore, with the smartness, sparkle, tiny splendour, and minikin speed of his witty shafts. In comparison with even these masters of the art, the good Bishop does not dwindle; and he challenges precedence over most of them in the purpose, tact, and good sense which blend with the whole of his satiric poetry.

13

SATIRE I.

Time was, and that was term'd the time of gold,
When world and time were young, that now are old,
(When quiet Saturn sway'd the mace of lead,
And pride was yet unborn, and yet unbred;)
Time was, that whiles the autumn fall did last,
Our hungry sires gaped for the falling mast
    Of the Dodonian oaks;
Could no unhusked acorn leave the tree,
But there was challenge made whose it might be;
And if some nice and liquorous appetite
Desired more dainty dish of rare delight,
They scaled the stored crab with clasped knee,
Till they had sated their delicious eye:
Or search'd the hopeful thicks of hedgy rows,
For briary berries, or haws, or sourer sloes:
Or when they meant to fare the fin'st of all,
They lick'd oak-leaves besprint with honey fall.
As for the thrice three-angled beech nutshell,
Or chestnut's armed husk, and hide kernel,
No squire durst touch, the law would not afford,
Kept for the court, and for the king's own board.
Their royal plate was clay, or wood, or stone;
The vulgar, save his hand, else he had none.
Their only cellar was the neighbour brook:
None did for better care, for better look.
Was then no plaining of the brewer's 'scape,
Nor greedy vintner mix'd the stained grape.
The king's pavilion was the grassy green,
Under safe shelter of the shady treen.
Under each bank men laid their limbs along,
Not wishing any ease, not fearing wrong:
Clad with their own, as they were made of old,

14

Not fearing shame, not feeling any cold.
But when by Ceres' huswifery and pain,
Men learn'd to bury the reviving grain,
And father Janus taught the new-found vine
Rise on the elm, with many a friendly twine:
And base desire bade men to delven low,
For needless metals, then 'gan mischief grow.
Then farewell, fairest age, the world's best days,
Thriving in all as it in age decays.
Then crept in pride, and peevish covetise,
And men grew greedy, discordous, and nice.
Now man, that erst hail-fellow was with beast,
Wox on to ween himself a god at least.
Nor aery fowl can take so high a flight,
Though she her daring wings in clouds have dight;
Nor fish can dive so deep in yielding sea,
Though Thetis' self should swear her safëty;
Nor fearful beast can dig his cave so low,
As could he further than earth's centre go;
As that the air, the earth, or ocean,
Should shield them from the gorge of greedy man.
Hath utmost Ind ought better than his own?
Then utmost Ind is near, and rife to gone,
O nature! was the world ordain'd for nought
But fill man's maw, and feed man's idle thought?
Thy grandsire's words savour'd of thrifty leeks,
Or manly garlic; but thy furnace reeks
Hot steams of wine; and can aloof descry
The drunken draughts of sweet autumnitie.
They naked went; or clad in ruder hide,
Or home-spun russet, void of foreign pride:
But thou canst mask in garish gauderie,
To suit a fool's far-fetched livery.
A French head join'd to neck Italian:

Thy thighs from Germany, and breast from Spain:
An Englishman in none, a fool in all:
Many in one, and one in several.
Then men were men; but now the greater part
Beasts are in life, and women are in heart.
Good Saturn self, that homely emperor,
In proudest pomp was not so clad of yore,
As is the under-groom of the ostlery,
Husbanding it in work-day yeomanry.
Lo! the long date of those expired days,
Which the inspired Merlin's word foresays;
When dunghill peasants shall be dight as kings,
Then one confusion another brings:
Then farewell, fairest age, the world's best days,
Thriving in ill, as it in age decays.

SATIRE VII.

Seest thou how gaily my young master goes,
Vaunting himself upon his rising toes;
And pranks his hand upon his dagger's side,
And picks his glutted teeth since late noontide?
'Tis Ruffio: Trow'st thou where he dined to-day?
In sooth I saw him sit with Duke Humphray.
Many good welcomes, and much gratis cheer,
Keeps he for every straggling cavalier,
And open house, haunted with great resort;
Long service mix'd with musical disport.
Many fair younker with a feather'd crest,
Chooses much rather be his shot-free guest,
To fare so freely with so little cost,
Than stake his twelvepence to a meaner host.
Hadst thou not told me, I should surely say
He touch'd no meat of all this livelong day.

16

For sure methought, yet that was but a guess,
His eyes seem'd sunk for very hollowness;
But could he have (as I did it mistake)
So little in his purse, so much upon his back?
So nothing in his maw? yet seemeth by his belt,
That his gaunt gut no too much stuffing felt.
Seest thou how side it hangs beneath his hip?
Hunger and heavy iron makes girdles slip;
Yet for all that, how stiffly struts he by,
All trapped in the new-found bravery.
The nuns of new-won Calais his bonnet lent,
In lieu of their so kind a conquerment.
What needed he fetch that from furthest Spain.
His grandam could have lent with lesser pain?
Though he perhaps ne'er pass'd the English shore,
Yet fain would counted be a conqueror.
His hair, French-like, stares on his frighted head,
One lock, Amazon-like, dishevelled,
As if he meant to wear a native cord,
If chance his fates should him that bane afford.
All British bare upon the bristled skin,
Close notched is his beard both lip and chin;
His linen collar labyrinthian set,
Whose thousand double turnings never met:
His sleeves half hid with elbow pinionings,
As if he meant to fly with linen wings.
But when I look, and cast mine eyes below,
What monster meets mine eyes in human show?
So slender waist with such an abbot's loin,
Did never sober nature sure conjoin,
Lik'st a strawn scarecrow in the new-sown field,
Rear'd on some stick, the tender corn to shield;
Or if that semblance suit not every deal,
Like a broad shake-fork with a slender steel.

Despised nature, suit them once aright,
Their body to their coat, both now misdight.
Their body to their clothes might shapen be,
That nill their clothës shape to their body.
Meanwhile I wonder at so proud a back,
Whiles the empty guts loud rumblen for long lack:
The belly envieth the back's bright glee,
And murmurs at such inequality.
The back appears unto the partial eyne,
The plaintive belly pleads they bribed been:
And he, for want of better advocate,
Doth to the ear his injury relate.
The back, insulting o'er the belly's need,
Says, Thou thyself, I others' eyes must feed.
The maw, the guts, all inward parts complain
The back's great pride, and their own secret pain.
Ye witless gallants, I beshrew your hearts,
That sets such discord 'twixt agreeing parts,
Which never can be set at onement more,
Until the maw's wide mouth be stopt with store.

RICHARD LOVELACE.

THIS unlucky cavalier and bard was born in 1618. He was
the son of Sir William Lovelace, of Woolwich, in Kent. He
was educated some say at Oxford, and others at Cambridge—
took a master's degree, and was afterwards presented at Court.
Anthony Wood thus describes his personal appearance at the
age of sixteen:—' He was the most amiable and beautiful person that eye ever beheld,—a person also of innate modesty,
virtue, and courtly deportment, which made him then, but
especially after when he retired to the great city, much admired
and adored by the fair sex.' Soon after this, he was chosen by
the county of Kent to deliver a petition from the inhabitants to

18

the House of Commons, praying them to restore the King to his rights, and to settle the government. Such offence was given by this to the Long Parliament, that Lovelace was thrown into prison, and only liberated on heavy bail. His paternal estate, which amounted to £500 a-year, was soon exhausted in his efforts to promote the royal cause. In 1646, he formed a regiment for the service of the King of France, became its colonel, and was wounded at Dunkirk. Ere leaving England, he had formed a strong attachment to a Miss Lucy Sacheverell, and had written much poetry in her praise, designating her as *Lux-Casta*. Unfortunately, hearing a report that Lovelace had died at Dunkirk of his wounds, she married another, so that, on his return home in 1648, he met a deep disappointment; and to complete his misery, the ruling powers cast him again into prison, where he lay till the death of Charles. Like some other men of genius, he beguiled his confinement by literary employment; and in 1649, he published a book under the title of ' Lucasta,' consisting of odes, sonnets, songs, and miscellaneous poems, most of which had been previously composed. After the execution of the King, he was liberated; but his funds were exhausted, his heart broken, and his constitution probably injured. He gradually sunk; and Wood says that he became very poor in body and purse, was the object of charity, 'went in ragged clothes, and mostly lodged in obscure and dirty places.' Alas for the Adonis of sixteen, the beloved of Lucasta, and the envied of all! Some have doubted these stories about his extreme poverty; and one of his biographers asserts, that his daughter and sole heir (but who, pray, was his wife and her mother?) married the son of Lord Chief-Justice Coke, and brought to her husband the estates of her father at Kingsdown, in Kent. Aubrey, however, corroborates the statements of Wood; and, at all events, Lovelace seems to have died, in 1658, in a wretched alley near Shoe Lane.

There is not much to be said about his poetry. It may be compared to his person—beautiful, but dressed in a stiff mode. We do not, in every point, homologate the opinions of Prynne, as to the ' unloveliness of love-locks;' but we do certainly look with a mixture of contempt and pity on the self-imposed tram-

mels of affectation in style and manner which bound many of
the poets of that period. The wits of Charles II. were more
disgustingly licentious; but their very carelessness saved them
from the conceits of their predecessors; and, while lowering the
tone of morality, they raised unwittingly the standard of taste.
Some of the songs of Lovelace, however, such as 'To Althea,
from Prison,' are exquisitely simple, as well as pure. Sir
Egerton Brydges has found out that Byron, in one of his be-
praised paradoxical beauties, either copied, or coincided with,
our poet. In the 'Bride of Abydos' he says of Zuleika—

'The mind, the *music* breathing from her face.'

Lovelace had, long before, in the song of 'Orpheus Mourning
for his Wife,' employed the words—

> ' Oh, could you view the melody
>   Of every grace,
> And *music of her face*,
>   You'd drop a tear ;
> Seeing more harmony
>   In her bright eye
> Than now you hear.'

While many have praised, others have called this idea nonsense; although, if we are permitted to speak of the harmony
of the tones of a cloud, why not of the harmony produced by
the consenting lines of a countenance, where every grace melts
into another, and the various features and expressions fluctuate
into a fine whole? Whatever, whether it be the beauty of the
human face, or the quiet lustre of statuary, or the mild glory of
moonlight, gives the effects of music, and, like that divine art,

'Pours on mortals a beautiful disdain,'

may surely become music's metaphor and poetic analogy.

SONG.

TO ALTHEA, FROM PRISON.

1 When Love, with unconfined wings,
      Hovers within my gates,
   And my divine Althea brings
      To whisper at my grates ;

When I lie tangled in her hair,
    And fetter'd to her eye,
The birds, that wanton in the air,
    Know no such liberty.

2 When flowing cups run swiftly round
    With no allaying Thames,
Our careless heads with roses bound,
    Our hearts with loyal flames ;
When thirsty grief in wine we steep,
    When healths and draughts go free,
Fishes, that tipple in the deep,
    Know no such liberty.

3 When, like committed linnets, I
    With shriller throat shall sing
The sweetness, mercy, majesty,
    And glories of my king ;*
When I shall voice aloud how good
    He is, how great should be,
Enlarged winds, that curl the flood,
    Know no such liberty.

4 Stone walls do not a prison make,
    Nor iron bars a cage ;
Minds innocent and quiet take
    That for an hermitage.
If I have freedom in my love,
    And in my soul am free,
Angels alone, that soar above,
    Enjoy such liberty.

* Charles I., in whose cause Lovelace was then in prison.

SONG.

1 Amarantha, sweet and fair,
  Forbear to braid that shining hair;
  As my curious hand or eye,
  Hovering round thee, let it fly:

2 Let it fly as unconfined
  As its ravisher, the wind,
  Who has left his darling east,
  To wanton o'er this spicy nest.

3 Every tress must be confess'd
  But neatly tangled at the best,
  Like a clew of golden thread
  Most excellently ravelled:

4 Do not then wind up that light
  In ribands, and o'ercloud the night;
  Like the sun in his early ray,
  But shake your head and scatter day.

A LOOSE SARABAND.

1 Ah me! the little tyrant thief,
    As once my heart was playing,
  He snatch'd it up, and flew away,
    Laughing at all my praying.

2 Proud of his purchase, he surveys,
    And curiously sounds it;
  And though he sees it full of wounds,
    Cruel, still on he wounds it.

3 And now this heart is all his sport,
   Which as a ball he boundeth,
From hand to hand, from breast to lip,
   And all its rest confoundeth.

4 Then as a top he sets it up,
   And pitifully whips it ;
Sometimes he clothes it gay and fine,
   Then straight again he strips it.

5 He cover'd it with false belief,
   Which gloriously show'd it ;
And for a morning cushionet
   On 's mother he bestow'd it.

6 Each day with her small brazen stings
   A thousand times she raced it ;
But then at night, bright with her gems,
   Once near her breast she placed it.

7 Then warm it 'gan to throb and bleed,
   She knew that smart, and grieved ;
At length this poor condemned heart,
   With these rich drugs reprieved.

8 She wash'd the wound with a fresh tear,
   Which my Lucasta dropped ;
And in the sleeve silk of her hair
   'Twas hard bound up and wrapped.

9 She probed it with her constancy,
   And found no rancour nigh it ;
Only the anger of her eye
   Had wrought some proud flesh nigh it.

10 Then press'd she hard in every vein,
   Which from her kisses thrilled,
   And with the balm heal'd all its pain
   That from her hand distilled.

11 But yet this heart avoids me still,
   Will not by me be owned;
   But, fled to its physician's breast,
   There proudly sits enthroned.

ROBERT HERRICK.

THIS poet—a bird with tropical plumage, and norland sweetness of song—was born in Cheapside, London, in 1591. His father was an eminent goldsmith. Herrick was sent to Cambridge; and having entered into holy orders, and being patronised by the Earl of Exeter, he was, in 1629, presented by Charles I. to the vicarage of Dean Prior, in Devonshire. Here he resided for twenty years, till ejected by the civil war. He seems all this time to have felt little relish either for his profession or parishioners. In the former, the cast of his poems shews that he must have been 'detained before the Lord;' and the latter he describes as a 'wild, amphibious race,' rude almost as 'salvages,' and 'churlish as the seas.' When he quitted his charge, he became an author at the mature age of fifty-six—publishing first, in 1647, his 'Noble Numbers; or, Pious Pieces;' and next, in 1648, his 'Hesperides; or, Works both Human and Divine of Robert Herrick, Esq.'—his ministerial prefix being now laid aside. Some of these poems were sufficiently unclerical—being wild and licentious in cast—although he himself alleges that his life was, sexually at least, blameless. Till the Restoration he lived in Westminster, supported by the rich among the Royalists, and keeping company with the popular dramatists and poets. It would seem that he had been in the habit of visiting London previously, while still acting as a clergyman, and had become a boon companion of Ben Jonson. Hence his well-known lines—

<blockquote>
'Ah, Ben !
Say how or when
Shall we, thy guests,
Meet at those lyric feasts,
Made at the " Sun,"
The " Dog," the " Triple Tun,"
Where we such clusters had
As made us nobly wild, not mad ?
And yet each verse of thine
Outdid the meat, outdid the frolic wine.
My Ben !
Or come again,
Or send to us
Thy wit's great overplus.
But teach us yet
Wisely to husband it ;
Lest we that talent spend,
And having once brought to an end
That precious stock, the store
Of such a wit, the world should have no more.'
</blockquote>

With the Restoration, fortune began again to smile on our poet. He was replaced in his old charge, and seems to have spent the rest of his life quietly in the country, enjoying the fresh air and the old English sports—'repenting at leisure moments,' as Shakspeare has it, of the early pruriencies of his muse ; or, as the same immortal bard says of Falstaff, 'patching up his old body' for a better place. The date of his death is not exactly ascertained ; but he seems to have got considerably to the shady side of seventy years of age.

Herrick's poetry was for a long time little known, till worthy Nathan Drake, in his ' Literary Hours,' performed to him, as to some others, the part of a friendly resurrectionist. He may be called the English Anacreon, and resembles the Greek poet, not only in graceful, lively, and voluptuous elegance and richness, but also in that deeper sentiment which often underlies the lighter surface of his verse. It is a great mistake to suppose that Anacreon was a mere contented sensualist and shallow songster of love and wine. Some of his odes shew that, if he yielded to the destiny of being a Cicada, singing amidst the vines of Bacchus, it was despair—the despair produced by a degraded age and a bad religion—which reduced him to the necessity. He was by nature an eagle; but he was an eagle in a sky where there was no sun. The cry of a noble being, placed in the most untoward circumstances, is here and there heard in his verses, and reminds you of the voice of one of the transmuted victims of Circe, or of Ariel from that cloven pine, where he

'howl'd away twelve winters.'

Herrick might be by constitution a voluptuary,—and he has unquestionably degraded his genius in not a few of his rhymes, —but in him, as well as in Anacreon, Horace, and Burns, there lay a better and a higher nature, which the critics have ignored, because it has not found a frequent or full utterance in his poetry. In proof that our author possessed profound sentiment, mingling and sometimes half-lost in the loose, luxuriant leafage of his imagery, we need only refer our readers to his ' Blossoms ' and his ' Daffodils.' Besides gaiety and gracefulness, his verse is exceedingly musical—his lines not only move but dance.

SONG.

1 Gather the rose-buds, while ye may,
    Old Time is still a-flying ;
And this same flower that smiles to-day
    To-morrow will be dying.

2 The glorious lamp of heaven, the Sun,
    The higher he 's a-getting,
The sooner will his race be run,
    And nearer he 's to setting.

3 The age is best which is the first,
    When youth and blood are warmer ;
But being spent, the worse and worst
    Times, still succeed the former.

4 Then be not coy, but use your time,
    And, whilst ye may, go marry;
For having lost but once your prime,
    You may for ever tarry.

CHERRY-RIPE.

Cherry-ripe, ripe, ripe, I cry;
Full and fair ones; come, and buy!
If so be you ask me where
They do grow? I answer, there,
Where my Julia's lips do smile;
There's the land or cherry isle,
Whose plantations fully show,
All the year, where cherries grow.

THE KISS: A DIALOGUE.

1. Among thy fancies, tell me this:
    What is the thing we call a kiss?—
2. I shall resolve ye what it is:

    It is a creature, born and bred
    Between the lips, all cherry red;
    By love and warm desires 'tis fed;
Chor.—And makes more soft the bridal bed:

2. It is an active flame, that flies
    First to the babies of the eyes,
    And charms them there with lullabies;
Chor.—And stills the bride too when she cries:

2. Then to the chin, the cheek, the ear,
    It frisks and flies; now here, now there;
    'Tis now far off, and then 'tis near;
Chor.—And here, and there, and everywhere.

1. Has it a speaking virtue ?—2. Yes.
1. How speaks it, say ?—2. Do you but this,
　　Part your join'd lips, then speaks your kiss;
Chor.—And this love's sweetest language is.

1. Has it a body ?—2. Aye, and wings,
　　With thousand rare encolourings;
　　And, as it flies, it gently sings,
Chor.—Love honey yields, but never stings.

TO DAFFODILS.

1 Fair daffodils, we weep to see
　　You haste away so soon;
As yet the early-rising sun
　　Has not attain'd his noon:
　　　　Stay, stay
　　Until the hast'ning day
　　　　Has run
　　But to the even-song;
And, having pray'd together, we
　　Will go with you along!

2 We have short time to stay, as you;
　　We have as short a spring,
As quick a growth to meet decay,
　　As you, or anything:
　　　　We die,
　　As your hours do; and dry
　　　　Away
　　Like to the summer's rain,
Or as the pearls of morning dew
　　Ne'er to be found again.

TO PRIMROSES.

1 Why do ye weep, sweet babes?   Can tears
        Speak grief in you,
        Who are but born
        Just as the modest morn
        Teem'd her refreshing dew?
    Alas! you have not known that shower
        That mars a flower;
        Nor felt the unkind
        Breath of a blasting wind;
        Nor are ye worn with years;
        Or warp'd, as we,
        Who think it strange to see
    Such pretty flowers, like to orphans young,
    To speak by tears before ye have a tongue.

2 Speak, whimpering younglings; and make known
        The reason why
        Ye droop and weep.
        Is it for want of sleep,
        Or childish lullaby?
    Or that ye have not seen as yet
        The violet?
        Or brought a kiss
        From that sweetheart to this?
        No, no; this sorrow shown
        By your tears shed,
        Would have this lecture read,
    'That things of greatest, so of meanest worth,
    Conceived with grief are, and with tears brought
        forth.'

TO BLOSSOMS.

1 Fair pledges of a fruitful tree,
        Why do ye fall so fast?
        Your date is not so past,
But you may stay yet here awhile
        To blush and gently smile
                And go at last.

2 What, were ye born to be
        An hour or half's delight,
        And so to bid good night?
'Tis pity Nature brought ye forth
        Merely to show your worth,
                And lose you quite.

3 But you are lovely leaves, where we
        May read how soon things have
        Their end, though ne'er so brave:
And after they have shown their pride,
        Like you, awhile, they glide
                Into the grave.

OBERON'S PALACE.

                Thus to a grove
Sometimes devoted unto love,
Tinsell'd with twilight, he and they,
Led by the shine of snails, a way
Beat with their num'rous feet, which by
Many a neat perplexity,
Many a turn, and many a cross
Tract, they redeem a bank of moss,
Spongy and swelling, and far more
Soft than the finest Lemster ore,

Mildly disparkling like those fires
Which break from the enjewell'd tires
Of curious brides, or like those mites
Of candied dew in moony nights;
Upon this convex all the flowers
Nature begets by the sun and showers,
Are to a wild digestion brought;
As if Love's sampler here was wrought
Or Cytherea's ceston, which
All with temptation doth bewitch.
Sweet airs move here, and more divine
Made by the breath of great-eyed kine
Who, as they low, impearl with milk
The four-leaved grass, or moss-like silk.
The breath of monkeys, met to mix
With musk-flies, are the aromatics
Which cense this arch; and here and there,
And further off, and everywhere
Throughout that brave mosaic yard,
Those picks or diamonds in the card,
With pips of hearts, of club, and spade,
Are here most neatly interlaid.
Many a counter, many a die,
Half-rotten and without an eye,
Lies hereabout; and for to pave
The excellency of this cave,
Squirrels' and children's teeth, late shed,
Are neatly here inchequered
With brownest toadstones, and the gum
That shines upon the bluer plumb.
       *   *   *   Art's
Wise hand enchasing here those warts
Which we to others from ourselves
Sell, and brought hither by the elves.

The tempting mole, stolen from the neck
Of some shy virgin, seems to deck
The holy entrance; where within
The room is hung with the blue skin
Of shifted snake, enfriezed throughout
With eyes of peacocks' trains, and trout-
Flies' curious wings; and these among
Those silver pence, that cut the tongue
Of the red infant, neatly hung.
The glow-worm's eyes, the shining scales
Of silvery fish, wheat-straws, the snail's
Soft candlelight, the kitling's eyne,
Corrupted wood, serve here for shine;
No glaring light of broad-faced day,
Or other over-radiant ray
Ransacks this room, but what weak beams
Can make reflected from these gems,
And multiply; such is the light,
But ever doubtful, day or night.
By this quaint taper-light he winds
His errors up; and now he finds
His moon-tann'd Mab as somewhat sick,
And, love knows, tender as a chick.
Upon six plump dandelions high-
Rear'd lies her elvish majesty,
Whose woolly bubbles seem'd to drown
Her Mabship in obedient down.

*   *   *   *   *

And next to these two blankets, o'er-
Cast of the finest gossamer;
And then a rug of carded wool,
Which, sponge-like, drinking in the dull
Light of the moon, seem'd to comply,
Cloud-like, the dainty deity:

Thus soft she lies; and overhead
A spinner's circle is bespread
With cobweb curtains, from the roof
So neatly sunk, as that no proof
Of any tackling can declare
What gives it hanging in the air.

   *   *   *   *   *

OBERON'S FEAST.

Shapcot, to thee the fairy state
I with discretion dedicate;
Because thou prizest things that are
Curious and unfamiliar.
Take first the feast; these dishes gone,
We 'll see the fairy court anon.
A little mushroom table spread;
After short prayers, they set on bread,
A moon-parch'd grain of purest wheat,
With some small glittering grit, to eat
His choicest bits with; then in a trice
They make a feast less great than nice.
But, all this while his eye is served,
We must not think his ear was starved;
But there was in place, to stir
His spleen, the chirring grasshopper,
The merry cricket, puling fly,
The piping gnat, for minstrelsy.
And now we must imagine first
The elves present, to quench his thirst,
A pure seed-pearl of infant dew,
Brought and besweeten'd in a blue
And pregnant violet; which done,
His kitling eyes begin to run

Quite through the table, where he spies
The horns of pap'ry butterflies,
Of which he eats; and tastes a little
Of what we call the cuckoo's spittle:
A little furze-ball pudding stands
By, yet not blessed by his hands—
That was too coarse; but then forthwith
He ventures boldly on the pith
Of sugar'd rush, and eats the sag
And well-bestrutted bee's sweet bag;
Gladding his palate with some store
Of emmets' eggs : what would he more
But beards of mice, a newt's stew'd thigh,
A bloated earwig, and a fly :
With the red-capp'd worm, that is shut
Within the concave of a nut,
Brown as his tooth; a little moth,
Late fatten'd in a piece of cloth;
With wither'd cherries; mandrakes' ears;
Moles' eyes; to these, the slain stag's tears;
The unctuous dewlaps of a snail;
The broke heart of a nightingale
O'ercome in music; with a wine
Ne'er ravish'd from the flatt'ring rine,
But gently press'd from the soft side
Of the most sweet and dainty bride,
Brought in a dainty daisy, which
He fully quaffs up to bewitch
His blood to height?   This done, commended
Grace by his priest, the feast is ended.

THE MAD MAID'S SONG.

1 Good-morrow to the day so fair;
    Good-morning, sir, to you;
Good-morrow to mine own torn hair,
    Bedabbled with the dew :

2 Good-morning to this primrose too;
    Good-morrow to each maid,
That will with flowers the tomb bestrew
    Wherein my love is laid.

3 Ah, woe is me; woe, woe is me!
    Alack, and well-a-day!
For pity, sir, find out this bee
    Which bore my love away.

4 I 'll seek him in your bonnet brave,
    I 'll seek him in your eyes;
Nay, now I think they 've made his grave
    I' th' bed of strawberries:

5 I 'll seek him there; I know ere this
    The cold, cold earth doth shake him;
But I will go, or send a kiss
    By you, sir, to awake him.

6 Pray hurt him not; though he be dead,
    He knows well who do love him,
And who with green turfs rear his head,
    And who do rudely move him.

7 He 's soft and tender, pray take heed,
    With bands of cowslips bind him,
And bring him home;—but 'tis decreed
    That I shall never find him!

CORINNA'S GOING A-MAYING.

1 Get up, get up for shame; the blooming morn
  Upon her wings presents the god unshorn:
     See how Aurora throws her fair
     Fresh-quilted colours through the air:
     Get up, sweet slug-a-bed, and see
     The dew bespangling herb and tree:
  Each flower has wept, and bow'd toward the east,
  Above an hour since; yet you are not drest;
     Nay, not so much as out of bed;
     When all the birds have matins said,
     And sung their thankful hymns; 'tis sin,
     Nay, profanation, to keep in;
  When as a thousand virgins on this day,
  Spring sooner than the lark, to fetch in May!

2 Rise and put on your foliage, and be seen
  To come forth like the spring-time, fresh and green,
     And sweet as Flora. Take no care
     For jewels for your gown, or hair:
     Fear not, the leaves will strew
     Gems in abundance upon you:
  Besides, the childhood of the day has kept,
  Against you come, some orient pearls unwept:
     Come and receive them, while the light
     Hangs on the dew-locks of the night,
     And Titan on the eastern hill
     Retires himself, or else stands still
  Till you come forth. Wash, dress, be brief in praying;
  Few beads are best, when once we go a-Maying!

3 Come, my Corinna, come; and, coming, mark
  How each field turns a street, each street a park
36

Made green, and trimm'd with trees; see how
Devotion gives each house a bough,
Or branch; each porch, each door, ere this
An ark, a tabernacle is
Made up of whitethorn newly interwove,
As if here were those cooler shades of love.
Can such delights be in the street
And open fields, and we not see 't ?
Come, we 'll abroad ; and let 's obey
The proclamation made for May,
And sin no more, as we have done, by staying;
But, my Corinna, come, let 's go a-Maying!

4 There 's not a budding boy or girl this day
But is got up, and gone to bring in May:
A deal of youth, ere this, is come
Back, and with whitethorn laden home:
Some have despatch'd their cakes and cream,
Before that we have left to dream;
And some have wept, and woo'd, and plighted troth,
And chose their priest, ere we can cast off sloth :
Many a green gown has been given;
Many a kiss, both odd and even;
Many a glance too has been sent
From out the eye, love's firmament;
Many a jest told of the key's betraying
This night, and locks pick'd; yet we 're not a-Maying!

5 Come, let us go, while we are in our prime,
And take the harmless folly of the time:
We shall grow old apace, and die
Before we know our liberty:
Our life is short, and our days run
As fast away as does the sun:

And, as a vapour, or a drop of rain,
Once lost, can ne'er be found again,
   So when or you, or I, are made
   A fable, song, or fleeting shade,
   All love, all liking, all delight
   Lies drown'd with us in endless night.
Then, while time serves, and we are but decaying,
Come, my Corinna, come, let's go a-Maying!

JEPHTHAH'S DAUGHTER.

1 O thou, the wonder of all days!
  O paragon and pearl of praise!
  O Virgin Martyr! ever bless'd
        Above the rest
  Of all the maiden train! we come,
  And bring fresh strewings to thy tomb.

2 Thus, thus, and thus we compass round
  Thy harmless and enchanted ground;
  And, as we sing thy dirge, we will
        The daffodil
  And other flowers lay upon
  The altar of our love, thy stone.

3 Thou wonder of all maids! list here,
  Of daughters all the dearest dear;
  The eye of virgins, nay, the queen
        Of this smooth green,
  And all sweet meads, from whence we get
  The primrose and the violet.

4 Too soon, too dear did Jephthah buy,
  By thy sad loss, our liberty:

His was the bond and cov'nant; yet
         Thou paid'st the debt,
Lamented maid!   He won the day,
But for the conquest thou didst pay.

5 Thy father brought with him along
The olive branch and victor's song:
He slew the Ammonites, we know,
         But to thy woe;
And, in the purchase of our peace,
The cure was worse than the disease.

6 For which obedient zeal of thine,
We offer thee, before thy shrine,
Our sighs for storax, tears for wine;
         And to make fine
And fresh thy hearse-cloth, we will here
Four times bestrew thee every year.

7 Receive, for this thy praise, our tears;
Receive this offering of our hairs;
Receive these crystal vials, fill'd
         With tears distill'd
From teeming eyes; to these we bring,
Each maid, her silver filleting,

8 To gild thy tomb; besides, these cauls,
These laces, ribands, and these fauls,
These veils, wherewith we used to hide
         The bashful bride,
When we conduct her to her groom:
All, all, we lay upon thy tomb.

9 No more, no more, since thou art dead,
Shall we e'er bring coy brides to bed;

No more at yearly festivals
              We cowslip balls
Or chains of columbines shall make
For this or that occasion's sake.

10 No, no; our maiden pleasures be
    Wrapt in a winding-sheet with thee;
    'Tis we are dead, though not i' th' grave,
                  Or if we have
    One seed of life left, 'tis to keep
    A Lent for thee, to fast and weep.

11 Sleep in thy peace, thy bed of spice,
    And make this place all paradise:
    May sweets grow here! and smoke from hence
                  Fat frankincense.
    Let balm and cassia send their scent
    From out thy maiden-monument.

12 May no wolf howl or screech-owl stir
    A wing upon thy sepulchre!
    No boisterous winds or storms
                  To starve or wither
    Thy soft, sweet earth! but, like a spring,
    Love keep it ever flourishing.

13 May all thy maids, at wonted hours,
    Come forth to strew thy tomb with flowers:
    May virgins, when they come to mourn,
                  Male-incense burn
    Upon thine altar! then return
    And leave thee sleeping in thy urn.

THE COUNTRY LIFE.

Sweet country life, to such unknown
Whose lives are others', not their own!
But serving courts and cities, be
Less happy, less enjoying thee!
Thou never plough'st the ocean's foam
To seek and bring rough pepper home;
Nor to the Eastern Ind dost rove,
To bring from thence the scorched clove:
Nor, with the loss of thy loved rest,
Bring'st home the ingot from the West.
No: thy ambition's masterpiece
Flies no thought higher than a fleece;
Or how to pay thy hinds, and clear
All scores, and so to end the year;
But walk'st about thy own dear bounds,
Not envying others' larger grounds:
For well thou know'st, 'tis not the extent
Of land makes life, but sweet content.
When now the cock, the ploughman's horn,
Calls forth the lily-wristed morn,
Then to thy corn-fields thou dost go,
Which though well-soil'd, yet thou dost know
That the best compost for the lands
Is the wise master's feet and hands.
There at the plough thou find'st thy team,
With a hind whistling there to them;
And cheer'st them up by singing how
The kingdom's portion is the plough.
This done, then to th' enamell'd meads,
Thou go'st; and as thy foot there treads,
Thou seest a present godlike power
Imprinted in each herb and flower;

And smell'st the breath of great-eyed kine,
Sweet as the blossoms of the vine.
Here thou behold'st thy large sleek neat
Unto the dewlaps up in meat;
And, as thou look'st, the wanton steer,
The heifer, cow, and ox, draw near,
To make a pleasing pastime there.
These seen, thou go'st to view thy flocks
Of sheep, safe from the wolf and fox;
And find'st their bellies there as full
Of short sweet grass, as backs with wool;
And leav'st them as they feed and fill;
A shepherd piping on a hill.
For sports, for pageantry, and plays,
Thou hast thy eves and holidays;
On which the young men and maids meet,
To exercise their dancing feet;
Tripping the comely country round,
With daffodils and daisies crown'd.
Thy wakes, thy quintels, here thou hast;
Thy May-poles too, with garlands graced;
Thy morris-dance, thy Whitsun-ale,
Thy shearing feast, which never fail;
Thy harvest-home, thy wassail-bowl,
That's toss'd up after fox i' the hole;
Thy mummeries, thy Twelfth-night kings
And queens, thy Christmas revellings;
Thy nut-brown mirth, thy russet wit;
And no man pays too dear for it.
To these thou hast thy times to go,
And trace the hare in the treacherous snow;
Thy witty wiles to draw, and get
The lark into the trammel net;
Thou hast thy cockrood, and thy glade

To take the precious pheasant made;
Thy lime-twigs, snares, and pitfalls, then,
To catch the pilfering birds, not men.
  O happy life, if that their good
The husbandmen but understood!
Who all the day themselves do please,
And younglings, with such sports as these;
And, lying down, have nought to affright
Sweet sleep, that makes more short the night.

SIR RICHARD FANSHAWE.

THIS gallant knight was son to Sir Henry Fanshawe, who was
Remembrancer to the Irish Exchequer, and brother to Thomas
Lord Fanshawe. He was born at Ware, in Hertfordshire, in
1607–8. He became a vehement Royalist, and acted for some
time as Secretary to Prince Rupert, and was, in truth, a kindred
spirit, worthy of recording the orders of that fiery spirit—the
Murat of the Royal cause—to whom the dust of the *mêlée* of
battle was the very breath of life. After the Restoration,
Fanshawe was appointed ambassador to Spain and Portugal.
He acted in this capacity at Madrid in 1666. He had issued
translations of the ‘ Lusiad ’ of Camoens, and the ‘ Pastor Fido ’
of Guarini. Along with the latter, which appeared in 1648, he
published some original poems of considerable merit. He holds
altogether a respectable, if not a very high place among our
early translators and minor poets.

THE SPRING, A SONNET.
FROM THE SPANISH.

Those whiter lilies which the early morn
  Seems to have newly woven of sleaved silk,
To which, on banks of wealthy Tagus born,
  Gold was their cradle, liquid pearl their milk.

These blushing roses, with whose virgin leaves
　　The wanton wind to sport himself presumes,
Whilst from their rifled wardrobe he receives
　　For his wings purple, for his breath perfumes.

Both those and these my Cælia's pretty foot
　　Trod up; but if she should her face display,
And fragrant breast, they'd dry again to the root,
　　As with the blasting of the mid-day's ray;
And this soft wind, which both perfumes and cools,
　　Pass like the unregarded breath of fools.

ABRAHAM COWLEY.

The 'melancholy' and musical Cowley was born in London in
the year 1618.　He was the posthumous son of a worthy grocer,
who lived in Fleet Street, near the end of Chancery Lane, and
who is supposed, from the omission of his name in the register
of St Dunstan's parish, to have been a Dissenter.　His mother
was left poor, but had a strong desire for her son's education,
and influence to get him admitted as a king's scholar into
Westminster.　His mind was almost preternaturally precocious,
and received early a strong and peculiar stimulus.　A copy of
Spenser lay in the window of his mother's apartment, and in it
he delighted to read, and became the devoted slave of poetry
ever after.　When only ten he wrote 'The Tragical History of
Pyramus and Thisbe,' and at twelve 'Constantia and Philetus.'
Pope wrote a lampoon about the same age as Cowley these
romantic narratives; and we have seen a pretty good copy of
verses on Napoleon, written at the age of seven, by one of the
most distinguished rising poets of our own day.　When fifteen
(Johnson calls it thirteen, but he and some other biographers
were misled by the portrait of the poet being, by mistake,
marked thirteen) Cowley published some of his early effusions,
under the title of 'Poetical Blossoms.'　While at school he

44

produced a comedy of a pastoral kind, entitled, 'Love's Riddle,' but it was not published till he went to Cambridge. To that university he proceeded in 1636, and two years after, there appeared the above-mentioned comedy, with a poetical dedication to Sir Kenelm Digby, one of the marvellous men of that age; and also 'Naufragium Joculare,' a comedy in Latin, inscribed to Dr Comber, master of the college. When the Prince of Wales afterwards visited Cambridge, the fertile Cowley got up the rough draft of another comedy, called 'The Guardian,' which was repeated to His Royal Highness by the scholars. This was afterwards, to the poet's great annoyance, printed during his absence from the country. In 1643 he took his degree of A.M., and was, the same year, through the prevailing influence of the Parliament, ejected, with many others, from Cambridge. He took refuge in St John's College, Oxford, where he published a satire, entitled 'The Puritan and Papist,' and where, by his loyalty and genius, he gained the favour of such distinguished courtiers as Lord Falkland. During this agitated period he resided a good deal in the family of the Lord St Albans; and when Oxford fell into the hands of the Parliament he followed the Queen to Paris, and there acted as Secretary to the same noble lord. He remained abroad about ten years, and during that period made various journeys in the furtherance of the Royal cause, visiting Flanders, Holland, Jersey, Scotland, &c. His chief employment, however, was carrying on a correspondence in cipher between the King and the Queen. Sprat says, 'he ciphered and deciphered with his own hand the greatest part of the letters that passed between their Majesties, and managed a vast intelligence in other parts, which, for some years together, took up all his days and two or three nights every week.' This does not seem employment very suitable to a man of genius. He seems, however, to have found time for more congenial avocations; and, in 1647, he published his 'Mistress,' a work which seems to glow with amorous fire, although Barnes relates of the author that he was never in love but once, and then had not resolution to reveal his passion. And yet he wrote 'The Chronicle,' from which we might infer that his heart was completely tinder, and that his series of love attachments had been an infinite one!

45

In 1556, being of no more use in Paris, Cowley was sent back to England, that 'under pretence of privacy and retirement he might take occasion of giving notice of the posture of things in this nation.' For some time he lay concealed in London, but was at length seized by mistake for another gentleman of the Royal party; and being thus discovered, he was continued in confinement, was several times examined, and ultimately succeeded, although with some difficulty, in obtaining his liberation, Dr Scarborough becoming his bail for a thousand pounds. In the same year he published a collection of his poems, with a querulous preface, in which he expresses a strong desire to 'retire to some of the American plantations, and to forsake the world for ever.' Meanwhile he gave himself out as a physician till the death of Cromwell, when he returned to France, resumed his former occupation, and remained till the Restoration. In 1657 he was created Doctor of Medicine at Oxford. Having studied botany to qualify himself for his physician's degree, he was induced to publish in Latin some books on plants, flowers, and trees.

The Restoration brought him less advantage than he had anticipated. Probably he expected too much, and had expressed his sanguine hopes in a song of triumph on the occasion. He had been promised, both by Charles I. and Charles II., the Mastership of the Savoy, (a forgotten sinecure office;) but lost it, says Wood, 'by certain persons, enemies to the Muses.' He brought on the stage at this time his old comedy of 'The Guardian,' under the title of 'Cutter of Coleman Street;' but it was thought a satire on the debauchery of the King's party, and was received with coldness. Cowley, according to Dryden, 'received the news of his ill success not with so much firmness as might have been expected from so great a man.' There are few who, like Dr Johnson, have been able to declare, after the rejection of a play or poem, that they felt 'like the Monument.' Cowley not only entertained, but printed his dissatisfaction, in the form of a poem called 'The Complaint,' which, like all selfish complaints, attracted little sympathy or attention. In this he calls himself the 'melancholy Cowley,' an epithet which has stuck to his memory.

He had always, according to his own statement, loved retirement. When he was a young boy at school, instead of running about on holidays, and playing with his fellows, he was wont to steal from them, and walk into the fields alone with a book. This passion had been overlaid, but not extinguished, during his public life; and now, swelled by disgust, it came back upon him in great strength. He seems, too, if we can believe Sprat, to have had an extraordinary attachment to Nature, as it 'was God's;' to the whole 'compass of the creation, and all the wonderful effects of the Divine wisdom.' At all events, he retired first to Barn Elms, and then to Chertsey in Surrey. He had obtained, through Lord St Albans and the Duke of Buckingham, the lease of some lands belonging to the Queen, which brought him in an income of £300 a year. Here, then, having, at the age of forty-two, reached 'the peaceful hermitage,' he set himself with all his might to enjoy it. He cultivated his fields, and renewed his botanical studies in his woods and garden. He wrote letters to his friends,. which are said to have been admirable, and might have ranked with those of Gray and Cowper, but unfortunately they have not been preserved. He renewed his intimacy with the Greek and Latin poets, and he set himself to retouch the 'Davideis,' which he had begun in early youth, but which he never lived to finish, and to compose his beautiful prose essays. But he soon found that Chertsey, no more than Paris, was Paradise. He had no wife nor children. He had sweet solitude, but no one near him to whom to whisper 'how sweet this solitude is!' The peasants were boors. His tenants would pay him no rent, and the cattle of his neighbours devoured his meadows. He was troubled with rheums and colds. He met a severe fall when he first came to Chertsey, of which he says, half in jest and half in earnest—'What this signifies, or may come to in time, God knows; if it be ominous, it can end in nothing less than hanging.' Robert Hall said of Bishop Watson that he seemed to have wedded political integrity in early life, and to have spent all the rest of his days in quarrelling with his wife. So Cowley wedded his long-sought-for bride, Solitude, and led a miserable life with her ever after. Fortunately for him, if not for the world, his career soon came to a close.

One hot day in summer, he stayed too long among his labourers
in the meadows, and was seized with a cold, which, being
neglected, carried him off on the 28th of July 1667. He was
not forty-nine years old. He died at the Porch House, Chertsey, and his remains were buried with great pomp near Chaucer
and Spenser; and King Charles, who had neglected him during
life, pronounced his panegyric after death, declaring that 'Mr
Cowley had not left behind him a better man in England.' It
was in keeping with the character of Charles to make up for
his deficiency in action, by his felicity of phrase.

If we may differ from such a high authority as 'Old Rowley,'
we would venture to doubt whether Cowley was the best—certainly he was not the greatest—man then in England. Milton
was alive, and the 'Paradise Lost' appeared in the very year
when the author of the 'Davideis' departed. Cowley gives
us the impression of having been an amiable and blameless,
rather than a good or great man. At all events, there was
nothing *active* in his goodness, and his greatness could not be
called magnanimity. He was a scholar and a poet misplaced
during early life; and when he gained that retirement for which
he sighed, he had, by his habits of life, lost his capacity of
relishing it. 'He that would enjoy solitude,' it has been said,
'must either be a wild beast or a god;' and Cowley was neither.
How different his grounds of dissatisfaction with the world from
those of Milton! Cowley was wearied of ciphering, and his
'Cutter of Coleman Street' had been cut; that was nearly the
whole matter of his complaint; while Milton had fallen from
being the second man in England into poverty, blindness, contempt, danger, and the disappointment of the most glorious
hopes which ever heaved the bosom of patriot or saint.

. We find the want of greatness which marked the man charac-
terising the poet. Infinite ingenuity, a charming flexibility and
abundance of fancy, a perception of remote analogies almost
unrivalled, great command of versification and language,
learning without bounds, and an occasional gracefulness and
sparkling ease (as in 'The Chronicle') superior to even Herrick
or Suckling,—are qualities that must be conceded to Cowley.
But the most of his writings are cold and glittering as the

sun-smitten glacier. He is seldom warm, except when he is proclaiming his own merits, or bewailing his own misfortunes. Hence his 'Wish,' and even his 'Complaint,' are very pleasing and natural specimens of poetry. But his 'Pindaric Odes,' his 'Hymn to Light,' and most of his 'Davideis,' while displaying great power, shew at least equal perversion, and are more memorable for their faults than for their beauties. In the 'Davideis,' he describes the attire of Gabriel in the spirit and language of a tailor; and there is no path so sacred or so lofty but he must sow it with conceits,—forced, false, and chilly. His 'Anacreontics,' on the other hand, are in general felicitous in style and aerial in motion. And in his Translations, although too free, he is uniformly graceful and spirited; and his vast command of language and imagery enables him often to improve his author—to gild the refined gold, to paint the lily, and to throw a new perfume on the violet, of the Grecian and Roman masters.

In prose, Cowley is uniformly excellent. The prefaces to his poems, especially his defence of sacred song in the prefix to the 'Davideis,' his short autobiography, the fragments of his letters which remain, and his posthumous essays, are all distinguished by a rich simplicity of style and by a copiousness of matter which excite in equal measure delight and surprise. He had written, it appears, three books on the Civil War, to the time of the battle of Newbury, which he destroyed. It is a pity, perhaps, that he had not preserved and completed the work. His intimacy with many of the leading characters and the secret springs of that remarkable period,—his clear and solid judgment, always so except when he was following the Dædalus Pindar upon waxen Icarian wings, or competing with Dr Donne in the number of conceits which he could stuff, like cloves, into his subject-matter,—and the bewitching ease and elegance of his prose style, would have combined to render it an important contribution to English history, and a worthy monument of its author's highly-accomplished and diversified powers.

THE CHRONICLE, A BALLAD.

1 Margarita first possess'd,
  If I remember well, my breast,
  Margarita first of all;
  But when a while the wanton maid
  With my restless heart had play'd,
  Martha took the flying ball.

2 Martha soon did it resign
  To the beauteous Catharine:
  Beauteous Catharine gave place
  (Though loth and angry she to part
  With the possession of my heart)
  To Eliza's conquering face.

3 Eliza till this hour might reign,
  Had she not evil counsels ta'en:
  Fundamental laws she broke
  And still new favourites she chose,
  Till up in arms my passions rose,
  And cast away her yoke.

4 Mary then, and gentle Anne,
  Both to reign at once began;
  Alternately they sway'd,
  And sometimes Mary was the fair,
  And sometimes Anne the crown did wear,
  And sometimes both I obey'd.

5 Another Mary then arose,
  And did rigorous laws impose;
  A mighty tyrant she!
  Long, alas! should I have been
  Under that iron-sceptred queen,
  Had not Rebecca set me free.

6 When fair Rebecca set me free,
  'Twas then a golden time with me:
  But soon those pleasures fled;
  For the gracious princess died
  In her youth and beauty's pride,
  And Judith reign'd in her stead.

7 One month, three days, and half an hour,
  Judith held the sovereign power:
  Wondrous beautiful her face,
  But so weak and small her wit,
  That she to govern was unfit,
  And so Susanna took her place.

8 But when Isabella came,
  Arm'd with a resistless flame,
  And the artillery of her eye,
  Whilst she proudly march'd about,
  Greater conquests to find out,
  She beat out Susan by the bye.

9 But in her place I then obey'd
  Black-eyed Bess, her viceroy made,
  To whom ensued a vacancy.
  Thousand worst passions then possess'd
  The interregnum of my breast.
  Bless me from such an anarchy!

10 Gentle Henrietta then,
  And a third Mary, next began:
  Then Joan, and Jane, and Audria;
  And then a pretty Thomasine,
  And then another Catharine,
  And then a long *et cætera*.

11 But should I now to you relate
    The strength and riches of their state,
    The powder, patches, and the pins,
    The ribands, jewels, and the rings,
    The lace, the paint, and warlike things,
    That make up all their magazines:

12 If I should tell the politic arts
    To take and keep men's hearts,
    The letters, embassies, and spies,
    The frowns, the smiles, and flatteries,
    The quarrels, tears, and perjuries,
    Numberless, nameless mysteries!

13 And all the little lime-twigs laid
    By Mach'avel the waiting-maid;
    I more voluminous should grow
    (Chiefly if I like them should tell
    All change of weathers that befell)
    Than Holinshed or Stow.

14 But I will briefer with them be,
    Since few of them were long with me.
    An higher and a nobler strain
    My present Emperess does claim,
    Helconora! first o' the name,
    Whom God grant long to reign.

THE COMPLAINT.

    In a deep vision's intellectual scene,
    Beneath a bower for sorrow made,
    The uncomfortable shade
    Of the black yew's unlucky green,

Mixed with the mourning willow's careful gray,
Where rev'rend Cam cuts out his famous way,
The melancholy Cowley lay;
And, lo! a Muse appeared to his closed sight
(The Muses oft in lands of vision play,)
Bodied, arrayed, and seen by an internal light:
A golden harp with silver strings she bore,
A wondrous hieroglyphic robe she wore,
In which all colours and all figures were
That Nature or that Fancy can create,
That Art can never imitate,
And with loose pride it wantoned in the air,
In such a dress, in such a well-clothed dream,
She used of old near fair Ismenus' stream
Pindar, her Theban favourite, to meet;
A crown was on her head, and wings were on her feet.

She touched him with her harp and raised him
    from the ground;
The shaken strings melodiously resound.
'Art thou returned at last,' said she,
'To this forsaken place and me ?
Thou prodigal! who didst so loosely waste
Of all thy youthful years the good estate;
Art thou returned here, to repent too late ?
And gather husks of learning up at last,
Now the rich harvest-time of life is past,
And winter marches on so fast ?
But when I meant to adopt thee for my son,
And did as learned a portion assign
As ever any of the mighty nine
Had to their dearest children done;
When I resolved to exalt thy anointed name
Among the spiritual lords of peaceful fame;

Thou changeling! thou, bewitch'd with noise and
　　show,
Wouldst into courts and cities from me go;
Wouldst see the world abroad, and have a share
In all the follies and the tumults there;
Thou wouldst, forsooth, be something in a state,
And business thou wouldst find, and wouldst create:
Business! the frivolous pretence
Of human lusts, to shake off innocence;
Business! the grave impertinence;
Business! the thing which I of all things hate;
Business! the contradiction of thy fate.

'Go, renegado! cast up thy account,
And see to what amount
Thy foolish gains by quitting me:
The sale of knowledge, fame, and liberty,
The fruits of thy unlearned apostasy.
Thou thoughtst, if once the public storm were past,
All thy remaining life should sunshine be:
Behold the public storm is spent at last,
The sovereign is tossed at sea no more,
And thou, with all the noble company,
Art got at last to shore:
But whilst thy fellow-voyagers I see,
All marched up to possess the promised land,
Thou still alone, alas! dost gaping stand,
Upon the naked beach, upon the barren sand.
As a fair morning of the blessed spring,
After a tedious, stormy night,
Such was the glorious entry of our king;
Enriching moisture dropped on every thing:
Plenty he sowed below, and cast about him light.
But then, alas! to thee alone
54

One of old Gideon's miracles was shown,
For every tree, and every hand around,
With pearly dew was crowned,
And upon all the quickened ground
The fruitful seed of heaven did brooding lie,
And nothing but the Muse's fleece was dry.
It did all other threats surpass,
When God to his own people said,
The men whom through long wanderings he had led,
That he would give them even a heaven of brass:
They looked up to that heaven in vain,
That bounteous heaven! which God did not restrain
Upon the most unjust to shine and rain.

'The Rachel, for which twice seven years and more,
Thou didst with faith and labour serve,
And didst (if faith and labour can) deserve,
Though she contracted was to thee,
Given to another, thou didst see, who had store
Of fairer and of richer wives before,
And not a Leah left, thy recompense to be.
Go on, twice seven years more, thy fortune try,
Twice seven years more God in his bounty may
Give thee to fling away
Into the court's deceitful lottery:
But think how likely 'tis that thou,
With the dull work of thy unwieldy plough,
Shouldst in a hard and barren season thrive,
Shouldst even able be to live;
Thou! to whose share so little bread did fall
In the miraculous year, when manna rain'd on all.'

Thus spake the Muse, and spake it with a smile,
That seemed at once to pity and revile:

And to her thus, raising his thoughtful head,
The melancholy Cowley said:
'Ah, wanton foe! dost thou upbraid
The ills which thou thyself hast made?
When in the cradle innocent I lay,
Thou, wicked spirit, stolest me away,
And my abused soul didst bear
Into thy new-found worlds, I know not where,
Thy golden Indies in the air;
And ever since I strive in vain
My ravished freedom to regain;
Still I rebel, still thou dost reign;
Lo, still in verse, against thee I complain.
There is a sort of stubborn weeds,
Which, if the earth but once it ever breeds,
No wholesome herb can near them thrive,
No useful plant can keep alive:
The foolish sports I did on thee bestow
Make all my art and labour fruitless now;
Where once such fairies dance, no grass doth
  ever grow.

'When my new mind had no infusion known,
Thou gavest so deep a tincture of thine own,
That ever since I vainly try
To wash away the inherent dye:
Long work, perhaps, may spoil thy colours quite,
But never will reduce the native white.
To all the ports of honour and of gain
I often steer my course in vain;
Thy gale comes cross, and drives me back again,
Thou slacken'st all my nerves of industry,
By making them so oft to be
The tinkling strings of thy loose minstrelsy.

Whoever this world's happiness would see
Must as entirely cast off thee,
As they who only heaven desire
Do from the world retire.
This was my error, this my gross mistake,
Myself a demi-votary to make.
Thus with Sapphira and her husband's fate,
(A fault which I, like them, am taught too late,)
For all that I give up I nothing gain,
And perish for the part which I retain.
Teach me not then, O thou fallacious Muse!
The court and better king t' accuse;
The heaven under which I live is fair,
The fertile soil will a full harvest bear:
Thine, thine is all the barrenness, if thou
Makest me sit still and sing when I should plough.
When I but think how many a tedious year
Our patient sovereign did attend
His long misfortune's fatal end;
How cheerfully, and how exempt from fear,
On the Great Sovereign's will he did depend,
I ought to be accursed if I refuse
To wait on his, O thou fallacious Muse!
Kings have long hands, they say, and though I be
So distant, they may reach at length to me.
However, of all princes thou
Shouldst not reproach rewards for being small or
        slow;
Thou! who rewardest but with popular breath,
And that, too, after death!'

THE DESPAIR.

1 Beneath this gloomy shade,
   By Nature only for my sorrows made,

I 'll spend this voice in cries,
In tears I 'll waste these eyes,
By love so vainly fed;
So lust of old the deluge punished.
Ah, wretched youth, said I;
Ah, wretched youth! twice did I sadly cry;
Ah, wretched youth! the fields and floods reply.

2 When thoughts of love I entertain,
I meet no words but Never, and In vain:
Never! alas! that dreadful name
Which fuels the infernal flame:
Never! my time to come must waste;
In vain! torments the present and the past:
In vain, in vain! said I,
In vain, in vain! twice did I sadly cry;
In vain, in vain! the fields and floods reply.

3 No more shall fields or floods do so,
For I to shades more dark and silent go:
All this world's noise appears to me
A dull, ill-acted comedy:
No comfort to my wounded sight,
In the sun's busy and impert'nent light.
Then down I laid my head,
Down on cold earth, and for a while was dead,
And my freed soul to a strange somewhere fled.

4 Ah, sottish soul! said I,
When back to its cage again I saw it fly:
Fool! to resume her broken chain,
And row her galley here again!
Fool! to that body to return,
Where it condemned and destined is to burn!

58

Once dead, how can it be
Death should a thing so pleasant seem to thee,
That thou shouldst come to live it o'er again in me ?

OF WIT.

1 Tell me, O tell! what kind of thing is Wit,
Thou who master art of it;
For the first matter loves variety less;
Less women love it, either in love or dress:
A thousand different shapes it bears,
Comely in thousand shapes appears:
Yonder we saw it plain, and here 'tis now,
Like spirits, in a place, we know not how.

2 London, that vends of false ware so much store,
In no ware deceives us more:
For men, led by the colour and the shape,
Like Zeuxis' birds, fly to the painted grape.
Some things do through our judgment pass,
As through a multiplying-glass;
And sometimes, if the object be too far,
We take a falling meteor for a star.

3 Hence 'tis a wit, that greatest word of fame,
Grows such a common name;
And wits by our creation they become,
Just so as tit'lar bishops made at Rome.
'Tis not a tale, 'tis not a jest,
Admired with laughter at a feast,
Nor florid talk, which can that title gain;
The proofs of wit for ever must remain.

4 'Tis not to force some lifeless verses meet
With their five gouty feet;

All everywhere, like man's, must be the soul,
And reason the inferior powers control.
Such were the numbers which could call
The stones into the Theban wall.
Such miracles are ceased; and now we see
No towns or houses raised by poetry.

5 Yet 'tis not to adorn and gild each part;
That shows more cost than art.
Jewels at nose and lips but ill appear;
Rather than all things wit, let none be there.
Several lights will not be seen,
If there be nothing else between.
Men doubt, because they stand so thick i' the sky,
If those be stars which paint the galaxy.

6 'Tis not when two like words make up one noise,
Jests for Dutch men and English boys;
In which who finds out wit, the same may see
In an'grams and acrostics poetry.
Much less can that have any place
At which a virgin hides her face;
Such dross the fire must purge away; 'tis just
The author blush there where the reader must.

7 'Tis not such lines as almost crack the stage,
When Bajazet begins to rage:
Nor a tall met'phor in the bombast way,
Nor the dry chips of short-lunged Seneca:
Nor upon all things to obtrude
And force some old similitude.
What is it then, which, like the Power Divine,
We only can by negatives define?
60

8 In a true piece of wit all things must be,
   Yet all things there agree:
   As in the ark, joined without force or strife,
   All creatures dwelt, all creatures that had life.
   Or as the primitive forms of all,
   If we compare great things with small,
   Which without discord or confusion lie,
   In that strange mirror of the Deity.

OF SOLITUDE.

1 Hail, old patrician trees, so great and good!
   Hail, ye plebeian underwood!
   Where the poetic birds rejoice,
   And for their quiet nests and plenteous food
   Pay with their grateful voice.

2 Hail the poor Muse's richest manor-seat!
   Ye country houses and retreat,
   Which all the happy gods so love,
   That for you oft they quit their bright and great
   Metropolis above.

3 Here Nature does a house for me erect,
   Nature! the fairest architect,
   Who those fond artists does despise
   That can the fair and living trees neglect,
   Yet the dead timber prize.

4 Here let me, careless and unthoughtful lying,
   Hear the soft winds above me flying,
   With all their wanton boughs dispute,
   And the more tuneful birds to both replying,
   Nor be myself, too, mute.

5 A silver stream shall roll his waters near,
   Gilt with the sunbeams here and there,
   On whose enamelled bank I'll walk,
   And see how prettily they smile,
   And hear how prettily they talk.

6 Ah! wretched, and too solitary he,
   Who loves not his own company!
   He'll feel the weight of it many a day,
   Unless he calls in sin or vanity
   To help to bear it away.

7 O Solitude! first state of humankind!
   Which bless'd remained till man did find
   Even his own helper's company:
   As soon as two, alas! together joined,
   The serpent made up three.

8 Though God himself, through countless ages, thee
   His sole companion chose to be,
   Thee, sacred Solitude! alone,
   Before the branchy head of number's tree
   Sprang from the trunk of one;

9 Thou (though men think thine an unactive part)
   Dost break and tame the unruly heart,
   Which else would know no settled pace,
   Making it move, well managed by thy art,
   With swiftness and with grace.

10 Thou the faint beams of reason's scattered light
    Dost, like a burning glass, unite,
    Dost multiply the feeble heat,
    And fortify the strength, till thou dost bright
    And noble fires beget.

11 Whilst this hard truth I teach, methinks I see
  The monster London laugh at me;
  I should at thee, too, foolish city!
  If it were fit to laugh at misery;
  But thy estate I pity.

12 Let but thy wicked men from out thee go,
  And all the fools that crowd thee so,
  Even thou, who dost thy millions boast,
  A village less than Islington wilt grow,
  A solitude almost.

THE WISH.

I.

Lest the misjudging world should chance to say
I durst not but in secret murmurs pray,
To whisper in Jove's ear
How much I wish that funeral,
Or gape at such a great one's fall;
This let all ages hear,
And future times in my soul's picture see
What I abhor, what I desire to be.

II.

I would not be a Puritan, though he
Can preach two hours, and yet his sermon be
But half a quarter long;
Though from his old mechanic trade
By vision he's a pastor made,
His faith was grown so strong;
Nay, though he think to gain salvation
By calling the Pope the Whore of Babylon.

III.

I would not be a Schoolmaster, though to him
His rods no less than Consuls' fasces seem ;
Though he in many a place,
Turns Lily oftener than his gowns,
Till at the last he makes the nouns
Fight with the verbs apace ;
Nay, though he can, in a poetic heat,
Figures, born since, out of poor Virgil beat.

IV.

I would not be a Justice of Peace, though he
Can with equality divide the fee,
And stakes with his clerk draw ;
Nay, though he sits upon the place
Of judgment, with a learned face
Intricate as the law ;
And whilst he mulcts enormities demurely,
Breaks Priscian's head with sentences securely.

V.

I would not be a Courtier, though he
Makes his whole life the truest comedy;
Although he be a man
In whom the tailor's forming art,
And nimble barber, claim more part
Than Nature herself can ;
Though, as he uses men, 'tis his intent
To put off Death too with a compliment.

VI.

From Lawyers' tongues, though they can spin with ease
The shortest cause into a paraphrase,
From Usurers' conscience

(For swallowing up young heirs so fast,
Without all doubt they'll choke at last)
Make me all innocence,
Good Heaven! and from thy eyes, O Justice! keep;
For though they be not blind, they're oft asleep.

VII.

From Singing-men's religion, who are
Always at church, just like the crows, 'cause there
They build themselves a nest;
From too much poetry, which shines
With gold in nothing but its lines,
Free, O you Powers! my breast;
And from astronomy, which in the skies
Finds fish and bulls, yet doth but tantalise.

VIII.

From your Court-madam's beauty, which doth carry
At morning May, at night a January;
From the grave City-brow
(For though it want an R, it has
The letter of Pythagoras)
Keep me, O Fortune! now,
And chines of beef innumerable send me,
Or from the stomach of the guard defend me.

IX.

This only grant me, that my means may lie
Too low for envy, for contempt too high.
Some honour I would have,
Not from great deeds, but good alone:
The unknown are better than ill known:
Rumour can ope the grave.
Acquaintance I would have, but when 't depends
Not from the number, but the choice of friends.

X.

Books should, not business, entertain the light,
And sleep, as undisturbed as death, the night.
My house a cottage more
Than palace, and should fitting be
For all my use, not luxury;
My garden, painted o'er
With Nature's hand, not Art's, that pleasure yield
Horace might envy in his Sabine field.

XI.

Thus would I double my life's fading space;
For he that runs it well twice runs his race;
And in this true delight,
These unbought sports, and happy state,
I would not fear, nor wish my fate,
But boldly say each night,
To-morrow let my sun his beams display,
Or in clouds hide them, I have lived to-day.

UPON THE SHORTNESS OF MAN'S LIFE.

1 Mark that swift arrow, how it cuts the air,
How it outruns thy following eye!
Use all persuasions now, and try
If thou canst call it back, or stay it there.
That way it went, but thou shalt find
No track is left behind.

2 Fool! 'tis thy life, and the fond archer thou.
Of all the time thou 'st shot away,
I 'll bid thee fetch but yesterday,
And it shall be too hard a task to do.
Besides repentance, what canst find
That it hath left behind?

3 Our life is carried with too strong a tide,
  A doubtful cloud our substance bears,
  And is the horse of all our years :
  Each day doth on a winged whirlwind ride.
  We and our glass run out, and must
  Both render up our dust.

4 But his past life who without grief can see,
  Who never thinks his end too near,
  But says to Fame, Thou art mine heir ;
  That man extends life's natural brevity—
  This is, this is the only way
  To outlive Nestor in a day.

ON THE PRAISE OF POETRY.

'Tis not a pyramid of marble stone,
Though high as our ambition ;
'Tis not a tomb cut out in brass, which can
Give life to the ashes of a man,
But verses only ; they shall fresh appear,
Whilst there are men to read or hear,
When time shall make the lasting brass decay,
And eat the pyramid away,
Turning that monument wherein men trust
Their names, to what it keeps, poor dust ;
Then shall the epitaph remain, and be
New graven in eternity.
Poets by death are conquered, but the wit
Of poets triumph over it.
What cannot verse ? When Thracian Orpheus took
His lyre, and gently on it strook,
The learned stones came dancing all along,

67

And kept time to the charming song.
With artificial pace the warlike pine,
The elm and his wife, the ivy-twine,
With all the better trees which erst had stood
Unmoved, forsook their native wood.
The laurel to the poet's hand did bow,
Craving the honour of his brow;
And every loving arm embraced, and made
With their officious leaves a shade.
The beasts, too, strove his auditors to be,
Forgetting their old tyranny.
The fearful hart next to the lion came,
And wolf was shepherd to the lamb.
Nightingales, harmless Syrens of the air,
And Muses of the place, were there;
Who, when their little windpipes they had found
Unequal to so strange a sound,
O'ercome by art and grief, they did expire,
And fell upon the conquering lyre.
Happy, oh happy they! whose tomb might be,
Mausolus! envied by thee!

THE MOTTO.

TENTANDA VIA EST, ETC.

What shall I do to be for ever known,
And make the age to come my own?
I shall like beasts or common people die,
Unless you write my elegy;
Whilst others great by being born are grown,
Their mother's labour, not their own.
In this scale gold, in the other fame does lie;
The weight of that mounts this so high.

These men are Fortune's jewels, moulded bright,
Brought forth with their own fire and light.
If I, her vulgar stone, for either look,
Out of myself it must be strook.
Yet I must on :   What sound is 't strikes mine ear ?
Sure I Fame's trumpet hear :
It sounds like the last trumpet, for it can
Raise up the buried man.
Unpass'd Alps stop me, but I 'll cut through all,
And march, the Muse's Hannibal.
Hence, all the flattering vanities that lay
Nets of roses in the way;
Hence, the desire of honours or estate,
And all that is not above Fate;
Hence, Love himself, that tyrant of my days,
Which intercepts my coming praise.
Come, my best friends ! my books ! and lead me on,
'Tis time that I were gone.
Welcome, great Stagyrite ! and teach me now
All I was born to know:
Thy scholar's victories thou dost far outdo;
He conquered th' earth, the whole world you,
Welcome, learn'd Cicero ! whose bless'd tongue
    and wit
Preserves Rome's greatness yet;
Thou art the first of orators; only he
Who best can praise thee next must be.
Welcome the Mantuan swan ! Virgil the wise,
Whose verse walks highest, but not flies;
Who brought green Poesy to her perfect age,
And made that art which was a rage.
Tell me, ye mighty Three ! what shall I do
To be like one of you?
But you have climb'd the mountain's top, there sit

On the calm flourishing head of it,
And whilst, with wearied steps, we upward go,
See us and clouds below.

DAVIDEIS.

BOOK II.

THE CONTENTS.

The friendship betwixt Jonathan and David; and, upon that occasion, a digression concerning the nature of love. A discourse between Jonathan and David, upon which the latter absents himself from court, and the former goes thither to inform himself of Saul's resolution. The feast of the Newmoon; the manner of the celebration of it; and therein a digression of the history of Abraham. Saul's speech upon David's absence from the feast, and his anger against Jonathan. David's resolution to fly away. He parts with Jonathan, and falls asleep under a tree. A description of Fancy. An angel makes up a vision in David's head. The vision itself; which is a prophecy of all the succession of his race, till Christ's time, with their most remarkable actions. At his awaking, Gabriel assumes a human shape, and confirms to him the truth of his vision.

But now the early birds began to call
The morning forth; up rose the sun and Saul:
Both, as men thought, rose fresh from sweet repose;
But both, alas! from restless labours rose:
For in Saul's breast Envy, the toilsome sin,
Had all that night active and tyrannous been:
She expelled all forms of kindness, virtue, grace,
Of the past day no footstep left, or trace;
The new-blown sparks of his old rage appear,
Nor could his love dwell longer with his fear.
So near a storm wise David would not stay,
Nor trust the glittering of a faithless day:
He saw the sun call in his beams apace,
And angry clouds march up into their place:
The sea itself smooths his rough brow awhile,
Flatt'ring the greedy merchant with a smile;
But he whose shipwrecked bark it drank before,
Sees the deceit, and knows it would have more.
Such is the sea, and such was Saul;

But Jonathan his son, and only good,
Was gentle as fair Jordan's useful flood;
Whose innocent stream, as it in silence goes,
Fresh honours and a sudden spring bestows
On both his banks, to every flower and tree;
The manner how lies hid, the effect we see:
But more than all, more than himself, he loved
The man whose worth his father's hatred moved;
For when the noble youth at Dammin stood,
Adorned with sweat, and painted gay with blood,
Jonathan pierced him through with greedy eye,
And understood the future majesty
Then destined in the glories of his look:
He saw, and straight was with amazement strook,
To see the strength, the feature, and the grace
Of his young limbs; he saw his comely face,
Where love and reverence so well-mingled were,
And head, already crowned with golden hair:
He saw what mildness his bold sp'rit did tame,
Gentler than light, yet powerful as a flame:
He saw his valour by their safety proved;
He saw all this, and as he saw, he loved.
    What art thou, Love! thou great mysterious thing?
From what hid stock does thy strange nature spring?
'Tis thou that movst the world through every part,
And holdst the vast frame close, that nothing start
From the due place and office first ordained;
By thee were all things made, and are sustained.
Sometimes we see thee fully, and can say
From hence thou tookst thy rise, and wentst that way;
But oftener the short beams of Reason's eye
See only there thou art, not how, nor why.
How is the loadstone, Nature's subtle pride,
By the rude iron woo'd, and made a bride?

How was the weapon wounded? what hid flame
The strong and conquering metal overcame?
Love (this world's grace) exalts his natural state;
He feels thee, Love! and feels no more his weight.
Ye learned heads whom ivy garlands grace,
Why does that twining plant the oak embrace?
The oak, for courtship most of all unfit,
And rough as are the winds that fight with it.
How does the absent pole the needle move?
How does his cold and ice beget hot love?
Which are the wings of lightness to ascend?
Or why does weight to the centre downwards bend?
Thus creatures void of life obey thy laws,
And seldom we, they never, know the cause.
In thy large state, life gives the next degree,
Where sense and good apparent places thee;
But thy chief palace is man's heart alone;
Here are thy triumphs and full glories shown:
Handsome desires, and rest, about thee flee,
Union, inheritance, zeal, and ecstasy,
With thousand joys, cluster around thine head,
O'er which a gall-less dove her wings does spread:
A gentle lamb, purer and whiter far
Than consciences of thine own martyrs are,
Lies at thy feet; and thy right hand does hold
The mystic sceptre of a cross of gold.
Thus dost thou sit (like men, ere sin had framed
A guilty blush) naked, but not ashamed.
What cause, then, did the fab'lous ancients find,
When first their superstition made thee blind?
'Twas they, alas! 'twas they who could not see,
When they mistook that monster, Lust, for thee. .
Thou art a bright, but not consuming, flame;
Such in the amazed bush to Moses came,

When that, secure, its new-crown'd head did rear,
And chid the trembling branches' needless fear;
Thy darts are healthful gold, and downwards fall,
Soft as the feathers that they are fletched withal.
Such, and no other, were those secret darts
Which sweetly touched this noblest pair of hearts:
Still to one end they both so justly drew,
As courteous doves together yoked would do:
No weight of birth did on one side prevail;
Two twins less even lie in Nature's scale:
They mingled fates, and both in each did share;
They both were servants, they both princes were.
If any joy to one of them was sent,
It was most his to whom it least was meant;
And Fortune's malice betwixt both was cross'd,
For striking one, it wounded the other most.
Never did marriage such true union find,
Or men's desires with so glad violence bind;
For there is still some tincture left of sin,
And still the sex will needs be stealing in.
Those joys are full of dross, and thicker far;
These, without matter, clear and liquid are.
Such sacred love does heaven's bright spirits fill,
Where love is but to understand and will,
With swift and unseen motions such as we
Somewhat express in heighten'd charity.
O ye bless'd One! whose love on earth became
So pure, that still in heaven 'tis but the same!
There now ye sit, and with mix'd souls embrace,
Gazing upon great Love's mysterious face,
And pity this base world, where friendship's made
A bait for sin, or else at best a trade.
Ah, wondrous prince! who a true friend couldst be
When a crown flatter'd, and Saul threaten'd thee!

Who held'st him dear whose stars thy birth did cross,
And bought'st him nobly at a kingdom's loss!
Israel's bright sceptre far less glory brings,
There have been fewer friends on earth than kings.
   To this strong pitch their high affections flew,
Till Nature's self scarce looked on them as two.
Hither flies David for advice and aid,
As swift as love and danger could persuade ;
As safe in Jonathan's trust his thoughts remain,
As when himself but dreams them o'er again.
   ' My dearest lord! farewell,' said he, ' farewell;
Heaven bless the King ; may no misfortune tell
The injustice of his hate when I am dead:
They 're coming now; perhaps my guiltless head
Here, in your sight, must then a-bleeding lie,
And scarce your own stand safe for being nigh.
Think me not scared with death, howe'er 't appear;
I know thou canst not think so : it is a fear
From which thy love and Dammin speaks me free;
I 've met him face to face, and ne'er could see
One terror in his looks to make me fly
When virtue bids me stand; but I would die
So as becomes my life, so as may prove
Saul's malice, and at least excuse your love.'
   He stopped, and spoke some passion with his eyes.
' Excellent friend!' the gallant prince replies ;
' Thou hast so proved thy virtues, that they 're known
To all good men, more than to each his own.
Who lives in Israel that can doubtful be
Of thy great actions ? for he lives by thee.
Such is thy valour, and thy vast success,
That all things but thy loyalty are less ;
And should my father at thy ruin aim,
'Twould wound as much his safety as his fame.

74

Think them not coming, then, to slay thee here,
But doubt mishaps as little as you fear;
For, by thy loving God, whoe'er design
Against thy life, must strike at it through mine,
But I my royal father must acquit
From such base guilt, or the low thought of it.
Think on his softness, when from death he freed
The faithless king of Am'lek's cursed seed;
Can he t' a friend, t' a son, so bloody grow,
He who even sinned but now to spare a foe?
Admit he could; but with what strength or art
Could he so long close and seal up his heart?
Such counsels jealous of themselves become,
And dare not fix without consent of some;
Few men so boldly ill great sins to do,
Till licensed and approved by others too.
No more (believe it) could he hide this from me,
Than I, had he discovered it, from thee.'
  Here they embraces join, and almost tears,
Till gentle David thus new-proved his fears:
'The praise you pleased, great prince! on me to spend,
Was all outspoken, when you styled me friend:
That name alone does dangerous glories bring,
And gives excuse to the envy of a king.
What did his spear, force, and dark plots, impart
But some eternal rancour in his heart?
Still does he glance the fortune of that day
When, drowned in his own blood, Goliath lay,
And covered half the plain; still hears the sound
How that vast monster fell, and strook the ground:
The dance, and, David his ten thousand slew,
Still wound his sickly soul, and still are new.
Great acts t' ambitious princes treason grow,
So much they hate that safety which they owe.

Tyrants dread all whom they raise high in place;
From the good danger, from the bad disgrace.
They doubt the lords, mistrust the people's hate,
Till blood become a principle of state.
Secured not by their guards nor by their right,
But still they fear even more than they affright.
Pardon me, sir; your father's rough and stern;
His will too strong to bend, too proud to learn.
Remember, sir, the honey's deadly sting!
Think on that savage justice of the King,
When the same day that saw you do before
Things above man, should see you man no more.
'Tis true, the accursed Agag moved his ruth;
He pitied his tall limbs and comely youth;
Had seen, alas! the proof of Heaven's fierce hate,
And feared no mischief from his powerless fate;
Remember how the old seer came raging down,
And taught him boldly to suspect his crown.
Since then, his pride quakes at the Almighty's rod,
Nor dares he love the man beloved by God.
Hence his deep rage and trembling envy springs;
Nothing so wild as jealousy of kings.
Whom should he counsel ask, with whom advise,
Who reason and God's counsel does despise?
Whose headstrong will no law or conscience daunt,
Dares he not sin, do you think, without your grant?
Yes, if the truth of our fixed love he know,
He would not doubt, believe it, to kill even you.'
    The prince is moved, and straight prepares to find
The deep resolves of his grieved father's mind.
The danger now appears, love can soon show it,
And force his stubborn piety to know it.
They agree that David should concealed abide,
Till his great friend had the Court's temper tried;

Till he had Saul's most sacred purpose found,
And searched the depth and rancour of his wound.
  'Twas the year's seventh-born moon; the solemn feast,
That with most noise its sacred mirth express'd.
From opening morn till night shuts in the day,
On trumpets and shrill horns the Levites play:
Whether by this in mystic type we see
The new-year's day of great eternity,
When the changed moon shall no more changes make,
And scattered death's by trumpets' sound awake;
Or that the law be kept in memory still,
Given with like noise on Sinai's shining hill;
Or that (as some men teach) it did arise
From faithful Abram's righteous sacrifice,
Who, whilst the ram on Isaac's fire did fry,
His horn with joyful tunes stood sounding by;
Obscure the cause, but God his will declared,
And all nice knowledge then with ease is spared.
At the third hour Saul to the hallowed tent,
'Midst a large train of priests and courtiers, went;
The sacred herd marched proud and softly by,
Too fat and gay to think their deaths so nigh.
Hard fate of beasts more innocent than we!
Prey to our luxury and our piety!
Whose guiltless blood on boards and altars spilt,
Serves both to make and expiate, too, our guilt!
Three bullocks of free neck, two gilded rams,
Two well-washed goats, and fourteen spotless lambs,
With the three vital fruits, wine, oil, and bread,
(Small fees to Heaven of all by which we're fed)
Are offered up: the hallowed flames arise,
And faithful prayers mount with them to the skies.
From thence the King to the utmost court is brought,
Where heavenly things an inspired prophet taught,

And from the sacred tent to his palace gates,
With glad kind shouts the assembly on him waits;
The cheerful horns before him loudly play,
And fresh-strewed flowers paint his triumphant way.
Thus in slow pace to the palace-hall they go,
Rich dressed for solemn luxury and show:
Ten pieces of bright tapestry hung the room,
The noblest work e'er stretched on Syrian loom,
For wealthy Adriel in proud Sidon wrought,
And given to Saul when Saul's best gift he sought,
The bright-eyed Merab; for that mindful day
No ornament so proper seemed as they.
    There all old Abram's story you might see,
And still some angel bore him company.
His painful but well-guided travels show
The fate of all his sons, the church below.
Here beauteous Sarah to great Pharaoh came ;
He blushed with sudden passion, she with shame :
Troubled she seemed, and labouring in the strife,
'Twixt her own honour and her husband's life.
Here on a conquering host, that careless lay,
Drowned in the joys of their new-gotten prey,
The patriarch falls ; well-mingled might you see
The confused marks of death and luxury.
In the next piece bless'd Salem's mystic king
Does sacred presents to the victor bring ;
Like Him whose type he bears, his rights receives,
Strictly requires his due, yet freely gives:
Even in his port, his habit, and his face,
The mild and great, the priest and prince, had place.
Here all their starry host the heavens display;
And, lo! a heavenly youth, more fair than they,
Leads Abram forth ; points upwards; 'Such,' said he,
'So bright and numberless thy seed shall be.'
   78

Here he with God a new alliance makes,
And in his flesh the marks of homage takes:
Here he the three mysterious persons feasts,
Well paid with joyful tidings by his guests:
Here for the wicked town he prays, and near,
Scarce did the wicked town through flames appear:
And all his fate, and all his deeds, were wrought,
Since he from Ur to Ephron's cave was brought.
But none 'mongst all the forms drew then their eyes
Like faithful Abram's righteous sacrifice:
The sad old man mounts slowly to the place,
With Nature's power triumphant in his face
O'er the mind's courage ; for, in spite of all,
From his swoln eyes resistless waters fall.
The innocent boy his cruel burden bore
With smiling looks, and sometimes walked before,
And sometimes turned to talk : above was made
The altar's fatal pile, and on it laid
The hope of mankind : patiently he lay,
And did his sire, as he his God, obey.
The mournful sire lifts up at last the knife,
And on one moment's string depends his life,
In whose young loins such brooding wonders lie.
A thousand sp'rits peeped from the affrighted sky,
Amazed at this strange scene, and almost fear'd,
For all those joyful prophecies they'd heard;
Till one leaped nimbly forth, by God's command,
Like lightning from a cloud, and stopped his hand.
The gentle sp'rit smiled kindly as he spoke;
New beams of joy through Abram's wonder broke.
The angel points to a tuft of bushes near,
Where an entangled ram does half appear,
And struggles vainly with that fatal net,
Which, though but slightly wrought, was firmly set:

For, lo! anon, to this sad glory doomed,
The useful beast on Isaac's pile consumed;
Whilst on his horns the ransomed couple played,
And the glad boy danced to the tunes he made.
  Near this hall's end a shittim table stood,
Yet well-wrought plate strove to conceal the wood;
For from the foot a golden vine did sprout,
And cast his fruitful riches all about.
Well might that beauteous ore the grape express,
Which does weak man intoxicate no less.
Of the same wood the gilded beds were made,
And on them large embroidered carpets laid,
From Egypt, the rich shop of follies, brought;
But arts of pride all nations soon are taught.
Behold seven comely blooming youths appear,
And in their hands seven silver washpots bear,
Curled, and gay clad, the choicest sons that be
Of Gibeon's race, and slaves of high degree.
Seven beauteous maids marched softly in behind,
Bright scarves their clothes, their hair fresh garlands bind,
And whilst the princes wash, they on them shed
Rich ointments, which their costly odours spread
O'er the whole room; from their small prisons free,
With such glad haste through the wide air they flee.
The King was placed alone, and o'er his head
A well-wrought heaven of silk and gold was spread,
Azure the ground, the sun in gold shone bright,
But pierced the wandering clouds with silver light.
The right-hand bed the King's three sons did grace,
The third was Abner's, Adriel's, David's place:
And twelve large tables more were filled below,
With the prime men Saul's court and camp could show.
The palace did with mirth and music sound,
And the crowned goblets nimbly moved around:
  80

But though bright joy in every guest did shine,
The plenty, state, music, and sprightful wine,
Were lost on Saul: an angry care did dwell
In his dark breast, and all gay forms expel.
David's unusual absence from the feast,
To his sick sp'rit did jealous thoughts suggest:
Long lay he still, nor drank, nor ate, nor spoke,
And thus at last his troubled silence broke.
 'Where can he be?' said he. 'It must be so.'
With that he paused awhile. 'Too well we know
His boundless pride: he grieves, and hates to see
The solemn triumphs of my court and me.
Believe me, friends! and trust what I can show
From thousand proofs; the ambitious David now
Does those vast things in his proud soul design,
That too much business give for mirth or wine.
He's kindling now, perhaps, rebellious fire
Among the tribes, and does even now conspire
Against my crown, and all our lives, whilst we
Are loth even to suspect what we might see.
By the Great Name 'tis true.'
With that he strook the board, and no man there,
But Jonathan, durst undertake to clear
The blameless prince: and scarce ten words he spoke,
When thus his speech the enraged tyrant broke:
 'Disloyal wretch! thy gentle mother's shame!
Whose cold, pale ghost even blushes at thy name!
Who fears lest her chaste bed should doubted be,
And her white fame stained by black deeds of thee!
Canst thou be mine? A crown sometimes does hire
Even sons against their parents to conspire;
But ne'er did story yet, or fable, tell
Of one so wild who, merely to rebel,
Quitted the unquestioned birthright of a throne,

And bought his father's ruin with his own.
Thou need'st not plead the ambitious youth's defence;
Thy crime clears his, and makes that innocence :
Nor can his foul ingratitude appear,
Whilst thy unnatural guilt is placed so near.
Is this that noble friendship you pretend?
Mine, thine own foe, and thy worst enemy's friend?
If thy low spirit can thy great birthright quit,
The thing's but just, so ill deserv'st thou it.
I, and thy brethren here, have no such mind,
Nor such prodigious worth in David find,
That we to him should our just rights resign,
Or think God's choice not made so well as thine.
Shame of thy house and tribe! hence from mine eye;
To thy false friend and servile master fly;
He's ere this time in arms expecting thee ;
Haste, for those arms are raised to ruin me.
Thy sin that way will nobler much appear,
Than to remain his spy and agent here.
When I think this, Nature, by thee forsook,
Forsakes me too.'   With that his spear he took
To strike at him : the mirth and music cease ;
The guests all rise this sudden storm t' appease.
The prince his danger and his duty knew,
And low he bowed, and silently withdrew.
    To David straight, who in a forest nigh
Waits his advice, the royal friend does fly.
The sole advice, now, like the danger clear,
Was in some foreign land this storm t' outwear.
All marks of comely grief in both are seen,
And mournful kind discourses passed between.
Now generous tears their hasty tongues restrain;
Now they begin, and talk all o'er again :
A reverent oath of constant love they take,

And God's high name their dreaded witness make :
Not that at all their faiths could doubtful prove,
But 'twas the tedious zeal of endless love.
Thus, ere they part, they the short time bestow
In all the pomp friendship and grief could show.
And David now, with doubtful cares oppressed,
Beneath a shade borrows some little rest ;
When by command divine thick mists arise,
And stop the sense, and close the conquered eyes.
There is a place which man most high doth rear,
The small world's heaven, where reason moves the
    sphere ;
Here in a robe which does all colours show,
(The envy of birds, and the clouds' gaudy bow,)
Fancy, wild dame, with much lascivious pride,
By twin-chameleons drawn, does gaily ride :
Her coach there follows, and throngs round about
Of shapes and airy forms an endless rout.
A sea rolls on with harmless fury here ;
Straight 'tis a field, and trees and herbs appear.
Here in a moment are vast armies made,
And a quick scene of war and blood displayed.
Here sparkling wines, and brighter maids come in,
The bawds for Sense, and lying baits of sin.
Some things arise of strange and quarrelling kind,
The forepart lion, and a snake behind.
Here golden mountains swell the covetous place,
And Centaurs ride themselves, a painted race.
Of these slight wonders Nature sees the store,
And only then accounts herself but poor.
    Hither an angel comes in David's trance,
And finds them mingled in an antique dance ;
Of all the numerous forms fit choice he takes,
And joins them wisely, and this vision makes.

First, David there appears in kingly state,
Whilst the Twelve Tribes his dread commands await:
Straight to the wars with his joined strength he goes,
Settles new friends, and frights his ancient foes.
To Solima, Canaan's old head, they came,
(Since high in note, then not unknown to Fame,)
The blind and lame the undoubted wall defend,
And no new wounds or dangers apprehend.
The busy image of great Joab there
Disdains the mock, and teaches them to fear:
He climbs the airy walls, leaps raging down,
New-minted shapes of slaughter fill the town.
They curse the guards their mirth and bravery chose,
All of them now are slain, or made like those.
Far through an inward scene an army lay,
Which with full banners a fair Fish display.
From Sidon plains to happy Egypt's coast
They seem all met, a vast and warlike host.
Thither hastes David to his destined prey,
Honour and noble danger lead the way.
The conscious trees shook with a reverent fear
Their unblown tops: God walked before him there.
Slaughter the wearied Rephaims' bosom fills,
Dead corpse emboss the vale with little hills.
On the other side, Sophenes' mighty king
Numberless troops of the bless'd East does bring:
Twice are his men cut off, and chariots ta'en;
Damascus and rich Adad help in vain;
Here Nabathæan troops in battle stand,
With all the lusty youth of Syrian land;
Undaunted Joab rushes on with speed,
Gallantly mounted on his fiery steed;
He hews down all, and deals his deaths around;
The Syrians leave, or possess, dead, the ground.

On the other wing does brave Abishai ride,
Reeking in blood and dust: on every side
The perjured sons of Ammon quit the field;
Some basely die, and some more basely yield.
Through a thick wood the wretched Hanun flies,
And far more justly then fears Hebrew spies.
Moloch, their bloody god, thrusts out his head,
Grinning through a black cloud: him they'd long fed
In his seven chambers, and he still did eat
New-roasted babes, his dear delicious meat.
Again they rise, more angered and dismayed;
Euphrates and swift Tigris sends them aid:
In vain they send it, for again they're slain,
And feast the greedy birds on Healy plain.
Here Rabba with proud towers affronts the sky,
And round about great Joab's trenches lie :
They force the walls, and sack the helpless town;
On David's head shines Ammon's massy crown.
'Midst various torments the cursed race expires;
David himself his severe wrath admires.
  Next upon Israel's throne does bravely sit
A comely youth, endowed with wondrous wit:
Far, from the parched line, a royal dame,
To hear his tongue and boundless wisdom, came :
She carried back in her triumphant womb
The glorious stock of thousand kings to come.
Here brightest forms his pomp and wealth display;
Here they a temple's vast foundations lay;
A mighty work; and with fit glories filled,
For God to inhabit, and that King to build.
Some from the quarries hew out massy stone,
Some draw it up with cranes ; some breathe and groan
In order o'er the anvil; some cut down
Tall cedars, the proud mountain's ancient crown;

Some carve the trunks, and breathing shapes bestow,
Giving the trees more life than when they grow.
But, oh! alas! what sudden cloud is spread
About this glorious King's eclipsed head?
It all his fame benights, and all his store,
Wrapping him round ; and now he 's seen no more.
    When straight his son appears at Sichem crown'd,
With young and heedless council circled round;
Unseemly object! but a falling state
Has always its own errors joined with Fate.
Ten tribes at once forsake the Jessian throne,
And bold Adoram at his message stone ;
'Brethren of Israel!'—More he fain would say,
But a flint stopped his mouth, and speech in the way..
Here this fond king's disasters but begin;
He 's destined to more shame by his father's sin.
Susac comes up, and under his command
A dreadful army from scorched Afric's sand,
As numberless as that: all is his prey;
The temple's sacred wealth they bear away;
Adrazar's shields and golden loss they take ;
Even David in his dream does sweat and shake.
Thus fails this wretched prince; his loins appear
Of less weight now than Solomon's fingers were.
    Abijah next seeks Israel to regain,
And wash in seas of blood his father's stain.
Ne'er saw the aged sun so cruel sight;
Scarce saw he this, but hid his bashful light.
Nebat's cursed son fled with not half his men;
Where were his gods of Dan and Bethel then?
Yet could not this the fatal strife decide;
God punished one, but blessed not the other side.
    Asan, a just and virtuous prince, succeeds,
High raised by Fame for great and godly deeds :

He cut the solemn groves where idols stood,
And sacrificed the gods with their own wood.
He vanquished thus the proud weak powers of hell;
Before him next their doting servants fell:
So huge an host of Zerah's men he slew,
As made even that Arabia desert too.
Why feared he then the perjured Baasha's sight?
Or bought the dangerous aid of Syrian's might?
Conquest, Heaven's gift, cannot by man be sold;
Alas! what weakness trusts he? man and gold.
    Next Josaphat possessed the royal state;
A happy prince, well worthy of his fate:
His oft oblations on God's altar, made
With thousand flocks, and thousand herds, are paid,
Arabian tribute!   What mad troops are those,
Those mighty troops that dare to be his foes?
He prays them dead; with mutual wounds they fall;
One fury brought, one fury slays them all.
Thus sits he still, and sees himself to win,
Never o'ercome but by his friend Ahab's sin;
On whose disguise Fates then did only look,
And had almost their God's command mistook:
Him from whose danger Heaven securely brings,
And for his sake too ripely wicked kings.
Their armies languish, burnt with thirst, at Seere,
Sighs all their cold, tears all their moisture there:
They fix their greedy eyes on the empty sky,
And fancy clouds, and so become more dry.
Elisha calls for waters from afar
To come; Elisha calls, and here they are.
In helmets they quaff round the welcome flood,
And the decrease repair with Moab's blood.
Jehoram next, and Ochoziah, throng
For Judah's sceptre; both shortlived too long.

A woman, too, from murder title claims;
Both with her sins and sex the crown she shames.
Proud, cursed woman! but her fall at last
To doubting men clears Heaven for what was past.
Joas at first does bright and glorious show;
In life's fresh morn his fame did early crow:
Fair was the promise of his dawning ray,
But prophet's angry blood o'ercast his day:
From thence his clouds, from thence his storms, begin,
It cries aloud, and twice lets Aram in.
So Amaziah lives, so ends his reign,
Both by their traitorous servants justly slain.
Edom at first dreads his victorious hand;
Before him thousand captives trembling stand.
Down a precipice, deep down he casts them all;
The mimic shapes in several postures fall:
But then (mad fool!) he does those gods adore,
Which when plucked down had worshipped him before.
Thus all his life to come is loss and shame :
No help from gods, who themselves helped not, came.
　　All this Uzziah's strength and wit repairs,
Leaving a well-built greatness to his heirs;
Till leprous scurf, o'er his whole body cast,
Takes him at first from men, from earth at last.
As virtuous was his son, and happier far;
Buildings his peace, and trophies graced his war:
But Achaz heaps up sins, as if he meant
To make his worst forefathers innocent:
He burns his son at Hinnon, whilst around
The roaring child drums and loud trumpets sound:
This to the boy a barbarous mercy grew,
And snatched him from all miseries to ensue.
Here Peca comes, and hundred thousands fall;
Here Rezin marches up, and sweeps up all;

Till like a sea the great Belochus' son
Breaks upon both, and both does overrun.
The last of Adad's ancient stock is slain,
Israel captived, and rich Damascus ta'en;
All his wild rage to revenge Judah's wrong;
But woe to kingdoms that have friends too strong!
    Thus Hezekiah the torn empire took,
And Assur's king with his worse gods forsook;
Who to poor Judah worlds of nations brings,
There rages, utters vain and mighty things.
Some dream of triumphs, and exalted names,
Some of dear gold, and some of beauteous dames;
Whilst in the midst of their huge sleepy boast,
An angel scatters death through all the host.
The affrighted tyrant back to Babel hies,
There meets an end far worse than that he flies.
Here Hezekiah's life is almost done!
So good, and yet, alas! so short 'tis spun.
The end of the line was ravelled, weak, and old;
Time must go back, and afford better hold,
To tie a new thread to it of fifteen years.
'Tis done; the almighty power of prayer and tears!
Backward the sun, an unknown motion, went;
The stars gazed on, and wondered what he meant.
Manasses next (forgetful man!) begins,
Enslaved and sold to Ashur by his sins;
Till by the rod of learned Misery taught,
Home to his God and country both he 's brought.
It taught not Ammon, nor his hardness brake,
He 's made the example he refused to take.
    Yet from this root a goodly scion springs,
Josiah! best of men, as well as kings.
Down went the calves, with all their gold and cost;
The priests then truly grieved, Osiris lost.

These mad Egyptian rites till now remained;
Fools! they their worser thraldom still retained!
In his own fires Moloch to ashes fell,
And no more flames must have besides his hell.
Like end Astartes' horned image found,
And Baal's spired stone to dust was ground.
No more were men in female habit seen,
Or they in men's, by the lewd Syrian queen;
No lustful maids at Benos' temple sit,
And with their body's shame their marriage get.
The double Dagon neither nature saves,
Nor flies she back to the Erythræan waves.
The travelling sun sees gladly from on high
His chariots burn, and Nergal quenched lie.
The King's impartial anger lights on all,
From fly-blown Accaron to the thundering Baal.
Here David's joy unruly grows and bold,
Nor could sleep's silken chain its violence hold,
Had not the angel, to seal fast his eyes,
The humours stirred, and bid more mists arise;
When straight a chariot hurries swift away,
And in it good Josiah bleeding lay:
One hand 's held up, one stops the wound; in vain
They both are used.   Alas! he 's slain, he 's slain.
    Jehoias and Jehoiakim next appear;
Both urge that vengeance which before was near.
He in Egyptian fetters captive dies,
This by more courteous Anger murdered lies.
His son and brother next to bonds sustain,
Israel's now solemn and imperial chain.
Here 's the last scene of this proud city's state;
All ills are met, tied in one knot of Fate.
Their endless slavery in this trial lay;
Great God had heaped up ages in one day:
    90

Strong works around the walls the Chaldees build,
The town with grief and dreadful business filled:
To their carved gods the frantic women pray,
Gods which as near their ruin were as they:
At last in rushes the prevailing foe,
Does all the mischief of proud conquest show.
The wondering babes from mothers' breasts are rent,
And suffer ills they neither feared nor meant.
No silver reverence guards the stooping age,
No rule or method ties their boundless rage.
The glorious temple shines in flames all o'er,
Yet not so bright as in its gold before.
Nothing but fire or slaughter meets the eyes;
Nothing the ear but groans and dismal cries.
The walls and towers are levelled with the ground,
And scarce aught now of that vast city's found,
But shards and rubbish, which weak signs might keep,
Of forepast glory, and bid travellers weep.
Thus did triumphant Assur homewards pass,
And thus Jerus'lem left, Jerusalem that was!
  Thus Zedechia saw, and this not all;
Before his face his friends and children fall,
The sport of insolent victors : this he views,
A king and father once : ill Fate could use
His eyes no more to do their master spite;
All to be seen she took, and next his sight.
Thus a long death in prison he outwears,
Bereft of grief's last solace, even his tears.
  Then Jeconiah's son did foremost come,
And he who brought the captived nation home;
A row of Worthies in long order passed
O'er the short stage; of all old Joseph last.
Fair angels passed by next in seemly bands,
All gilt, with gilded baskets in their hands.

Some as they went the blue-eyed violets strew,
Some spotless lilies in loose order threw.
Some did the way with full-blown roses spread,
Their smell divine, and colour strangely red;
Not such as our dull gardens proudly wear,
Whom weather's taint, and wind's rude kisses tear.
Such, I believe, was the first rose's hue,
Which, at God's word, in beauteous Eden grew;
Queen of the flowers, which made that orchard gay,
The morning-blushes of the Spring's new day.
      With sober pace an heavenly maid walks in,
Her looks all fair, no sign of native sin
Through her whole body writ; immoderate grace
Spoke things far more than human in her face:
It casts a dusky gloom o'er all the flowers,
And with full beams their mingled light devours.
An angel straight broke from a shining cloud,
And pressed his wings, and with much reverence bowed;
Again he bowed, and grave approach he made,
And thus his sacred message sweetly said:
      'Hail! full of grace! thee the whole world shall call
Above all bless'd; thee, who shall bless them all.
Thy virgin womb in wondrous sort shall shroud
Jesus the God; (and then again he bowed)
Conception the great Spirit shall breathe on thee:
Hail thou! who must God's wife, God's mother be.'
With that his seeming form to heaven he reared,
(She low obeisance made) and disappeared.
Lo! a new star three Eastern sages see;
(For why should only earth a gainer be?)
They saw this Phosphor's infant light, and knew
It bravely ushered in a sun as new;
They hasted all this rising sun t' adore;
With them rich myrrh, and early spices, bore.

Wise men! no fitter gift your zeal could bring;
You 'll in a noisome stable find your king.
Anon a thousand devils run roaring in;
Some with a dreadful smile deform'dly grin;
Some stamp their cloven paws, some frown, and tear
The gaping snakes from their black-knotted hair;
As if all grief, and all the rage of hell
Were doubled now, or that just now they fell:
But when the dreaded maid they entering saw,
All fled with trembling fear and silent awe:
In her chaste arms the Eternal Infant lies,
The Almighty Voice changed into feeble cries.
Heaven contained virgins oft, and will do more;
Never did virgin contain Heaven before.
Angels peep round to view this mystic thing,
And halleluiah round, all halleluiah sing.

No longer could good David quiet bear
The unwieldy pleasure which o'erflowed him here:
It broke the fetter, and burst ope his eye;
Away the timorous Forms together fly.
Fixed with amaze he stood, and time must take,
To learn if yet he were at last awake.
Sometimes he thinks that Heaven this vision sent,
And ordered all the pageants as they went:
Sometimes that only 'twas wild Fancy's play,
The loose and scattered relics of the day.

When Gabriel (no bless'd sp'rit more kind or fair)
Bodies and clothes himself with thickened air;
All like a comely youth in life's fresh bloom,
Rare workmanship, and wrought by heavenly loom!
He took for skin a cloud most soft and bright
That o'er the mid-day sun pierced through with light;
Upon his cheeks a lively blush he spread,
Washed from the morning beauty's deepest red;

A harmless flaming meteor shone for hair,
And fell adown his shoulders with loose care:
He cuts out a silk mantle from the skies,
Where the most sprightly azure please the eyes;
This he with starry vapours spangles all,
Took in their prime ere they grow ripe, and fall:
Of a new rainbow, ere it fret or fade,
The choicest piece took out, a scarf is made;
Small streaming clouds he does for wings display,
Not virtuous lovers' sighs more soft than they;
These he gilds o'er with the sun's richest rays,
Caught gliding o'er pure streams on which he plays.
    Thus dressed, the joyful Gabriel posts away,
And carries with him his own glorious day
Through the thick woods; the gloomy shades a while
Put on fresh looks, and wonder why they smile;
The trembling serpents close and silent lie;
The birds obscene far from his passage fly;
A sudden spring waits on him as he goes,
Sudden as that which by creation rose.
Thus he appears to David; at first sight
All earth-bred fears and sorrows take their flight:
In rushes joy divine, and hope, and rest;
A sacred calm shines through his peaceful breast.
'Hail, man belov'd! from highest heaven,' said he,
'My mighty Master sends thee health by me.
The things thou saw'st are full of truth and light,
Shaped in the glass of the divine foresight.
Even now old Time is harnessing the Years
To go in order thus: hence, empty fears!
Thy fate's all white; from thy bless'd seed shall spring
The promised Shilo, the great mystic King.
Round the whole earth his dreaded Name shall sound,
And reach to worlds that must not yet be found:

94

The Southern clime him her sole Lord shall style,
Him all the North, even Albion's stubborn isle.
My fellow-servant, credit what I tell.'
Straight into shapeless air unseen he fell.

LIFE.

'NASCENTES MORIMUR.'—*Manil.*

1 We're ill by these grammarians used:
  We are abused by words, grossly abused;
  From the maternal tomb
  To the grave's fruitful womb
  We call here Life; but Life's a name
  That nothing here can truly claim:
  This wretched inn, where we scarce stay to bait,
  We call our dwelling-place;
  We call one step a race:
  But angels in their full-enlightened state,
  Angels who live, and know what 'tis to be,
  Who all the nonsense of our language see,
  Who speak things, and our words their ill-drawn
      picture scorn.
  When we by a foolish figure say,
  Behold an old man dead! then they
  Speak properly, and cry, Behold a man-child born!

2 My eyes are opened, and I see
  Through the transparent fallacy:
  Because we seem wisely to talk
  Like men of business, and for business walk
  From place to place,
  And mighty voyages we take,
  And mighty journeys seem to make
  O'er sea and land, the little point that has no space;

Because we fight, and battles gain,
Some captives call, and say the rest are slain;
Because we heap up yellow earth, and so
Rich, valiant, wise, and virtuous seem to grow;
Because we draw a long nobility
From hieroglyphic proofs of heraldry,
And impudently talk of a posterity;
And, like Egyptian chroniclers,
Who write of twenty thousand years,
With maravedies make the account,
That single time might to a sum amount;
We grow at last by custom to believe
That really we live;
Whilst all these shadows that for things we take,
Are but the empty dreams which in death's sleep
  we make.

3 But these fantastic errors of our dream
Lead us to solid wrong;
We pray God our friends' torments to prolong.
And wish uncharitably for them
To be as long a-dying as Methusalem.
The ripened soul longs from his prison to come,
But we would seal and sew up, if we could, the
  womb.
We seek to close and plaster up by art
The cracks and breaches of the extended shell,
And in that narrow cell
Would rudely force to dwell
The noble, vigorous bird already winged to part.

THE PLAGUES OF EGYPT.

I.

Is this thy bravery, Man! is this thy pride!
Rebel to God, and slave to all beside!
Captived by everything! and only free
To fly from thine own liberty!
All creatures, the Creator said, were thine;
No creature but might since say, Man is mine!
In black Egyptian slavery we lie,
And sweat and toil in the vain dru
Of tyrant Sin,
To which we trophies raise, and wear out all our
        breath
In building up the monuments of death.
We, the choice race, to God and angels kin!
In vain the prophets and apostles come
To call us home,
Home to the promised Canaan above,
Which does with nourishing milk and pleasant
        honey flow,
And even i' th' way to which we should be fed
With angels' tasteful bread:
But we, alas! the flesh-pots love;
We love the very leeks and sordid roots below.

II.

In vain we judgments feel, and wonders see;
In vain did God to descend hither deign,
He was his own Ambassador in vain,
Our Moses and our guide himself to be.
We will not let ourselves to go,
And with worse hardened hearts, do our own
        Pharaohs grow;

Ah! lest at last we perish so,
Think, stubborn Man! think of the Egyptian prince,
(Hard of belief and will, but not so hard as thou,)
Think with what dreadful proofs God did convince
The feeble arguments that human power could show;
Think what plagues attend on thee,
Who Moses' God dost now refuse more oft than Moses he.

III.

'If from some God you come,' said the proud king,
With half a smile and half a frown,
'But what God can to Egypt be unknown?
What sign, what powers, what credence do you bring?'
'Behold his seal! behold his hand!'
Cries Moses, and casts down the almighty wand:
The almighty wand scarce touched the earth,
When, with an undiscerned birth,
The almighty wand a serpent grew,
And his long half in painted folds behind him drew:
Upwards his threatening tail he threw,
Upwards he cast his threatening head,
He gaped and hissed aloud,
With flaming eyes surveyed the trembling crowd,
And, like a basilisk, almost looked the assembly dead:
Swift fled the amazed king, the guards before him fled.

IV.

Jannes and Jambres stopped their flight,
And with proud words allayed the affright.
'The God of slaves!' said they, 'how can he be
More powerful than their master's deity?'
And down they cast their rods,
And muttered secret sounds that charm the servile gods.
The evil spirits their charms obey,

And in a subtle cloud they snatch the rods away,
And serpents in their place the airy jugglers lay:
Serpents in Egypt's monstrous land
Were ready still at hand,
And all at the Old Serpent's first command:
And they, too, gaped, and they, too, hissed,
And they their threatening tails did twist;
But straight on both the Hebrew serpent flew,
Broke both their active backs, and both it slew,
And both almost at once devoured;
So much was overpowered
By God's miraculous creation
His servant Nature's slightly wrought and feeble genera-
    tion.

v.

On the famed bank the prophets stood,
Touched with their rod, and wounded all the flood;
Flood now no more, but a long vein of putrid blood;
The helpless fish were found
In their strange current drowned;
The herbs and trees washed by the mortal tide
About it blushed and died:
The amazed crocodiles made haste to ground;
From their vast trunks the dropping gore they spied,
Thought it their own, and dreadfully aloud they cried:
Nor all thy priests, nor thou,
O King! couldst ever show
From whence thy wandering Nile begins his course;
Of this new Nile thou seest the sacred source,
And as thy land that does o'erflow,
Take heed lest this do so.
What plague more just could on thy waters fall?
The Hebrew infants' murder stains them all.

99

The kind, instructing punishment enjoy;
Whom the red river cannot mend, the Red Sea shall
    destroy.

VI.

The river yet gave one instruction more,
And from the rotting fish and unconcocted gore,
Which was but water just before,
A loathsome host was quickly made,
That scaled the banks, and with loud noise did all the
    country invade;
As Nilus when he quits his sacred bed,
(But like a friend he visits all the land
With welcome presents in his hand,)
So did this living tide the fields o'erspread.
In vain the alarmed country tries
To kill their noisome enemies,
From the unexhausted source still new recruits arise:
Nor does the earth these greedy troops suffice;
The towns and houses they possess,
The temples and the palaces,
Nor Pharaoh nor his gods they fear,
Both their importune croakings hear:
Unsatiate yet they mount up higher,
Where never sun-born frog durst to aspire,
And in the silken beds their slimy members place,
A luxury unknown before to all the watery race.

VII.

The water thus her wonders did produce,
But both were to no use:
As yet the sorcerer's mimic power served for excuse.
Try what the earth will do, said God, and lo!
They struck the earth a fertile blow,

    100

And all the dust did straight to stir begin,
One would have thought some sudden wind had been,
But, lo! 'twas nimble life was got within!
And all the little springs did move,
And every dust did an armed vermin prove,
Of an unknown and new-created kind,
Such as the magic gods could neither make or find.
The wretched shameful foe allowed no rest
Either to man or beast;
Not Pharaoh from the unquiet plague could be,
With all his change of raiments, free;
The devils themselves confessed
This was God's hand; and 'twas but just
To punish thus man's pride, to punish dust with dust.

VIII.

Lo! the third element does his plagues prepare,
And swarming clouds of insects fill the air;
With sullen noise they take their flight,
And march in bodies infinite;
In vain 'tis day above, 'tis still beneath them night;
Of harmful flies the nations numberless
Composed this mighty army's spacious boast;
Of different manners, different languages,
And different habits, too, they wore,
And different arms they bore:
And some, like Scythians, lived on blood,
And some on green, and some on flowery food,
And Accaron, the airy prince, led on this various host.
Houses secure not men; the populous ill
Did all the houses fill:
The country all around,
Did with the cries of tortured cattle sound;

About the fields enraged they flew,
And wished the plague that was t' ensue.

IX.

From poisonous stars a mortal influence came,
(The mingled malice of their flame,)
A skilful angel did the ingredients take,
And with just hands the sad composure make,
And over all the land did the full viol shake.
Thirst, giddiness, faintness, and putrid heats,
And pining pains, and shivering sweats,
On all the cattle, all the beasts, did fall;
With deformed death the country's covered all.
The labouring ox drops down before the plough;
The crowned victims to the altar led
Sink, and prevent the lifted blow:
The generous horse from the full manger turns his head,
Does his loved floods and pastures scorn,
Hates the shrill trumpet and the horn,
Nor can his lifeless nostril please
With the once-ravishing smell of all his dappled mis-
        tresses ;
The starving sheep refuse to feed,
They bleat their innocent souls out into air;
The faithful dogs lie gasping by them there;
The astonished shepherd weeps, and breaks his tuneful
        reed.

X.

Thus did the beasts for man's rebellion die;
God did on man a gentler medicine try,
And a disease for physic did apply.
Warm ashes from the furnace Moses took,
The sorcerers did with wonder on him look,

And smiled at the unaccustomed spell
Which no Egyptian rituals tell.
He flings the pregnant ashes through the air,
And speaks a mighty prayer,
Both which the minist'ring winds around all Egypt bear;
As gentle western blasts, with downy wings
Hatching the tender springs,
To the unborn buds with vital whispers say,
Ye living buds, why do ye stay?
The passionate buds break through the bark their way;
So wheresoe'er this tainted wind but blew,
Swelling pains and ulcers grew;
It from the body called all sleeping poisons out,
And to them added new;
A noisome spring of sores as thick as leaves did sprout.

XI.

Heaven itself is angry next;
Woe to man when Heaven is vexed;
With sullen brow it frowned,
And murmured first in an imperfect sound;
Till Moses, lifting up his hand,
Waves the expected signal of his wand,
And all the full-charged clouds in ranged squadrons
        move,
And fill the spacious plains above;
Through which the rolling thunder first does play,
And opens wide the tempest's noisy way:
And straight a stony shower
Of monstrous hail does downward pour,
Such as ne'er Winter yet brought forth,
From all her stormy magazines of the north:
It all the beasts and men abroad did slay,
O'er the defaced corpse, like monuments, lay;

The houses and strong-bodied trees it broke,
Nor asked aid from the thunder's stroke:
The thunder but for terror through it flew,
The hail alone the work could do.
The dismal lightnings all around,
Some flying through the air, some running on the ground,
Some swimming o'er the waters' face,
Filled with bright horror every place;
One would have thought, their dreadful day to have seen,
The very hail and rain itself had kindled been.

XII.

The infant corn, which yet did scarce appear,
Escaped this general massacre
Of every thing that grew,
And the well-stored Egyptian year
Began to clothe her fields and trees anew;
When, lo! a scorching wind from the burnt countries
      blew,
And endless legions with it drew
Of greedy locusts, who, where'er
With sounding wings they flew,
Left all the earth depopulate and bare,
As if Winter itself had marched by there,
Whate'er the sun and Nile
Gave with large bounty to the thankful soil,
The wretched pillagers bore away,
And the whole Summer was their prey;
Till Moses with a prayer,
Breathed forth a violent western wind,
Which all these living clouds did headlong bear
(No stragglers left behind)
Into the purple sea, and there bestow
On the luxurious fish a feast they ne'er did know.

With untaught joy Pharaoh the news does hear,
And little thinks their fate attends on him and his so
  near.

XIII.

What blindness and what darkness did there e'er
Like this undocile king's appear?
Whate'er but that which now does represent
And paint the crime out in the punishment?
From the deep baleful caves of hell below,
Where the old mother Night does grow,
Substantial Night, that does disclaim
Privation's empty name,
Through secret conduits monstrous shapes arose,
Such as the sun's whole force could not oppose;
They with a solid cloud
All heaven's eclipsed face did shroud;
Seemed with large wings spread o'er the sea and earth,
To brood up a new Chaos his deformed birth;
And every lamp, and every fire,
Did, at the dreadful sight, wink and expire,
To the empyrean source all streams of light seemed to
  retire.
The living men were in their standing houses buried,
But the long night no slumber knows,
But the short death finds no repose.
Ten thousand terrors through the darkness fled,
And ghosts complained, and spirits murmured,
And fancy's multiplying sight
Viewed all the scenes invisible of night.

XIV.

Of God's dreadful anger these
Were but the first light skirmishes;
The shock and bloody battle now begins,

105

The plenteous harvest of full-ripened sins.
It was the time when the still moon
Was mounted softly to her noon,
And dewy sleep, which from Night's secret springs arose,
Gently as Nile the land o'erflows;
When, lo! from the high countries of refined day,
The golden heaven without allay,
Whose dross, in the creation purged away,
Made up the sun's adulterate ray,
Michael, the warlike prince, does downwards fly,
Swift as the journeys of the sight,
Swift as the race of light,
And with his winged will cuts through the yielding sky.
He passed through many a star, and as he passed
Shone (like a star in them) more brightly there
Than they did in their sphere :
On a tall pyramid's pointed head he stopped at last,
And a mild look of sacred pity cast
Down on the sinful land where he was sent
To inflict the tardy punishment.
' Ah! yet,' said he, ' yet, stubborn King! repent,
Whilst thus unarmed I stand,
Ere the keen sword of God fill my commanded hand;
Suffer but yet thyself and thine to live.
Who would, alas! believe
That it for man,' said he,
' So hard to be forgiven should be,
And yet for God so easy to forgive!'

XV.

He spoke, and downwards flew,
And o'er his shining form a well-cut cloud he threw,
Made of the blackest fleece of night,
And close-wrought to keep in the powerful light;

106

Yet, wrought so fine, it hindered not his flight,
But through the key-holes and the chinks of doors,
And through the narrowest walks of crooked pores,
He passed more swift and free
Than in wide air the wanton swallows flee:
He took a pointed pestilence in his hand,
The spirits of thousand mortal poisons made
The strongly-tempered blade,
The sharpest sword that e'er was laid
Up in the magazines of God to scourge a wicked land:
Through Egypt's wicked land his march he took,
And as he marched the sacred first-born struck
Of every womb; none did he spare;
None from the meanest beast to Cenchre's purple heir.

XVI.

The swift approach of endless night
Breaks ope the wounded sleepers' rolling eyes;
They awake the rest with dying cries,
And darkness doubles the affright.
The mixéd sounds of scattered deaths they hear,
And lose their parted souls 'twixt grief and fear.
Louder than all, the shrieking women's voice
Pierces this chaos of confused noise;
As brighter lightning cuts a way,
Clear and distinguished through the day:
With less complaints the Zoan temples sound
When the adored heifer 's drowned,
And no true marked successor to be found:
While health, and strength, and gladness does possess
The festal Hebrew cottages;
The bless'd destroyer comes not there,
To interrupt the sacred cheer,
That now begins their well-reformed year.

107

Upon their doors he read and understood
God's protection writ in blood;
Well was he skilled i' th' character divine,
And though he passed by it in haste,
He bowed, and worshipped as he passed
The mighty mystery through its humble sign.

XVII.

The sword strikes now too deep and near,
Longer with its edge to play,
No diligence or cost they spare
To haste the Hebrews now away,
Pharaoh himself chides their delay;
So kind and bountiful is fear!
But, oh! the bounty which to fear we owe,
Is but like fire struck out of stone,
So hardly got, and quickly gone,
That it scarce outlives the blow.
Sorrow and fear soon quit the tyrant's breast,
Rage and revenge their place possess'd:
With a vast host of chariots and of horse,
And all his powerful kingdom's ready force,
The travelling nation he pursues,
Ten times o'ercome, he still the unequal war renews.
Filled with proud hopes, 'At least,' said he,
'The Egyptian gods, from Syrian magic free,
Will now revenge themselves and me;
Behold what passless rocks on either hand,
Like prison walls, about them stand!
Whilst the sea bounds their flight before,
And in our injured justice they must find
A far worse stop than rocks and seas behind;
Which shall with crimson gore
New paint the water's name, and double dye the shore.'

XVIII.

He spoke; and all his host
Approved with shouts the unhappy boast;
A bidden wind bore his vain words away,
And drowned them in the neighbouring sea.
No means to escape the faithless travellers spy,
And with degenerous fear to die,
Curse their new-gotten liberty :
But the great Guide well knew he led them right,
And saw a path hid yet from human sight:
He strikes the raging waves; the waves on either side
Unloose their close embraces, and divide,
And backwards press, as in some solemn show
The crowding people do,
(Though just before no space was seen,)
To let the admired triumph pass between.
The wondering army saw, on either hand,
The no less wondering waves like rocks of crystal stand.
They marched betwixt, and boldly trod
The secret paths of God:
And here and there, all scattered in their way,
The sea's old spoils and gaping fishes lay
Deserted on the sandy plain:
The sun did with astonishment behold
The inmost chambers of the opened main,
For whatsoe'er of old
By his own priests, the poets, has been said,
He never sunk till then into the Ocean's bed.

XIX.

Led cheerfully by a bright captain, Flame,
To the other shore at morning-dawn they came,
And saw behind the unguided foe
March disorderly and slow:

The prophet straight from the Idumean strand
Shakes his imperious wand;
The upper waves, that highest crowded lie,
The beckoning wand espy;
Straight their first right-hand files begin to move,
And with a murmuring wind
Give the word march to all behind;
The left-hand squadrons no less ready prove,
But with a joyful, louder noise,
Answer their distant fellows' voice,
And haste to meet them make,
As several troops do all at once a common signal take.
What tongue the amazement and the affright can tell,
Which on the Chamian army fell,
When on both sides they saw the roaring main
Broke loose from his invisible chain?
They saw the monstrous death and watery war
Come rolling down loud ruin from afar;
In vain some backward and some forwards fly
With helpless haste, in vain they cry
To their celestial beasts for aid;
In vain their guilty king they upbraid,
In vain on Moses he, and Moses' God, does call,
With a repentance true too late:
They're compassed round with a devouring fate
That draws, like a strong net, the mighty sea upon them
    all.

GEORGE WITHER.

THIS remarkable man was born in Hampshire, at Bentworth, near Alton, in 1588. He was sent to Magdalene College, Oxford, but had hardly been there till his father remanded him home to hold the plough—a reversal of the case of Cincinnatus which did not please the aspiring spirit of our poet. He took an early opportunity of breaking loose from this occupation, and of going to London with the romantic intention of making his fortune at Court. Finding that to rise at Court, flattery was indispensable, and determined not to flatter, he, in 1613, published his 'Abuses Whipt and Stript,' for which he was committed for some months to the Marshalsea. Here he wrote his beautiful poem, 'The Shepherd's Hunting;' and is said to have gained his manumission by a satire to the King, in which he defends his former writings. Soon after his liberation, he published his 'Hymns and Songs of the Church,' a book which embroiled him with the clergy, but procured him the favour of King James, who encouraged him to finish a translation of the Psalms. He travelled to the court of the Queen of Bohemia, (James's daughter,) in fulfilment of a vow, and presented her with a copy of his completed translation.

In 1639, he was a captain of horse in the expedition against the Scotch. When the Civil War broke out, he sold his estate to raise a troop of horse on the Parliamentary side, and soon after was made a major. In 1642, he was appointed captain and commander of Farnham Castle, in Surrey; but owing to some neglect or cowardice on his part, it was ceded the same year to Sir William Waller. He was made prisoner by the Royalists some time after this, and would have been put to death had not Denham interfered, alleging that as long as Wither survived, he (Denham) could not be accounted the worst poet in England. He was afterwards appointed Cromwell's major-general of all the horse and foot in the county of Surrey. He made money at this time by Royalist sequestrations, but lost it all at the Restoration. He had, on the death of Cromwell, hailed Richard with enthusiasm, and predicted him a happy reign; which makes Campbell remark, 'He never but once in his life foreboded good, and in that prophecy he was mistaken.' Wither was by no means pleased with the loss of his fortune, and remonstrated bitterly; but for so doing he was thrown into prison again. Here his mind continued as active as ever, and he poured out treatises, poems, and satires—sometimes, when pen and ink were denied him, inscribing his thoughts with red ochre upon a trencher. After three years, he was, in 1663, released from Newgate, under bond for good behaviour; and four years afterwards he died in London. This was on the 2d of May 1667. He was buried between the east door and the south end of the Savoy church, in the Strand.

Wither was a man of real genius, but seems to have been partially insane. His political zeal was a frenzy; and his religion was deeply tinged with puritanic gloom. His 'Collection of Emblems' never became so popular as those of Quarles, and are now nearly as much forgotten as his satires, his psalms, and his controversial treatises. But his early poems are delightful—full of elegant and playful fancy, ease of language, and delicacy of sentiment. Some passages in 'The Shepherd's Hunting,' and in the 'Address to Poetry,' resemble the style of Milton in his 'L'Allegro' and 'Penseroso.' His 'Christmas' catches the full spirit of that joyous carnival of Christian England. Altogether, it is refreshing to turn from the gnarled oak of Wither's struggling and unhappy life, to the beautiful flowers, nodding over it, of his poesy.

FROM 'THE SHEPHERD'S HUNTING.'

See'st thou not, in clearest days,
Oft thick fogs could heavens raise?
And the vapours that do breathe
From the earth's gross womb beneath,
Seem they not with their black steams
To pollute the sun's bright beams,
And yet vanish into air,
Leaving it unblemished, fair?
So, my Willy, shall it be
With Detraction's breath and thee:

It shall never rise so high
As to stain thy poesy.
As that sun doth oft exhale
Vapours from each rotten vale ;
Poesy so sometimes drains
Gross conceits from muddy brains ;
Mists of envy, fogs of spite,
'Twixt men's judgments and her light ;
But so much her power may do
That she can dissolve them too.
If thy verse do bravely tower,
As she makes wing, she gets power !
Yet the higher she doth soar,
She 's affronted still the more :
Till she to the high'st hath past,
Then she rests with Fame at last.
Let nought therefore thee affright,
But make forward in thy flight :
For if I could match thy rhyme,
To the very stars I 'd climb ;
There begin again, and fly
Till I reached eternity.
But, alas ! my Muse is slow ;
For thy pace she flags too low.
Yes, the more 's her hapless fate,
Her short wings were clipped of late ;
And poor I, her fortune ruing,
Am myself put up a-muing.
But if I my cage can rid,
I 'll fly where I never did.
And though for her sake I 'm cross'd,
Though my best hopes I have lost,
And knew she would make my trouble
Ten times more than ten times double ;

I would love and keep her too,
Spite of all the world could do.
For though banished from my flocks,
And confined within these rocks,
Here I waste away the light,
And consume the sullen night;
She doth for my comfort stay,
And keeps many cares away.
Though I miss the flowery fields,
With those sweets the springtide yields;
Though I may not see those groves,
Where the shepherds chant their loves,
And the lasses more excel
Than the sweet-voiced Philomel;
Though of all those pleasures past,
Nothing now remains at last,
But remembrance, poor relief,
That more makes than mends my grief:
She's my mind's companion still,
Maugre Envy's evil will:
Whence she should be driven too,
Were 't in mortals' power to do.
She doth tell me where to borrow
Comfort in the midst of sorrow;
Makes the desolatest place
To her presence be a grace,
And the blackest discontents
Be her fairest ornaments.
In my former days of bliss,
His divine skill taught me this,
That from everything I saw,
I could some invention draw;
And raise pleasure to her height
Through the meanest object's sight:

By the murmur of a spring,
Or the least bough's rustling;
By a daisy, whose leaves spread,
Shut when Titan goes to bed;
Or a shady bush or tree,
She could more infuse in me,
Than all Nature's beauties can,
In some other wiser man.
By her help I also now
Make this churlish place allow
Some things that may sweeten gladness
In the very gall of sadness:
The dull loneness, the black shade
That these hanging vaults have made,
The strange music of the waves,
Beating on these hollow caves,
This black den, which rocks emboss,
Overgrown with eldest moss;
The rude portals, that give light
More to terror than delight,
This my chamber of neglect,
Walled about with disrespect,
From all these, and this dull air,
A fit object for despair,
She hath taught me by her might
To draw comfort and delight.
　　Therefore, then, best earthly bliss,
I will cherish thee for this!
Poesy, thou sweet'st content
That e'er Heaven to mortals lent;
Though they as a trifle leave thee,
Whose dull thoughts can not conceive thee,
Though thou be to them a scorn
That to nought but earth are born;

Let my life no longer be
Than I am in love with thee!
Though our wise ones call it madness,
Let me never taste of gladness
If I love not thy madd'st fits
Above all their greatest wits!
And though some, too seeming holy,
Do account thy raptures folly,
Thou dost teach me to contemn
What makes knaves and fools of them!

THE SHEPHERD'S RESOLUTION.

1 Shall I, wasting in despair,
  Die because a woman 's fair?
  Or make pale my cheeks with care,
  'Cause another's rosy are?
  Be she fairer than the day,
  Or the flowery meads in May;
     If she be not so to me,
     What care I how fair she be?

2 Shall my foolish heart be pined,
  'Cause I see a woman kind?
  Or a well-disposed nature
  Joined with a lovely feature?
  Be she meeker, kinder, than
  The turtle-dove or pelican;
     If she be not so to me,
     What care I how kind she be?

3 Shall a woman's virtues 'move
  Me to perish for her love?
  Or, her well-deservings known,
  Make me quite forget mine own?

Be she with that goodness blest,
Which may merit name of Best;
    If she be not such to me,
    What care I how good she be?

4 'Cause her fortune seems too high,
Shall I play the fool and die?
Those that bear a noble mind,
Where they want of riches find,
Think what with them they would do,
That without them dare to woo;
    And, unless that mind I see,
    What care I how great she be?

5 Great, or good, or kind, or fair,
I will ne'er the more despair:
If she love me, this believe—
I will die ere she shall grieve.
If she slight me when I woo,
I can scorn and let her go:
    If she be not fit for me,
    What care I for whom she be?

THE STEADFAST SHEPHERD.

1 Hence away, thou Siren, leave me,
  Pish! unclasp these wanton arms;
Sugared words can ne'er deceive me,
  Though thou prove a thousand charms.
    Fie, fie, forbear;
    No common snare
Can ever my affection chain:
    Thy painted baits,
    And poor deceits,
Are all bestowed on me in vain.

2 I'm no slave to such as you be;
   Neither shall that snowy breast,
Rolling eye, and lip of ruby,
   Ever rob me of my rest:
      Go, go, display
      Thy beauty's ray
To some more soon enamoured swain:
      Those common wiles
      Of sighs and smiles
Are all bestowed on me in vain.

3 I have elsewhere vowed a duty;
   Turn away thy tempting eye:
Show not me a painted beauty:
   These impostures I defy:
      My spirit loathes
      Where gaudy clothes
And feigned oaths may love obtain:
      I love her so,
      Whose look swears No,
That all your labours will be vain.

4 Can he prize the tainted posies
   Which on every breast are worn,
That may pluck the virgin roses
   From their never-touched thorn?
      I can go rest
      On her sweet breast
That is the pride of Cynthia's train:
      Then stay thy tongue,
      Thy mermaid song
Is all bestowed on me in vain.

5 He 's a fool that basely dallies,
  Where each peasant mates with him:
Shall I haunt the thronged valleys,
  Whilst there 's noble hills to climb?
    No, no, though clowns
    Are scared with frowns,
I know the best can but disdain;
    And those I 'll prove:
    So will thy love
Be all bestowed on me in vain.

6 I do scorn to vow a duty
  Where each lustful lad may woo;
Give me her whose sun-like beauty
  Buzzards dare not soar unto:
    She, she it is
    Affords that bliss
For which I would refuse no pain:
    But such as you,
    Fond fools, adieu!
You seek to captive me in vain.

7 Leave me then, you Siren, leave me:
  Seek no more to work my harms:
Crafty wiles cannot deceive me,
  Who am proof against your charms:
    You labour may
    To lead astray
The heart that constant shall remain;
    And I the while
    Will sit and smile
To see you spend your time in vain.

THE SHEPHERD'S HUNTING.

ARGUMENT.

Cuddy tells how all the swains
Pity Roget on the plains;
Who, requested, doth relate
The true cause of his estate;
Which broke off, because 'twas long,
They begin a three-man song.

WILLY.   CUDDY.   ROGET.

WILLY.

Roget, thy old friend Cuddy here, and I,
Are come to visit thee in these thy bands,
Whilst both our flocks in an enclosure by
Do pick the thin grass from the fallowed lands.
He tells me thy restraint of liberty,
Each one throughout the country understands:
   And there is not a gentle-natured lad,
   On all these downs, but for thy sake is sad.

CUDDY.

Not thy acquaintance and thy friends alone
Pity thy close restraint, as friends should do:
But some that have but seen thee for thee moan:
Yea, many that did never see thee too.
Some deem thee in a fault, and most in none;
So divers ways do divers rumours go:
   And at all meetings where our shepherds be,
   Now the main news that 's extant is of thee.

ROGET.

Why, this is somewhat yet: had I but kept
Sheep on the mountains till the day of doom,
My name should in obscurity have slept,
In brakes, in briars, shrubbed furze and broom.
120

Into the world's wide care it had not crept,
Nor in so many men's thoughts found a room :
　　But what cause of my sufferings do they know ?
　　Good Cuddy, tell me how doth rumour go ?

CUDDY.

Faith, 'tis uncertain ; some speak this, some that :
Some dare say nought, yet seem to think a cause,
And many a one, prating he knows not what,
Comes out with proverbs and old ancient saws,
As if he thought thee guiltless, and yet not :
Then doth he speak half-sentences, then pause :
　　That what the most would say, we may suppose :
　　But what to say, the rumour is, none knows.

ROGET.

Nor care I greatly, for it skills not much
What the unsteady common-people deems ;
His conscience doth not always feel least touch,
That blameless in the sight of others seems :
My cause is honest, and because 'tis such
I hold it so, and not for men's esteems :
　　If they speak justly well of me, I'm glad ;
　　If falsely evil, it ne'er makes me sad.

WILLY.

I like that mind ; but, Roget, you are quite
Beside the matter that I long to hear :
Remember what you promised yesternight,
You 'd put us off with other talk, I fear ;
Thou know'st that honest Cuddy's heart 's upright,
And none but he, except myself, is near :
　　Come therefore, and betwixt us two relate,
　　The true occasion of thy present state.

ROGET.

My friends, I will; you know I am a swain,
That keep a poor flock here upon this plain:
Who, though it seems I could do nothing less,
Can make a song, and woo a shepherdess;
And not alone the fairest where I live
Have heard me sing, and favours deigned to give;
But though I say 't, the noblest nymph of Thame,
Hath graced my verse unto my greater fame.
Yet being young, and not much seeking praise,
I was not noted out for shepherds' lays,
Nor feeding flocks, as you know others be:
For the delight that most possessed me
Was hunting foxes, wolves, and beasts of prey;
That spoil our folds, and bear our lambs away.
For this, as also for the love I bear
Unto my country, I laid by all care
Of gain, or of preferment, with desire
Only to keep that state I had entire,
And like a true-grown huntsman sought to speed
Myself with hounds of rare and choicest breed,
Whose names and natures ere I further go,
Because you are my friends, I 'll let you know.
My first esteemed dog that I did find,
Was by descent of old Actæon's kind;
A brach, which if I do not aim amiss,
For all the world is just like one of his:
She 's named Love, and scarce yet knows her duty;
Her dam 's my lady's pretty beagle Beauty,
I bred her up myself with wondrous charge,
Until she grew to be exceeding large,
And waxed so wanton that I did abhor it,
And put her out amongst my neighbours for it.
The next is Lust, a hound that 's kept abroad,

'Mongst some of mine acquaintance, but a toad
Is not more loathsome : 'tis a cur will range
Extremely, and is ever full of mange;
And 'cause it is infectious, she 's not wont
To come among the rest, but when they hunt.
Hate is the third, a hound both deep and long.
His sire is true or else supposed Wrong.
He 'll have a snap at all that pass him by,
And yet pursues his game most eagerly.
With him goes Envy coupled, a lean cur,
And she 'll hold out, hunt we ne'er so far :
She pineth much, and feedeth little too,
Yet stands and snarleth at the rest that do.
Then there 's Revenge, a wondrous deep-mouthed dog,
So fleet, I 'm fain to hunt him with a clog,
Yet many times he 'll much outstrip his bounds,
And hunts not closely with the other hounds :
He 'll venture on a lion in his ire ;
Curst Choler was his dam, and Wrong his sire.
This Choler is a brach that 's very old,
And spends her mouth too much to have it hold :
She 's very testy, an unpleasing cur,
That bites the very stones, if they but stir :
Or when that ought but her displeasure moves,
She 'll bite and snap at any one she loves :
But my quick-scented'st dog is Jealousy,
The truest of this breed 's in Italy :
The dam of mine would hardly fill a glove,
It was a lady's little dog, called Love :
The sire, a poor deformed cur, named Fear,
As shagged and as rough as is a bear :
And yet the whelp turned after neither kind,
For he is very large, and near-hand blind ;
At the first sight he hath a pretty colour,

But doth not seem so, when you view him fuller;
A vile suspicious beast, his looks are bad,
And I do fear in time he will grow mad.
To him I couple Avarice, still poor ;
Yet she devours as much as twenty more :
A thousand horse she in her paunch can put,
Yet whine as if she had an empty gut :
And having gorged what might a land have found,
She 'll catch for more, and hide it in the ground.
Ambition is a hound as greedy full;
But he for all the daintiest bits doth cull :
He scorns to lick up crumbs beneath the table,
He 'll fetch 't from boards and shelves, if he be able :
Nay, he can climb if need be ; and for that,
With him I hunt the martin and the cat :
And yet sometimes in mounting he 's so quick,
He fetches falls are like to break his neck.
Fear is well-mouth'd, but subject to distrust;
A stranger cannot make him take a crust :
A little thing will soon his courage quail,
And 'twixt his legs he ever claps his tail;
With him Despair now often coupled goes,
Which by his roaring mouth each huntsman knows.
None hath a better mind unto the game,
But he gives off, and always seemeth lame.
My bloodhound Cruelty, as swift as wind,
Hunts to the death, and never comes behind;
Who but she 's strapp'd and muzzled too withal,
Would eat her fellows, and the prey and all;
And yet she cares not much for any food,
Unless it be the purest harmless blood.
All these are kept abroad at charge of many,
They do not cost me in a year a penny.
But there 's two couple of a middling size,

That seldom pass the sight of my own eyes.
Hope, on whose head I 've laid my life to pawn;
Compassion, that on every one will fawn.
This would, when 'twas a whelp, with rabbits play
Or lambs, and let them go unhurt away:
Nay, now she is of growth, she 'll now and then
Catch you a hare, and let her go again.
The two last, Joy and Sorrow, 'tis a wonder,
Can ne'er agree, nor ne'er bide far asunder.
Joy 's ever wanton, and no order knows:
She 'll run at larks, or stand and bark at crows.
Sorrow goes by her, and ne'er moves his eye;
Yet both do serve to help make up the cry.
Then comes behind all these to bear the base,
Two couple more of a far larger race,
Such wide-mouth'd trollops, that 'twould do you good
To hear their loud loud echoes tear the wood.
There 's Vanity, who, by her gaudy hide,
May far away from all the rest be spied,
Though huge, yet quick, for she 's now here, now there;
Nay, look about you, and she 's everywhere:
Yet ever with the rest, and still in chase.
Right so, Inconstancy fills every place;
And yet so strange a fickle-natured hound,
Look for her, and she 's nowhere to be found.
Weakness is no fair dog unto the eye,
And yet she hath her proper quality;
But there 's Presumption, when he heat hath got,
He drowns the thunder and the cannon-shot:
And when at start he his full roaring makes,
The earth doth tremble, and the heaven shakes.
These were my dogs, ten couple just in all,
Whom by the name of Satyrs I do call:
Mad curs they be, and I can ne'er come nigh them,

But I'm in danger to be bitten by them.
Much pains I took, and spent days not a few,
To make them keep together, and hunt true:
Which yet I do suppose had never been,
But that I had a scourge to keep them in.
Now when that I this kennel first had got,
Out of my own demesnes I hunted not,
Save on these downs, or among yonder rocks,
After those beasts that spoiled our parish flocks;
Nor during that time was I ever wont
With all my kennel in one day to hunt:
Nor had done yet, but that this other year,
Some beasts of prey, that haunt the deserts here,
Did not alone for many nights together
Devour, sometime a lamb, sometime a wether,
And so disquiet many a poor man's herd,
But that of losing all they were afeard:
Yea, I among the rest did fare as bad,
Or rather worse, for the best ewes[1] I had
(Whose breed should be my means of life and gain)
Were in one evening by these monsters slain:
Which mischief I resolved to repay,
Or else grow desperate, and hunt all away;
For in a fury (such as you shall see
Huntsmen in missing of their sport will be)
I vowed a monster should not lurk about,
In all this province, but I'd find him out,
And thereupon, without respect or care,
How lame, how full, or how unfit they were,
In haste unkennell'd all my roaring crew,
Who were as mad as if my mind they knew,
And ere they trail'd a flight-shot, the fierce curs
Had roused a hart, and thorough brakes and furs

<hr>

[1] 'Ewes:' hopes.

Follow'd at gaze so close, that Love and Fear
Got in together, so had surely there
Quite overthrown him, but that Hope thrust in
'Twixt both, and saved the pinching of his skin,
Whereby he 'scaped, till coursing o'erthwart,
Despair came in, and griped him to the heart:
I hallowed in the res'due to the fall,
And for an entrance, there I fleshed them all:
Which having done, I dipped my staff in blood,
And onward led my thunder to the wood;
Where what they did, I 'll tell you out anon,
My keeper calls me, and I must be gone.
Go if you please a while, attend your flocks,
And when the sun is over yonder rocks,
Come to this cave again, where I will be,
If that my guardian so much favour me.
　　Yet if you please, let us three sing a strain,
　　Before you turn your sheep into the plain.

WILLY.

I am content.

CUDDY.

　　As well content am I.

ROGET.

Then, Will, begin, and we 'll the rest supply.

SONG.

WILLY.

　　Shepherd, would these gates were ope,
　　Thou might'st take with us thy fortune.

ROGET.

　　No, I 'll make this narrow scope,
　　Since my fate doth so importune
　　Means unto a wider hope.

127

CUDDY.

Would thy shepherdess were here,
Who belov'd, loves thee so dearly!

ROGET.

Not for both your flocks, I swear,
And the gain they yield you yearly,
Would I so much wrong my dear.
Yet to me, nor to this place,
Would she now be long a stranger;
She would hold it no disgrace,
(If she feared not more my danger,)
Where I am to show her face.

WILLY.

Shepherd, we would wish no harms,
But something that might content thee.

ROGET.

Wish me then within her arms,
And that wish will ne'er repent me,
If your wishes might prove charms.

WILLY.

Be thy prison her embrace,
Be thy air her sweetest breathing.

CUDDY.

Be thy prospect her fair face,
For each look a kiss bequeathing,
And appoint thyself the place.

ROGET.

Nay pray, hold there, for I should scantly then
Come meet you here this afternoon again:
But fare you well, since wishes have no power,
Let us depart, and keep the 'pointed hour.

128

SIR WILLIAM DAVENANT,

THE author of 'Gondibert,' was the son of a vintner in Oxford, and born in February 1605. Gossip says—but says with her usual carelessness about truth—that he was the son of no less a person than William Shakspeare, who used, in his journeys between London and Stratford, to stop at the Crown, an inn kept by Davenant's reputed father. This story is hinted at by Wood, was told to Pope by Betterton the player, and believed by Malone, but seems to be a piece of mere scandal. It is true that Davenant had a great veneration for Shakspeare, and expressed it, when only ten years old, in lines ' In remembrance of Master William Shakspeare,' beginning thus:—

> ' Beware, delighted poets, when you sing,
> To welcome nature in the early spring,
>   Your numerous feet not tread
>   The banks of Avon, for each flower
> (As it ne'er knew a sun or shower)
>   Hangs there the pensive head.'

Southey says—' The father was a man of melancholy temperament, the mother handsome and lively; and as Shakspeare used to put up at the house on his journeys between Stratford and London, Davenant is said to have affected the reputation of being Shakspeare's son. If he really did this, there was a levity, or rather a want of feeling, in the boast, for which social pleasantry, and the spirits which are induced by wine, afford but little excuse.'

He was entered at Lincoln College; he next became page to the Duchess of Richmond; and we find him afterwards in the family of Fulk Greville, Lord Brooke—famous as the friend of Sir Philip Sidney. He began to write for the stage in 1628; and on the death of Ben Jonson he was made Poet Laureate—to the disappointment of Thomas May, so much praised by Johnson and others for his proficiency in Latin poetry, as displayed in his supplement to Lucan's 'Pharsalia.' He became afterwards manager of Drury Lane; but owing to his connexion with the intrigues of that unhappy period, he was imprisoned in the Tower, and subsequently made his escape to France. On his return to England, he distinguished himself greatly in the Royal cause; and when that became desperate, he again took refuge in France, and wrote part of his 'Gondibert.' He projected a scheme for carrying over a colony to Virginia; but his vessel was seized by one of the Parliamentary ships—he himself was conveyed a prisoner to Cowes Castle, in the Isle of Wight, and thence to the Tower, preparatory to being tried by the High Commission. But a giant hand, worthy of having saved him had he been Shakspeare's veritable son, was now stretched forth to his rescue—the hand of Milton. In this generous act Milton was seconded by Whitelocke, and by two aldermen of York, to whom our poet had rendered some services. Liberated from the Tower, Davenant was also permitted, through the influence of Whitelocke, to open, in defiance of Puritanic prohibition, a kind of theatre at Rutland House, and by enacting his own plays there, he managed to support himself till the Restoration. He then, it is supposed, repaid to Milton his friendly service, and shielded him from the wrath of the Court. From this period Davenant continued to write for the stage—having received the patent of the Duke's Theatre, in Lincoln's Inn—till his death. This event took place on April 7, 1668. His last play, written in conjunction with Dryden, was an alteration and pollution of Shakspeare's 'Tempest,' which was more worthy of Trinculo than of the authors of 'Absalom and Ahithophel' and of 'Gondibert.' Supposing Davenant the son of Shakspeare, his act to his father's masterpiece reminds us, in the excess of its filial impiety, of Ham's conduct to Noah.

'Gondibert' is a large and able, without being a great poem. It has the incurable and indefensible defect of dulness. 'The line labours, and the words move slow.' The story is interesting of itself, but is lost in the labyrinthine details. It has many fine lines, and some highly and successfully wrought passages; but as a whole we may say of it as Porson said of certain better productions, 'It will be read when the works of Homer and Virgil are forgotten—but *not till then.*'

FROM 'GONDIBERT'—CANTO II.

THE ARGUMENT.

The hunting which did yearly celebrate
The Lombards' glory, and the Vandals' fate:
The hunters praised; how true to love they are,
How calm in peace and tempest-like in war.
The stag is by the numerous chase subdued,
And straight his hunters are as hard pursued.

1 Small are the seeds Fate does unheeded sow
    Of slight beginnings to important ends;
Whilst wonder, which does best our reverence show
    To Heaven, all reason's sight in gazing spends.

2 For from a day's brief pleasure did proceed,
    A day grown black in Lombard histories,
Such lasting griefs as thou shalt weep to read,
    Though even thine own sad love had drained thine
        eyes.

3 In a fair forest, near Verona's plain,
    Fresh as if Nature's youth chose there a shade,
The Duke, with many lovers in his train,
    Loyal and young, a solemn hunting made.

4 Much was his train enlarged by their resort
    Who much his grandsire loved, and hither came
To celebrate this day with annual sport,
    On which by battle here he earned his fame,

5 And many of these noble hunters bore
    Command amongst the youth at Bergamo;
'Whose fathers gathered here the wreaths they wore,
    When in this forest they interred the foe.

6 Count Hurgonil, a youth of high descent,
    Was listed here, and in the story great;
  He followed honour, when towards death it went;
    Fierce in a charge, but temperate in retreat.

7 His wondrous beauty, which the world approved,
    He blushing hid, and now no more would own
  (Since he the Duke's unequalled sister loved)
    Than an old wreath when newly overthrown.

8 And she, Orna the shy! did seem in life
    So bashful too, to have her beauty shown,
  As I may doubt her shade with Fame at strife,
    That in these vicious times would make it known.

9 Not less in public voice was Arnold here;
    He that on Tuscan tombs his trophies raised;
  And now Love's power so willingly did bear,
    That even his arbitrary reign he praised.

10 Laura, the Duke's fair niece, enthralled his heart,
    Who was in court the public morning glass,
  Where those, who would reduce nature to art,
    Practised by dress the conquests of the face.

11 And here was Hugo, whom Duke Gondibert
    For stout and steadfast kindness did approve;
  Of stature small, but was all over heart,
    And, though unhappy, all that heart was love.

12 In gentle sonnets he for Laura pined,
    Soft as the murmurs of a weeping spring,
  Which ruthless she did as those murmurs mind:
    So, ere their death, sick swans unheeded sing.

13 Yet, whilst she Arnold favoured, he so grieved,
    As loyal subjects quietly bemoan
Their yoke, but raise no war to be relieved,
    Nor through the envied fav'rite wound the throne.

14 Young Goltho next these rivals we may name,
    Whose manhood dawned early as summer light;
As sure and soon did his fair day proclaim,
    And was no less the joy of public sight.

15 If love's just power he did not early see,
    Some small excuse we may his error give;
Since few, though learn'd, know yet blest love to be
    That secret vital heat by which we live:

16 But such it is; and though we may be thought
    To have in childhood life, ere love we know,
Yet life is useless till by reason taught,
    And love and reason up together grow.

17 Nor more the old show they outlive their love,
    If, when their love 's decayed, some signs they give
Of life, because we see them pained and move,
    Than snakes, long cut, by torment show they live.

18 If we call living, life, when love is gone,
    We then to souls, God's coin, vain reverence pay;
Since reason, which is love, and his best known
    And current image, age has worn away.

19 And I, that love and reason thus unite,
    May, if I old philosophers control,
Confirm the new by some new poet's light,
    Who, finding love, thinks he has found the soul.

20 From Goltho, to whom love yet tasteless seemed,
    We to ripe Tybalt are by order led;
  Tybalt, who love and valour both esteemed,
    And he alike from either's wounds had bled.

21 Public his valour was, but not his love,
    One filled the world, the other he contained;
  Yet quietly alike in both did move,
    Of that ne'er boasted, nor of this complained.

22 With these, whose special names verse shall preserve,
    Many to this recorded hunting came;
  Whose worth authentic mention did deserve,
    But from Time's deluge few are saved by Fame.

23 Now like a giant lover rose the sun
    From the ocean queen, fine in his fires and great;
  Seemed all the morn for show, for strength at noon,
    As if last night she had not quenched his heat.

24 And the sun's servants, who his rising wait,
    His pensioners, for so all lovers are,
  And all maintained by him at a high rate
    With daily fire, now for the chase prepare.

25 All were, like hunters, clad in cheerful green,
    Young Nature's livery, and each at strife
  Who most adorned in favours should be seen,
    Wrought kindly by the lady of his life.

26 These martial favours on their waists they wear,
    On which, for now they conquest celebrate,
  In an embroidered history appear
    Like life, the vanquished in their fears and fate.

27 And on these belts, wrought with their ladies' care,
    Hung cimeters of Akon's trusty steel;
  Goodly to see, and he who durst compare
    Those ladies' eyes, might soon their temper feel.

28 Cheered as the woods, where new-waked choirs they
      meet,
    Are all; and now dispose their choice relays
  Of horse and hounds, each like each other fleet;
    Which best, when with themselves compared, we
      praise.

29 To them old forest spies, the harbourers,
    With haste approach, wet as still weeping night,
  Or deer that mourn their growth of head with tears,
    When the defenceless weight does hinder flight.

30 And dogs, such whose cold secrecy was meant
    By Nature for surprise, on these attend;
  Wise, temperate lime-hounds that proclaim no scent,
    Nor harb'ring will their mouths in boasting spend.

31 Yet vainlier far than traitors boast their prize,
    On which their vehemence vast rates does lay,
  Since in that worth their treason's credit lies,
    These harb'rers praise that which they now betray.

32 Boast they have lodged a stag, that all the race
    Outruns of Croton horse, or Rhegian hounds;
  A stag made long since royal in the chase,
    If kings can honour give by giving wounds.

33 For Aribert had pierced him at a bay,
    Yet 'scaped he by the vigour of his head;
  And many a summer since has won the day,
    And often left his Rhegian followers dead.

34 His spacious beam, that even the rights outgrew,
    From antler to his troch had all allowed,
By which his age the aged woodmen knew,
    Who more than he were of that beauty proud.

35 Now each relay a several station finds,
    Ere the triumphant train the copse surrounds;
Relays of horse, long breathed as winter winds,
    And their deep cannon-mouthed experienced
       hounds.

36 The huntsmen, busily concerned in show,
    As if the world were by this beast undone,
And they against him hired as Nature's foe,
    In haste uncouple, and their hounds outrun.

37 Now wind they a recheat, the roused deer's knell,
    And through the forest all the beasts are awed;
Alarmed by Echo, Nature's sentinel,
    Which shows that murderous man is come abroad.

38 Tyrannic man! thy subjects' enemy!
    And 'more through wantonness than need or hate,
From whom the winged to their coverts fly,
    And to their dens even those that lay in wait.

39 So this, the most successful of his kind,
    Whose forehead's force oft his opposers pressed,
Whose swiftness left pursuers' shafts behind,
    Is now of all the forest most distressed!

40 The herd deny him shelter, as if taught
    To know their safety is to yield him lost;
Which shows they want not the results of thought,
    But speech, by which we ours for reason boast.

41 We blush to see our politics in beasts,
    Who many saved by this one sacrifice;
And since through blood they follow interests,
    Like us when cruel should be counted wise.

42 His rivals, that his fury used to fear
    For his loved female, now his faintness shun ;
But were his season hot, and she but near,
    (O mighty love!) his hunters were undone.

43 From thence, well blown, he comes to the relay,
    Where man's famed reason proves but cowardice,
And only serves him meanly to betray;
    Even for the flying, man in ambush lies.

44 But now, as his last remedy to live,
    (For every shift for life kind Nature makes,
Since life the utmost is which she can give,)
    Cool Adice from the swoln bank he takes.

45 But this fresh bath the dogs will make him leave,
    Whom he sure-nosed as fasting tigers found;
Their scent no north-east wind could e'er deceive
    Which drives the air, nor flocks that soil the ground.

46 Swift here the fliers and pursuers seem;
    The frighted fish swim from their Adice,
The dogs pursue the deer, he the fleet stream,
    And that hastes too to the Adriatic sea.

47 Refreshed thus in this fleeting clement,
    He up the steadfast shore did boldly rise;
And soon escaped their view, but not their scent,
    That faithful guide, which even conducts their eyes.

48 This frail relief was like short gales of breath,
      Which oft at sea a long dead calm prepare;
    Or like our curtains drawn at point of death,
      When all our lungs are spent, to give us air.

49 For on the shore the hunters him attend:
      And whilst the chase grew warm as is the day,
    (Which now from the hot zenith does descend,)
      He is embossed, and wearied to a bay.

50 The jewel, life, he must surrender here,
      Which the world's mistress, Nature, does not give,
    But like dropped favours suffers us to wear,
      Such as by which pleased lovers think they live.

51 Yet life he so esteems, that he allows
      It all defence his force and rage can make;
    And to the eager dogs such fury shows,
      As their last blood some unrevenged forsake.

52 But now the monarch murderer comes in,
      Destructive man! whom Nature would not arm,
    As when in madness mischief is foreseen,
      We leave it weaponless for fear of harm.

53 For she defenceless made him, that he might
      Less readily offend; but art arms all,
    From single strife makes us in numbers fight;
      And by such art this royal stag did fall.

54 He weeps till grief does even his murderers pierce;
      Grief which so nobly through his anger strove,
    That it deserved the dignity of verse,
      And had it words, as humanly would move.

138

55 Thrice from the ground his vanquished head he reared,
    And with last looks his forest walks did view;
  Where sixty summers he had ruled the herd,
    And where sharp dittany now vainly grew:

56 Whose hoary leaves no more his wounds shall heal;
    For with a sigh (a blast of all his breath)
  That viewless thing, called life, did from him steal,
    And with their bugle-horns they wind his death.

57 Then with their annual wanton sacrifice,
    Taught by old custom, whose decrees are vain,
  And we, like humorous antiquaries, that prize
    Age, though deformed, they hasten to the plain.

58 Thence homeward bend as westward as the sun,
    Where Gondibert's allies proud feasts prepare,
  That day to honour which his grandsire won;
    Though feasts the eves to funerals often are.

59 One from the forest now approached their sight,
    Who them did swiftly on the spur pursue;
  One there still resident as day and night,
    And known as the eldest oak which in it grew:

60 Who, with his utmost breath advancing, cries,
    (And such a vehemence no heart could feign,)
  'Away! happy the man that fastest flies!
    Fly, famous Duke! fly with thy noble train!'

61 The Duke replied: 'Though with thy fears disguised,
    Thou dost my sire's old ranger's image bear,
  And for thy kindness shalt not be despised;
    Though counsels are but weak which come from
      fear.

62 'Were dangers here, great as thy love can shape,
    And love with fear can danger multiply,
Yet when by flight thou bidst us meanly 'scape,
    Bid trees take wings, and rooted forests fly.'

63 Then said the ranger: 'You are bravely lost!'
    (And like high anger his complexion rose.)
'As little know I fear as how to boast;
    But shall attend you through your many foes.

64 'See where in ambush mighty Oswald lay!
    And see, from yonder lawn he moves apace,
With lances armed to intercept thy way,
    Now thy sure steeds are wearied with the chase.

65 'His purple banners you may there behold,
    Which, proudly spread, the fatal raven bear;
And full five hundred I by rank have told,
    Who in their gilded helms his colours wear.'

66 The Duke this falling storm does now discern;
    Bids little Hugo fly! but 'tis to view
The foe, and timely their first count'nance learn,
    Whilst firm he in a square his hunters drew.

67 And Hugo soon, light as his courser's heels,
    Was in their faces troublesome as wind;
And like to it so wingedly he wheels,
    No one could catch, what all with trouble find.

68 But everywhere the leaders and the led
    He temperately observed with a slow sight;
Judged by their looks how hopes and fears were fed,
    And by their order their success in fight.

140

69 Their number, 'mounting to the ranger's guess,
    In three divisions evenly was disposed;
  And that their enemies might judge it less,
    It seemed one gross with all the spaces closed.

70 The van fierce Oswald led, where Paradine
    And manly Dargonet, both of his blood,
  Outshined the noon, and their minds' stock within
    Promised to make that outward glory good.

71 The next, bold, but unlucky Hubert led,
    Brother to Oswald, and no less allied
  To the ambitions which his soul did wed;
    Lowly without, but lined with costly pride.

72 Most to himself his valour fatal was,
    Whose glories oft to others dreadful were;
  So comets, though supposed destruction's cause,
    But waste themselves to make their gazers fear.

73 And though his valour seldom did succeed,
    His speech was such as could in storms persuade;
  Sweet as the hopes on which starved lovers feed,
    Breathed in the whispers of a yielding maid.

74 The bloody Borgio did conduct the rear,
    Whom sullen Vasco heedfully attends;
  To all but to themselves they cruel were,
    And to themselves chiefly by mischief friends.

75 War, the world's art, nature to them became;
    In camps begot, born, and in anger bred;
  The living vexed till death, and then their fame,
    Because even fame some life is to the dead.

76 Cities, wise statesmen's folds for civil sheep,
    They sacked, as painful shearers of the wise;
For they like careful wolves would lose their sleep,
    When others' prosperous toils might be their prize.

77 Hugo amongst these troops spied many more,
    Who had, as brave destroyers, got renown;
And many forward wounds in boast they wore,
    Which, if not well revenged, had ne'er been shown.

78 Such the bold leaders of these lancers were,
    Which of the Brescian veterans did consist;
Whose practised age might charge of armies bear,
    And claim some rank in Fame's eternal list.

79 Back to his Duke the dexterous Hugo flies,
    What he observed he cheerfully declares;
With noble pride did what he liked despise;
    For wounds he threatened whilst he praised their
        scars.

80 Lord Arnold cried, 'Vain is the bugle-horn,
    Where trumpets men to manly work invite!
That distant summons seems to say, in scorn,
    We hunters may be hunted hard ere night.'

81 'Those beasts are hunted hard that hard can fly,'
    Replied aloud the noble Hurgonil;
'But we, not used to flight, know best to die;
    And those who know to die, know how to kill.

82 'Victors through number never gained applause;
    If they exceed our count in arms and men,
It is not just to think that odds, because
    One lover equals any other ten.'

142

FROM 'GONDIBERT'—CANTO IV.

1 The King, who never time nor power misspent
    In subject's bashfulness, whiling great deeds
Like coward councils, who too late consent, .
    Thus to his secret will aloud proceeds:

2 'If to thy fame, brave youth, I could add wings,
    Or make her trumpet louder by my voice,
I would, as an example drawn for kings,
    Proclaim the cause why thou art now my choice.

*   *   *   *   *

3 'For she is yours, as your adoption free;
    And in that gift my remnant life I give;
But 'tis to you, brave youth! who now are she;
    And she that heaven where secondly I live.

4 'And richer than that crown, which shall be thine
    When life's long progress I have gone with fame,
Take all her love; which scarce forbears to shine,
    And own thee, through her virgin curtain, shame.'

5 Thus spake the king; and Rhodalind appeared
    Through published love, with so much bashfulness,
As young kings show, when by surprise o'erheard,
    Moaning to favourite ears a deep distress.

6 For love is a distress, and would be hid
    Like monarchs' griefs, by which they bashful grow;
And in that shame beholders they forbid;
    Since those blush most, who most their blushes
      show.

143

7 And Gondibert, with dying eyes, did grieve
    At her vailed love, a wound he cannot heal,
  As great minds mourn, who cannot then relieve
    The virtuous, when through shame they want
      conceal.

8 And now cold Birtha's rosy looks decay;
    Who in fear's frost had like her beauty died,
  But that attendant hope persuades her stay
    A while, to hear her Duke; who thus replied:

9 'Victorious King! abroad your subjects are,
    Like legates, safe; at home like altars free!
  Even by your fame they conquer, as by war;
    And by your laws safe from each other be.

10 'A king you are o'er subjects so, as wise
    And noble husbands seem o'er loyal wives;
  Who claim not, yet confess their liberties,
    And brag to strangers of their happy lives.

11 'To foes a winter storm; whilst your friends bow,
    Like summer trees, beneath your bounty's load;
  To me, next him whom your great self, with low
    And cheerful duty, serves, a giving God.

12 'Since this is you, and Rhodalind, the light
    By which her sex fled virtue find, is yours,
  Your diamond, which tests of jealous sight,
    The stroke, and fire, and Oisel's juice endures;

13 'Since she so precious is, I shall appear
    All counterfeit, of art's disguises made;
  And never dare approach her lustre near,
    Who scarce can hold my value in the shade.

14 'Forgive me that I am not what I seem;
    But falsely have dissembled an excess
Of all such virtues as you most esteem;
    But now grow good but as I ills confess.

15 'Far in ambition's fever am I gone!
    Like raging flame aspiring is my love;
Like flame destructive too, and, like the sun,
    Does round the world tow'rds change of objects
        move.

16 'Nor is this now through virtuous shame confessed;
    But Rhodalind does force my conjured fear,
As men whom evil spirits have possessed,
    Tell all when saintly votaries appear.

17 'When she will grace the bridal dignity,
    It will be soon to all young monarchs known;
Who then by posting through the world will try
    Who first can at her feet present his crown.

18 'Then will Verona seem the inn of kings,
    And Rhodalind shall at her palace gate
Smile, when great love these royal suitors brings;
    Who for that smile would as for empire wait.

19 'Amongst this ruling race she choice may take
    For warmth of valour, coolness of the mind,
Eyes that in empire's drowsy calms can wake,
    In storms look out, in darkness dangers find;

20 'A prince who more enlarges power than lands,
    Whose greatness is not what his map contains;
But thinks that his where he at full commands,
    Not where his coin does pass, but power remains.

21 'Who knows that power can never be too high
      When by the good possessed, for 'tis in them
   The swelling Nile, from which though people fly,
      They prosper most by rising of the stream.

22 'Thus, princes, you should choose; and you will find,
      Even he, since men are wolves, must civilise,
   As light does tame some beasts of savage kind,
      Himself yet more, by dwelling in your eyes.'

23 Such was the Duke's reply; which did produce
      Thoughts of a diverse shape through several ears:
   His jealous rivals mourn at his excuse;
      But Astragon it cures of all his fears.

24 Birtha his praise of Rhodalind bewails;
      And now her hope a weak physician seems;
   For hope, the common comforter, prevails
      Like common medicines, slowly in extremes.

25 The King (secure in offered empire) takes
      This forced excuse as troubled bashfulness,
   And a disguise which sudden passion makes,
      To hide more joy than prudence should express.

26 And Rhodalind, who never loved before,
      Nor could suspect his love was given away,
   Thought not the treasure of his breast so poor,
      But that it might his debts of honour pay.

27 To hasten the rewards of his desert,
      The King does to Verona him command;
   And, kindness so imposed, not all his art
      Can now instruct his duty to withstand.
   146

28 Yet whilst the King does now his time dispose
        In seeing wonders, in this palace shown,
    He would a parting kindness pay to those
        Who of their wounds are yet not perfect grown.

29 And by this fair pretence, whilst on the King
        Lord Astragon through all the house attends,
    Young Orgo does the Duke to Birtha bring,
        Who thus her sorrows to his bosom sends:

30 'Why should my storm your life's calm voyage vex?
        Destroying wholly virtue's race in one:
    So by the first of my unlucky sex,
        All in a single ruin were undone.

31 'Make heavenly Rhodalind your bride! whilst I,
        Your once loved maid, excuse you, since I know
    That virtuous men forsake so willingly
        Long-cherished life, because to heaven they go.

32 'Let me her servant be: a dignity,
        Which if your pity in my fall procures,
    I still shall value the advancement high,
        Not as the crown is hers, but she is yours.'

33 Ere this high sorrow up to dying grew,
        The Duke the casket opened, and from thence,
    Formed like a heart, a cheerful emerald drew;
        Cheerful, as if the lively stone had sense.

34 The thirtieth caract it had doubled twice;
        Not taken from the Attic silver mine,
    Nor from the brass, though such, of nobler price,
        Did on the necks of Parthian ladies shine:

35 Nor yet of those which make the Ethiop proud;
    Nor taken from those rocks where Bactrians climb:
But from the Scythian, and without a cloud;
    Not sick at fire, nor languishing with time.

36 Then thus he spake: 'This, Birtha, from my male
    Progenitors, was to the loyal she
On whose kind heart they did in love prevail,
    The nuptial pledge, and this I give to thee:

37 'Seven centuries have passed, since it from bride
    To bride did first succeed; and though 'tis known
From ancient lore, that gems much virtue hide,
    And that the emerald is the bridal stone:

38 'Though much renowned because it chastens loves,
    And will, when worn by the neglected wife,
Show when her absent lord disloyal proves,
    By faintness, and a pale decay of life.

39 'Though emeralds serve as spies to jealous brides,
    Yet each compared to this does counsel keep;
Like a false stone, the husband's falsehood hides,
    Or seems born blind, or feigns a dying sleep.

40 'With this take Orgo, as a better spy,
    Who may in all your kinder fears be sent
To watch at court, if I deserve to die
    By making this to fade, and you lament.'

41 Had now an artful pencil Birtha drawn,
    With grief all dark, then straight with joy all light,
He must have fancied first, in early dawn,
    A sudden break of beauty out of night.

42 Or first he must have marked what paleness fear,
    Like nipping frost, did to her visage bring;
Then think he sees, in a cold backward year,
    A rosy morn begin a sudden spring.

43 Her joys, too vast to be contained in speech,
    Thus she a little spake: 'Why stoop you down,
My plighted lord, to lowly Birtha's reach,
    Since Rhodalind would lift you to a crown?

44 'Or why do I, when I this plight embrace,
    Boldly aspire to take what you have given?
But that your virtue has with angels place,
    And 'tis a virtue to aspire to heaven.

45 'And as towards heaven all travel on their knees,
    So I towards you, though love aspire, will move:
And were you crowned, what could you better please
    Then awed obedience led by bolder love?

46 'If I forget the depth from whence I rise,
    Far from your bosom banished be my heart;
Or claim a right by beauty to your eyes;
    Or proudly think my chastity desert.

47 'But thus ascending from your humble maid
    To be your plighted bride, and then your wife,
Will be a debt that shall be hourly paid,
    Till time my duty cancel with my life.

48 'And fruitfully, if heaven e'er make me bring
    Your image to the world, you then my pride
No more shall blame than you can tax the spring
    For boasting of those flowers she cannot hide.

49 'Orgo I so receive as I am taught
    By duty to esteem whate'er you love;
  And hope the joy he in this jewel brought
    Will luckier than his former triumphs prove.

50 'For though but twice he has approached my sight,
    He twice made haste to drown me in my tears:
  But now I am above his planet's spite,
    And as for sin beg pardon for my fears.'

51 Thus spake she: and with fixed, continued sight
    The Duke did all her bashful beauties view;
  Then they with kisses sealed their sacred plight,
    Like flowers, still sweeter as they thicker grew.

52 Yet must these pleasures feel, though innocent,
    The sickness of extremes, and cannot last;
  For power, love's shunned impediment, has sent
    To tell the Duke his monarch is in haste:

53 And calls him to that triumph which he fears
    So as a saint forgiven, whose breast does all
  Heaven's joys contain, wisely loved pomp forbears,
    Lest tempted nature should from blessings fall.

54 He often takes his leave, with love's delay,
    And bids her hope he with the King shall find,
  By now appearing forward to obey,
    A means to serve him less in Rhodalind.

55 She weeping to her closet window hies,
    Where she with tears doth Rhodalind survey;
  As dying men, who grieve that they have eyes,
    When they through curtains spy the rising day.
    150

DR HENRY KING.

OF this poetical divine we know nothing, except that he was born in 1591, and died in 1669,—that he was chaplain to James I., and Bishop of Chichester,—and that he indited some poetry as pious in design as it is pretty in execution.

SIC VITA.

Like to the falling of a star,
Or as the flights of eagles are;
Or like the fresh spring's gaudy hue,
Or silver drops of morning dew;
Or like a wind that chafes the flood,
Or bubbles which on water stood:
Even such is man, whose borrowed light
Is straight called in, and paid to-night.

The wind blows out, the bubble dies;
The spring entombed in autumn lies;
The dew dries up, the star is shot:
The flight is past—and man forgot.

SONG.

1 Dry those fair, those crystal eyes,
Which like growing fountains rise
To drown their banks! Grief's sullen brooks
Would better flow in furrowed looks:
Thy lovely face was never meant
To be the shore of discontent.

2 Then clear those waterish stars again,
Which else portend a lasting rain;

Lest the clouds which settle there
Prolong my winter all the year,
And thy example others make
In love with sorrow, for thy sake.

LIFE.

1 What is the existence of man's life
But open war or slumbered strife?
Where sickness to his sense presents
The combat of the elements,
And never feels a perfect peace
Till death's cold hand signs his release.

2 It is a storm—where the hot blood
Outvies in rage the boiling flood:
And each loud passion of the mind
Is like a furious gust of wind,
Which beats the bark with many a wave,
Till he casts anchor in the grave.

3 It is a flower—which buds, and grows,
And withers as the leaves disclose;
Whose spring and fall faint seasons keep,
Like fits of waking before sleep,
Then shrinks into that fatal mould
Where its first being was enrolled.

4 It is a dream—whose seeming truth
Is moralised in age and youth;
Where all the comforts he can share
As wandering as his fancies are,
Till in a mist of dark decay
The dreamer vanish quite away.

5 It is a dial—which points out
   The sunset as it moves about;
   And shadows out in lines of night
   The subtle stages of Time's flight,
   Till all-obscuring earth hath laid
   His body in perpetual shade.

6 It is a weary interlude—
   Which doth short joys, long woes, include:
   The world the stage, the prologue tears;
   The acts vain hopes and varied fears;
   The scene shuts up with loss of breath,
   And leaves no epilogue but Death!

JOHN CHALKHILL.

THIS author was of the age of Spenser, and is said to have been
an acquaintance and friend of that poet. It was not, however,
till 1683 that good old Izaak Walton published 'Thealma and
Clearchus,' a pastoral romance, which, he stated, had been written long since by John Chalkhill, Esq. He says of the author,
'that he was in his time a man generally known, and as well
beloved; for he was humble and obliging in his behaviour—a
gentleman, a scholar, very innocent and prudent, and indeed his
whole life was useful, quiet, and virtuous.' Some have suspected
that this production proceeded from the pen of Walton himself.
This, however, is rendered extremely unlikely—first, by the fact
that Walton, when he printed 'Thealma,' was ninety years of
age; and, secondly, by the difference in style and purpose between that poem and Walton's avowed productions. The mind
of Walton was quietly ingenious; that of the author of 'Thealma'
is adventurous and fantastic. Walton loved 'the green pastures
and the still waters' of the Present; the other, the golden groves
and ideal wildernesses of the Golden Age in the Past.

'Thealma and Clearchus' may be called an 'Arcadia' in

rhyme. It resembles that work of Sir Philip Sidney, not only in subject, but in execution. Its plot is dark and puzzling, its descriptions are rich to luxuriance, its narrative is tedious, and its characters are mere shadows. But although a dream, it is a dream of genius, and brings beautifully before our imagination that early period in the world's history, in which poets and painters have taught us to believe, when the heavens were nearer, the skies clearer, the fat of the earth richer, the foam of the sea brighter, than in our degenerate days;—when shepherds, reposing under broad, umbrageous oaks, saw, or thought they saw, in the groves the shadow of angels, and on the mountain-summits the descending footsteps of God. Chalkhill resembles, of all our modern poets, perhaps Shelley most, in the ideality of his conception, the enthusiasm of his spirit, and the unmitigated gorgeousness of his imagination.

ARCADIA.

Arcadia, was of old, a state,
Subject to none but their own laws and fate;
Superior there was none, but what old age
And hoary hairs had raised; the wise and sage,
Whose gravity, when they are rich in years,
Begat a civil reverence more than fears
In the well-mannered people; at that day,
All was in common, every man bare sway
O'er his own family; the jars that rose
Were soon appeased by such grave men as those:
This mine and thine, that we so cavil for,
Was then not heard of; he that was most poor
Was rich in his content, and lived as free
As they whose flocks were greatest; nor did he
Envy his great abundance, nor the other
Disdain the low condition of his brother,
But lent him from his store to mend his state,
And with his love he quits him, thanks his fate;

And, taught by his example, seeks out such
As want his help, that they may do as much.
Their laws, e'en from their childhood, rich and poor
Had written in their hearts, by conning o'er
The legacies of good old men, whose memories
Outlive their monuments, the grave advice
They left behind in writing;—this was that
That made Arcadia then so blest a state;
Their wholesome laws had linked them so in one,
They lived in peace and sweet communion.
Peace brought forth plenty, plenty bred content,
And that crowned all their plans with merriment.
They had no foe, secure they lived in tents,
All was their own they had, they paid no rents;
Their sheep found clothing, earth provided food,
And labour dressed them as their wills thought good;
On unbought delicates their hunger fed,
And for their drink the swelling clusters bled;
The valleys rang with their delicious strains,
And pleasure revelled on those happy plains;
Content and labour gave them length of days,
And peace served in delight a thousand ways.

THEALMA, A DESERTED SHEPHERDESS.

Scarce had the ploughman yoked his horned team,
And locked their traces to the crooked beam,
When fair Thealma, with a maiden scorn,
That day before her rise, outblushed the morn;
Scarce had the sun gilded the mountain-tops,
When forth she leads her tender ewes.
    *   *   *   *   *
Down in a valley, 'twixt two rising hills,
From whence the dew in silver drops distils

To enrich the lowly plain, a river ran,
Hight Cygnus, (as some think, from Leda's swan
That there frequented;) gently on it glides,
And makes indentures in her crooked sides,
And with her silent murmurs rocks asleep
Her watery inmates; 'twas not very deep,
But clear as that Narcissus looked in, when
His self-love made him cease to live with men.
Close by the river was a thick-leafed grove,
Where swains of old sang stories of their love,
But unfrequented now since Colin died—
Colin, that king of shepherds, and the pride
Of all Arcadia;—here Thealma used
To feed her milky droves; and as they browsed,
Under the friendly shadow of a beech
She sat her down; grief had tongue-tied her speech,
Her words were sighs and tears—dumb eloquence—
Heard only by the sobs, and not the sense.
With folded arms she sat, as if she meant
To hug those woes which in her breast were pent;
Her looks were nailed to earth, that drank
Her tears with greediness, and seemed to thank
Her for those briny showers, and in lieu
Returns her flowery sweetness for her dew.

*   *   *   *   *

' O my Clearchus!' said she, and with tears
Embalms his name : ' oh, if the ghosts have ears,
Or souls departed condescend so low,
To sympathise with mortals in their woe,
Vouchsafe to lend a gentle ear to me,
Whose life is worse than death, since not with thee.
What privilege have they that are born great
More than the meanest swain?   The proud waves beat

With more impetuousness upon high lands,
Than on the flat and less-resisting strands: -
The lofty cedar, and the knotty oak,
Are subject more unto the thunder-stroke,
Than the low shrubs that no such shocks endure;
Even their contempt doth make them live secure.
Had I been born the child of some poor swain,
Whose thoughts aspire no higher than the plain,
I had been happy then; t' have kept these sheep,
Had been a princely pleasure; quiet sleep
Had drowned my cares, or sweetened them with dreams:
Love and content had been my music's themes;
Or had Clearchus lived the life I lead,
I had been blest!'

PRIESTESS OF DIANA.

Within a little silent grove hard by,
Upon a small ascent, he might espy
A stately chapel, richly gilt without,
Beset with shady sycamores about:
And ever and anon he might well hear
A sound of music steal in at his ear
As the wind gave it being; so sweet an air
Would strike a syren mute.—
   *   *   *   *   *
A hundred virgins there he might espy
Prostrate before a marble deity,
Which, by its portraiture, appeared to bo
The image of Diana; on their knee
They tendered their devotions, with sweet airs,
Offering the incense of their praise and prayers.
Their garments all alike; beneath their paps
Buckled together with a silver claps,

And 'cross their snowy silken robes, they wore
An azure scarf, with stars embroidered o'er.
Their hair in curious tresses was knit up,
Crowned with a silver crescent on the top.
A silver bow their left hand held, their right,
For their defence, held a sharp-headed flight
Drawn from their broidered quiver, neatly tied
In silken cords, and fastened to their side.
Under their vestments, something short before,
White buskins, laced with ribanding, they wore.
It was a catching sight for a young eye,
That love had fired before.   He might espy
One, whom the rest had sphere-like circled round,
Whose head was with a golden chaplet crowned.
He could not see her face, only his ear
Was blessed with the sweet sounds that came from her.

THEALMA IN FULL DRESS.

—— Tricked herself in all her best attire,
As if she meant this day to invite desire
To fall in love with her; her loose hair
Hung on her shoulders, sporting with the air;
Her brow a coronet of rosebuds crowned,
With loving woodbines' sweet embraces bound.
Two globe-like pearls were pendant to her ears,
And on her breast a costly gem she wears,
An adamant, in fashion like a heart,
Whereon Love sat, a-plucking out a dart,
With this same motto graven round about,
On a gold border, 'Sooner in than out.'
This gem Clearchus gave her, when, unknown,
At tilt his valour won her for his own.
Instead of bracelets on her wrists, she wore
A pair of golden shackles, chained before

Unto a silver ring, enamelled blue,
Whereon in golden letters to the view
This motto was presented, 'Bound, yet free,'
And in a true-love's knot, a T and C
Buckled it fast together; her silk gown
Of grassy green, in equal plaits hung down
Unto the earth; and as she went, the flowers,
Which she had broidered on it at spare hours,
Were wrought so to the life, they seemed to grow
In a green field; and as the wind did blow,
Sometimes a lily, then a rose, takes place,
And blushing seems to hide it in the grass:
And here and there good oats 'mong pearls she strew,
That seemed like spinning glow-worms in the dew.
Her sleeves were tinsel, wrought with leaves of green
In equal distance spangeled between,
And shadowed over with a thin lawn cloud,
Through which her workmanship more graceful showed.

DWELLING OF THE WITCH ORANDRA.

Down in a gloomy valley, thick with shade,
Which two aspiring hanging rocks had made,
That shut out day, and barred the glorious sun
From prying into the actions there done;
Set full of box and cypress, poplar, yew,
And hateful elder that in thickets grew,
Among whose boughs the screech-owl and night-crow
Sadly recount their prophecies of woe,
Where leather-winged bats, that hate the light,
Fan the thick air, more sooty than the night.
The ground o'ergrown with weeds and bushy shrubs,
Where milky hedgehogs nurse their prickly cubs:
And here and there a mandrake grows, that strikes
The hearers dead with their loud fatal shrieks;

Under whose spreading leaves the ugly toad,
The adder, and the snake, make their abode.
Here dwelt Orandra ; so the witch was hight,
And hither had she toiled him by a sleight:
She knew Anaxus was to go to court,
And, envying virtue, she made it her sport
To hinder him, sending her airy spies
Forth with delusion to entrap his eyes,
As would have fired a hermit's chill desires
Into a flame ; his greedy eye admires
The more than human beauty of her face,
And much ado he had to shun the grace ;
Conceit had shaped her out so like his love,
That he was once about in vain to prove
Whether 'twas his Clarinda, yea or no,
But he bethought him of his herb, and so
The shadow vanished; many a weary step
It led the prince, that pace with it still kept,
Until it brought him by a hellish power
Unto the entrance of Orandra's bower,
Where underneath an elder-tree he spied
His man Pandevius, pale and hollow-eyed;
Inquiring of the cunning witch what fate
Betid his master; they were newly sate
When his approach disturbed them; up she rose,
And toward Anaxus (envious hag) she goes;
Pandevius she had charmed into a maze,
And struck him mute, all he could do was gaze.
He called him by his name, but all in vain,
Echo returns 'Pandevius' back again;
Which made him wonder, when a sudden fear
Shook all his joints: she, cunning hag, drew near,
And smelling to his herb, he recollects
His wandering spirits, and with anger checks

160

His coward fears; resolved now to outdare
The worst of dangers, whatsoe'er they were;
He eyed her o'er and o'er, and still his eye
Found some addition to deformity.
An old decrepit hag she was, grown white
With frosty age, and withered with despite
And self-consuming hate; in furs yclad,
And on her head a thrummy cap she had.
Her knotty locks, like to Alecto's snakes,
Hang down about her shoulders, which she shakes
Into disorder; on her furrowed brow
One might perceive Time had been long at plough.
Her eyes, like candle-snuffs, by age sunk quite
Into their sockets, yet like cats' eyes bright:
And in the darkest night like fire they shined,
The ever-open windows of her mind.
Her swarthy cheeks, Time, that all things consumes,
Had hollowed flat into her toothless gums.
Her hairy brows did meet above her nose,
That like an eagle's beak so crooked grows,
It well-nigh kissed her chin; thick bristled hair
Grew on her upper lip, and here and there
A rugged wart with grisly hairs behung;
Her breasts shrunk up, her nails and fingers long;
Her left leant on a staff, in her right hand
She always carried her enchanting wand.
Splay-footed, beyond nature, every part
So patternless deformed, 'twould puzzle art
To make her counterfeit; only her tongue,
Nature had that most exquisitely strung,
Her oily language came so smoothly from her,
And her quaint action did so well become her,
Her winning rhetoric met with no trips,
But chained the dull'st attention to her lips.

With greediness he heard, and though he strove
To shake her off, the more her words did move.
She wooed him to her cell, called him her son,
And with fair promises she quickly won
Him to her beck; or rather he, to try
What she could do, did willingly comply
With her request.   *   *   *
Her cell was hewn out of the marble rock
By more than human art; she did not knock,
The door stood always open, large and wide,
Grown o'er with woolly moss on either side,
And interwove with ivy's flattering twines,
Through which the carbuncle and diamond shines.
Not set by Art, but there by Nature sown
At the world's birth, so star-like bright they shone.
They served instead of tapers to give light
To the dark entry, where perpetual Night,
Friend to black deeds, and sire of Ignorance,
Shuts out all knowledge, lest her eye by chance
Might bring to light her follies: in they went,
The ground was strewed with flowers, whose sweet scent,
Mixed with the choice perfumes from India brought,
Intoxicates his brain, and quickly caught
His credulous sense ; the walls were gilt, and set
With precious stones, and all the roof was fret
With a gold vine, whose straggling branches spread
All o'er the arch; the swelling grapes were red;
This Art had made of rubies, clustered so,
To the quick'st eye they more than seemed to grow;
About the wall lascivious pictures hung,
Such as were of loose Ovid sometimes sung.
On either side a crew of dwarfish elves
Held waxen tapers, taller than themselves:
Yet so well shaped unto their little stature,

So angel-like in face, so sweet in feature;
Their rich attire so differing; yet so well
Becoming her that wore it, none could tell
Which was the fairest, which the handsomest decked,
Or which of them desire would soon'st affect.
After a low salute they all 'gan sing,
And circle in the stranger in a ring.
Orandra to her charms was stepped aside,
Leaving her guest half won and wanton-eyed.
He had forgot his herb: cunning delight
Had so bewitched his ears, and bleared his sight,
And captivated all his senses so,
That he was not himself; nor did he know
What place he was in, or how he came there,
But greedily he feeds his eye and ear
With what would ruin him;—

  *   *   *   *   *

       Next unto his view
She represents a banquet, ushered in
By such a shape as she was sure would win
His appetite to taste; so like she was
To his Clarinda, both in shape and face;
So voiced, so habited, of the same gait
And comely gesture; on her brow in state
Sat such a princely majesty, as he
Had noted in Clarinda; save that she
Had a more wanton eye, that here and there
Rolled up and down, not settling any where.
Down on the ground she falls his hand to kiss,
And with her tears bedews it; cold as ice
He felt her lips, that yet inflamed him so,
That he was all on fire the truth to know,
Whether she was the same she did appear,
Or whether some fantastic form it were,

Fashioned in his imagination
By his still working thoughts, so fixed upon
His loved Clarinda, that his fancy strove,
Even with her shadow, to express his love.

CATHARINE PHILLIPS.

VERY little is known of the life of this lady-poet. She was
born in 1631. Her maiden name was Fowler. She married
James Phillips, Esq., of the Priory of Cardigan. Her poems,
published under the name of "Orinda," were very popular in her
lifetime, although it was said they were published without her
consent. She translated two of the tragedies of Corneille, and
left a volume of letters to Sir Charles Cotterell. These, however, did not appear till after her death. She died of small-pox
—then a deadly disease—in 1664. She seems to have been a
favourite alike with the wits and the divines of her age. Jeremy
Taylor addressed to her his "Measures and Offices of Friendship;" Dryden praised her; and Flatman and Cowley, besides
imitating her poems while she was living, paid rhymed tributes
to her memory when dead. Her verses are never commonplace,
and always sensible, if they hardly attain to the measure and
the stature of lofty poetry.

THE INQUIRY.

1 If we no old historian's name
      Authentic will admit,
   But think all said of friendship's fame
      But poetry or wit;
   Yet what 's revered by minds so pure
   Must be a bright idea sure.

2 But as our immortality
      By inward sense we find,
   Judging that if it could not be,
      It would not be designed:

So here how could such copies fall,
If there were no original?

3 But if truth be in ancient song,
    Or story we believe;
If the inspired and greater throng
    Have scorned to deceive;
There have been hearts whose friendship gave
Them thoughts at once both soft and grave.

4 Among that consecrated crew
    Some more seraphic shade
Lend me a favourable clew,
    Now mists my eyes invade.
Why, having filled the world with fame,
Left you so little of your flame?

5 Why is't so difficult to see
    Two bodies and one mind?
And why are those who else agree
    So difficultly kind?
Hath Nature such fantastic art,
That she can vary every heart?

6 Why are the bands of friendship tied
    With so remiss a knot,
That by the most it is defied,
    And by the most forgot?
Why do we step with so light sense
From friendship to indifference?

7 If friendship sympathy impart,
    Why this ill-shuffled game,
That heart can never meet with heart,
    Or flame encounter flame?

What does this cruelty create?
Is 't the intrigue of love or fate?

8 Had friendship ne'er been known to men,
   (The ghost at last confessed)
The world had then a stranger been
   To all that heaven possessed.
 But could it all be here acquired,
Not heaven itself would be desired.

A FRIEND.

1 Love, nature's plot, this great creation's soul,
   The being and the harmony of things,
Doth still preserve and propagate the whole,
   From whence man's happiness and safety springs:
The earliest, whitest, blessed'st times did draw
From her alone their universal law.

2 Friendship's an abstract of this noble flame,
   'Tis love refined and purged from all its dross,
The next to angels' love, if not the same,
   As strong in passion is, though not so gross:
It antedates a glad eternity,
And is an heaven in epitome.

    *   *   *   *   *

3 Essential honour must be in a friend,
   Not such as every breath fans to and fro;
But born within, is its own judge and end,
   And dares not sin though sure that none should
     know.
Where friendship 's spoke, honesty 's understood;
For none can be a friend that is not good.

    *   *   *   *   *

4 Thick waters show no images of things;
   Friends are each other's mirrors, and should be
Clearer than crystal or the mountain springs,
   And free from clouds, design, or flattery.
For vulgar souls no part of friendship share;
Poets and friends are born to what they are.

MARGARET, DUCHESS OF NEWCASTLE.

This lady, if not more of a woman than Mrs Phillips, was considerably more of a poet. She was born (probably) about 1625. She was the daughter of Sir Charles Lucas, and became a maid-of-honour to Henrietta Maria. Accompanying the Queen to France, she met with the Marquis, afterwards Duke of Newcastle, and married him at Paris in 1645. They removed to Antwerp, and there, in 1653, this lady published a volume, entitled 'Poems and Fancies.' The pair aided each other in their studies, and the result was a number of enormous folios of poems, plays, speeches, and philosophical disquisitions. These volumes were, we are told, great favourites of Coleridge and Charles Lamb, for the sake, we presume, of the wild sparks of insight and genius which break irresistibly through the scholastic smoke and bewildered nonsense. When Charles II. was restored, the Marquis and his wife returned to England, and spent their life in great harmony. She died in 1673, leaving behind her some beautiful fantasias, where the meaning is often finer than the music, such as the 'Pastime and Recreation of Fairies in Fairyland.' Her poetry, particularly her contrasted pictures of Mirth and Melancholy, present fine accumulations of imagery drawn direct from nature, and shewn now in brightest sunshine, and now in softest moonlight, as the change of her subject and her tone of feeling require.

MELANCHOLY DESCRIBED BY MIRTH.

Her voice is low, and gives a hollow sound;
She hates the light, and is in darkness found;

Or sits with blinking lamps, or tapers small,
Which various shadows make against the wall.
She loves nought else but noise which discord makes,
As croaking frogs, whose dwelling is in lakes;
The raven's hoarse, the mandrake's hollow groan,
And shrieking owls which fly i' the night alone;
The tolling bell, which for the dead rings out;
A mill, where rushing waters run about;
The roaring winds, which shake the cedars tall,
Plough up the seas, and beat the rocks withal.
She loves to walk in the still moonshine night,
And in a thick dark grove she takes delight;
In hollow caves, thatched houses, and low cells,
She loves to live, and there alone she dwells.

MELANCHOLY DESCRIBING HERSELF.

I dwell in groves that gilt are with the sun;
Sit on the banks by which clear waters run;
In summers hot, down in a shade I lie;
My music is the buzzing of a fly;
I walk in meadows, where grows fresh green grass;
In fields, where corn is high, I often pass;
Walk up the hills, where round I prospects see,
Some brushy woods, and some all champaigns be;
Returning back, I in fresh pastures go,
To hear how sheep do bleat, and cows do low;
In winter cold, when nipping frosts come on,
Then I do live in a small house alone;
Although 'tis plain, yet cleanly 'tis within,
Like to a soul that's pure, and clear from sin;
And there I dwell in quiet and still peace,
Not filled with cares how riches to increase;
I wish nor seek for vain and fruitless pleasures;
No riches are, but what the mind intreasures.

Thus am I solitary, live alone,
Yet better loved, the more that I am known;
And though my face ill-favoured at first sight,
After acquaintance, it will give delight.
Refuse me not, for I shall constant be;
Maintain your credit and your dignity.

THOMAS STANLEY.

THOMAS STANLEY, like Thomas Brown in later days, was both a philosopher and a poet; but his philosophical reputation at the time eclipsed his poetical. He was the only son of Sir Thomas Stanley of Camberlow Green, in Hertfordshire, and was born in 1620. He received his education at Pembroke College, Oxford; and after travelling for some years abroad, he took up his abode in the Middle Temple. Here he seems to have spent the rest of his life in patient and multifarious studies. He made translations of some merit from Anacreon, Bion, Moschus, and the 'Kisses' of Secundus, as well as from Marino, Boscan, Tristan, and Gongora. He wrote a work of great pretensions as a compilation, entitled 'The History of Philosophy,' containing the lives, opinions, actions, and discourses of philosophers of every sect, of which he published the first volume in 1655, and completed it in a fourth in 1662. It is rather a vast collection of the materials for a history, than a history itself. He is a Cudworth in magnitude and learning, but not in strength and comprehension, and is destitute of precision and clearness of style. Stanley also wrote some poems, which discover powers that might have been better employed in original composition than in translation. His style, rich of itself, is enriched to repletion by conceits, and sometimes by voluptuous sentiments and language. He adds a new flush to the cheek of Anacreon himself; and his grapes are so heavy, that not a staff, but a wain were required to bear them. Stanley died in 1678.

CELIA SINGING.

1 Roses in breathing forth their scent,
  Or stars their borrowed ornament;
  Nymphs in their watery sphere that move,
  Or angels in their orbs above;
  The winged chariot of the light,
  Or the slow, silent wheels of night;
  The shade which from the swifter sun
  Doth in a swifter motion run,
Or souls that their eternal rest do keep,
Make far less noise than Celia's breath in sleep.

2 But if the angel which inspires
  This subtle flame with active fires,
  Should mould this breath to words, and those
  Into a harmony dispose,
  The music of this heavenly sphere
  Would steal each soul (in) at the ear,
  And into plants and stones infuse
  A life that cherubim would choose,
And with new powers invert the laws of fate,
Kill those that live, and dead things animate.

SPEAKING AND KISSING.

1 The air which thy smooth voice doth break,
    Into my soul like lightning flies;
  My life retires while thou dost speak,
    And thy soft breath its room supplies.

2 Lost in this pleasing ecstasy,
    I join my trembling lips to thine,
  And back receive that life from thee
    Which I so gladly did resign.

3 Forbear, Platonic fools! t' inquire
    What numbers do the soul compose;
No harmony can life inspire,
    But that which from these accents flows.

LA BELLE CONFIDANTE.

You earthly souls that court a wanton flame
    Whose pale, weak influence
Can rise no higher than the humble name
    And narrow laws of sense,
Learn, by our friendship, to create
        An immaterial fire,
Whose brightness angels may admire,
        But cannot emulate.
Sickness may fright the roses from her cheek,
        Or make the lilies fade,
But all the subtle ways that death doth seek
        Cannot my love invade.

THE LOSS.

1   Yet ere I go,
    Disdainful Beauty, thou shalt be
        So wretched as to know
    What joys thou fling'st away with me.

2   A faith so bright,
    As Time or Fortune could not rust;
        So firm, that lovers might
    Have read thy story in my dust,

3   And crowned thy name
    With laurel verdant as thy youth,
        Whilst the shrill voice of Fame
    Spread wide thy beauty and my truth.

4   This thou hast lost,
For all true lovers, when they find
    That my just aims were crossed,
Will speak thee lighter than the wind.

5   And none will lay
Any oblation on thy shrine,
    But such as would betray
Thy faith to faiths as false as thine.

6   Yet, if thou choose
On such thy freedom to bestow,
    Affection may excuse,
For love from sympathy doth flow.

NOTE ON ANACREON.

Let's not rhyme the hours away;
Friends! we must no longer play:
Brisk Lyæus—see!—invites
To more ravishing delights.
Let's give o'er this fool Apollo,
Nor his fiddle longer follow:
Fie upon his forked hill,
With his fiddlestick and quill;
And the Muses, though they're gamesome,
They are neither young nor handsome;
And their freaks in sober sadness
Are a mere poetic madness:
Pegasus is but a horse;
He that follows him is worse.
See, the rain soaks to the skin,
Make it rain as well within.
Wine, my boy; we'll sing and laugh,
All night revel, rant, and quaff;

Till the morn, stealing behind us,
At the table sleepless find us.
When our bones, alas! shall have
A cold lodging in the grave;
When swift Death shall overtake us,
We shall sleep and none can wake us.
Drink we then the juice o' the vine
Make our breasts Lyæus' shrine;
Bacchus, our debauch beholding,
By thy image I am moulding,
Whilst my brains I do replenish
With this draught of unmixed Rhenish;
By thy full-branched ivy twine;
By this sparkling glass of wine;
By thy Thyrsus so renowned:
By the healths with which th' art crowned;
By the feasts which thou dost prize;
By thy numerous victories;
By the howls by Mœnads made;
By this haut-gout carbonade;
By thy colours red and white;
By the tavern, thy delight;
By the sound thy orgies spread;
By the shine of noses red;
By thy table free for all;
By the jovial carnival;
By thy language cabalistic;
By thy cymbal, drum, and his stick;
By the tunes thy quart-pots strike up;
By thy sighs, the broken hiccup;
By thy mystic set of ranters;
By thy never-tamed panthers;
By this sweet, this fresh and free air;
By thy goat, as chaste as we are;

By thy fulsome Cretan lass;
By the old man on the ass;
By thy cousins in mixed shapes;
By the flower of fairest grapes;
By thy bisks famed far and wide;
By thy store of neats'-tongues dried;
By thy incense, Indian smoke;
By the joys thou dost provoke;
By this salt Westphalia gammon;
By these sausages that inflame one;
By thy tall majestic flagons;
By mass, tope, and thy flapdragons;
By this olive's unctuous savour;
By this orange, the wine's flavour;
By this cheese o'errun with mites;
By thy dearest favourites;
To thy frolic order call us,
Knights of the deep bowl install us;
And to show thyself divine,
Never let it want for wine.

ANDREW MARVELL.

This noble-minded patriot and poet, the friend of Milton, the
Abdiel of a dark and corrupt age,—'faithful found among the
faithless, faithful only he,'—was born in Hull in 1620. He was
sent to Cambridge, and is said there to have nearly fallen a
victim to the proselytising Jesuits, who enticed him to London.
His father, however, a clergyman in Hull, went in search of and
brought him back to his university, where speedily, by exten-
sive culture and the vigorous exercise of his powerful faculties,
he emancipated himself for ever from the dominion, and the
danger of the dominion, of superstition and bigotry. We know
little more about the early days of our poet. When only twenty,

he lost his father in remarkable circumstances. In 1640, he had embarked on the Humber in company with a youthful pair whom he was to marry at Barrow, in Lincolnshire. The weather was calm; but Marvell, seized with a sudden presentiment of danger, threw his staff ashore, and cried out, 'Ho for heaven!' A storm came on, and the whole company perished. In consequence of this sad event, the gentleman, whose daughter was to have been married, conceiving that the father had sacrificed his life while performing an act of friendship, adopted young Marvell as his son. Owing to this, he received a better education, and was sent abroad to travel. It is said that at Rome he met and formed a friendship with Milton, then engaged on his immortal continental tour. We find Marvell next at Constantinople, as Secretary to the English Embassy at that Court. We then lose sight of him till 1653, when he was engaged by the Protector to superintend the education of a Mr Dutton at Eton. For a year and a half after Cromwell's death, Marvell assisted Milton as Latin Secretary to the Protector. Our readers are all familiar with the print of Cromwell and Milton seated together at the council-table,—the one the express image of active power and rugged grandeur, the other of thoughtful majesty and ethereal grace. Marvell might have been added as a third, and become the emblem of strong English sense and incorruptible integrity. A letter of Milton's was, not long since, discovered, dated February 1652, in which he speaks of Marvell as fitted, by his knowledge of Latin and his experience of teaching, to be his assistant. He was not appointed, however, till 1657. In 1660, he became member for Hull, and was re-elected as long as he lived. He was absent, however, from England for two years, in the beginning of the reign, in Germany and Holland. Afterwards he sought leave from his constituents to act as Ambassador's Secretary to Lord Carlisle at the Northern Courts; but from the year 1665 to his death, his attention to his parliamentary duties was unremitting. He constantly corresponded with his constituents; and after the longest sittings, he used to write out for their use a minute account of public proceedings ere he went to bed, or took any refreshment. He was one of the last members who received pay from the town he represented; (2s. a-day was probably the sum;) and his constituents were wont, besides, to send him barrels of ale as tokens of their regard. Marvell spoke little in the House; but his heart and vote were always in the right place. Even Prince Rupert continually consulted him, and was sometimes persuaded by him to support the popular side; and King Charles having met him once in private, was so delighted with his wit and agreeable manners, that he thought him worth trying to bribe. He sent Lord Danby to offer him a mark of his Majesty's consideration. Marvell, who was seated in a dingy room up several flights of stairs, declined the proffer, and, it is said, called his servant to witness that he had dined for three successive days on the same shoulder of mutton, and was not likely, therefore, to care for or need a bribe. When the Treasurer was gone, he had to send to a friend to borrow a guinea. Although a silent senator, Marvell was a copious and popular writer. He attacked Bishop Parker for his slavish principles, in a piece entitled 'The Rehearsal Transposed,' in which he takes occasion to vindicate and panegyrise his old colleague Milton. His anonymous 'Account of the Growth of Arbitrary Power and Popery in England' excited a sensation, and a reward was offered for the apprehension of the author and printer. Marvell had many of the elements of a first-rate political pamphleteer. He had wit of a most pungent kind, great though coarse fertility of fancy, and a spirit of independence that nothing could subdue or damp. He was the undoubted ancestor of the Defoes, Swifts, Steeles, Juniuses, and Burkes, in whom this kind of authorship reached its perfection, ceased to be fugitive, and assumed classical rank.

Marvell had been repeatedly threatened with assassination, and hence, when he died suddenly on the 16th of August 1678, it was surmised that he had been removed by poison. The Corporation of Hull voted a sum to defray his funeral expenses, and for raising a monument to his memory; but owing to the interference of the Court, through the rector of the parish, this votive tablet was not at the time erected. He was buried in St Giles-in-the-Fields.

'Out of the strong came forth sweetness,' saith the Hebrew

record. And so from the sturdy Andrew Marvell have proceeded such soft and lovely strains as 'The Emigrants,' 'The Nymph complaining for the Death of her Fawn,' 'Young Love,' &c. The statue of Memnon became musical at the dawn; and the stern patriot, whom no bribe could buy and no flattery melt, is found sympathising in song with a boatful of banished Englishmen in the remote Bermudas, and inditing 'Thoughts in a Garden,' from which you might suppose that he had spent his life more with melons than with men, and was better acquainted with the motions of a bee-hive than with the contests of Parliament, and the distractions of a most distracted age. It was said (not with thorough truth) of Milton, that he could cut out a Colossus from a rock, but could not carve heads upon cherry-stones—a task which his assistant may be said to have performed in his stead, in his small but delectable copies of verse.

THE EMIGRANTS.

1 Where the remote Bermudas ride,
  In the ocean's bosom unespied,
  From a small boat that rowed along,
  The listening winds received this song.

2 'What should we do but sing His praise
  That led us through the watery maze,
  Unto an isle so long unknown,
  And yet far kinder than our own!

3 'Where he the huge sea-monsters racks,
  That lift the deep upon their backs;
  He lands us on a grassy stage,
  Safe from the storms and prelates' rage.

4 'He gave us this eternal spring
  Which here enamels everything,
  And sends the fowls to us in care,
  On daily visits through the air.

5 'He hangs in shades the orange bright,
  Like golden lamps in a green night;
  *   *   *   *   *
  And in these rocks for us did frame
  A temple where to sound his name.

6 'Oh, let our voice his praise exalt
  Till it arrive at heaven's vault,
  Which then perhaps rebounding may
  Echo beyond the Mexique bay.'

7 Thus sung they in the English boat,
  A holy and a cheerful note;
  And all the way, to guide their chime,
  With falling oars they kept the time.

THE NYMPH COMPLAINING FOR THE DEATH OF HER FAWN.

The wanton troopers riding by   .
Have shot my fawn, and it will die.
Ungentle men! they cannot thrive
Who killed thee. Thou ne'er didst alive
Them any harm; alas! nor could
Thy death to them do any good.
I'm sure I never wished them ill;
Nor do I for all this; nor will:
But, if my simple prayers may yet
Prevail with Heaven to forget
Thy murder, I will join my tears,
Rather than fail. But, O my fears!
It cannot die so. Heaven's King
Keeps register of every thing,
And nothing may we use in vain:
Even beasts must be with justice slain.
    *   *   *   *   *

178

Inconstant Sylvio, when yet
I had not found him counterfeit,
One morning (I remember well)
Tied in this silver chain and bell,
Gave it to me: nay, and I know
What he said then: I 'm sure I do.
Said he, 'Look how your huntsman here
Hath taught a fawn to hunt his deer.'
But Sylvio soon had me beguiled.
This waxed tame while he grew wild,
And, quite regardless of my smart,
Left me his fawn, but took his heart.
Thenceforth I set myself to play
My solitary time away
With this, and very well content
Could so my idle life have spent;
For it was full of sport, and light
Of foot and heart; and did invite
Me to its game; it seemed to bless
Itself in me.   How could I less
Than love it?   Oh, I cannot be
Unkind to a beast that loveth me!
Had it lived long, I do not know
Whether it too might have done so
As Sylvio did; his gifts might be
Perhaps as false, or more, than he.
But I am sure, for aught that I
Could in so short a time espy,
Thy love was far more better than
The love of false and cruel man.
With sweetest milk and sugar first
I it at my own fingers nursed;
And as it grew, so every day
It waxed more white and sweet than they:

It had so sweet a breath; and oft
I blushed to see its foot more soft
And white, shall I say, than my hand?
Nay, any lady's of the land.
It is a wondrous thing how fleet
'Twas on those little silver feet;
With what a pretty skipping grace
It oft would challenge me the race;
And when 't had left me far away,
'Twould stay, and run again, and stay;
For it was nimbler much than hinds,
And trod as if on the four winds.
I have a garden of my own,
But so with roses overgrown,
And lilies, that you would it guess
To be a little wilderness,
And all the spring-time of the year
It only loved to be there.
Among the beds of lilies I
Have sought it oft where it should lie,
Yet could not, till itself would rise,
Find it, although before mine eyes;
For in the flaxen lilies' shade
It like a bank of lilies laid;
Upon the roses it would feed,
Until its lips e'en seemed to bleed;
And then to me 'twould boldly trip,
And print those roses on my lip.
But all its chief delight was still
On roses thus itself to fill,
And its pure virgin limbs to fold
In whitest sheets of lilies cold.
Had it lived long, it would have been
Lilies without, roses within.   *   *   *

ON PARADISE LOST.

When I beheld the poet blind, yet bold,
In slender book his vast design unfold,
Messiah crowned, God's reconciled decree,
Rebelling angels, the forbidden tree,
Heaven, Hell, Earth, Chaos, all; the argument
Held me a while misdoubting his intent,
That he would ruin (for I saw him strong)
The sacred truths to fable and old song;
(So Sampson groped the temple's posts in spite)
The world o'erwhelming to revenge his sight.

    Yet as I read, still growing less severe,
I liked his project, the success did fear;
Through that wild field how he his way should find,
O'er which lame Faith leads Understanding blind;
Lest he 'd perplex the things he would explain,
And what was easy he should render vain.

    Or if a work so infinite be spanned,
Jealous I was that some less skilful hand
(Such as disquiet always what is well,
And, by ill imitating, would excel)
Might hence presume the whole creation's day
To change in scenes, and show it in a play.

    Pardon me, mighty poet, nor despise
My causeless, yet not impious, surmise.
But I am now convinced, and none will dare
Within thy labours to pretend a share.
Thou hast not missed one thought that could be fit.
And all that was improper dost omit;
So that no room is here for writers left,
But to detect their ignorance or theft.

    That majesty, which through thy work doth reign,
Draws the devout, deterring the profane.

And things divine thou treat'st of in such state
As them preserves, and thee, inviolate.
At once delight and horror on us seize,
Thou sing'st with so much gravity and ease;
And above human flight dost soar aloft
With plume so strong, so equal, and so soft.
The bird named from that Paradise you sing,
So never flags, but always keeps on wing.
      Where couldst thou words of such a compass find?
Whence furnish such a vast expanse of mind?
Just Heaven thee, like Tiresias, to requite,
Rewards with prophecy thy loss of sight.
      Well mightst thou scorn thy readers to allure
With tinkling rhyme, of thy own sense secure;
While the Town-Bays writes all the while and spells,
And like a pack-horse tires without his bells:
Their fancies like our bushy points appear;
The poets tag them, we for fashion wear.
I too, transported by the mode, offend,
And while I meant to praise thee, must commend.
Thy verse created, like thy theme, sublime,
In number, weight, and measure, needs not rhyme.

THOUGHTS IN A GARDEN.

1 How vainly men themselves amaze,
   To win the palm, the oak, or bays!
   And their incessant labours see
   Crowned from some single herb or tree,
   Whose short and narrow-verged shade
   Does prudently their toils upbraid;
   While all the flowers and trees do close,
   To weave the garlands of repose.

2 Fair Quiet, have I found thee here,
And Innocence, thy sister dear?
Mistaken long, I sought you then
In busy companies of men.
Your sacred plants, if here below,
Only among the plants will grow.
Society is all but rude
To this delicious solitude.

3 No white nor red was ever seen
So amorous as this lovely green.
Fond lovers, cruel as their flame,
Cut in these trees their mistress' name.
Little, alas, they know or heed,
How far these beauties her exceed!
Fair trees! where'er your barks I wound,
No name shall but your own be found.

4 What wondrous life in this I lead!
Ripe apples drop about my head.
The luscious clusters of the vine
Upon my mouth do crush their wine.
The nectarine, and curious peach,
Into my hands themselves do reach.
Stumbling on melons as I pass,
Ensnared with flowers, I fall on grass.

5 Meanwhile the mind from pleasure less
Withdraws into its happiness.
The mind, that ocean where each kind
Does straight its own resemblance find;
Yet it creates, transcending these,
Far other worlds and other seas;
Annihilating all that's made
To a green thought in a green shade.

6 Here at the fountain's sliding foot,
  Or at some fruit-tree's mossy root,
  Casting the body's vest aside,
  My soul into the boughs does glide;
  There, like a bird, it sits and sings,
  Then whets and claps its silver wings,
  And, till prepared for longer flight,
  Waves in its plumes the various light.

7 Such was the happy garden state,
  While man there walked without a mate:
  After a place so pure and sweet,
  What other help could yet be meet!
  But 'twas beyond a mortal's share
  To wander solitary there:
  Two paradises are in one,
  To live in paradise alone.

8 How well the skilful gard'ner drew
  Of flowers and herbs this dial new!
  Where, from above, the milder sun
  Does through a fragrant zodiac run:
  And, as it works, the industrious bee
  Computes its time as well as we.
  How could such sweet and wholesome hours
  Be reckoned but with herbs and flowers?

SATIRE ON HOLLAND.

Holland, that scarce deserves the name of land,
As but the offscouring of the British sand;
And so much earth as was contributed
By English pilots when they heaved the lead;
Or what by the ocean's slow alluvion fell,
Of shipwrecked cockle and the mussel-shell;

This indigested vomit of the sea
Fell to the Dutch by just propriety.
Glad then, as miners who have found the ore,
They, with mad labour, fished the land to shore:
And dived as desperately for each piece
Of earth, as if 't had been of ambergris;
Collecting anxiously small loads of clay,
Less than what building swallows bear away;
Or than those pills which sordid beetles roll,
Transfusing into them their dunghill soul.
How did they rivet, with gigantic piles,
Thorough the centre their new-catched miles;
And to the stake a struggling country bound,
Where barking waves still bait the forced ground;
Building their watery Babel far more high
To reach the sea, than those to scale the sky.
Yet still his claim the injured Ocean laid,
And oft at leap-frog o'er their steeples played;
As if on purpose it on land had come
To show them what's their *mare liberum.*
A daily deluge over them does boil;
The earth and water play at level-coil.
The fish oft-times the burgher dispossessed,
And sat, not as a meat, but as a guest;
And oft the Tritons, and the sea-nymphs, saw
Whole shoals of Dutch served up for Cabillau;
Or, as they over the new level ranged,
For pickled herring, pickled heeren changed.
Nature, it seem'd, ashamed of her mistake,
Would throw their land away at duck and drake,
Therefore necessity, that first made kings,
Something like government among them brings.
For, as with Pigmies, who best kills the crane,
Among the hungry he that treasures grain,

Among the blind the one-eyed blinkard reigns,
So rules among the drowned he that drains.
Not who first see the rising sun commands,
But who could first discern the rising lands.
Who best could know to pump an earth so leak,
Him they their lord, and country's father, speak.
To make a bank was a great plot of state;
Invent a shovel, and be a magistrate.
Hence some small dikegrave unperceived invades
The power, and grows, as 'twere, a king of spades;
But, for less envy some joined states endures,
Who look like a commission of the sewers:
For these half-anders, half-wet and half-dry,
Nor bear strict service, nor pure liberty.
'Tis probable religion, after this,
Came next in order; which they could not miss.
How could the Dutch but be converted, when
The apostles were so many fishermen?
Besides, the waters of themselves did rise,
And, as their land, so them did re-baptize;
Though herring for their God few voices missed,
And Poor-John to have been the Evangelist.
Faith, that could never twins conceive before,
Never so fertile, spawned upon this shore
More pregnant than their Marg'ret, that laid down
For Hands-in-Kelder of a whole Hans-Town.
Sure, when religion did itself embark,
And from the east would westward steer its ark,
It struck, and splitting on this unknown ground,
Each one thence pillaged the first piece he found:
Hence Amsterdam, Turk, Christian, Pagan, Jew,
Staple of sects, and mint of schism grew;
That bank of conscience, where not one so strange
Opinion, but finds credit, and exchange.

In vain for Catholics ourselves we bear:
The universal church is only there.   *   *   *

IZAAK WALTON.

THIS amiable enemy of the finny tribe was born in Stafford, in August 1593. We hear of him first as settled in London, following the trade of a sempster, or linen-draper, having a shop in the Royal Burse, in Cornhill, which was 'seven feet and a half long, and five wide,' and where he became possessed of a moderate fortune. He spent his leisure time in fishing 'with honest Nat and R. Roe.' From the Royal Burse, he removed to Fleet Street, where he had 'one half of a shop,' a hosier occupying the other half. In 1632, he married Anne, the daughter of Thomas Ken of Furnival's Inn, and sister of Dr Ken, the celebrated Bishop of Bath and Wells. Through her and her kindred, he became acquainted with many eminent men of the day. His wife, 'a woman of remarkable prudence and primitive piety,' died long before him. He retired from business in 1643, and lived, for forty years after, a life of leisure and quiet enjoyment, spending much of his time in the houses of his friends, and much of it by the still waters, which he so dearly loved. Walton commenced his literary career by writing a Life of Dr Donne, and followed with another of Sir Henry Wotton, prefixed to his literary remains. In 1653 appeared his 'Complete Angler,' four editions of which were called for before his decease. He wrote, in 1662, a Life of Richard Hooker; in 1670, a Life of George Herbert; and, in 1678, a Life of Bishop Sanderson—all distinguished by *naïveté* and heart. In 1680, he published an anonymous discourse on the 'Distempers of the Times.' In 1683, he printed, as we have seen, Chalkhill's 'Thealma and Clearchus;' and on the 15th of December in the same year, he died at Winchester, while residing with his son-in-law, Dr Hawkins, Prebendary of Winchester Cathedral.

Walton is one of the most loveable of all authors. Your admiration of him is always melting into affection. Red as his hand is with the blood of fish, you pant to grasp it and press it to yours. You go with him to the fishing as you would with a bright-eyed boy, relishing his simple-hearted enthusiasm, and leaning down to listen to his precocious remarks, and to pat his curly head. It is the prevalence of the childlike element which makes Walton's 'Angler' rank with Bunyan's 'Pilgrim,' 'Robinson Crusoe,' and White's 'Natural History of Selborne,' as among the most delightful books in the language. Its descriptions of nature, too, are so fresh, that you smell to them as to a green leaf. Walton would not have been at home fishing in the Forth or Clyde, or in such rivers as are found in Norway, the milk-blue Logen, or the grass-green Rauma, uniting, with its rich mediation, Romsdale Horn to the tremendous Witch-Peaks which lower on the opposite side of the valley;—the waters of his own dear England, going softly and somewhat drowsily on their path, are the sources of his inspiration, and seem to sound like the echoes of his own subdued but gladsome spirit. Johnson defined angling as a rod with a fish at one end, and a fool at the other; in Walton's case, we may correct the expression to 'a rod with a fish at one end, and a fine old fellow—the " ae best fellow in the world "—at the other '—

' In wit a man, simplicity a child.'

We have given a specimen of the verse he intersperses sparingly in a book which *is itself a complete poem.*

THE ANGLER'S WISH.

1 I in these flowery meads would be:
 These crystal streams should solace me,
 To whose harmonious bubbling noise
 I with my angle would rejoice:
 Sit here and see the turtle-dove
 Court his chaste mate to acts of love:

2 Or on that bank feel the west wind
 Breathe health and plenty: please my mind
 To see sweet dew-drops kiss these flowers,
 And then washed off by April showers!

> Here hear my Kenna sing a song,
> There see a blackbird feed her young,
>
> 3 Or a leverock build her nest:
> Here give my weary spirits rest,
> And raise my low-pitched thoughts above
> Earth, or what poor mortals love;
> Or, with my Bryan[1] and my book,
> Loiter long days near Shawford brook:
>
> 4 There sit by him and eat my meat,
> There see the sun both rise and set,
> There bid good morning to next day,
> There meditate my time away,
> And angle on, and beg to have
> A quiet passage to the grave.

JOHN WILMOT, EARL OF ROCHESTER.

WE hear of the Spirit of Evil on one occasion entering into swine, but, if possible, a stranger sight is that of the Spirit of Poesy finding a similar incarnation. Certainly the connexion of genius in the Earl of Rochester with a life of the most degrading and desperate debauchery is one of the chief marvels of this marvellous world.

John Wilmot was the son of Henry, Lord Rochester, and was born April 10, 1647, at Ditchley in Oxfordshire. He was taught grammar at the school of Burford. He then ' entered a nobleman' into Wadham College, when twelve years old, and at 1661, when only fourteen, he was, in conjunction with some others of rank, made M.A. by Lord Clarendon in person. Pursuing his travels in France and Italy, he went in 1665 to sea with the Earl of Sandwich, and distinguished himself at Bergen in an attack on the Dutch fleet. Next year, while

[1] Probably his dog.

serving under Sir Edward Spragge, his commander sent him in
the heat of an engagement with a reproof to one of his captains—
a duty which Wilmot gallantly accomplished amidst a storm of
shot. With this early courage some of his biographers have
contrasted his subsequent reputation for cowardice, his slinking
away out of street-quarrels, his refusing to fight the Duke of
Buckingham, &c. This diversity at different periods may
perhaps be accounted for on the ground of the nervousness
which continued dissipation produces, and perhaps from his
poetical temperament. A poet, we are persuaded, is often the
bravest, and often the most pusillanimous of men. Byron was
unquestionably in general a brave, almost a pugnacious man;
and yet he confesses that at certain times, had one proceeded to
horsewhip him, he would not have had the hardihood to resist.
Shelley, who, in a tremendous storm, behaved with dauntless
heroism, and who would at any time have acted on the example
of his own character in ' Prometheus,' who, in a shipwreck,

' gave an enemy
His plank, then plunged aside to die,'

was yet subject to paroxysms of nervous horror, which made him
perspire and tremble like a spirit-seeing steed. Rochester had
the same temperament, and a similar creed, with these men,
although inferior to them both in *morale* and in genius.

His character was certainly very depraved. He told Burnet
on his deathbed that for five years he had not known the sensation of sobriety, having been all that time either totally drunk,
or mad through the dregs of drunkenness. He on one occasion,
while in this state, erected a stage on Tower Hill, and addressed
the mob as a naked mountebank. Even after he became more
temperate, he continued and even increased his licentiousness—
one devil went out, and seven entered in. He pursued low
amours in disguise; he practised occasionally as a quack doctor;
and at other times he retired to the country, and, like Byron,
amused himself by libelling all his acquaintances—every line
in each libel being a lie. Notwithstanding all this, he was a
favourite with Charles II., who made him one of the gentlemen
of the bedchamber, and comptroller of Woodstock Park. In
his lucid intervals he recurred to his studies, wrote occasional

verses, read in French Boileau and in English Cowley, and is called by Wood·the best scholar among all the nobility.

At last, ere he was thirty-one, the 'dreary old sort of feel,' and the 'rigid fibre and stiffening limbs,' of which Byron and Burns, when scarcely older, complained, began to assail Rochester. He had exhausted his capacity of enjoyment by excess, and had deprived himself of the consolations of religion by infidelity. His unbelief was not like Shelley's—the growth of his own mind, and the fruit of unbridled, though earnest, speculation;—it was merely a drug which he snatched from the laboratories of others to deaden his remorse, and enable him to look with desperate calmness to the blotted Past and the lowering Future. At this stage of his career, he became acquainted with Bishop Burnet, who has recorded his conversion and edifying end in a book which, says Johnson, 'the critic ought to read for its elegance, the philosopher for its arguments, and the saint for its piety.' To this, after Johnson's example, we refer our readers. Rochester died July 26, 1680, before he had completed his thirty-fourth year. He was married, and left three daughters and a son named Charles, who did not long survive his father. With him the male line ceased, and the title was conferred on a younger son of Lord Clarendon. His poems appeared in the year of his death, professing on the title-page to be printed at Antwerp. They contain much that is spurious, but some productions that are undoubtedly Rochester's. They are at the best, poor fragmentary exhibitions of a vigorous, but undisciplined mind. His songs are rather easy than lively. His imitations are distinguished by grace and spirit. His 'Nothing' is a tissue of clever conceits, like gaudy weeds growing on a sterile soil, but here and there contains a grand and gloomy image, such as—

'And rebel Light obscured thy reverend dusky face.'

His 'Satire against Man' might be praised for its vigorous misanthropy, but is chiefly copied from Boileau.

Rochester may be signalised as the first thoroughly depraved and vicious person, so far as we remember, who assumed the office of the satirist,—the first, although not, alas! the last human imitator of 'Satan accusing Sin.' Some satirists before

him had been faulty characters, while rather inconsistently assailing the faults of others; but here, for the first time, was a
man of no virtue, or belief in virtue whatever, (his tenderness to
his family, revealed in his letters, is just that of the tiger fondling his cubs, and seeming, perhaps, to *them* a ' much-misrepresented character,') and whose life was one mass of wounds,
bruises, and putrefying sores,—a naked satyr who gloried in his
shame,—becoming a severe castigator of public morals and of
private character. Surely there was a gross anomaly implied in
this, which far greater genius than Rochester's could never have
redeemed.

SONG.

1 Too late, alas! I must confess,
    You need not arts to move me;
Such charms by nature you possess,
    'Twere madness not to love ye.

2 Then spare a heart you may surprise,
    And give my tongue the glory
To boast, though my unfaithful eyes
    Betray a tender story.

SONG.

1 My dear mistress has a heart
    Soft as those kind looks she gave me,
When with love's resistless art,
    And her eyes, she did enslave me.
But her constancy 's so weak,
    She 's so wild and apt to wander,
That my jealous heart would break
    Should we live one day asunder.

2 Melting joys about her move,
    Killing pleasures, wounding blisses:
She can dress her eyes in love,
    And her lips can warm with kisses.

192

Angels listen when she speaks,
  She's my delight, all mankind's wonder;
But my jealous heart would break,
  Should we live one day asunder.

THE EARL OF ROSCOMMON.

WENTWORTH DILLON, Earl of Roscommon, was the son of James
Dillon and Elizabeth Wentworth. She was the sister of the
infamous Strafford, who was at once uncle and godfather to our
poet. In what exact year Dillon was born is uncertain, but it
was some time about 1633. His father had been converted from
Popery by Usher; and when the Irish Rebellion broke out,
Strafford, afraid of the fury of the Irish, sent for his godson, and
took him to his own seat in Yorkshire, where he was. taught
Latin with great care. He was sent afterwards to Caen, where
he studied under Bochart. It is said that while playing extra-
vagantly there at the customary games of boys, he suddenly
paused, became grave, and cried out, 'My father is dead,' and
that a fortnight after arrived tidings from Ireland confirming his
impression. Johnson is inclined to believe this story, and we
are more than inclined. Since the lexicographer's day, many of
what used to be called his 'superstitions' have been established
as certain facts, although their explanation is still shrouded in
darkness. Roscommon was then only ten years of age.

From Caen he travelled to Italy, where he obtained a profound knowledge of medals. At the Restoration he returned
to England, where he was made Captain of the Band of Pen-
sioners, and subsequently Master of the Horse to the Duchess
of York. He became unfortunately addicted to gambling, and,
through this miserable habit, he got embroiled in endless quar-
rels, as well as in pecuniary embarassments.

Business compelled him to visit Ireland, where the Duke of
Ormond made him Captain of the Guards. On his return to
England in 1662, he married the Lady Frances, daughter of the
Earl of Burlington. By her he had no issue. His second

wife, whom he married in 1674, was Isabella, daughter of Matthew Beynton of Barmister, in Yorkshire.

Roscommon now began to meditate and execute literary projects. He produced an 'Essay on Translated Verse,' (in 1681,) a translation of Horace's 'Art of Poetry,' and other pieces. He projected, in conjunction with his friend Dryden, a plan for refining our language and fixing its standard, as if Time were not the great refiner, fixer, and enricher of a tongue. While busy with these schemes and occupations, the troubles of James II.'s reign commenced. Roscommon determined to retire to Rome, saying, 'It is best to sit near the chimney when the chamber smokes.' Death, however, prevented him from reaching the beloved and desired focus of Roman Catholic darkness. He was assailed by gout, and an ignorant French empiric, whom he consulted, contrived to drive the disease into the bowels. Roscommon expired, uttering with great fervour two lines from his own translation of the 'Dies Iræ,'—

> 'My God, my Father, and my Friend,
> Do not forsake me in my end.'

This was in 1684. He received a pompous interment in Westminster Abbey.

Roscommon does not deserve the name of a great poet. He was a man of varied accomplishments and exquisite taste rather than of genius. His 'Essay on Translated Verse' is a sound and sensible, not a profound and brilliant production. In one point he went before his age. He praises Milton's 'Paradise Lost,' although unfortunately he selects for encomium the passage in the sixth book describing the angels fighting against each other with fire-arms—a passage which most critics have considered a blot upon the poem.

FROM "AN ESSAY ON TRANSLATED VERSE."

Immodest words admit of no defence;
For want of decency is want of sense.
What moderate fop would rake the park or stews,
Who among troops of faultless nymphs may choose?
Variety of such is to be found:

Take then a subject proper to expound;
But moral, great, and worth a poet's voice;
For men of sense despise a trivial choice;
And such applause it must expect to meet,
As would some painter busy in a street,
To copy bulls and bears, and every sign
That calls the staring sots to nasty wine.
   Yet 'tis not all to have a subject good:
It must delight us when 'tis understood.
He that brings fulsome objects to my view,
As many old have done, and many new,
With nauseous images my fancy fills,
And all goes down like oxymel of squills.
Instruct the listening world how Maro sings
Of useful subjects and of lofty things.
These will such true, such bright ideas raise,
As merit gratitude, as well as praise:
But foul descriptions are offensive still,
Either for being like, or being ill:
For who, without a qualm, hath ever looked
On holy garbage, though by Homer cooked?
Whose railing heroes, and whose wounded gods
Make some suspect he snores, as well as nods.
But I offend—Virgil begins to frown,
And Horace looks with indignation down:
My blushing Muse with conscious fear retires,
And whom they like implicitly admires.
   On sure foundations let your fabric rise,
And with attractive majesty surprise;
Not by affected meretricious arts,
But strict harmonious symmetry of parts;
Which through the whole insensibly must pass,
With vital heat to animate the mass:
A pure, an active, an auspicious flame;

And bright as heaven, from whence the blessing came:
But few, oh! few souls, preordained by fate,
The race of gods, have reached that envied height.
No rebel Titan's sacrilegious crime,
By heaping hills on hills can hither climb:
The grizzly ferryman of hell denied
Æneas entrance, till he knew his guide.
How justly then will impious mortals fall,
Whose pride would soar to heaven without a call!
    Pride, of all others the most dangerous fault,
Proceeds from want of sense, or want of thought.
The men who labour and digest things most,
Will be much apter to despond than boast:
For if your author be profoundly good,
'Twill cost you dear before he 's understood.
How many ages since has Virgil writ!
How few are they who understand him yet!
Approach his altars with religious fear:
No vulgar deity inhabits there.
Heaven shakes not more at Jove's imperial nod,
Than poets should before their Mantuan god.
Hail, mighty Maro! may that sacred name
Kindle my breast with thy celestial flame,
Sublime ideas and apt words infuse;
The Muse instruct my voice, and thou inspire the Muse!
    What I have instanced only in the best,
Is, in proportion, true of all the rest.
Take pains the genuine meaning to explore!
There sweat, there strain: tug the laborious oar;
Search every comment that your care can find;
Some here, some there, may hit the poet's mind:
Yet be not blindly guided by the throng:
The multitude is always in the wrong.
When things appear unnatural or hard,

Consult your author, with himself compared.
Who knows what blessing Phœbus may bestow,
And future ages to your labour owe ?
Such secrets are not easily found out;
But, once discovered, leave no room for doubt.
Truth stamps conviction in your ravished breast;
And peace and joy attend the glorious guest.

   Truth still is one; Truth is divinely bright;
No cloudy doubts obscure her native light;
While in your thoughts you find the least debate,
You may confound, but never can translate.
Your style will this through all disguises show;
For none explain more clearly than they know.
He only proves he understands a text,
Whose exposition leaves it unperplexed.
They who too faithfully on names insist,
Rather create than dissipate the mist;
And grow unjust by being over nice,
For superstitious virtue turns to vice.
Let Crassus' ghost and Labienus tell
How twice in Parthian plains their legions fell.
Since Rome hath been so jealous of her fame
That few know Pacorus' or Monæses' name.

   Words in one language elegantly used,
Will hardly in another be excused;
And some that Rome admired in Cæsar's time,
May neither suit our genius nor our clime.
The genuine sense, intelligibly told,
Shows a translator both discreet and bold.

   Excursions are inexpiably bad;
And 'tis much safer to leave out than add.
Abstruse and mystic thought you must express
With painful care, but seeming easiness;
For truth shines brightest through the plainest dress.

The Æncan Muse, when she appears in state,
Makes all Jove's thunder on her verses wait;
Yet writes sometimes as soft and moving things
As Venus speaks, or Philomela sings.
Your author always will the best advise,
Fall when he falls, and when he rises, rise.
Affected noise is the most wretched thing,
That to contempt can empty scribblers bring.
Vowels and accents, regularly placed,
On even syllables (and still the last)
Though gross innumerable faults abound,
In spite of nonsense, never fail of sound,
But this is meant of even verse alone,
As being most harmonious and most known:
For if you will unequal numbers try,
There accents on odd syllables must lie.
Whatever sister of the learned Nine
Does to your suit a willing ear incline,
Urge your success, deserve a lasting name,
She'll crown a grateful and a constant flame.
But if a wild uncertainty prevail,
And turn your veering heart with every gale,
You lose the fruit of all your former care,
For the sad prospect of a just despair.
    A quack, too scandalously mean to name,
Had, by man-midwifery, got wealth and fame;
As if Lucina had forgot her trade,
The labouring wife invokes his surer aid.
Well-seasoned bowls the gossip's spirits raise,
Who, while she guzzles, chats the doctor's praise;
And largely, what she wants in words, supplies,
With maudlin eloquence of trickling eyes.
But what a thoughtless animal is man!
How very active in his own trepan!

For, greedy of physicians' frequent fees,
From female mellow praise he takes degrees;
Struts in a new unlicensed gown, and then
From saving women falls to killing men.
Another such had left the nation thin,
In spite of all the children he brought in.
His pills as thick as hand grenadoes flew;
And where they fell, as certainly they slew:
His name struck everywhere as great a damp,
As Archimedes' through the Roman camp.
With this, the doctor's pride began to cool;
For smarting soundly may convince a fool.
But now repentance came too late for grace;
And meagre famine stared him in the face:
Fain would he to the wives be reconciled,
But found no husband left to own a child.
The friends, that got the brats, were poisoned too:
In this sad case, what could our vermin do?
Worried with debts, and past all hope of bail,
The unpitied wretch lies rotting in a jail:
And there, with basket-alms scarce kept alive,
Shows how mistaken talents ought to thrive.
    I pity, from my soul, unhappy men,
Compelled by want to prostitute their pen;
Who must, like lawyers, either starve or plead,
And follow, right or wrong, where guineas lead!
But you, Pompilian, wealthy, pampered heirs,
Who to your country owe your swords and cares,
Let no vain hope your easy mind seduce,
For rich ill poets are without excuse;
'Tis very dangerous tampering with the Muse,
The profit's small, and you have much to lose;
For though true wit adorns your birth or place,
Degenerate lines degrade the attainted race.

No poet any passion can excite,
But what they feel transport them when they write.
Have you been led through the Cumæan cave,
And heard the impatient maid divinely rave?
I hear her now; I see her rolling eyes;
And panting, 'Lo! the God, the God,' she cries:
With words not hers, and more than human sound,
She makes the obedient ghosts peep trembling through
    the ground.
But, though we must obey when Heaven commands,
And man in vain the sacred call withstands,
Beware what spirit rages in your breast;
For ten inspired, ten thousand are possess'd:
Thus make the proper use of each extreme,
And write with fury, but correct with phlegm.
As when the cheerful hours too freely pass,
And sparkling wine smiles in the tempting glass,
Your pulse advises, and begins to beat
Through every swelling vein a loud retreat:
So when a Muse propitiously invites,
Improve her favours, and indulge her flights;
But when you find that vigorous heat abate,
Leave off, and for another summons wait.
Before the radiant sun, a glimmering lamp,
Adulterate measures to the sterling stamp,
Appear not meaner than mere human lines,
Compared with those whose inspiration shines:
These, nervous, bold; those, languid and remiss;
There cold salutes; but here a lover's kiss.
Thus have I seen a rapid headlong tide,
With foaming waves the passive Saone divide;
Whose lazy waters without motion lay,
While he, with eager force, urged his impetuous way.

CHARLES COTTON.

HEARTY, careless 'Charley Cotton' was born in 1630. His father, Sir George Cotton, was improvident and intemperate in his latter days, and left the poet an encumbered estate situated at Ashbourne, in Derbyshire, near the river Dove. This place will recall the words quoted by O'Connell in Parliament in reference to the present Lord Derby :—

> 'Down thy fair banks, romantic Ashbourne, glides
> The Derby dilly, with its six insides.'

Charles studied at Cambridge; and after travelling abroad, married the daughter of Sir Thomas Owthorp in Nottinghamshire, who does not appear to have lived long. His extravagance keeping him poor, he was compelled to eke out his means by translating works from the French and Italian, including those of a spirit somewhat kindred to his own—Montaigne. At the age of forty, he obtained a captain's commission in the army, and went to Ireland. There he met with his second wife, Mary, Countess Dowager of Ardglass, the widow of Lord Cornwall. She possessed a jointure of £1500 a-year, secured, however, after marriage, from her husband's imprudent and reckless management. He returned to his English estate, where he became passionately fond of fishing,—intimate with Izaak Walton, whom he invited in a poem, although now eighty-three years old, to visit him in the country—and where he built a fishing-house, with the initials of Izaak's name and his own united in ciphers over the door; the walls, too, being painted with fishing scenes, and the portraits of Cotton and Walton appearing upon the beaufet. Poor Charles had a less fortunate career than his friend, dying insolvent at Westminster in 1687.

Careless gaiety and reckless extravagance, blended with heart, sense, and sincerity, were the characteristics of Cotton as a man, and were, as is usually the case, transferred to his poetry. He squandered his pence and his powers with equal profusion. His travestie of the 'Æneid' is pronounced by Christopher North (who must have read it, however,) a beastly book. Campbell says, with striking justice, of another of Cotton's productions, 'His imitations of Lucian betray the grossest misconception of humorous effect, when he attempts to burlesque that which is ludicrous already.' It is like trying to turn the 'Tale of a Tub' into ridicule. But Cotton's own vein, as exhibited in his 'Invitation to Walton,' his 'New Year,' and his 'Voyage to Ireland,' (which anticipates in some measure the style of Anstey in the 'New Bath Guide,') is very rich and varied, full of ease, picturesque spirit, and humour, and stamps him a genuine, if not a great poet.

INVITATION TO IZAAK WALTON.

1 Whilst in this cold and blustering clime,
    Where bleak winds howl, and tempests roar,
We pass away the roughest time
    Has been of many years before;

2 Whilst from the most tempestuous nooks
    The chillest blasts our peace invade,
And by great rains our smallest brooks
    Are almost navigable made;

3 Whilst all the ills are so improved
    Of this dead quarter of the year,
That even you, so much beloved,
    We would not now wish with us here:

4 In this estate, I say, it is
    Some comfort to us to suppose,
That in a better clime than this,
    You, our dear friend, have more repose;

5 And some delight to me the while,
    Though Nature now does weep in rain,
To think that I have seen her smile,
    And haply may I do again.
202.

6 If the all-ruling Power please
   We live to see another May,
We'll recompense an age of these
   Foul days in one fine fishing day.

7 We then shall have a day or two,
   Perhaps a week, wherein to try
What the best master's hand can do
   With the most deadly killing fly.

8 A day with not too bright a beam;
   A warm, but not a scorching sun;
A southern gale to curl the stream;
   And, master, half our work is done.

9 Then, whilst behind some bush we wait
   The scaly people to betray,
We'll prove it just, with treacherous bait,
   To make the preying trout our prey;

10 And think ourselves, in such an hour,
   Happier than those, though not so high,
Who, like leviathans, devour
   Of meaner men the smaller fry.

11 This, my best friend, at my poor home,
   Shall be our pastime and our theme;
But then—should you not deign to come,
   You make all this a flattering dream.

A VOYAGE TO IRELAND IN BURLESQUE.

CANTO I.

The lives of frail men are compared by the sages
Or unto short journeys, or pilgrimages,

As men to their inns do come sooner or later,
That is, to their ends, to be plain in my matter;
From whence when one dead is, it currently follows,
He has run his race, though his goal be the gallows;
And this 'tis, I fancy, sets folks so a-madding,
And makes men and women so eager of gadding;
Truth is, in my youth I was one of these people
Would have gone a great way to have seen a high
    steeple,
And though I was bred 'mongst the wonders o' th' Peak,
Would have thrown away money, and ventured my neck
To have seen a great hill, a rock, or a cave,
And thought there was nothing so pleasant and brave:
But at forty years old you may, if you please,
Think me wiser than run such errands as these;
Or had the same humour still ran in my toes,
A voyage to Ireland I ne'er should have chose;
But to tell you the truth on't, indeed it was neither
Improvement nor pleasure for which I went thither;
I know then you 'll presently ask me for what?
Why, faith, it was that makes the old woman trot;
And therefore I think I 'm not much to be blamed
If I went to the place whereof Nick was ashamed.
    O Coryate! thou traveller famed as Ulysses,
In such a stupendous labour as this is,
Come lend me the aids of thy hands and thy feet,
Though the first be pedantic, the other not sweet,
Yet both are so restless in peregrination,
They 'll help both my journey, and eke my relation.
    'Twas now the most beautiful time of the year,
The days were now long, and the sky was now clear,
And May, that fair lady of splendid renown,
Had dressed herself fine, in her flowered tabby gown,
When about some two hours and an half after noon,

When it grew something late, though I thought it too
    soon,
With a pitiful voice, and a most heavy heart,
I tuned up my pipes to sing '*loth to depart;*'
The ditty concluded, I called for my horse,
And with a good pack did the jument endorse,
Till he groaned and he. f—d under the burden,
For sorrow had made me a cumbersome lurden:
And now farewell, Dove, where I've caught such brave
    dishes
Of over-grown, golden, and silver-scaled fishes;
Thy trout and thy grayling may now feed securely,
I've left none behind me can take 'em so surely;
Feed on then, and breed on, until the next year,
But if I return I expect my arrear.

    By pacing and trotting betimes in the even,
Ere the sun had forsaken one half of the heaven,
We all at fair Congerton took up our inn,
Where the sign of a king kept a King and his queen:
But who do you think came to welcome me there?
No worse a man, marry, than good master mayor,
With his staff of command, yet the man was not lame,
But he needed it more when he went, than he came;
After three or four hours of friendly potation,
We took leave each of other in courteous fashion,
When each one, to keep his brains fast in his head,
Put on a good nightcap, and straightway to bed.

    Next morn, having paid for boiled, roasted, and bacon,
And of sovereign hostess our leaves kindly taken,
(For her king, as 'twas rumoured, by late pouring down,
This morning had got a foul flaw in his crown,)
We mounted again, and full soberly riding,
Three miles we had rid ere we met with a biding;
But there, having over-night plied the tap well,

We now must needs water at a place called Holmes
    Chapel:
'A hay!' quoth the foremost, 'ho! who keeps the house?'
Which said, out an host comes as brisk as a louse;
His hair combed as sleek as a barber he 'd been,
A cravat with black ribbon tied under his chin;
Though by what I saw in him, I straight 'gan to fear
That knot would be one day slipped under his ear.
Quoth he (with low congé), 'What lack you, my lord?'
'The best liquor,' quoth I, 'that the house will afford.'
'You shall straight,' quoth he; and then calls out, 'Mary,
Come quickly, and bring us a quart of Canary.'
'Hold, hold, my spruce host! for i' th' morning so early,
I never drink liquor but what 's made of barley.'
Which words were scarce out, but, which made me admire,
My lordship was presently turned into 'squire:
    'Ale, 'squire, you mean?' quoth he nimbly again,
'What, must it be purled'—'No, I love it best plain.'
'Why, if you 'll drink ale, sir, pray take my advice,
Here 's the best ale i' th' land, if you 'll go to the price;
Better, I sure am, ne'er blew out a stopple;
But then, in plain truth, it is sixpence a bottle.'
'Why, faith,' quoth I, 'friend, if your liquor be such,
For the best ale in England, it is not too much:
Let 's have it, and quickly.'—'O sir! you may stay;
A pot in your pate is a mile in your way:
Come, bring out a bottle here presently, wife,
Of the best Cheshire hum he e'er drank in his life.'
Straight out comes the mistress in waistcoat of silk,
As clear as a milkmaid, as white as her milk,
With visage as oval and sleek as an egg,
As straight as an arrow, as right as my leg:
A curtsey she made, as demure as a sister,
I could not forbear, but alighted and kissed her:
    206

Then ducking another, with most modest mien,
The first word she said was, 'Will 't please you walk in?'
I thanked her; but told her, I then could not stay,
For the haste of my business did call me away.
She said, she was sorry it fell out so odd,
But if, when again I should travel that road,
I would stay there a night, she assured me the nation
Should nowhere afford better accommodation:
Meanwhile my spruce landlord has broken the cork,
And called for a bodkin, though he had a fork;
But I showed him a screw, which I told my brisk gull
A trepan was for bottles had broken their skull;
Which, as it was true, he believed without doubt,
But 'twas I that applied it, and pulled the cork out.
Bounce, quoth the bottle, the work being done,
It roared, and it smoked, like a new-fired gun;
But the shot missed us all, or else we 'd been routéd,
Which yet was a wonder, we were so about it.
Mine host poured and filled, till he could fill no fuller:
'Look here, sir,' quoth he, 'both for nap and for colour,
Sans bragging, I hate it, nor will I e'er do 't;
I defy Leek, and Lambhith, and Sandwich, to boot.'
By my troth, he said true, for I speak it with tears,
Though I have been a toss-pot these twenty good years,
And have drank so much liquor has made me a debtor,
In my days, that I know of, I never drank better:
We found it so good and we drank so profoundly,
That four good round shillings were whipt away roundly;
And then I conceived it was time to be jogging,
For our work had been done, had we stay'd t' other
     noggin.
  From thence we set forth with more metal and spright,
Our horses were empty, our coxcombs were light;
O'er Dellamore forest we, tantivy, posted,

Till our horses were basted as if they were roasted:
In truth, we pursued might have been by our haste,
And I think Sir George Booth did not gallop so fast,
Till about two o'clock after noon, God be blest,
We came, safe and sound, all to Chester i' th' west.

And now in high time 'twas to call for some meat,
Though drinking does well, yet some time we must eat:
And i' faith we had victuals both plenty and good,
Where we all laid about us as if we were wood:
Go thy ways, Mistress Anderton, for a good woman,
Thy guests shall by thee ne'er be turned to a common;
And whoever of thy entertainment complains,
Let him lie with a drab, and be poxed for his pains.

And here I must stop the career of my Muse,
The poor jade is weary, 'las! how should she choose?
And if I should further here spur on my course,
I should, questionless, tire both my wits and my horse:
To-night let us rest, for 'tis good Sunday's even,
To-morrow to church, and ask pardon of Heaven.
Thus far we our time spent, as here I have penned it,
An odd kind of life, and 'tis well if we mend it:
But to-morrow (God willing) we'll have t'other bout,
And better or worse be 't, for murder will out,
Our future adventures we'll lay down before ye,
For my Muse is deep sworn to use truth of the story.

CANTO II.

After seven hours' sleep, to commute for pains taken,
A man of himself, one would think, might awaken;
But riding, and drinking hard, were two such spells,
I doubt I 'd slept on, but for jangling of bells,
Which, ringing to matins all over the town,
Made me leap out of bed, and put on my gown,
With intent (so God mend me) t' have gone to the choir,

208

When straight I perceived myself all on a fire;
For the two forenamed things had so heated my blood,
That a little phlebotomy would do me good:
I sent for chirurgeon, who came in a trice,
And swift to shed blood, needed not be called twice,
But tilted stiletto quite thorough the vein,
From whence issued out the ill humours amain;
When having twelve ounces, he bound up my arm,
And I gave him two Georges, which did him no harm:
But after my bleeding, I soon understood
It had cooled my devotion as well as my blood;
For I had no more mind to look on my psalter,
Than (saving your presence) I had to a halter;
But, like a most wicked and obstinate sinner,
Then sat in my chamber till folks came to dinner:
I dined with good stomach, and very good cheer,
With a very fine woman, and good ale and beer;
When myself having stuffed than a bagpipe more full,
I fell to my smoking until I grew dull;
And, therefore, to take a fine nap thought it best,
For when belly full is, bones would be at rest:
I tumbled me down on my bed like a swad,
Where, oh! the delicious dream that I had!
Till the bells, that had been my morning molesters,
Now waked me again, chiming all in to vespers:
With that starting up, for my man I did whistle,
And combed out and powdered my locks that were
    grizzle;
Had my clothes neatly brushed, and then put on my
    sword,
Resolved now to go and attend on the word.
  Thus tricked, and thus trim, to set forth I begin,
Neat and cleanly without, but scarce cleanly within;
For why, Heaven knows it, I long time had been

A most humble obedient servant to sin;
And now in devotion was even so proud,
I scorned forsooth to join prayer with the crowd;
For though courted by all the bells as I went,
I was deaf, and regarded not the compliment,
But to the cathedral still held on my pace,
As 't were, scorning to kneel but in the best place.
I there made myself sure of good music at least,
But was something deceived, for 'twas none of the best:
But however I stay'd at the church's commanding
Till we came to the ' Peace passes all understanding,'
Which no sooner was ended, but whir and away,
Like boys in a school when they 've leave got to play;
All save master mayor, who still gravely stays
Till the rest had made room for his worship and 's mace:
Then he and his brethren in order appear,
I out of my stall, and fell into his rear;
For why, 'tis much safer appearing, no doubt,
In authority's tail, than the head of a rout.
    In this rev'rend order we marched from prayer;
The mace before me borne as well as the mayor;
Who looking behind him, and seeing most plain
A glorious gold belt in the rear of his train,
Made such a low congé, forgetting his place,
I was never so honoured before in my days:
But then off went my scalp-case, and down went my fist,
Till the pavement, too hard, by my knuckles was kissed;
By which, though thick-skulled, he must understand this,
That I was a most humble servant of his;
Which also so wonderful kindly he took,
(As I well perceived both b' his gesture and look,)
That to have me dogg'd home he straightway appointed,
Resolving, it seems, to be better acquainted.
I was scarce in my quarters, and set down on crupper,
    210

But his man was there too, to invite me to supper:
I start up, and after most respective fashion
Gave his worship much thanks for his kind invitation;
But begged his excuse, for my stomach was small,
And I never did eat any supper at all;
But that after supper I would kiss his hands,
And would come to receive his worship's commands.
Sure no one will say, but a patron of slander,
That this was not pretty well for a Moorlander:
And since on such reasons to sup I refused,
I nothing did doubt to be holden excused;
But my quaint repartee had his worship possess'd
With so wonderful good a conceit of the rest,
That with mere impatience he hoped in his breeches
To see the fine fellow that made such fine speeches:
'Go, sirrah!' quoth he, 'get you to him again,
And will and require, in his Majesty's name,
That he come; and tell him, obey he were best, or
I'll teach him to know that he's now in West-Chester.'
The man, upon this, comes me running again,
But yet minced his message, and was not so plain;
Saying to me only, 'Good sir, I am sorry
To tell you my master has sent again for you;
And has such a longing to have you his guest,
That I, with these ears, heard him swear and protest,
He would neither say grace, nor sit down on his bum,
Nor open his napkin, until you do come.'
With that I perceived no excuse would avail,
And, seeing there was no defence for a flail,
I said I was ready master may'r to obey,
And therefore desired him to lead me the way.
We went, and ere Malkin could well lick her ear,
(For it but the next door was, forsooth) we were there;
Where lights being brought me, I mounted the stairs,

The worst I e'er saw in my life at a mayor's:
But everything else must be highly commended.
I there found his worship most nobly attended,
Besides such a supper as well did convince,
A may'r in his province to be a great prince;
As he sat in his chair, he did not much vary,
In state nor in face, from our eighth English Harry;
But whether his face was swelled up with fat,
Or puffed up with glory, I cannot tell that.
Being entered the chamber half length of a pike,
And cutting of faces exceedingly like
One of those little gentlemen brought from the Indies,
And screwing myself into congés and cringes,
By then I was half-way advanced in the room,
His worship most rev'rendly rose from his bum,
And with the more honour to grace and to greet me,
Advanced a whole step and a half for to meet me;
Where leisurely doffing a hat worth a tester,
He bade me most heartily welcome to Chester.
I thanked him in language the best I was able,
And so we forthwith sat us all down to table.
    Now here you must note, and 'tis worth observation,
That as his chair at one end o' th' table had station;
So sweet mistress may'ress, in just such another,
Like the fair queen of hearts, sat in state at the other;
By which I perceived, though it seemed a riddle,
The lower end of this must be just in the middle:
But perhaps 'tis a rule there, and one that would mind it
Amongst the town-statutes 'tis likely might find it.
But now into the pottage each deep his spoon claps,
As in truth one might safely for burning one's chaps,
When straight, with the look and the tone of a scold,
Mistress may'ress complained that the pottage was cold;
'And all 'long of your fiddle-faddle,' quoth she.

'Why, what then, Goody Two-Shoes, what if it be?
'Hold you, if you can, your tittle-tattle,' quoth he.
I was glad she was snapped thus, and guessed by th'
    discourse,
The may'r, not the gray mare, was the better horse,
And yet for all that, there is reason to fear,
She submitted but out of respect to his year:
However 'twas well she had now so much grace,
Though not to the man, to submit to his place;
For had she proceeded, I verily thought
My turn would the next be, for I was in fault:
But this brush being past, we fell to our diet,
And every one there filled his belly in quiet.
Supper being ended, and things away taken,
Master mayor's curiosity 'gan to awaken;
Wherefore making me draw something nearer his chair,
He willed and required me there to declare
My country, my birth, my estate, and my parts,
And whether I was not a master of arts;
And eke what the business was had brought me thither,
With what I was going about now, and whither:
Giving me caution, no lie should escape me,
For if I should trip, he should certainly trap me.
I answered, my country was famed Staffordshire;
That in deeds, bills, and bonds, I was ever writ squire;
That of land I had both sorts, some good, and some evil,
But that a great part on't was pawned to the devil;
That as for my parts, they were such as he saw;
That, indeed, I had a small smatt'ring of law,
Which I lately had got more by practice than reading,
By sitting o' th' bench, whilst others were pleading;
But that arms I had ever more studied than arts,
And was now to a captain raised by my deserts;
That the business which led me through Palatine ground

Into Ireland was, whither now I was bound;
Where his worship's great favour I loud will proclaim,
And in all other places wherever I came.
He said, as to that, I might do what I list,
But that I was welcome, and gave me his fist;
When having my fingers made crack with his gripes,
He called to his man for some bottles and pipes.

To trouble you here with a longer narration
Of the several parts of our confabulation,
Perhaps would be tedious; I'll therefore remit ye
Even to the most rev'rend records of the city,
Where, doubtless, the acts of the may'rs are recorded,
And if not more truly, yet much better worded.

In short, then, we piped and we tippled Canary,
Till my watch pointed one in the circle horary;
When thinking it now was high time to depart,
His worship I thanked with a most grateful heart;
And because to great men presents are acceptable,
I presented the may'r, ere I rose from the table,
With a certain fantastical box and a stopper;
And he having kindly accepted my offer,
I took my fair leave, such my visage adorning,
And to bed, for I was to rise early i' th' morning.

CANTO III.

The sun in the morning disclosed his light,
With complexion as ruddy as mine over night;
And o'er th' eastern mountains peeping up 's head,
The casement being open, espied me in bed;
With his rays he so tickled my lids that I waked,
And was half ashamed, for I found myself naked;
But up I soon start, and was dressed in a trice,
And called for a draught of ale, sugar, and spice;
Which having turned off, I then call to pay,

214

And packing my nawls, whipt to horse, and away.
A guide I had got, who demanded great vails,
For conducting me over the mountains of Wales:
Twenty good shillings, which sure very large is;
Yet that would not serve, but I must bear his charges;
And yet for all that, rode astride on a beast,
The worst that e'er went on three legs, I protest:
It certainly was the most ugly of jades,
His hips and his rump made a right ace of spades;
His sides were two ladders, well spur-galled withal;
His neck was a helve, and his head was a mall;
For his colour, my pains and your trouble I'll spare,
For the creature was wholly denuded of hair;
And, except for two things, as bare as my nail,
A tuft of a mane, and a sprig of a tail;
And by these the true colour one can no more know,
Than by mouse-skins above stairs, the merkin below.
Now such as the beast was, even such was the rider,
With a head like a nutmeg, and legs like a spider;
A voice like a cricket, a look like a rat,
The brains of a goose, and the heart of a cat:
Even such was my guide and his beast; let them pass,
The one for a horse, and the other an ass.
But now with our horses, what sound and what rotten,
Down to the shore, you must know, we were gotten;
And there we were told, it concerned us to ride,
Unless we did mean to encounter the tide;
And then my guide lab'ring with heels and with hands,
With two up and one down, hopped over the sands,
Till his horse, finding the labour for three legs too sore,
Foaled out a new leg, and then he had four:
And now by plain dint of hard spurring and whipping,
Dry-shod we came where folks sometimes take shipping;
And where the salt sea, as the devil were in't,

Came roaring t' have hindered our journey to Flint;
But we, by good luck, before him got thither,
He else would have carried us, no man knows whither.
    And now her in Wales is, Saint Taph be her speed,
Gott splutter her taste, some Welsh ale her had need;
For her ride in great haste, and   *   *
For fear of her being catched up by the fishes:
But the lord of Flint castle's no lord worth a louse,
For he keeps ne'er a drop of good drink in his house;
But in a small house near unto 't there was store
Of such ale as, thank God, I ne'er tasted before;
And surely the Welsh are not wise of their fuddle,
For this had the taste and complexion of puddle.   .
From thence then we marched, full as dry as we came,
My guide before prancing, his steed no more lame,
O'er hills and o'er valleys uncouth and uneven,
Until 'twixt the hours of twelve and eleven,
More hungry and thirsty than tongue can well tell,
We happily came to Saint Winifred's well:
I thought it the pool of Bethesda had been,
By the cripples lay there; but I went to my inn
To speak for some meat, for so stomach did motion,
Before I did further proceed in devotion:
I went into th' kitchen, where victuals I saw,
Both beef, veal, and mutton, but all on't was raw;
And some on't alive, but soon went to slaughter,
For four chickens were slain by my dame and her
        daughter;
Of which to Saint Win. ere my vows I had paid,
They said I should find a rare fricasée made:
I thanked them, and straight to the well did repair,
Where some I found cursing, and others at prayer;
Some dressing, some stripping, some out and some in,
Some naked, where botches and boils might be seen;

Of which some were fevers of Venus I'm sure,
And therefore unfit for the virgin to cure:
But the fountain, in truth, is well worth the sight,
The beautiful virgin's own tears not more bright;
Nay, none but she ever shed such a tear,
Her conscience, her name, nor herself, were more clear.
In the bottom there lie certain stones that look white,
But streaked with pure red, as the morning with light,
Which they say is her blood, and so it may be,
But for that, let who shed it look to it for me.
Over the fountain a chapel there stands,
Which I wonder has 'scaped master Oliver's hands;
The floor's not ill paved, and the margin o' th' spring
Is inclosed with a certain octagonal ring;
From each angle of which a pillar does rise,
Of strength and of thickness enough to suffice
To support and uphold from falling to ground
A cupola wherewith the virgin is crowned.
Now 'twixt the two angles that fork to the north,
And where the cold nymph does her basin pour forth,
Under ground is a place where they bathe, as 'tis said,
And 'tis true, for I heard folks' teeth hack in their head;
For you are to know, that the rogues and the *   *
Are not let to pollute the spring-head with their sores.
But one thing I chiefly admired in the place,
That a saint and a virgin endued with such grace,
Should yet be so wonderful kind a well-willer
To that whoring and filching trade of a miller,
As within a few paces to furnish the wheels
Of I cannot tell how many water-mills:
I've studied that point much, you cannot guess why,
But the virgin was, doubtless, more righteous than I.
And now for my welcome, four, five, or six lasses,
With as many crystalline liberal glasses,

Did all importune me to drink of the water
Of Saint Winifred, good Thewith's fair daughter.
A while I was doubtful, and stood in a muse,
Not knowing, amidst all that choice, where to choose.
Till a pair of black eyes, darting full in my sight,
From the rest o' th' fair maidens did carry me quite;
I took the glass from her, and whip, off it went,
I half doubt I fancied a health to the saint:
But he was a great villain committed the slaughter,
For Saint Winifred made most delicate water.
I slipped a hard shilling into her soft hand,
Which had like to have made me the place have
        profaned;
And giving two more to the poor that were there,
Did, sharp as a hawk, to my quarters repair.
  My dinner was ready, and to it I fell,
I never ate better meat, that I can tell;
When having half dined, there comes in my host,
A catholic good, and a rare drunken toast;
This man, by his drinking, inflamed the scot,
And told me strange stories, which I have forgot;
But this I remember, 'twas much on's own life,
And one thing, that he had converted his wife.
  But now my guide told me, it time was to go,
For that to our beds we must both ride and row;
Wherefore calling to pay, and having accounted,
I soon was down-stairs, and as suddenly mounted:
On then we travelled, our guide still before,
Sometimes on three legs, and sometimes on four,
Coasting the sea, and over hills crawling,
Sometimes on all four, for fear we should fall in;
For underneath Neptune lay skulking to watch us,
And, had we but slipped once, was ready to catch us.
Thus in places of danger taking more heed,

And in safer travelling mending our speed:
Redland Castle and Abergoney we past,
And o'er against Connoway came at the last:
Just over against a castle there stood,
O' th' right hand the town, and o' th' left hand a wood;
'Twixt the wood and the castle they see at high water
The storm, the place makes it a dangerous matter;
And besides, upon such a steep rock it is founded,
As would break a man's neck, should he 'scape being
     drowned:
Perhaps though in time one may make them to yield,
But 'tis prettiest Cob-castle e'er I beheld.
   The sun now was going t' unharness his steeds,
When the ferry-boat brasking her sides 'gainst the weeds,
Came in as good time as good time could be,
To give us a cast o'er an arm of the sea;
And bestowing our horses before and abaft,
O'er god Neptune's wide cod-piece gave us a waft;
Where scurvily landing at foot of the fort,
Within very few paces we entered the port,
Where another King's Head invited me down,
For indeed I have ever been true to the crown.

DR HENRY MORE.

THIS eminent man was the son of a gentleman of good family
and estate in Grantham, Lincolnshire. He was born in 1614.
His father sent him to study at Eton, and thence, in 1631, he
repaired to Cambridge, where he was destined to spend the
most of his life. Philosophy attracted him early, in preference
to science or literature, and he became a follower of Plato, so
decided and enthusiastic as to gain for himself the title of 'The
Platonist' *par excellence.* In 1639, he graduated M.A.; and the

next year, he published the first part of 'Psychozoia; or, The Song of the Soul,' containing a Christiano-Platonical account of Man and Life. In preparing the materials of this poem, he had studied all the principal Platonists and mystical writers, and is said to have read himself almost to a shadow. And not only was his body emaciated, but his mind was so overstrung, that he imagined himself to see spiritual beings, to hear super-natural voices, and to converse, like Socrates, with a particular genius. He thought, too, that his body 'exhaled the perfume of violets!' Notwithstanding these little peculiarities, his genius and his learning, the simplicity of his character, and the inno-cence of his life, rendered him a general favourite; he was made a fellow of his college, and became a tutor to various persons of distinguished rank. One of these was Sir John Finch, whose sister, Lady Conway, an enthusiast herself, brought More ac-quainted with the famous John Baptist Van Helment, a man after whom, in the beginning of the seventeenth century, the whole of Europe wondered. He was a follower and imitator of Paracelsus, like him affected universal knowledge, aspired to revolutionise the science of medicine, and died with the re-putation of one who, with great powers and acquirements, instead of becoming a great man, ended as a brilliant pretender, and was rather an 'architect of ruin' to the systems of others, than the founder of a solid fabric of his own. More admired, of course, not the quackery, but the adventurous boldness of Helment's genius, and his devotion to chemistry; which is certainly the most spiritual of all the sciences, and must, especially in its trans-cendental forms, have had a great charm for a Platonic thinker. Our author was entirely devoted to study, and resisted every inducement to leave what he called his 'Paradise' at Cam-bridge. His friends once tried to decoy him into a bishopric, and got him the length of Whitehall to kiss the king's hand on the occasion; but when he understood their purpose, he refused to go a single step further. His life was a long, learned, happy, and holy dream. He was of the most benevolent disposition; and once observed to a friend, ' that he was thought by some to have a soft head, but he thanked God he had a soft heart.' In the heat of the Rebellion, the Republicans spared More, although

he had refused to take the Covenant. Campbell says of him,
'He corresponded with Descartes, was the friend of Cudworth,
and, as a divine and a moralist, was not only popular in his own
time, but has been mentioned with admiration both by Addison
and Blair.' One is rather amused at the latter clause. That a
man of More's massive learning, noble eloquence, and divine
genius should need the testimony of a mere elegant wordmonger
like Blair, seems ludicrous enough ; and Addison himself, except
in wit and humour, was not worthy to have untied the shoe-
latchets of the old Platonist. We were first introduced to this
writer by good Dr John Brown, late of Broughton Place, Edinburgh, and shall never forget hearing him, in his library, read
some splendid passages from More's work, in those deep, mellow, antique tones which flavoured whatever he read, like the
crust on old wine. His chief works are, ' A Discourse on the
Immortality of the Soul,' ' The Mystery of Godliness,' ' The
Mystery of Iniquity,' ' Divine Dialogues,' ' An Antidote against
Atheism,' ' Ethical and Metaphysical Manuals,' &c. In writing such books, and pursuing the recondite studies of which
they were the fruit, More spent his life happily. In 1661, he
became a Fellow of the Royal Society. For twenty years after
the Restoration, his works are said to have sold better than any
of their day—a curious and unaccountable fact, considering the
levity and licentiousness of the period. In September 1687, the
fine old spiritualist, aged seventy-three, went away to that land
of ' ideas ' to which his heart had been translated long before.

More's prose writings give us, on the whole, a higher idea of
his powers than his poem. This is not exactly, as a recent
critic calls it, ' dull and tedious,' but it is in some parts prosaic,
and in others obscure. The gleams of fancy in it are genuine,
but few and far between. But his prose works constitute, like
those of Cudworth, Charnock, Jeremy Taylor, and John Scott,
a vast old quarry, abounding both in blocks and in gems—blocks
of granite solidity, and gems of starry lustre. The peculiarity of
More is in that poetico-philosophic mist which, like the autum-
nal gossamer, hangs in light and beautiful festoons over his
thoughts, and which suggests pleasing memories of Plato and the
Alexandrian school. Like all the followers of the Grecian sage,

he dwells in a region of 'ideas,' which are to him the only realities, and are not cold, but warm; he sees all things in Divine solution; the visible is lost in the invisible, and nature retires before her God. Surely they are splendid reveries those of the Platonic school; but it is sad to reflect that they have not cast the slightest gleam of light on the dark, frightful, faith-shattering mysteries which perplex all inquirers. The old shadows of sin, death, damnation, evil, and hell, are found to darken the 'ideas' of Plato's world quite as deeply as they do the actualities of this weary, work-day earth, into which men have, for some inscrutable purpose, been sent to be, on the whole, miserable,—so often to toil without compensation, to suffer without benefit, and to hope without fulfilment.

OPENING OF SECOND PART OF 'PSYCHOZOIA.'

1 Whatever man he be that dares to deem
  True poets' skill to spring of earthly race,
  I must him tell, that he doth mis-esteem
  Their strange estate, and eke himself disgrace
  By his rude ignorance. For there's no place
  For forced labour, or slow industry,
  Of flagging wits, in that high fiery chase;
  So soon as of the Muse they quickened be,
At once they rise, and lively sing like lark in sky.

2 Like to a meteor, whose material
  Is low unwieldy earth, base unctuous slime,
  Whose inward hidden parts ethereal
  Lie close upwrapt in that dull sluggish fime,
  Lie fast asleep, till at some fatal time
  Great Phœbus' lamp has fired its inward sprite,
  And then even of itself on high doth climb:
  That erst was dark' becomes all eye, all sight,
Bright star, that to the wise of future things gives light.

222

3 Even so the weaker mind, that languid lies,
    Knit up in rags of dirt, dark, cold, and blind,
    So soon that purer flame of love unties
    Her clogging chains, and doth her sprite unbind,
    She soars aloft; for she herself doth find
    Well plumed; so raised upon her spreaden wing,
    She softly plays, and warbles in the wind,
    And carols out her inward life and spring
Of overflowing joy, and of pure love doth sing.

EXORDIUM OF THIRD PART.

1 Hence, hence, unhallowed ears, and hearts more hard
    Than winter clods fast froze with northern wind,
    But most of all, foul tongue! I thee discard,
    That blamest all that thy dark straitened mind
    Cannot conceive: but that no blame thou find;
    Whate'er my pregnant muse brings forth to light,
    She'll not acknowledge to be of her kind,
    Till eagle-like she turn them to the sight
Of the eternal Word, all decked with glory bright.

2 Strange sights do straggle in my restless thoughts,
    And lively forms with orient colours clad
    Walk in my boundless mind, as men ybrought
    Into some spacious room, who when they've had
    A turn or two, go out, although unbade.
    All these I see and know, but entertain
    None to my friend but who's most sober sad;
    Although, the time my roof doth them contain
Their presence doth possess me till they out again.

3 And thus possessed, in silver trump I sound
    Their guise, their shape, their gesture, and array;
    But as in silver trumpet nought is found

When once the piercing sound is passed away,
(Though while the mighty blast therein did stay,
Its tearing noise so terribly did shrill,
That it the heavens did shake, and earth dismay,)
As empty I of what my flowing quill
In needless haste elsewhere, or here, may hap to spill.

4 For 'tis of force, and not of a set will,
Nor dare my wary mind afford assent
To what is placed above all mortal skill;
But yet, our various thoughts to represent,
Each gentle wight will deem of good intent.
Wherefore, with leave the infinity I'll sing
Of time, of space; or without leave; I'm brent
With eager rage, my heart for joy doth spring,
And all my spirits move with pleasant trembeling.

5 An inward triumph doth my soul upheave
And spread abroad through endless 'spersed air.
My nimble mind this clammy clod doth leave,
And lightly stepping on from star to star
Swifter than lightning, passeth wide and far,
Measuring the unbounded heavens and wasteful sky;
Nor aught she finds her passage to debar,
For still the azure orb as she draws nigh
Gives back, new stars appear, the world's walls 'fore her fly.

DESTRUCTION AND RENOVATION OF ALL THINGS.

1   As the seas,
Boiling with swelling waves, aloft did rise,
And met with mighty showers and pouring rain
From heaven's spouts; so the broad flashing skies,
With brimstone thick and clouds of fiery bane,
Shall meet with raging Etna's and Vesuvius' flame.
   224

2 The burning bowels of this wasting ball
  Shall gallup up great flakes of rolling fire,
  And belch out pitchy flames, till over all
  Having long raged, Vulcan himself shall tire,
  And (the earth an ash-heap made) shall then expire:
  Here Nature, laid asleep in her own urn,
  With gentle rest right easily will respire,
  Till to her pristine task she do return
As fresh as Phœnix young under the Arabian morn.

3 Oh, happy they that then the first are born,
  While yet the world is in her vernal pride;
  For old corruption quite away is worn,
  As metal pure so is her mould well tried.
  Sweet dews, cool-breathing airs, and spaces wide
  Of precious spicery, wafted with soft wind:
  Fair comely bodies goodly beautified.

4 For all the while her purged ashes rest,
  These relics dry suck in the heavenly dew,
  And roscid manna rains upon her breast,
  And fills with sacred milk, sweet, fresh, and new,
  Where all take life and doth the world renew;
  And then renewed with pleasure be yfed.
  A green, soft mantle doth her bosom strew
  With fragrant herbs and flowers embellished,
Where without fault or shame all living creatures bed.

A DISTEMPERED FANCY.

1 Then the wild fancy from her horrid womb
  Will senden forth foul shapes.   O dreadful sight!
  Overgrown toads, fierce serpents, thence will come,
  Red-scaled dragons, with deep burning light

In their hollow eye-pits: with these she must fight:
Then think herself ill wounded, sorely stung.
Old fulsome hags, with scabs and scurf bedight,
Foul tarry spittle tumbling with their tongue
On their raw leather lips, these near will to her clung,

2 And lovingly salute against her will,
  Closely embrace, and make her mad with woe:
  She 'd lever thousand times they did her kill,
  Than force her such vile baseness undergo.
  Anon some giant his huge self will show,
  Gaping with mouth as vast as any cave,
  With stony, staring eyes, and footing slow:
  She surely deems him her live, walking grave,
From that dern hollow pit knows not herself to save.

3 After a while, tossed on the ocean main,
  A boundless sea she finds of misery;
  The fiery snorts of the leviathan,
  That makes the boiling waves before him fly,
  She hears, she sees his blazing morn-bright eye:
  If here she 'scape, deep gulfs and threatening rocks
  Her frighted self do straightway terrify;
  Steel-coloured clouds with rattling thunder knocks,
With these she is amazed, and thousand such-like mocks.

SOUL COMPARED TO A LANTERN.

1 Like to a light fast locked in lantern dark,
  Whereby by night our wary steps we guide
  In slabby streets, and dirty channels mark,
  Some weaker rays through the black top do glide,
  And flusher streams perhaps from horny side.
  But when we 've passed the peril of the way,

Arrived at home, and laid that case aside,
The naked light how clearly doth it ray,
And spread its joyful beams as bright as summer's day.

2 Even so, the soul, in this contracted state,
Confined to these strait instruments of sense,
More dull and narrowly doth operate.
At this hole hears, the sight must ray from thence,
Here tastes, there smells; but when she's gone from
        hence,
Like naked lamp, she is one shining sphere,
And round about has perfect cognoscence
Whate'er in her horizon doth appear:
She is one orb of sense, all eye, all airy ear.

WILLIAM CHAMBERLAYNE.

CHAMBERLAYNE was, during life, a poor man, and, till long
after his death, an unappreciated poet.   He was a physician at
Shaftesbury, Dorsetshire; born in 1619, and died in 1689.   He
appears to have been present among the Royalists at the battle
of Newbury.   He complains bitterly of his narrow circumstances,
and yet he lived to a long age.   He published, in 1658, a tragic
comedy, entitled 'Love's Victory,' and in 1659, 'Pharonnida,' a
heroic poem.

The latter is the main support of his literary reputation.   It
was discovered to be good by Thomas Campbell, who might
say,

'I was the first that ever burst
Into that silent sea.'

Silent, however, it continues since, and can never be expected
to be thronged by visitors.   The story is interesting, and many
of the separate thoughts, expressions, and passages are beautiful, as, for instance—

'The scholar stews his catholic brains for food;'

227

and this—

> ' Harsh poverty,
> That moth which frets the sacred robe of wit;'

but the style is often elliptical and involved; the story meanders too much, and is too long and intricate; and, on the whole, a few mutilated fragments are all that are likely to remain of an original and highly elaborate poem.

ARGALIA TAKEN PRISONER BY THE TURKS.

*   *   The Turks had ought
Made desperate onslaughts on the isle, but brought
Nought back but wounds and infamy; but now,
Wearied with toil, they are resolved to bow
Their stubborn resolutions with the strength
Of not-to-be-resisted want: the length
Of the chronical disease extended had
To some few months, since to oppress the sad
But constant islanders, the army lay,
Circling their confines.   Whilst this tedious stay
From battle rusts the soldier's valour in
His tainted cabin, there had often been,
With all variety of fortune, fought
Brave single combats, whose success had brought
Honour's unwithered laurels on the brow
Of either party; but the balance, now
Forced by the hand of a brave Turk, inclined   .
Wholly to them.   Thrice had his valour shined
In victory's refulgent rays, thrice heard
The shouts of conquest; thrice on his lance appeared
The heads of noble Rhodians, which had struck
A general sorrow 'mongst the knights.   All look
Who next the lists should enter; each desires
The task were his, but honour now requires
A spirit more than vulgar, or she dies
The next attempt, their valour's sacrifice;

228

To prop whose ruins, chosen by the free
Consent of all, Argalia comes to be
Their happy champion.   Truce proclaimed, until
The combat ends, the expecting people fill
The spacious battlements; the Turks forsake
Their tents, of whom the city ladies take
A dreadful view, till a more noble sight
Diverts their looks; each part behold their knight
With various wishes, whilst in blood and sweat
They toil for victory.   The conflict's heat
Raged in their veins, which honour more inflamed
Than burning calentures could do; both blamed
The feeble influence of their stars, that gave
No speedier conquest; each neglects to save
Himself, to seek advantage to offend
His eager foe   *   *   *   *
      *   *   *   But now so long
The Turks' proud champion had endured the strong
Assaults of the stout Christian, till his strength
Cooled, on the ground, with his blood—he fell at length,
Beneath his conquering sword.   The barbarous crew
O' the villains that did at a distance view
Their champion's fall, all bands of truce forgot,
Running to succour him, begin a hot
And desperate combat with those knights that stand
To aid Argalia, by whose conquering hand
Whole squadrons of them fall, but here he spent
His mighty spirit in vain, their cannons rent
His scattered troops.
          *   *   *   *   *

Argalia lies in chains, ordained to die
A sacrifice unto the cruelty
Of the fierce bashaw, whose loved favourite in
The combat late he slew; yet had not been

In that so much unhappy, had not he
That honoured then his sword with victory,
Half-brother to Janusa been, a bright
But cruel lady, whose refined delight
Her slave (though husband), Ammurat, durst not
Ruffle with discontent; wherefore, to cool that hot
Contention of her blood, which he foresaw
That heavy news would from her anger draw,
To quench with the brave Christian's death, he sent
Him living to her, that her anger, spent
In flaming torments, might not settle in
The dregs of discontent.   Staying to win
Some Rhodian castles, all the prisoners were
Sent with a guard into Sardinia, there
To meet their wretched thraldom.   From the rest
Argalia severed, soon hopes to be bless'd
With speedy death, though waited on by all
The hell-instructed torments that could fall
Within invention's reach; but he 's not yet
Arrived to his period, his unmoved stars sit
Thus in their orbs secured.   It was the use
Of the Turkish pride, which triumphs in the abuse
Of suffering Christians, once, before they take
The ornaments of nature off, to make
Their prisoners public to the view, that all
Might mock their miseries: this sight did call
Janusa to her palace-window, where,
Whilst she beholds them, love resolved to bear
Her ruin on her treacherous eye-beams, till
Her heart infected grew; their orbs did fill,
As the most pleasing object, with the sight
Of him whose sword opened a way for the flight
Of her loved brother's soul.

*   *   *   *   *

HENRY VAUGHAN.

VAUGHAN was born in Wales, on the banks of the Uske, in Brecknockshire, in 1614. His father was a gentleman, but, we presume, poor, as his son was bred to a profession. Young Vaughan became first a lawyer, and then a physician; and we suppose, had it not been for his advanced life, he would have become latterly a clergyman, since he grew, when old, exceedingly devout. In life, he was not fortunate, and we find him, like Chamberlayne, complaining bitterly of the poverty of the poetical tribe. In 1651, he published a volume of verse, in which nascent excellence struggles with dim obscurities, like a young moon with heavy clouds. But his ' Silex Scintillans,' or ' Sacred Poems,' produced in later life, attests at once the depth of his devotion, and the truth and originality of his genius. He died in 1695.

Campbell, always prone to be rather severe on pious poets, and whose taste, too, was finical at times, says of Vaughan— ' He is one of the harshest even of the inferior order of the school of conceit; but he has some few scattered thoughts that meet the eye amidst his harsh pages, like wild flowers on a barren heath.' Surely this is rather ' harsh ' judgment. At the same time, it is not a little laughable to find that Campbell has himself appropriated one of these ' wild flowers.' In his beautiful ' Rainbow,' he cries—

> ' How came the world's gray fathers forth
>   To mark thy sacred sign ! '

Vaughan had said—

> ' How bright wert thou when Shem's admiring eye,
>   Thy burnished, flaming arch did first descry;
>   When Terah, Nahor, Haran, Abram, Lot,
>   The youthful world's gray fathers in one knot,
>   Did with intentive looks watch every hour
>   For thy new light, and trembled at each shower !'

Indeed, all Campbell's ' Rainbow' is just a reflection of Vaughan's, and reminds you of those faint, pale shadows of the heavenly bow you sometimes see in the darkened and disarranged skies of spring. To steal from, and then strike down the victim, is more suitable to robbers than to poets.

Perhaps the best criticism on Vaughan may be found in the title of his own poems, ' Silex Scintillans.' He had a good deal of the dulness and hardness of the flint about his mind, but the influence of poverty and suffering,—for true it is that

> ' Wretched men
> Are cradled into poetry by wrong ;
> They learn in suffering what they teach in song,'—

and latterly the power of a genuine, though somewhat narrow piety, struck out glorious scintillations from the bare but rich rock. He ranks with Crashaw, Quarles, and Herbert, as one of the best of our early religious poets ; like them in their faults, and superior to all of them in refinement and beauty, if not in strength of genius.

ON A CHARNEL-HOUSE.

Where are you, shoreless thoughts, vast-tentered[1] hope,
Ambitious dreams, aims of an endless scope,
Whose stretched excess runs on a string too high,
And on the rack of self-extension die?
Chameleons of state, air-mongering[2] band,
Whose breath, like gunpowder, blows up a land,
Come, see your dissolution, and weigh
What a loathed nothing you shall be one day.
As the elements by circulation pass
From one to the other, and that which first was
Is so again, so 'tis with you. The grave
And nature but complete : what the one gave,
The other takes. Think, then, that in this bed
There sleep the relics of as proud a head,
As stern and subtle as your own ; that hath
Performed or forced as much ; whose tempest-wrath
Hath levelled kings with slaves ; and wisely, then,

[1] ' Vast-tentered:' extended.—[2] ' Air-mongering:' dealing in air or unsubstantial visions.

Calm these high furies, and descend to men.
Thus Cyrus tamed the Macedon ; a tomb
Checked him who thought the world too strait a room.
Have I obeyed the powers of a face,
A beauty, able to undo the race
Of easy man ?   I look but here, and straight
I am informed; the lovely counterfeit
Was but a smoother clay.   That famished slave,
Beggared by wealth, who starves that he may save,
Brings hither but his sheet.   Nay, the ostrich-man,
That feeds on steel and bullet, he that can
Outswear his lordship, and reply as tough
To a kind word, as if his tongue were buff,
Is chapfallen here : worms, without wit or fear,
Defy him now ; death has disarmed the bear.
Thus could I run o'er all the piteous score
Of erring men, and having done, meet more.
Their shuffled wills, abortive, vain intents,
Fantastic humours, perilous ascents,
False, empty honours, traitorous delights,
And whatsoe'er a blind conceit invites,—
But these, and more, which the weak vermins swell,
Are couched in this accumulative cell,
Which I could scatter ; but the grudging sun
Calls home his beams, and warns me to be gone :
Day leaves me in a double night, and I
Must bid farewell to my sad library,
Yet with these notes.   Henceforth with thought of thee
I 'll season all succeeding jollity,
Yet damn not mirth, nor think too much is fit :
Excess hath no religion, nor wit ;
But should wild blood swell to a lawless strain,
One check from thee shall channel it again.

ON GOMBAULD'S ENDYMION.

I 've read thy soul's fair night-piece, and have seen
The amours and courtship of the silent queen;
Her stolen descents to earth, and what did move her
To juggle first with heaven, then with a lover;
With Latmos' louder rescue, and, alas!
To find her out, a hue and cry in brass;
Thy journal of deep mysteries, and sad
Nocturnal pilgrimage; with thy dreams, clad
In fancies darker than thy cave; thy glass
Of sleepy draughts; and as thy soul did pass
In her calm voyage, what discourse she heard
Of spirits; what dark groves and ill-shaped guard
Ismena led thee through; with thy proud flight
O'er Periardes, and deep-musing night
Near fair Eurotas' banks; what solemn green
The neighbour shades wear; and what forms are seen
In their large bowers; with that sad path and seat
Which none but light-heeled nymphs and fairies beat,
Their solitary life, and how exempt
From common frailty, the severe contempt
They have of man, their privilege to live
A tree or fountain, and in that reprieve
What ages they consume: with the sad vale
Of Diophania; and the mournful tale
Of the bleeding, vocal myrtle:—these and more,
Thy richer thoughts, we are upon the score
To thy rare fancy for.   Nor dost thou fall
From thy first majesty, or ought at all
Betray consumption.   Thy full vigorous bays
Wear the same green, and scorn the lean decays
Of style or matter; just as I have known
Some crystal spring, that from the neighbour down

Derived her birth, in gentle murmurs steal
To the next vale, and proudly there reveal
Her streams in louder accents, adding still
More noise and waters to her channel, till
At last, swollen with increase, she glides along
The lawns and meadows, in a wanton throng
Of frothy billows, and in one great name
Swallows the tributary brooks' drowned fame.
Nor are they mere inventions, for we
In the same piece find scattered philosophy,
And hidden, dispersed truths, that folded lie
In the dark shades of deep allegory,
So neatly weaved, like arras, they descry
Fables with truth, fancy with history.
So that thou hast, in this thy curious mould,
Cast that commended mixture wished of old,
Which shall these contemplations render far
Less mutable, and lasting as their star;
And while there is a people, or a sun,
Endymion's story with the moon shall run.

APOSTROPHE TO FLETCHER THE DRAMATIST.

I did believe, great Beaumont being dead,
Thy widowed muse slept on his flowery bed.
But I am richly cozened, and can see
Wit transmigrates—his spirit stayed with thee;
Which, doubly advantaged by thy single pen,
In life and death now treads the stage again.
And thus are we freed from that dearth of wit
Which starved the land, since into schisms split,
Wherein th' hast done so much, we must needs guess
Wit's last edition is now i' the press.
For thou hast drained invention, and he
That writes hereafter, doth but pillage thee.

But thou hast plots; and will not the Kirk strain
At the designs of such a tragic brain?
Will they themselves think safe, when they shall see
Thy most abominable policy?
Will not the Ears assemble, and think 't fit
Their synod fast and pray against thy wit?
But they 'll not tire in such an idle quest—
Thou dost but kill and circumvent in jest;
And when thy angered muse swells to a blow,
'Tis but for Field's or Swanstoed's overthrow.
Yet shall these conquests of thy bays outlive
Their Scottish zeal, and compacts made to grieve
The peace of spirits; and when such deeds fail
Of their foul ends, a fair name is thy bail.
But, happy! thou ne'er saw'st these storms our air
Teemed with, even in thy time, though seeming fair.
Thy gentle soul, meant for the shade and ease
Withdrew betimes into the land of peace.
So, nested in some hospitable shore,
The hermit-angler, when the mid seas roar,
Packs up his lines, and ere the tempest raves,
Retires, and leaves his station to the waves. .
Thus thou diedst almost with our peace; and we,
This breathing time, thy last fair issue see,
Which I think such, if needless ink not soil
So choice a muse, others are but thy foil;
This or that age may write, but never see
A wit that dares run parallel with thee.
True Ben must live; but bate him, and thou hast
Undone all future wits, and matched the past.

PICTURE OF THE TOWN.

Abominable face of things!—here 's noise
Of banged mortars, blue aprons, and boys,

Pigs, dogs, and drums; with the hoarse, hellish notes
Of politicly-deaf usurers' throats;
With new fine worships, and the old cast team
Of justices, vexed with the cough and phlegm.
'Midst these, the cross looks sad; and in the shire-
Hall furs of an old Saxon fox appear,
With brotherly ruffs and beards, and a strange sight
Of high, monumental hats, ta'en at the fight
Of Eighty-eight; while every burgess foots
The mortal pavement in eternal boots.
Hadst thou been bachelor, I had soon divined
Thy close retirements, and monastic mind;
Perhaps some nymph had been to visit; or
The beauteous churl was to be waited for,
And, like the Greek, ere you the sport would miss,
You stayed and stroked the distaff for a kiss.

*   *   *   *   *

Why, two months hence, if thou continue thus,
Thy memory will scarce remain with us.
The drawers have forgot thee, and exclaim
They have not seen thee here since Charles' reign;
Or, if they mention thee, like some old man
That at each word inserts—Sir, as I can
Remember—so the cipherers puzzle me
With a dark, cloudy character of thee;
That, certes, I fear thou wilt be lost, and we
Must ask the fathers ere 't be long for thee.
Come! leave this sullen state, and let not wine
And precious wit lie dead for want of thine.
Shall the dull market landlord, with his rout
Of sneaking tenants, dirtily swill out
This harmless liquor? shall they knock and beat
For sack, only to talk of rye and wheat?
Oh, let not such preposterous tippling be;

237

In our metropolis, may I ne'er see
Such tavern sacrilege, nor lend a line
To weep the rapes and tragedy of wine!
Here lives that chemic quick-fire, which betrays
Fresh spirits to the blood, and warms our lays;
I have reserved, 'gainst thy approach, a cup,
That, were thy muse stark dead, should raise her up,
And teach her yet more charming words and skill,
Than ever Cœlia, Chloris, Astrophil,
Or any of the threadbare names inspired
Poor rhyming lovers, with a mistress fired.
Come, then, and while the snow-icicle hangs
At the stiff thatch, and winter's frosty fangs
Benumb the year, blithe as of old, let us,
'Midst noise and war, of peace and mirth discuss.
This portion thou wert born for: why should we
Vex at the times' ridiculous misery?
An age that thus hath fooled itself, and will,
Spite of thy teeth and mine, persist so still.
Let's sit, then, at this fire, and while we steal
A revel in the town, let others seal,
Purchase, or cheat, and who can, let them pay,
Till those black deeds bring on a darksome day.
Innocent spenders we!   A better use
Shall wear out our short lease, and leave th' obtuse
Rout to their husks : they and their bags, at best,
Have cares in earnest—we care for a jest.

THE GOLDEN AGE.

Happy that first white age ! when we
Lived by the earth's mere charity;
No soft luxurious diet then
Had effeminated men—
No other meat nor wine had any

Than the coarse mast, or simple honey;
And, by the parents' care laid up,
Cheap berries did the children sup.
No pompous wear was in those days,
Of gummy silks, or scarlet baize.
Their beds were on some flowery brink,
And clear spring water was their drink.
The shady pine, in the sun's heat,
Was their cool and known retreat;
For then 'twas not cut down, but stood
The youth and glory of the wood.
The daring sailor with his slaves
Then had not cut the swelling waves,
Nor, for desire of foreign store,
Seen any but his native shore.
No stirring drum had scared that age,
Nor the shrill trumpet's active rage;
No wounds, by bitter hatred made,
With warm blood soiled the shining blade;
For how could hostile madness arm
An age of love to public harm,
When common justice none withstood,
Nor sought rewards for spilling blood?
Oh that at length our age would raise
Into the temper of those days!
But—worse than Ætna's fires!—debate
And avarice inflame our state.
Alas! who was it that first found
Gold hid of purpose under ground—
That sought out pearls, and dived to find
Such precious perils for mankind?

REGENERATION.

1 A ward, and still in bonds, one day
        I stole abroad;
It was high spring, and all the way
        Primrosed, and hung with shade;
        Yet was it frost within,
        And surly wind
Blasted my infant buds, and sin,
        Like clouds, eclipsed my mind.

2 Stormed thus, I straight perceived my spring
        Mere stage and show,
My walk a monstrous, mountained thing,
        Rough-cast with rocks and snow;
        And as a pilgrim's eye,
        Far from relief,
Measures the melancholy sky,
        Then drops, and rains for grief,

3 So sighed I upwards still; at last,
        'Twixt steps and falls,
I reached the pinnacle, where placed
        I found a pair of scales;
        I took them up, and laid
        In the one late pains,
The other smoke and pleasures weighed,
        But proved the heavier grains.

4 With that some cried, Away; straight I
        Obeyed, and led
Full east, a fair, fresh field could spy—
        Some called it Jacob's Bed—
        A virgin soil, which no

Rude feet e'er trod,
Where, since he stept there, only go
Prophets and friends of God.

5 Here I reposed, but scarce well set,
  A grove descried
Of stately height, whose branches met
  And mixed on every side;
I entered, and, once in,
  (Amazed to see 't,)
Found all was changed, and a new spring
  Did all my senses greet.

6 The unthrift sun shot vital gold
  A thousand pieces,
And heaven its azure did unfold,
  Chequered with snowy fleeces.
The air was all in spice,
  And every bush
A garland wore; thus fed my eyes,
  But all the ear lay hush.

7 Only a little fountain lent
  Some use for ears,
And on the dumb shades language spent,
  The music of her tears;
I drew her near, and found
  The cistern full
Of divers stones, some bright and round,
  Others ill-shaped and dull.

8 The first, (pray mark,) as quick as light
  Danced through the flood;
But the last, more heavy than the night,
  Nailed to the centre stood;

I wondered much, but tired
At last with thought,
My restless eye, that still desired,
As strange an object brought.

9 It was a bank of flowers, where I descried
(Though 'twas mid-day)
Some fast asleep, others broad-eyed
And taking in the ray;
Here musing long I heard
A rushing wind,
Which still increased, but whence it stirred,
Nowhere I could not find.

10 I turned me round, and to each shade
Despatched an eye,
To see if any leaf had made
Least motion or reply;
But while I, listening, sought
My mind to ease
By knowing where 'twas, or where not,
It whispered, 'Where I please.'

'Lord,' then said I, 'on me one breath,
And let me die before my death!'

'Arise, O north, and come, thou south wind; and blow upon my garden, that the spices thereof may flow out.'—CANT. iv. 16.

RESURRECTION AND IMMORTALITY.

'By that new and living way, which he hath prepared for us, through the veil, which is his flesh.'—HEB. x. 20.

BODY.

1 Oft have I seen, when that renewing breath
That binds and loosens death

Inspired a quickening power through the dead
        Creatures abed,
        Some drowsy silk-worm creep
        From that long sleep,
And in weak, infant hummings chime and knell
        About her silent cell,
Until at last, full with the vital ray,
        She winged away,
        And, proud with life and sense,
        Heaven's rich expense,
Esteemed (vain things!) of two whole elements
        As mean, and span-extents.
Shall I then think such providence will be
        Less friend to me,
    Or that he can endure to be unjust
    Who keeps his covenant even with our dust?

SOUL.

2 Poor querulous handful! was't for this
        I taught thee all that is?
Unbowelled nature, showed thee her recruits,
        And change of suits,
        And how of death we make
        A mere mistake;
For no thing can to nothing fall, but still
        Incorporates by skill,
And then returns, and from the womb of things
        Such treasure brings,
        As phœnix-like renew'th
        Both life and youth;
For a preserving spirit doth still pass
        Untainted through this mass,
Which doth resolve, produce, and ripen all
        That to it fall;

243

Nor are those births, which we
Thus suffering see,
Destroyed at all; but when time's restless wave
Their substance doth deprave,
And the more noble essence finds his house
Sickly and loose,
He, ever young, doth wing
Unto that spring
And source of spirits, where he takes his lot,
Till time no more shall rot
His passive cottage; which, (though laid aside,)
Like some spruce bride,
Shall one day rise, and, clothed with shining light,
All pure and bright,
Remarry to the soul, for 'tis most plain
Thou only fall'st to be refined again.

3 Then I that here saw darkly in a glass
But mists and shadows pass,
And, by their own weak shine, did search the springs
And course of things,
Shall with enlightened rays
Pierce all their ways;
And as thou saw'st, I in a thought could go
To heaven or earth below,
To read some star, or mineral, and in state
There often sate;
So shalt thou then with me,
Both winged and free,
Rove in that mighty and eternal light,
Where no rude shade or night
Shall dare approach us; we shall there no more
Watch stars, or pore
Through melancholy clouds, and say,

'Would it were day!'
One everlasting Sabbath there shall run
Without succession, and without a sun.

'But go thou thy way until the end be: for thou shalt rest, and stand in thy lot at the end of the days.'—DAN. xii. 13.

THE SEARCH.

'Tis now clear day: I see a rose·
Bud in the bright east, and disclose
The pilgrim-sun.   All night have I
Spent in a roving ecstasy
To find my Saviour.   I have been
As far as Bethlehem, and have seen
His inn and cradle; being there
I met the wise men, asked them where
He might be found, or what star can
Now point him out, grown up a man?
To Egypt hence I fled, ran o'er
All her parched bosom to Nile's shore,
Her yearly nurse; came back, inquired
Amongst the doctors, and desired
To see the temple, but was shown
A little dust, and for the town
A heap of ashes, where, some said,
A small bright sparkle was abed,
Which would one day (beneath the pole)
Awake, and then refine the whole.
  Tired here, I came to Sychar, thence
To Jacob's well, bequeathed since
Unto his sons, where often they,
In those calm, golden evenings, lay
Watering their flocks, and having spent
Those white days, drove home to the tent

Their well-fleeced train; and here (O fate!)
I sit where once my Saviour sate.
The angry spring in bubbles swelled,
Which broke in sighs still, as they filled,
And whispered, Jesus had been there,
But Jacob's children would not hear.
Loth hence to part, at last I rise,
But with the fountain in mine eyes,
And here a fresh search is decreed:
He must be found where he did bleed.
I walk the garden, and there see
Ideas of his agony,
And moving anguishments, that set
His blest face in a bloody sweat;
I climbed the hill, perused the cross,
Hung with my gain, and his great loss:
Never did tree bear fruit like this,
Balsam of souls, the body's bliss.
But, O his grave! where I saw lent
(For he had none) a monument,
An undefiled, a new-hewed one,
But there was not the Corner-stone.
Sure then, said I, my quest is vain,
He'll not be found where he was slain;
So mild a Lamb can never be
'Midst so much blood and cruelty.
I 'll to the wilderness, and can
Find beasts more merciful than man;
He lived there safe, 'twas his retreat
From the fierce Jew, and Herod's heat,
And forty days withstood the fell
And high temptations of hell;
With seraphim there talked he,
His Father's flaming ministry,

He heavened their walks, and with his eyes
Made those wild shades a paradise.
Thus was the desert sanctified
To be the refuge of his bride.
I 'll thither then; see, it is day!
The sun 's broke through to guide my way.
　　But as I urged thus, and writ down
What pleasures should my journey crown,
What silent paths, what shades and cells,
Fair virgin-flowers and hallowed wells,
I should rove in, and rest my head
Where my dear Lord did often tread,
Sugaring all dangers with success,
Methought I heard one singing thus:

　　　1 Leave, leave thy gadding thoughts;
　　　　　Who pores
　　　　　And spies
　　　Still out of doors,
　　　　　Descries
　　　Within them nought.

　　　2 The skin and shell of things,
　　　　　Though fair,
　　　　　Are not
　　　Thy wish nor prayer,
　　　　　But got
　　　By mere despair
　　　　　Of wings.

　　　3 To rack old elements,
　　　　　Or dust,
　　　　　And say,

Sure here he must
Needs stay,
Is not the way,
Nor just.

Search well another world; who studies this,
Travels in clouds, seeks manna where none is.

'That they should seek the Lord, if haply they might feel after him, and find him, though he be not far off from every one of us: for in him we live, and move, and have our being.'—ACTS xvii. 27, 28.

ISAAC'S MARRIAGE.

'And Isaac went out to pray in the field at the eventide, and he lifted up his eyes, and saw, and, behold, the camels were coming.'—GEN. xxiv. 63.

Praying! and to be married! It was rare,
But now 'tis monstrous; and that pious care
Though of ourselves, is so much out of date,
That to renew 't were to degenerate.
But thou a chosen sacrifice wert given,
And offered up so early unto Heaven,
Thy flames could not be out; religion was
Rayed into thee like beams into a glass;
Where, as thou grew'st, it multiplied, and shined
The sacred constellation of thy mind.
But being for a bride, prayer was such
A decried course, sure it prevailed not much.
Hadst ne'er an oath nor compliment? thou wert
An odd, dull suitor; hadst thou but the art
Of these our days, thou couldst have coined thee twenty
New several oaths, and compliments, too, plenty.
O sad and wild excess! and happy those
White days, that durst no impious mirth expose:
When conscience by lewd use had not lost sense,
Nor bold-faced custom banished innocence!

Thou hadst no pompous train, nor antic crowd
Of young, gay swearers, with their needless, loud
Retinue; all was here smooth as thy bride,
And calm like her, or that mild evening-tide.
Yet hadst thou nobler guests : angels did wind
And rove about thee, guardians of thy mind;
These fetched thee home thy bride, and all the way
Advised thy servant what to do and say;
These taught him at the well, and thither brought
The chaste and lovely object of thy thought.
But here was ne'er a compliment, not one
Spruce, supple cringe, or studied look put on.
All was plain, modest truth : nor did she come
In rolls and curls, mincing and stately dumb;
But in a virgin's native blush and fears,
Fresh as those roses which the day-spring wears.
O sweet, divine simplicity!   O grace
Beyond a curled lock or painted face!
A pitcher too she had, nor thought it much
To carry that, which some would scorn to touch;
With which in mild, chaste language she did woo
To draw him drink, and for his camels too.
    And now thou knew'st her coming, it was time
To get thee wings on, and devoutly climb
Unto thy God; for marriage of all states
Makes most unhappy, or most fortunates.
This brought thee forth, where now thou didst undress
Thy soul, and with new pinions refresh
Her wearied wings, which, so restored, did fly
Above the stars, a track unknown and high;
And in her piercing flight perfumed the air,
Scattering the myrrh and incense of thy prayer.
So from Lahai-roi's[1] well some spicy cloud,

---

[1] 'Lahai-roi:' a well in the south country where Jacob dwelt, between Kadesh
and Bered; *Heb.*, The well of him that liveth and seeth me.

Wooed by the sun, swells up to be his shroud,
And from her moist womb weeps a fragrant shower,
Which, scattered in a thousand pearls, each flower
And herb partakes; where having stood awhile,
And something cooled the parched and thirsty isle,
The thankful earth unlocks herself, and blends
A thousand odours, which, all mixed, she sends
Up in one cloud, and so returns the skies
That dew they lent, a breathing sacrifice.
    Thus soared thy soul, who, though young, didst in-
        herit
Together with his blood thy father's spirit,
Whose active zeal and tried faith were to thee
Familiar ever since thy infancy.
Others were timed 'and trained up to 't, but thou
Didst thy swift years in piety outgrow.
Age made them reverend and a snowy head,
But thou wert so, ere time his snow could shed.
Then who would truly limn thee out must paint
First a young patriarch, then a married saint.

MAN'S FALL AND RECOVERY.

Farewell, you everlasting hills! I 'm cast
Here under clouds, where storms and tempests blast
    This sullied flower,
Robbed of your calm; nor can I ever make,
Transplanted thus, one leaf of his t' awake;
    But every hour
He sleeps and droops; and in this drowsy state
Leaves me a slave to passions and my fate.
    Besides I 've lost
A train of lights, which in those sunshine days
Were my sure guides; and only with me stays,
    Unto my cost,

One sullen beam, whose charge is to dispense
More punishment than knowledge to my sense.
                Two thousand years
I sojourned thus.   At last Jeshurun's king
Those famous tables did from Sinai bring.
                These swelled my fears,
Guilts, trespasses, and all this inward awe;
For sin took strength and vigour from the law.
                Yet have I found
A plenteous way, (thanks to that Holy One!)
To cancel all that e'er was writ in stone.
                His saving wound
Wept blood that broke this adamant, and gave
To sinners confidence, life to the grave.
                This makes me span
My fathers' journeys, and in one fair step
O'er all their pilgrimage and labours leap.
                For God, made man,
Reduced the extent of works of faith; so made
Of their Red Sea a spring: I wash, they wade.

'As by the offence of one the fault came on all men to condemnation; so by
the righteousness of one, the benefit abounded towards all men to the justification
of life.'—ROM. v. 18.

THE SHOWER.

1 'Twas so; I saw thy birth.   That drowsy lake
From her faint bosom breathed thee, the disease
Of her sick waters, and infectious ease.
                But now at even,
                Too gross for heaven,
Thou fall'st in tears, and weep'st for thy mistake.

2 Ah! it is so with me; oft have I pressed
Heaven with a lazy breath; but fruitless this

Pierced not; love only can with quick access
          Unlock the way,
          When all else stray,
The smoke and exhalations of the breast.

3 Yet if, as thou dost melt, and, with thy train
Of drops, make soft the earth, my eyes could weep
O'er my hard heart, that's bound up and asleep,
          Perhaps at last,
          Some such showers past,
My God would give a sunshine after rain.

BURIAL.

1 O thou! the first-fruits of the dead,
          And their dark bed,
When I am cast into that deep
          And senseless sleep,
The wages of my sin,
          O then,
Thou great Preserver of all men,
          Watch o'er that loose
          And empty house,
Which I sometime lived in!

2 It is in truth a ruined piece,
          Not worth thy eyes;
And scarce a room, but wind and rain
          Beat through and stain
The seats and cells within;
          Yet thou,
Led by thy love, wouldst stoop thus low,
          And in this cot,
          All filth and spot,
Didst with thy servant inn.

3 And nothing can, I hourly see,
      Drive thee from me.
Thou art the same, faithful and just,
      In life or dust.
        Though then, thus crumbed, I stray
        In blasts,
Or exhalations, and wastes,
      Beyond all eyes,
      Yet thy love spies
That change, and knows thy clay.

4 The world's thy box: how then, there tossed,
      Can I be lost?
But the delay is all; Time now
      Is old and slow;
      His wings are dull and sickly.
      Yet he
Thy servant is, and waits on thee.
      Cut then the sum,
      Lord, haste, Lord, come,
O come, Lord Jesus, quickly!

'And not only they, but ourselves also, which have the first-fruits of the Spirit, even we ourselves groan within ourselves, waiting for the adoption, to wit, the redemption of our body.'—Rom. viii. 23.

CHEERFULNESS.

1 Lord, with what courage and delight
      I do each thing,
When thy least breath sustains my wing!
      I shine and move
      Like those above,
      And, with much gladness
      Quitting sadness,
Make me fair days of every night.

2 Affliction thus mere pleasure is;
        And hap what will,
If thou be in't, 'tis welcome still.
        But since thy rays
        In sunny days
        Thou dost thus lend,
        And freely spend,
Ah! what shall I return for this?

3 Oh that I were all soul! that thou
        Wouldst make each part
Of this poor sinful frame pure heart!
        Then would I drown
        My single one;
        And to thy praise
        A concert raise
Of hallelujahs here below.

THE PASSION.

1 O my chief good!
    My dear, dear God!
    When thy blest blood
Did issue forth, forced by the rod,
        What pain didst thou
        Feel in each blow!
        How didst thou weep,
        And thyself steep
In thy own precious, saving tears!
        What cruel smart
        Did tear thy heart!
        How didst thou groan it
        In the spirit,
O thou whom my soul loves and fears!

2 Most blessed Vine!
    Whose juice so good
    I feel as wine,
But thy fair branches felt as blood,
    How wert thou pressed
    To be my feast!
    In what deep anguish
    Didst thou languish!
What springs of sweat and blood did drown thee!
    How in one path
    Did the full wrath
    Of thy great Father
    Crowd and gather,
Doubling thy griefs, when none would own thee!

3 How did the weight
    Of all our sins,
    And death unite
To wrench and rack thy blessed limbs!
    How pale and bloody
    Looked thy body!
    How bruised and broke,
    With every stroke!
How meek and patient was thy spirit!
    How didst thou cry,
    And groan on high,
    'Father, forgive,
    And let them live!
I die to make my foes inherit!'

4 O blessed Lamb!
    That took'st my sin,
    That took'st my shame,
How shall thy dust thy praises sing?

I would I were
One hearty tear!
One constant spring!
Then would I bring
Thee two small mites, and be at strife
Which should most vie,
My heart or eye,
Teaching my years
In smiles and tears
To weep, to sing, thy death, my life.

RULES AND LESSONS.

1 When first thy eyes unvail, give thy soul leave
To do the like; our bodies but forerun
The spirit's duty.   True hearts spread and heave
Unto their God, as flowers do to the sun.
   Give him thy first thoughts then; so shalt thou keep
   Him company all day, and in him sleep.

2 Yet never sleep the sun up.   Prayer should
Dawn with the day.   There are set, awful hours
'Twixt Heaven and us.   The manna was not good
After sun-rising; far-day sullies flowers.
   Rise to prevent the sun; sleep doth sins glut,
   And heaven's gate opens when this world's is shut.

3 Walk with thy fellow-creatures; note the hush
And whispers amongst them.   There 's not a spring
Or leaf but hath his morning-hymn.   Each bush
And oak doth know I AM.   Canst thou not sing?
   Oh, leave thy cares and follies! go this way,
   And thou art sure to prosper all the day.

4 Serve God before the world; let him not go
Until thou hast a blessing; then resign
  256

The whole unto him, and remember who
Prevailed by wrestling ere the sun did shine;
  Pour oil upon the stones; weep for thy sin;
  Then journey on, and have an eye to heaven.

5 Mornings are mysteries; the first world's youth,
Man's resurrection and the future's bud
Shroud in their births; the crown of life, light, truth
Is styled their star, the stone, and hidden food.
  Three blessings wait upon them, two of which
  Should move.   They make us holy, happy, rich.

6 When the world's up, and every swarm abroad,
Keep thou thy temper; mix not with each clay;
Despatch necessities; life hath a load
Which must be carried on, and safely may.
  Yet keep those cares without thee, let the heart
  Be God's alone, and choose the better part.

7 Through all thy actions, counsels, and discourse,
Let mildness and religion guide thee out;
If truth be thine, what needs a brutish force?
But what's not good and just ne'er go about.
  Wrong not thy conscience for a rotten stick;
  That gain is dreadful which makes spirits sick.

8 To God, thy country, and thy friend be true;
If priest and people change, keep thou thy ground.
Who sells religion is a Judas Jew;
And, oaths once broke, the soul cannot be sound.
  The perjurer's a devil let loose: what can
  Tie up his hands that dares mock God and man?

9 Seek not the same steps with the crowd; stick thou
To thy sure trot; a constant, humble mind

Is both his own joy, and his Maker's too;
Let folly dust it on, or lag behind.
   A sweet self-privacy in a right soul
   Outruns the earth, and lines the utmost pole.

10 To all that seek thee bear an open heart;
Make not thy breast a labyrinth or trap;
If trials come, this will make good thy part,
For honesty is safe, come what can hap;
   It is the good man's feast, the prince of flowers,
   Which thrives in storms, and smells best after
     showers.

11 Seal not thy eyes up from the poor, but give
Proportion to their merits, and thy purse;
Thou may'st in rags a mighty prince relieve,
Who, when thy sins call for 't, can fence a curse.
   Thou shalt not lose one mite.   Though waters stray,
   The bread we cast returns in fraughts one day.

12 Spend not an hour so as to weep another,
For tears are not thine own; if thou giv'st words,
Dash not with them thy friend, nor Heaven; oh,
    smother
A viperous thought; some syllables are swords.
   Unbitted tongues are in their penance double;
   They shame their owners, and their hearers trouble.

13 Injure not modest blood, while spirits rise
In judgment against lewdness; that 's base wit
That voids but filth and stench.   Hast thou no prize
But sickness or infection? stifle it.
   Who makes his jest of sins, must be at least,
   If not a very devil, worse than beast.

258

14 Yet fly no friend, if he be such indeed;
   But meet to quench his longings, and thy thirst;
   Allow your joys, religion: that done, speed,
   And bring the same man back thou wert at first.
       Who so returns not, cannot pray aright,
       But shuts his door, and leaves God out all night.

15 To heighten thy devotions, and keep low
   All mutinous thoughts, what business e'er thou hast,
   Observe God in his works; here fountains flow,
   Birds sing, beasts feed, fish leap, and the earth stands
           fast;
       Above are restless motions, running lights,
       Vast circling azure, giddy clouds, days, nights.

16 When seasons change, then lay before thine eyes
   His wondrous method; mark the various scenes
   In heaven; hail, thunder, rainbows, snow, and ice,
   Calms, tempests, light, and darkness, by his means;
       Thou canst not miss his praise; each tree, herb,
           flower
       Are shadows of his wisdom and his power.

17 To meals when thou dost come, give him the praise
   Whose arm supplied thee; take what may suffice,
   And then be thankful; oh, admire his ways
   Who fills the world's unemptied granaries!
       A thankless feeder is a thief, his feast
       A very robbery, and himself no guest.

18 High-noon thus past, thy time decays; provide
   Thee other thoughts; away with friends and mirth;
   The sun now stoops, and hastes his beams to hide
   Under the dark and melancholy earth.

All but preludes thy end.   Thou art the man
Whose rise, height, and descent is but a span.

19 Yet, set as he doth, and 'tis well.   Have all
Thy beams home with thee: trim thy lamp, buy oil,
And then set forth; who is thus dressed, the fall
Furthers his glory, and gives death the foil.
   Man is a summer's day; whose youth and fire
   Cool to a glorious evening, and expire.

20 When night comes, list[1] thy deeds; make plain the way
'Twixt heaven and thee; block it not with delays;
But perfect all before thou sleep'st; then say
'There 's one sun more strung on my bead of days.'
   What 's good score up for joy; the bad, well scanned,
   Wash off with tears, and get thy Master's hand.

21 Thy accounts thus made, spend in the grave one hour
Before thy time; be not a stranger there,
Where thou may'st sleep whole ages; life's poor flower
Lasts not a night sometimes.   Bad spirits fear
   This conversation; but the good man lies
   Entombed many days before he dies.

22 Being laid, and dressed for sleep, close not thy eyes
Up with thy curtains; give thy soul the wing
In some good thoughts; so, when the day shall rise,
And thou unrak'st thy fire, those sparks will bring
   New flames; besides where these lodge, vain heats mourn
   And die; that bush where God is shall not burn.

23 When thy nap 's over, stir thy fire, and rake
In that dead age; one beam i' the dark outvies

<hr>

[1] 'List:' weigh.

Two in the day; then from the damps and ache
Of night shut up thy leaves; be chaste; God pries
  Through thickest nights; though then the sun be
    far,
Do thou the works of day, and rise a star.

24 Briefly, do as thou wouldst be done unto,
Love God, and love thy neighbour; watch and pray.
These are the words and works of life; this do,
And live; who doth not thus, hath lost heaven's way.
  Oh, lose it not! look up, wilt change those lights
  For chains of darkness and eternal nights?

REPENTANCE.

Lord, since thou didst in this vile clay
    That sacred ray,
Thy Spirit, plant, quickening the whole
  With that one grain's infused wealth,
My forward flesh crept on, and subtly stole
  Both growth and power; checking the health
And heat of thine.   That little gate
  And narrow way, by which to thee
The passage is, he termed a grate
  And entrance to captivity;
Thy laws but nets, where some small birds,
  And those but seldom too, were caught;
Thy promises but empty words,
  Which none but children heard or taught.
This I believed: and though a friend
  Came oft from far, and whispered, No;
Yet, that not sorting to my end,
  I wholly listened to my foe.
Wherefore, pierced through with grief, my sad,
  Seduced soul sighs up to thee;

To thee, who with true light art clad,
  And seest all things just as they be.
Look from thy throne upon this roll
  Of heavy sins, my high transgressions,
Which I confess with all my soul;
  My God, accept of my confession!
        It was last day,
Touched with the guilt of my own way,
I sat alone, and taking up,
        The bitter cup,
Through all thy fair and various store,
Sought out what might outvie my score.
  The blades of grass thy creatures feeding;
  The trees, their leaves; the flowers, their seeding;
  The dust, of which I am a part;
  The stones, much softer than my heart;
  The drops of rain, the sighs of wind,
  The stars, to which I am stark blind;
  The dew thy herbs drink up by night,
  The beams they warm them at i' the light;
  All that have signature or life
  I summoned to decide this strife;
  And lest I should lack for arrears,
  A spring ran by, I told her tears;
  But when these came unto the scale,
  My sins alone outweighed them all.
O my dear God! my life, my love!
Most blessed Lamb! and mildest Dove!
Forgive your penitent offender,
And no more his sins remember;
Scatter these shades of death, and give
Light to my soul, that it may live;
Cut me not off for my transgressions,
Wilful rebellions, and suppressions;

But give them in those streams a part
Whose spring is in my Saviour's heart.
Lord, I confess the heinous score,
And pray I may do so no more;
Though then all sinners I exceed,
Oh, think on this, thy Son did bleed!
Oh, call to mind his wounds, his woes,
His agony, and bloody throes;
Then look on all that thou hast made,
And mark how they do fail and fade;
The heavens themselves, though fair and bright,
Are dark and unclean in thy sight;
How then, with thee, can man be holy,
Who dost thine angels charge with folly?
Oh, what am I, that I should breed
Figs on a thorn, flowers on a weed?
I am the gourd of sin and sorrow,
Growing o'er night, and gone to-morrow.
In all this round of life and death
Nothing 's more vile than is my breath;
Profaneness on my tongue doth rest,
Defects and darkness in my breast;
Pollutions all my body wed,
And even my soul to thee is dead;
Only in him, on whom I feast,
Both soul and body are well dressed;
    His pure perfection quits all score,
    And fills the boxes of his poor;
He is the centre of long life and light;
I am but finite, he is infinite.
Oh, let thy justice then in him confine,
And through his merits make thy mercy mine!

THE DAWNING.

Ah! what time wilt thou come? when shall that cry,
　‘The Bridegroom’s coming!’ fill the sky?
Shall it in the evening run
When our words and works are done?
Or will thy all-surprising light
　　　Break at midnight,
When either sleep or some dark pleasure
Possesseth mad man without measure?
Or shall these early, fragrant hours
　　　Unlock thy bowers,
And with their blush of light descry
Thy locks crowned with eternity?
Indeed, it is the only time
That with thy glory doth best chime;
All now are stirring, every field
　　　Full hymns doth yield;
The whole creation shakes off night,
And for thy shadow looks the light;
Stars now vanish without number,
Sleepy planets set and slumber,
The pursy clouds disband and scatter,
All expect some sudden matter;
Not one beam triumphs, but from far
　　　That morning-star.

Oh, at what time soever thou,
Unknown to us, the heavens wilt bow,
And, with thy angels in the van,
Descend to judge poor careless man,
Grant I may not like puddle lie
In a corrupt security,
Where, if a traveller water crave,

He finds it dead, and in a grave.
But as this restless, vocal spring
All day and night doth run and sing,
And though here born, yet is acquainted
Elsewhere, and flowing keeps untainted;
So let me all my busy age
In thy free services engage;
And though, while here, of force I must
Have commerce sometimes with poor dust,
And in my flesh, though vile and low,
As this doth in her channel flow,
Yet let my course, my aim, my love,
And chief acquaintance be above;
So when that day and hour shall come
In which thyself will be the Sun,
Thou'lt find me dressed and on my way,
Watching the break of thy great day.

THE TEMPEST.

1 How is man parcelled out! how every hour
    Shows him himself, or something he should see!
    This late, long heat may his instruction be;
    And tempests have more in them than a shower.

        When nature on her bosom saw
                Her infants die,
        And all her flowers withered to straw,
                Her breasts grown dry;
        She made the earth, their nurse and tomb,
                Sigh to the sky,
        Till to those sighs, fetched from her womb,
                Rain did reply;
        So in the midst of all her fears
                And faint requests,

> Her earnest sighs procured her tears
> And filled her breasts.

2 Oh that man could do so! that he would hear
    The world read to him! all the vast expense
    In the creation shed and slaved to sense,
Makes up but lectures for his eye and ear.

3 Sure mighty Love, foreseeing the descent
    Of this poor creature, by a gracious art
    Hid in these low things snares to gain his heart,
And laid surprises in each element.

4 All things here show him heaven; waters that fall
    Chide and fly up; mists of corruptest foam
Quit their first beds and mount; trees, herbs, flowers,
    all
Strive upwards still, and point him the way home.

5 How do they cast off grossness? only earth
    And man, like Issachar, in loads delight,
    Water's refined to motion, air to light,
Fire to all three,[1] but man hath no such mirth.

6 Plants in the root with earth do most comply,
    Their leaves with water and humidity,
    The flowers to air draw near and subtilty,
And seeds a kindred fire have with the sky.

7 All have their keys and set ascents; but man
    Though he knows these, and hath more of his
    own,
Sleeps at the ladder's foot; alas! what can
    These new discoveries do, except they drown?

[1] 'All three:' light, motion, heat.

8 Thus, grovelling in the shade and darkness, he
   Sinks to a dead oblivion; and though all
   He sees, like pyramids, shoot from this ball,
And lessening still, grow up invisibly,

9 Yet hugs he still his dirt; the stuff he wears,
   And painted trimming, takes down both his eyes;
   Heaven hath less beauty than the dust he spies,
And money better music than the spheres.

10 Life's but a blast; he knows it; what? shall straw
   And bulrush-fetters temper his short hour?
   Must he nor sip nor sing? grows ne'er a flower
To crown his temples? shall dreams be his law?

11 O foolish man! how hast thou lost thy sight?
   How is it that the sun to thee alone
   Is grown thick darkness, and thy bread a stone?
Hath flesh no softness now? mid-day no light?

12 Lord! thou didst put a soul here. If I must
   Be broke again, for flints will give no fire
   Without a steel, oh, let thy power clear
Thy gift once more, and grind this flint to dust!

THE WORLD.

1 I saw eternity the other night,
   Like a great ring of pure and endless light,
      All calm, as it was bright;
And round beneath it, time, in hours, days, years,
      Driven by the spheres,
Like a vast shadow moved, in which the world
      And all her train were hurled.
The doting lover in his quaintest strain
      Did there complain;

Near him, his lute, his fancy, and his flights,
    Wit's sour delights;
With gloves, and knots, the silly snares of pleasure,
    Yet his dear treasure,
All scattered lay, while he his eyes did pour
    Upon a flower.

2 The darksome statesman, hung with weights and woe,
  Like a thick midnight fog, moved there so slow,
    He did nor stay, nor go;
Condemning thoughts, like sad eclipses, scowl
    Upon his soul,
And clouds of crying witnesses without
    Pursued him with one shout.
Yet digged the mole, and, lest his ways be found,
    Worked under ground,
Where he did clutch his prey.   But one did see
    That policy.
Churches and altars fed him; perjuries
    Were gnats and flies;
It rained about him blood and tears; but he
    Drank them as free.

3 The fearful miser on a heap of rust
  Sat pining all his life there, did scarce trust
    His own hands with the dust,
Yet would not place one piece above, but lives
    In fear of thieves.
Thousands there were as frantic as himself,
    And hugged each one his pelf;
The downright epicure placed heaven in sense,
    And scorned pretence;
While others, slipped into a wide excess,
    Said little less;

The weaker sort slight, trivial wares enslave,
      Who think them brave,
And poor, despised truth sat counting by
      Their victory.

4 Yet some, who all this while did weep and sing,
   And sing and weep, soared up into the ring;
         But most would use no wing.
   'O fools,' said I, 'thus to prefer dark night
         Before true light!
   To live in grots and caves, and hate the day
         Because it shows the way,
   The way, which from this dead and dark abode
         Leads up to God,
   A way where you might tread the sun, and be
         More bright than he!'
   But, as I did their madness so discuss,
         One whispered thus,
   'This ring the bridegroom did for none provide,
         But for his bride.'

' All that is in the world, the lust of the flesh, the lust of the eye, and the pride
of life, is not of the Father, but is of the world. And the world passeth away,
and the lusts thereof; but he that doeth the will of God abideth for ever.'—1
JOHN ii. 16, 17.

THE CONSTELLATION.

1 Fair, ordered lights, whose motion without noise
      Resembles those true joys,
   Whose spring is on that hill where you do grow,
   And we here taste sometimes below.

2 With what exact obedience do you move,
      Now beneath, and now above!
   And in your vast progressions overlook
   The darkest night and closest nook!

3 Some nights I see you in the gladsome east,
   Some others near the west,
  And when I cannot see, yet do you shine,
   And beat about your endless line.

4 Silence and light and watchfulness with you
   Attend and wind the clue ;
  No sleep nor sloth assails you, but poor man
   Still either sleeps, or slips his span.

5 He gropes beneath here, and with restless care,
   First makes, then hugs a snare ;
  Adores dead dust, sets heart on corn and grass,
   But seldom doth make heaven his glass.

6 Music and mirth, if there be music here,
   Take up and tune his ear ;
  These things are kin to him, and must be had ;
   Who kneels, or sighs a life, is mad.

7 Perhaps some nights he 'll watch with you, and peep
   When it were best to sleep;
  Dares know effects, and judge them long before,
   When the herb he treads knows much, much more.

8 But seeks he your obedience, order, light,
   Your calm and well-trained flight?
  Where, though the glory differ in each star,
   Yet is there peace still and no war.

9 Since placed by him, who calls you by your names,
   And fixed there all your flames,
  Without command you never acted ought,
   And then you in your courses fought.

10 But here, commissioned by a black self-will,
　　　　The sons the father kill,
　　The children chase the mother, and would heal
　　　　The wounds they give by crying zeal.

11 Then cast her blood and tears upon thy book,
　　　　Where they for fashion look ;
　　And, like that lamb, which had the dragon's voice,
　　　　Seem mild, but are known by their noise.

12 Thus by our lusts disordered into wars,
　　　　Our guides prove wandering stars,
　　Which for these mists and black days were reserved,
　　　　What time we from our first love swerved.

13 Yet oh, for his sake who sits now by thee
　　　　All crowned with victory,
　　So guide us through this darkness, that we may
　　　　Be more and more in love with day!

14 Settle and fix our hearts, that we may move
　　　　In order, peace, and love ;
　　And, taught obedience by thy whole creation,
　　　　Become an humble, holy nation!

15 Give to thy spouse her perfect and pure dress,
　　　　Beauty and holiness ;
　　And so repair these rents, that men may see
　　　　And say, 'Where God is, all agree.'

MISERY.

　　　Lord, bind me up, and let me lie
　　　A prisoner to my liberty,
　　　If such a state at all can be
　　　As an impris'ment serving thee;

The wind, though gathered in thy fist,
Yet doth it blow still where it list,
And yet shouldst thou let go thy hold,
Those gusts might quarrel and grow bold.
　　As waters here, headlong and loose,
The lower grounds still chase and choose,
Where spreading all the way they seek
And search out every hole and creek;
So my spilt thoughts, winding from thee,
Take the down-road to vanity,
Where they all stray, and strive which shall
Find out the first and steepest fall.
I cheer their flow, giving supply
To what's already grown too high,
And having thus performed that part,
Feed on those vomits of my heart.
I break the fence my own hands made
Then lay that trespass in the shade;
Some fig-leaves still I do devise,
As if thou hadst not ears nor eyes.
Excess of friends, of words, and wine
Take up my day, while thou dost shine
All unregarded, and thy book
Hath not so much as one poor look.
If thou steal in amidst the mirth
And kindly tell me, I am earth,
I shut thee out, and let that slip;
Such music spoils good fellowship.
Thus wretched I and most unkind,
Exclude my dear God from my mind,
Exclude him thence, who of that cell
Would make a court, should he there dwell.
He goes, he yields; and troubled sore
His Holy Spirit grieves therefore;

The mighty God, the eternal King
Doth grieve for dust, and dust doth sing.
But I go on, haste to divest
Myself of reason, till oppressed
And buried in my surfeits, I
Prove my own shame and misery.
Next day I call and cry for thee
Who shouldst not then come near to me;
But now it is thy servant's pleasure,
Thou must and dost give him his measure.
Thou dost, thou com'st, and in a shower
Of healing sweets thyself dost pour
Into my wounds; and now thy grace
(I know it well) fills all the place;
I sit with thee by this new light,
And for that hour thou 'rt my delight;
No man can more the world despise,
Or thy great mercies better prize.
I school my eyes, and strictly dwell
Within the circle of my cell;
That calm and silence are my joys,
Which to thy peace are but mere noise.
At length I feel my head to ache,
My fingers itch, and burn to take
Some new employment, I begin
To swell and foam and fret within:
   'The age, the present times are not
   To snudge in and embrace a cot;
   Action and blood now get the game,
   Disdain treads on the peaceful name;
   Who sits at home too bears a load
   Greater than those that gad abroad.'
Thus do I make thy gifts given me
The only quarrellers with thee;

I 'd loose those knots thy hands did tie,
Then would go travel, fight, or die.
Thousands of wild and waste infusions
Like waves beat on my resolutions;
As flames about their fuel run,
And work and wind till all be done,
So my fierce soul bustles about,
And never rests till all be out.
Thus wilded by a peevish heart,
Which in thy music bears no part,
I storm at thee, calling my peace
A lethargy, and mere disease;
Nay those bright beams shot from thy eyes
To calm me in these mutinies,
I style mere tempers, which take place
At some set times, but are thy grace.

Such is man's life, and such is mine,
The worst of men, and yet still thine,
Still thine, thou know'st, and if not so,
Then give me over to my foe.
Yet since as easy 'tis for thee
To make man good as bid him be,
And with one glance, could he that gain,
To look him out of all his pain,
Oh, send me from thy holy hill
So much of strength as may fulfil
All thy delights, whate'er they be,
And sacred institutes in me!
Open my rocky heart, and fill
It with obedience to thy will;
Then seal it up, that as none see,
So none may enter there but thee.

Oh, hear, my God! hear him, whose blood
Speaks more and better for my good!

Oh, let my cry come to thy throne!
My cry not poured with tears alone,
(For tears alone are often foul,)
But with the blood of all my soul;
With spirit-sighs, and earnest groans,
Faithful and most repenting moans,
With these I cry, and crying pine,
Till thou both mend, and make me thine.

MOUNT OF OLIVES.

When first I saw true beauty, and thy joys,
Active as light, and calm without all noise,
Shined on my soul, I felt through all my powers
Such a rich air of sweets, as evening showers,
Fanned by a gentle gale, convey, and breathe
On some parched bank, crowned with a flowery wreath;
Odours, and myrrh, and balm in one rich flood
O'erran my heart, and spirited my blood;
My thoughts did swim in comforts, and mine eye
Confessed, 'The world did only paint and lie.'
And where before I did no safe course steer,
But wandered under tempests all the year;
Went bleak and bare in body as in mind,
And was blown through by every storm and wind,
I am so warmed now by this glance on me,
That 'midst all storms I feel a ray of thee.
So have I known some beauteous passage rise
In sudden flowers and arbours to my eyes,
And in the depth and dead of winter bring
To my cold thoughts a lively sense of spring.
    Thus fed by thee, who dost all beings nourish,
My withered leaves again look green and flourish;
I shine and shelter underneath thy wing,
Where, sick with love, I strive thy name to sing;

Thy glorious name ! which grant I may so do,
That these may be thy praise, and my joy too !

ASCENSION-DAY.

Lord Jesus ! with what sweetness and delights,
Sure, holy hopes, high joys, and quickening flights,
Dost thou feed thine !   O thou ! the hand that lifts
To him who gives all good and perfect gifts,
Thy glorious, bright ascension, though removed
So many ages from me, is so proved
And by thy Spirit sealed to me, that I
Feel me a sharer in thy victory !
        I soar and rise
        Up to the skies,
      Leaving the world their day;
        And in my flight
        For the true light
      Go seeking all the way;
I greet thy sepulchre, salute thy grave,
That blest enclosure, where the angels gave
The first glad tidings of thy early light,
And resurrection from the earth and night.
I see that morning in thy convert's[1] tears,
Fresh as the dew, which but this dawning wears.
I smell her spices; and her ointment yields
As rich a scent as the now primrosed fields.
The day-star smiles, and light with the deceased
Now shines in all the chambers of the east.
What stirs, what posting intercourse and mirth
Of saints and angels glorify the earth?
What sighs, what whispers, busy stops and stays,
Private and holy talk, fill all the ways?
They pass as at the last great day, and run

---

[1] 'Thy convert:' St Mary Magdalene.

In their white robes to seek the risen Sun;
I see them, hear them, mark their haste, and move
Amongst them, with them, winged with faith and love.
Thy forty days' more secret commerce here
After thy death and funeral, so clear
And indisputable, shows to my sight
As the sun doth, which to those days gave light.
I walk the fields of Bethany, which shine
All now as fresh as Eden, and as fine.
Such was the bright world on the first seventh day,
Before man brought forth sin, and sin decay;
When like a virgin clad in flowers and green
The pure earth sat, and the fair woods had seen
No frost, but flourished in that youthful vest
With which their great Creator had them dressed:
When heaven above them shined like molten glass,
While all the planets did unclouded pass;
And springs, like dissolved pearls, their streams did pour,
Ne'er marred with floods, nor angered with a shower.
With these fair thoughts I move in this fair place,
And the last steps of my mild Master trace.
I see him leading out his chosen train
All sad with tears, which like warm summer rain
In silent drops steal from their holy eyes,
Fixed lately on the cross, now on the skies.
And now, eternal Jesus! thou dost heave
Thy blessed hands to bless those thou dost leave.
The cloud doth now receive thee, and their sight
Having lost thee, behold two men in white!
Two and no more: 'What two attest is true,'
Was thine own answer to the stubborn Jew.
Come then, thou faithful Witness! come, dear Lord,
Upon the clouds again to judge this world!

277

COCK-CROWING.

1 Father of lights! what sunny seed,
   What glance of day hast thou confined
   Into this bird?   To all the breed
   This busy ray thou hast assigned;
       Their magnetism works all night,
       And dreams of paradise and light.

2 Their eyes watch for the morning hue,
   Their little grain-expelling night
   So shines and sings, as if it knew
   The path unto the house of light.
       It seems their candle, howe'er done,
       Was tinned and lighted at the sun.

3 If such a tincture, such a touch,
   So firm a longing can empower,
   Shall thy own image think it much
   To watch for thy appearing hour?
       If a mere blast so fill the sail,
       Shall not the breath of God prevail?

4 O thou immortal light and heat!
   Whose hand so shines through all this frame,
   That by the beauty of the seat,
   We plainly see who made the same,
       Seeing thy seed abides in me,
       Dwell thou in it, and I in thee!

5 To sleep without thee is to die;
   Yea, 'tis a death partakes of hell:
   For where thou dost not close the eye
   It never opens, I can tell.
       In such a dark, Egyptian border,
       The shades of death dwell, and disorder.

6 If joys, and hopes, and earnest throes,
  And hearts, whose pulse beats still for light,
  Are given to birds; who, but thee, knows
  A love-sick soul's exalted flight?
     Can souls be tracked by any eye
     But his, who gave them wings to fly?

7 Only this veil which thou hast broke,
  And must be broken yet in me,
  This veil, I say, is all the cloak
  And cloud which shadows me from thee.
     This veil thy full-eyed love denies,
     And only gleams and fractions spies.

8 Oh, take it off! make no delay;
  But brush me with thy light, that I
  May shine unto a perfect day,
  And warm me at thy glorious eye!
     Oh, take it off! or till it flee,
     Though with no lily, stay with me!

THE PALM-TREE.

1 Dear friend, sit down, and bear awhile this shade,
  As I have yours long since.   This plant you see
  So pressed and bowed, before sin did degrade
  Both you and it, had equal liberty

2 With other trees; but now, shut from the breath
  And air of Eden, like a malcontent
  It thrives nowhere.   This makes these weights, like
    death
  And sin, hang at him; for the more he's bent

3 The more he grows.   Celestial natures still
   Aspire for home.   This Solomon of old,
   By flowers, and carvings, and mysterious skill
   Of wings, and cherubims, and palms, foretold.

4 This is the life which, hid above with Christ
   In God, doth always (hidden) multiply,
   And spring, and grow, a tree ne'er to be priced,
   A tree whose fruit is immortality.

5 Here spirits that have run their race, and fought,
   And won the fight, and have not feared the frowns
   Nor loved the smiles of greatness, but have wrought
   Their Master's will, meet to receive their crowns.

6 Here is the patience of the saints: this tree
   Is watered by their tears, as flowers are fed
   With dew by night; but One you cannot see
   Sits here, and numbers all the tears they shed.

. 7 Here is their faith too, which if you will keep
   When we two part, I will a journey make
   To pluck a garland hence while you do sleep,
   And weave it for your head against you wake.

THE GARLAND.

1 Thou, who dost flow and flourish here below,
   To whom a falling star and nine days' glory,
   Or some frail beauty, makes the bravest show,
   Hark, and make use of this ensuing story.

         When first my youthful, sinful age
                Grew master of my ways,
         Appointing error for my page,
                And darkness for my days;

I flung away, and with full cry
    Of wild affections, rid
In post for pleasures, bent to try
    All gamesters that would bid.
I played with fire, did counsel spurn,
    Made life my common stake;
But never thought that fire would burn,
    Or that a soul could ache.
Glorious deceptions, gilded mists,
    False joys, fantastic flights,
Pieces of sackcloth with silk lists,
    These were my prime delights.
I sought choice bowers, haunted the spring,
    Culled flowers and made me posies;
Gave my fond humours their full wing,
    And crowned my head with roses.
But at the height of this career
    I met with a dead man,
Who, noting well my vain abear,
    Thus unto me began:
' Desist, fond fool, be not undone;
    What thou hast cut to-day
Will fade at night, and with this sun
    Quite vanish and decay.'

2 Flowers gathered in this world, die here; if thou
Wouldst have a wreath that fades not, let them grow,
And grow for thee.   Who spares them here, shall find
A garland, where comes neither rain nor wind.

LOVE-SICK.

Jesus, my life! how shall I truly love thee?
Oh that thy Spirit would so strongly move me,
That thou wert pleased to shed thy grace so far

As to make man all pure love, flesh a star!
A star that would ne'er set, but ever rise,
So rise and run, as to outrun these skies,
These narrow skies (narrow to me) that bar,
So bar me in, that I am still at war,
At constant war with them.   Oh, come, and rend
Or bow the heavens! Lord, bow them and descend,
And at thy presence make these mountains flow,
These mountains of cold ice in me!   Thou art
Refining fire; oh, then, refine my heart,
My foul, foul heart!   Thou art immortal heat;
Heat motion gives; then warm it, till it beat;
So beat for thee, till thou in mercy hear;
So hear, that thou must open; open to
A sinful wretch, a wretch that caused thy woe;
Thy woe, who caused his weal; so far his weal
That thou forgott'st thine own, for thou didst seal
Mine with thy blood, thy blood which makes thee mine,
Mine ever, ever; and me ever thine.

PSALM CIV.

1 Up, O my soul, and bless the Lord!   O God,
    My God, how great, how very great art thou !
Honour and majesty have their abode
        With thee, and crown thy brow.

2 Thou cloth'st thyself with light as with a robe,
    And the high, glorious heavens thy mighty hand
Doth spread like curtains round about this globe
        Of air, and sea, and land.

3 The beams of thy bright chambers thou dost lay
    In the deep waters, which no eye can find ;
The clouds thy chariots are, and thy pathway
        The wings of the swift wind.

4 In thy celestial, gladsome messages
    Despatched to holy souls, sick with desire
And love of thee, each willing angel is
        Thy minister in fire.

5 Thy arm unmoveable for ever laid
    And founded the firm earth; then with the deep
As with a vail thou hidd'st it; thy floods played
        Above the mountains steep.

6 At thy rebuke they fled, at the known voice
    Of their Lord's thunder they retired apace:
Some up the mountains passed by secret ways,
        Some downwards to their place.

7 For thou to them a bound hast set, a bound
    Which, though but sand, keeps in and curbs whole
        seas:
There all their fury, foam, and hideous sound,
        Must languish and decrease.

8 And as thy care bounds these, so thy rich love
    Doth broach the earth; and lesser brooks lets forth,
Which run from hills to valleys, and improve
        Their pleasure and their worth.

9 These to the beasts of every field give drink;
    There the wild asses swallow the cool spring:
And birds amongst the branches on their brink
        Their dwellings have, and sing.

10 Thou from thy upper springs above, from those
    Chambers of rain, where heaven's large bottles lie,
Dost water the parched hills, whose breaches close,
        Healed by the showers from high.

11 Grass for the cattle, and herbs for man's use
    Thou mak'st to grow; these, blessed by thee, the
        earth
  Brings forth, with wine, oil, bread; all which infuse
        To man's heart strength and mirth.

12 Thou giv'st the trees their greenness, even to those
    Cedars in Lebanon, in whose thick boughs
  The birds their nests build; though the stork doth
        The fir-trees for her house.   [choose

13 To the wild goats the high hills serve for folds,
    The rocks give conies a retiring place:
  Above them the cool moon her known course holds,
        And the sun runs his race.

14 Thou makest darkness, and then comes the night,
    In whose thick shades and silence each wild beast
  Creeps forth, and, pinched for food, with scent and sight
        Hunts in an eager quest.

15 The lion's whelps, impatient of delay,
    Roar in the covert of the woods, and seek
  Their meat from thee, who dost appoint the prey,
        And feed'st them all the week.

16 This past, the sun shines on the earth; and they
    Retire into their dens; man goes abroad
  Unto his work, and at the close of day
        Returns home with his load.

17 O Lord my God, how many and how rare
    Are thy great works! In wisdom hast thou made
  Them all; and this the earth, and every blade
        Of grass we tread declare.

18 So doth the deep and wide sea, wherein are
    Innumerable creeping things, both small
And great; there ships go, and the shipmen's fear,
    The comely, spacious whale.

19 These all upon thee wait, that thou mayst feed
    Them in due season: what thou giv'st they take;
Thy bounteous open hand helps them at need,
    And plenteous meals they make.

20 When thou dost hide thy face, (thy face which keeps
    All things in being,) they consume and mourn:
When thou withdraw'st their breath their vigour
    And they to dust return.   [sleeps,

21 Thou send'st thy Spirit forth, and they revive,
    The frozen earth's dead face thou dost renew.
Thus thou thy glory through the world dost drive,
    And to thy works art true.

22 Thine eyes behold the earth, and the whole stage
    Is moved and trembles, the hills melt and smoke
With thy least touch; lightnings and winds that rage
    At thy rebuke are broke.

23 Therefore as long as thou wilt give me breath
    I will in songs to thy great name employ
That gift of thine, and to my day of death
    Thou shalt be all my joy.

24 I 'll spice my thoughts with thee, and from thy word
    Gather true comforts; but the wicked liver
Shall be consumed. O my soul, bless thy Lord!
    Yea, bless thou him for ever!

THE TIMBER.

1 Sure thou didst flourish once! and many springs,
  Many bright mornings, much dew, many showers
Passed o'er thy head; many light hearts and wings,
  Which now are dead, lodged in thy living bowers.

2 And still a new succession sings and flies;
  Fresh groves grow up, and their green branches
Towards the old and still-enduring skies,   [shoot
  While the low violet thrives at their root.

3 But thou, beneath the sad and heavy line
  Of death, doth waste all senseless, cold, and dark;
Where not so much as dreams of light may shine,
  Nor any thought of greenness, leaf, or bark.

4 And yet, as if some deep hate and dissent,
  Bred in thy growth betwixt high winds and thee,
Were still alive, thou dost great storms resent,
  Before they come, and know'st how near they be.

5 Else all at rest thou liest, and the fierce breath
  Of tempests can no more disturb thy case;
But this thy strange resentment after death
  Means only those who broke in life thy peace.

6 So murdered man, when lovely life is done,
  And his blood freezed, keeps in the centre still
Some secret sense, which makes the dead blood run
  At his approach that did the body kill.

7 And is there any murderer worse than sin?
  Or any storms more foul than a lewd life?
Or what resentient can work more within
  Than true remorse, when with past sins at strife?
  286

8 He that hath left life's vain joys and vain care,
　　And truly hates to be detained on earth,
　Hath got an house where many mansions are,
　　And keeps his soul unto eternal mirth.

9 But though thus dead unto the world, and ceased
　　From sin, he walks a narrow, private way;
　Yet grief and old wounds make him sore displeased,
　　And all his life a rainy, weeping day.

10 For though he should forsake the world, and live
　　As mere a stranger as men long since dead;
　Yet joy itself will make a right soul grieve
　　To think he should be so long vainly led.

11 But as shades set off light, so tears and grief,
　　Though of themselves but a sad blubbered story,
　By showing the sin great, show the relief
　　Far greater, and so speak my Saviour's glory.

12 If my way lies through deserts and wild woods,
　　Where all the land with scorching heat is cursed;
　Better the pools should flow with rain and floods
　　To fill my bottle, than I die with thirst.

13 Blest showers they are, and streams sent from above;
　　Begetting virgins where they use to flow;
　The trees of life no other waters love,
　　Than upper springs, and none else make them grow.

14 But these chaste fountains flow not till we die.
　　Some drops may fall before; but a clear spring
　　And ever running, till we leave to fling
　Dirt in her way, will keep above the sky.

' He that is dead is freed from sin.'—Rom. vi. 7.

287

THE JEWS.

1   When the fair year
Of your Deliverer comes,
And that long frost which now benumbs
Your hearts shall thaw; when angels here
    Shall yet to man appear,
And familiarly confer
Beneath the oak and juniper;
    When the bright Dove,
Which now these many, many springs
    Hath kept above,
    Shall with spread wings
Descend, and living waters flow
To make dry dust, and dead trees grow;

2   Oh, then, that I
Might live, and see the olive bear
Her proper branches! which now lie
    Scattered each where;
And, without root and sap, decay;
Cast by the husbandman away.
    And sure it is not far!
For as your fast and foul decays,
Forerunning the bright morning star,
Did sadly note his healing rays
Would shine elsewhere, since you were blind,
And would be cross, when God was kind,—

3   So by all signs
Our fulness too is now come in;
And the same sun, which here declines
And sets, will few hours hence begin
To rise on you again, and look

Towards old Mamre and Eshcol's brook.
        For surely he
Who loved the world so as to give
His only Son to make it free,
Whose Spirit too doth mourn and grieve
To see man lost, will for old love
From your dark hearts this veil remove.

4 Faith sojourned first on earth in you,
        You were the dear and chosen stock:
The arm of God, glorious and true,
        Was first revealed to be your rock.

5 You were the eldest child, and when
        Your stony hearts despised love,
The youngest, even the Gentiles, then,
        Were cheered your jealousy to move.

6 Thus, righteous Father! dost thou deal
        With brutish men; thy gifts go round
By turns, and timely, and so heal
        The lost son by the newly found.

PALM-SUNDAY.

1 Come, drop your branches, strew the way,
        Plants of the day!
Whom sufferings make most green and gay.
The King of grief, the Man of sorrow,
Weeping still like the wet morrow,
Your shades and freshness comes to borrow.

2 Put on, put on your best array;
Let the joyed road make holyday,
And flowers, that into fields do stray,
Or secret groves, keep the highway.

3 Trees, flowers, and herbs; birds, beasts, and
          stones,
    That since man fell expect with groans
    To see the Lamb, come all at once,
    Lift up your heads and leave your moans;
          For here comes he
          Whose death will be
    Man's life, and your full liberty.

4 Hark! how the children shrill and high
          'Hosanna' cry;
    Their joys provoke the distant sky,
    Where thrones and seraphim reply;
    And their own angels shine and sing,
          In a bright ring:
          Such young, sweet mirth
          Makes heaven and earth
    Join in a joyful symphony.

5 The harmless, young, and happy ass,
    (Seen long before[1] this came to pass,)
    Is in these joys a high partaker,
    Ordained and made to bear his Maker.

6 Dear Feast of Palms, of flowers and dew!
      Whose fruitful dawn sheds hopes and lights;
    Thy bright solemnities did shew
      The third glad day through two sad nights.

7 I'll get me up before the sun,
      I'll cut me boughs off many a tree,
    And all alone full early run
      To gather flowers to welcome thee.

[1] Zechariah ix. 9.

8 Then, like the palm, though wronged I'll bear,
    I will be still a child, still meek
  As the poor ass which the proud jeer,
    And only my dear Jesus seek.

9 If I lose all, and must endure
    The proverbed griefs of holy Job,
  I care not, so I may secure
    But one green branch and a white robe.

PROVIDENCE.

1   Sacred and secret hand!
  By whose assisting, swift command
  The angel showed that holy well
      Which freed poor Hagar from her fears,
      And turned to smiles the begging tears
  Of young, distressed Ishmael.

2   How, in a mystic cloud,
  Which doth thy strange, sure mercies shroud,
  Dost thou convey man food and money,
      Unseen by him till they arrive
      Just at his mouth, that thankless hive,
  Which kills thy bees, and eats thy honey!

3   If I thy servant be,
  Whose service makes even captives free,
  A fish shall all my tribute pay,
      The swift-winged raven shall bring me meat,
      And I, like flowers, shall still go neat,
  As if I knew no month but May.

4   I will not fear what man
  With all his plots and power can.

Bags that wax old may plundered be;
But none can sequester or let
A state that with the sun doth set,
And comes next morning fresh as he.

5   Poor birds this doctrine sing,
And herbs which on dry hills do spring,
Or in the howling wilderness
    Do know thy dewy morning hours,
    And watch all night for mists or showers,
Then drink and praise thy bounteousness.

6   May he for ever die
Who trusts not thee, but wretchedly
Hunts gold and wealth, and will not lend
    Thy service nor his soul one day!
    May his crown, like his hopes, be clay;
And what he saves may his foes spend!

7   If all my portion here,
The measure given by thee each year,
Were by my causeless enemies
    Usurped; it never should me grieve,
    Who know how well thou canst relieve,
Whose hands are open as thine eyes.

8   Great King of love and truth!
Who wouldst not hate my froward youth,
And wilt not leave me when grown old,
    Gladly will I, like Pontic sheep,
    Unto my wormwood diet keep,
Since thou hast made thy arm my fold.

ST MARY MAGDALENE.

Dear, beauteous saint! more white than day,
When in his naked, pure array;
Fresher than morning-flowers, which shew,
As thou in tears dost, best in dew.
How art thou changed, how lively, fair,
Pleasing, and innocent an air,
Not tutored by thy glass, but free,
Native, and pure, shines now in thee!
But since thy beauty doth still keep
Bloomy and fresh, why dost thou weep?
This dusky state of sighs and tears
Durst not look on those smiling years,
When Magdal-castle was thy seat,
Where all was sumptuous, rare, and neat.
Why lies this hair despised now
Which once thy care and art did show?
Who then did dress the much-loved toy
In spires, globes, angry curls and coy,
Which with skilled negligence seemed shed
About thy curious, wild, young head?
Why is this rich, this pistic nard
Spilt, and the box quite broke and marred?
What pretty sullenness did haste
Thy easy hands to do this waste?
Why art thou humbled thus, and low
As earth thy lovely head dost bow?
Dear soul! thou knew'st flowers here on earth
At their Lord's footstool have their birth;
Therefore thy withered self in haste
Beneath his blest feet thou didst cast,
That at the root of this green tree
Thy great decays restored might be.

Thy curious vanities, and rare
Odorous ointments kept with care,
And dearly bought, when thou didst see
They could not cure nor comfort thee;
Like a wise, early penitent,
Thou sadly didst to him present,
Whose interceding, meek, and calm
Blood, is the world's all-healing balm.
This, this divine restorative
Called forth thy tears, which ran in live
And hasty drops, as if they had
(Their Lord so near) sense to be glad.
Learn, ladies, here the faithful cure
Makes beauty lasting, fresh, and pure;
Learn Mary's art of tears, and then
Say you have got the day from men.
Cheap, mighty art! her art of love,
Who loved much, and much more could move;
Her art! whose memory must last
Till truth through all the world be passed;
Till his abused, despised flame
Return to heaven, from whence it came,
And send a fire down, that shall bring
Destruction on his ruddy wing.
Her art! whose pensive, weeping eyes,
Were once sin's loose and tempting spies;
But now are fixed stars, whose light
Helps such dark stragglers to their sight.

Self-boasting Pharisee! how blind
A judge wert thou, and how unkind!
It was impossible that thou,
Who wert all false, shouldst true grief know.
Is 't just to judge her faithful tears

294

By that foul rheum thy false eye wears?
'This woman,' sayst thou, 'is a sinner!'
And sat there none such at thy dinner?
Go, leper, go! wash till thy flesh
Comes like a child's, spotless and fresh;
He is still leprous that still paints:
Who saint themselves, they are no saints.

THE RAINBOW.

Still young and fine! but what is still in view
We slight as old and soiled, though fresh and new.
How bright wert thou, when Shem's admiring eye
Thy burnished, flaming arch did first descry!
When Terah, Nahor, Haran, Abram, Lot,
The youthful world's gray fathers in one knot,
Did with intentive looks watch every hour
For thy new light, and trembled at each shower!
When thou dost shine, darkness looks white and fair,
Forms turn to music, clouds to smiles and air:
Rain gently spends his honey-drops, and pours
Balm on the cleft earth, milk on grass and flowers.
Bright pledge of peace and sunshine! the sure tie
Of thy Lord's hand, the object[1] of his eye!
When I behold thee, though my light be dim,
Distant, and low, I can in thine see him,
Who looks upon thee from his glorious throne,
And minds the covenant 'twixt all and one.
O foul, deceitful men! my God doth keep
His promise still, but we break ours and sleep.
After the fall the first sin was in blood,
And drunkenness quickly did succeed the flood;
But since Christ died, (as if we did devise
To lose him too, as well as paradise,)

[1] Genesis ix. 16.

These two grand sins we join and act together,
Though blood and drunkenness make but foul, foul
        weather.
Water, though both heaven's windows and the deep
Full forty days o'er the drowned world did weep,
Could not reform us, and blood in despite,
Yea, God's own blood, we tread upon and slight.
So those bad daughters, which God saved from fire,
While Sodom yet did smoke, lay with their sire.

Then, peaceful, signal bow, but in a cloud
Still lodged, where all thy unseen arrows shroud;
I will on thee as on a comet look,
A comet, the sad world's ill-boding book;
Thy light as luctual and stained with woes
I'll judge, where penal flames sit mixed and close.
For though some think thou shin'st but to restrain
Bold storms, and simply dost attend on rain;
Yet I know well, and so our sins require,
Thou dost but court cold rain, till rain turns fire.

THE SEED GROWING SECRETLY.

MARK IV. 26.

1 If this world's friends might see but once
        What some poor man may often feel,
    Glory and gold and crowns and thrones
        They would soon quit, and learn to kneel.

2 My dew, my dew! my early love,
        My soul's bright food, thy absence kills!
    Hover not long, eternal Dove!
        Life without thee is loose and spills.

3 Something I had, which long ago
        Did learn to suck and sip and taste;

But now grown sickly, sad, and slow,
    Doth fret and wrangle, pine and waste.

4 Oh, spread thy sacred wings, and shake
    One living drop! one drop life keeps!
If pious griefs heaven's joys awake,
    Oh, fill his bottle! thy child weeps!

5 Slowly and sadly doth he grow,
    And soon as left shrinks back to ill;
Oh, feed that life, which makes him blow
    And spread and open to thy will!

6 For thy eternal, living wells
    None stained or withered shall come near:
A fresh, immortal green there dwells,
    And spotless white is all the wear.

7 Dear, secret greenness! nursed below
    Tempests and winds and winter nights!
Vex not that but One sees thee grow,
    That One made all these lesser lights.

8 If those bright joys he singly sheds
    On thee, were all met in one crown,
Both sun and stars would hide their heads;
    And moons, though full, would get them down.

9 Let glory be their bait whose minds
    Are all too high for a low cell:
Though hawks can prey through storms and winds,
    The poor bee in her hive must dwell.

10 Glory, the crowd's cheap tinsel, still
    To what most takes them is a drudge;
And they too oft take good for ill,
    And thriving vice for virtue judge.

11 What needs a conscience calm and bright
     Within itself an outward test?
   Who breaks his glass to take more light,
     Makes way for storms into his rest.

12 Then bless thy secret growth, nor catch
     At noise, but thrive unseen and dumb;
   Keep clean, bear fruit, earn life, and watch,
     Till the white-winged reapers come!

CHILDHOOD.

I cannot reach it; and my striving eye
Dazzles at it, as at eternity.
      Were now that chronicle alive,
Those white designs which children drive,
And the thoughts of each harmless hour,
With their content too in my power,
Quickly would I make my path even,
And by mere playing go to heaven.

        Why should men love
A wolf more than a lamb or dove?
Or choose hell-fire and brimstone streams
Before bright stars and God's own beams?
Who kisseth thorns will hurt his face,
But flowers do both refresh and grace;
And sweetly living (fie on men!)
Are, when dead, medicinal then.
If seeing much should make staid eyes,
And long experience should make wise,
Since all that age doth teach is ill,
Why should I not love childhood still?
Why, if I see a rock or shelf,
Shall I from thence cast down myself,

Or by complying with the world,
From the same precipice be hurled?
Those observations are but foul,
Which make me wise to lose my soul.

And yet the practice worldlings call
Business and weighty action all,
Checking the poor child for his play,
But gravely cast themselves away.

Dear, harmless age! the short, swift span
Where weeping virtue parts with man;
Where love without lust dwells, and bends
What way we please without self-ends.

An age of mysteries! which he
Must live twice that would God's face see;
Which angels guard, and with it play,
Angels! which foul men drive away.

How do I study now, and scan
Thee more than ere I studied man,
And only see through a long night
Thy edges and thy bordering light!
Oh for thy centre and mid-day!
For sure that is the narrow way!

ABEL'S BLOOD.

Sad, purple well! whose bubbling eye
Did first against a murderer cry;
Whose streams, still vocal, still complain
  Of bloody Cain;
And now at evening are as red
As in the morning when first shed.
  If single thou,

Though single voices are but low,
Couldst such a shrill and long cry rear
As speaks still in thy Maker's ear,
What thunders shall those men arraign
Who cannot count those they have slain,
Who bathe not in a shallow flood,
But in a deep, wide sea of blood—
A sea whose loud waves cannot sleep,
But deep still calleth upon deep;
Whose urgent sound, like unto that
Of many waters, beateth at
The everlasting doors above,
Where souls behind the altar move,
And with one strong, incessant cry
Inquire 'How long?' of the Most High?
          Almighty Judge!
At whose just laws no just men grudge;
Whose blessed, sweet commands do pour
Comforts and joys and hopes each hour
On those that keep them; oh, accept
Of his vowed heart, whom thou hast kept
From bloody men! and grant I may
That sworn memorial duly pay
To thy bright arm, which was my light
And leader through thick death and night!
          Aye may that flood,
That proudly spilt and despised blood,
Speechless and calm as infants sleep!
Or if it watch, forgive and weep
For those that spilt it!   May no cries
From the low earth to high heaven rise,
But what, like his whose blood peace brings,
Shall, when they rise, speak better things
Than Abel's doth!   May Abel be

Still single heard, while these agree
With his mild blood in voice and will,
Who prayed for those that did him kill!

RIGHTEOUSNESS.

1 Fair, solitary path! whose blessed shades
  The old, white prophets planted first and dressed;
Leaving for us, whose goodness quickly fades,
  A shelter all the way, and bowers to rest;

2 Who is the man that walks in thee? who loves
  Heaven's secret solitude, those fair abodes,
Where turtles build, and careless sparrows move,
  Without to-morrow's evils and future loads?

3 Who hath the upright heart, the single eye,
  The clean, pure hand, which never meddled pitch?
Who sees invisibles, and doth comply
  With hidden treasures that make truly rich?

4   He that doth seek and love
            The things above,
  Whose spirit ever poor is, meek, and low;
          Who simple still and wise,
            Still homeward flies,
  Quick to advance, and to retreat most slow.

5   Whose acts, words, and pretence
            Have all one sense,
  One aim and end; who walks not by his sight;
          Whose eyes are both put out,
            And goes about
  Guided by faith, not by exterior light.

6   Who spills no blood, nor spreads
          Thorns in the beds
Of the distressed, hasting their overthrow;
       Making the time they had
          Bitter and sad,
Like chronic pains, which surely kill, though slow.

7   Who knows earth nothing hath
          Worth love or wrath,
But in his Hope and Rock is ever glad.
       Who seeks and follows peace,
          When with the ease
And health of conscience it is to be had.

8   Who bears his cross with joy,
          And doth employ
His heart and tongue in prayers for his foes;
       Who lends not to be paid,
          And gives full aid
Without that bribe which usurers impose.

9   Who never looks on man
          Fearful and wan,
But firmly trusts in God; the great man's measure,
       Though high and haughty, must
          Be ta'en in dust;
But the good man is God's peculiar treasure.

10   Who doth thus, and doth not
          These good deeds blot
With bad, or with neglect; and heaps not wrath
       By secret filth, nor feeds
          Some snake, or weeds,
Cheating himself—That man walks in this path.

JACOB'S PILLOW AND PILLAR.

I see the temple in thy pillar reared,
And that dread glory which thy children feared,
In mild, clear visions, without a frown,
Unto thy solitary self is shown.
'Tis number makes a schism: throngs are rude,
And God himself died by the multitude.
This made him put on clouds, and fire, and smoke;
Hence he in thunder to thy offspring spoke.
The small, still voice at some low cottage knocks,
But a strong wind must break thy lofty rocks.

The first true worship of the world's great King
From private and selected hearts did spring;
But he most willing to save all mankind,
Enlarged that light, and to the bad was kind.
Hence catholic or universal came
A most fair notion, but a very name.
For this rich pearl, like some more common stone,
When once made public, is esteemed by none.
Man slights his Maker when familiar grown,
And sets up laws to pull his honour down.
This God foresaw: and when slain by the crowd,
Under that stately and mysterious cloud
Which his death scattered, he foretold the place
And form to serve him in should be true grace,
And the meek heart; not in a mount, nor at
Jerusalem, with blood of beasts and fat.
A heart is that dread place, that awful cell,
That secret ark, where the mild Dove doth dwell,
When the proud waters rage: when heathens rule
By God's permission, and man turns a mule,
This little Goshen, in the midst of night

And Satan's seat, in all her coasts hath light;
Yea, Bethel shall have tithes, saith Israel's stone,
And vows and visions, though her foes cry, None.
Thus is the solemn temple sunk again
Into a pillar, and concealed from men.
And glory be to his eternal name,
Who is contented that this holy flame
Shall lodge in such a narrow pit, till he
With his strong arm turns our captivity!

But blessed Jacob, though thy sad distress
Was just the same with ours, and nothing less;
For thou a brother, and bloodthirsty too,
Didst fly,[1] whose children wrought thy children's woe:
Yet thou in all thy solitude and grief,
On stones didst sleep, and found'st but cold relief;
Thou from the Day-star a long way didst stand,
And all that distance was law and command.
But we a healing Sun, by day and night,
Have our sure guardian and our leading light.
What thou didst hope for and believe we find
And feel, a Friend most ready, sure, and kind.
Thy pillow was but type and shade at best,
But we the substance have, and on him rest.

THE FEAST.

1   Oh, come away,
Make no delay,
Come while my heart is clean and steady!
While faith and grace
Adorn the place,
Making dust and ashes ready!

1 Obadiah 10; Amos i. 11.

304

2   No bliss here lent
     Is permanent,
  Such triumphs poor flesh cannot merit;
     Short sips and sights
     Endear delights:
  Who seeks for more he would inherit.

3   Come then, true bread,
     Quickening the dead,
  Whose eater shall not, cannot die!
     Come, antedate
     On me that state,
  Which brings poor dust the victory.

4   Aye victory,
     Which from thine eye
  Breaks as the day doth from the east,
     When the spilt dew
     Like tears doth shew
  The sad world wept to be released.

5   Spring up, O wine,
     And springing shine
  With some glad message from his heart,
     Who did, when slain,
     These means ordain
  For me to have in him a part!

6   Such a sure part
     In his blest heart,
  The well where living waters spring,
     That, with it fed,
     Poor dust, though dead,
  Shall rise again, and live, and sing.

7   O drink and bread,
          Which strikes death dead,
    The food of man's immortal being!
          Under veils here
          Thou art my cheer,
    Present and sure without my seeing.

8   How dost thou fly
          And search and pry
    Through all my parts, and, like a quick
          And knowing lamp,
          Hunt out each damp,
    Whose shadow makes me sad or sick!

9   O what high joys!
          The turtle's voice
    And songs I hear! O quickening showers
        .   Of my Lord's blood,
          You make rocks bud,
    And crown dry hills with wells and flowers!

10   For this true ease,
          This healing peace,
    For this [brief] taste of living glory, ·
          My soul and all,
          Kneel down and fall,
    And sing his sad victorious story!

11   O thorny crown,
          More soft than down!
    O painful cross, my bed of rest!
          O spear, the key
        .   Opening the way!
    O thy worst state, my only best!

12   O all thy griefs
      Are my reliefs,
  As all my sins thy sorrows were!
      And what can I,
      To this reply?
  What, O God! but a silent tear?

13   Some toil and sow
      That wealth may flow,
  And dress this earth for next year's meat:
      But let me heed
      Why thou didst bleed,
  And what in the next world to eat.

'Blessed are they which are called unto the marriage supper of the Lamb.'—
Rev. xix. 9.

THE WATERFALL.

With what deep murmurs, through time's silent
  stealth,
Does thy transparent, cool, and watery wealth
    Here flowing fall,
    And chide and call,
As if his liquid, loose retinue staid
Lingering, and were of this steep place afraid:
    The common pass,
    Where, clear as glass,
    All must descend
    Not to an end,
But quickened by this deep and rocky grave,
Rise to a longer course more bright and brave.

  Dear stream! dear bank! where often I
  Have sat, and pleased my pensive eye;
  Why, since each drop of thy quick store

Runs thither whence it flowed before,
Should poor souls fear a shade or night,
Who came (sure) from a sea of light?
Or, since those drops are all sent back
So sure to thee that none doth lack,
Why should frail flesh doubt any more
That what God takes he 'll not restore?

O useful element and clear!
My sacred wash and cleanser here;
My first consigner unto those
Fountains of life, where the Lamb goes!
What sublime truths and wholesome themes
Lodge in thy mystical, deep streams!
Such as dull man can never find,
Unless that Spirit lead his mind,
Which first upon thy face did move
And hatched all with his quickening love.
As this loud brook's incessant fall
In streaming rings re-stagnates all,
Which reach by course the bank, and then
Are no more seen: just so pass men.
O my invisible estate,
My glorious liberty, still late!
Thou art the channel my soul seeks,
Not this with cataracts and creeks.

DR JOSEPH BEAUMONT.

THIS writer, though little known, appears to us to stand as high almost as any name in the present volume, and we are proud to reprint here some considerable specimens of his magnificent poetry.

Joseph Beaumont was sprung from a collateral branch of the ancient family of the Beaumonts, that family from which sprung Sir John Beaumont, the author of 'Bosworth Field,' and Francis Beaumont, the celebrated dramatist. He was born at Hadleigh, in Suffolk. Of his early life nothing is known. He received his education at Cambridge, where, during the Civil War, he was fellow and tutor of Peterhouse. Ejected by the Republicans from his offices, he retired to Hadleigh, and spent his time in the composition of his *magnum opus*, 'Psyche.' This poem appeared in 1648; and in 1702, three years after the author's death, his son published a second edition, with numerous corrections, and the addition of four cantos by the author. Beaumont also wrote several minor pieces in English and Latin, a controversial tract in reply to Henry More's 'Mystery of Godliness,' and several theological works which are still in MS., according to a provision in his will to that effect. Peace and perpetuity to their slumbers!

After the Restoration, our author was not only reinstated in his former situations, but received from his patron, Bishop Wren, several valuable pieces of preferment besides. Afterwards, he exercised successively the offices of Master of Jesus and of Peterhouse, and was King's Professor of Divinity from 1670 to 1699. In the latter year he died.

While praising the genius of Beaumont, we are far from commending his 'Psyche,' either as an artistic whole, or as a readable book. It is, sooth to say, a dull allegory, in twenty-four immense cantos, studded with the rarest beauties. It is considerably longer than the 'Faery Queen,' nearly four times the length of the 'Paradise Lost,' and five or six times as long as the 'Excursion.' To read it through now-a-days were to perform a purgatorial penance. But the imagination and fancy are

'nenserian, his colouring is often Titianesque in gorgeousness,
and his pictures of shadows, abstractions, and all fantastic forms,
are so forcible as to seem to start from the canvas.   In painting
the beautiful, his verse becomes careless and flowing as a
loosened zone; in painting the frightful and the infernal, his
language, like his feeling, seems to curdle and stiffen in horror,
as where, speaking of Satan, he says—

> ' His tawny teeth
> Were ragged grown, by endless *gnashing at*
> *The dismal riddle of his living death.*'

The ' Psyche' may be compared to a palace of Fairyland, where
successive doors fly open to the visitor—one revealing a banquet-
ing-room filled with the materials of exuberant mirth; another,
an enchanted garden, with streams stealing from grottos, and
nymphs gliding through groves; a third conducting you to a
dungeon full of dead men's bones and all uncleanness; a fourth,
to a pit which seems the mouth of hell, and whence cries of tor-
ture come up, shaking the smoke that ascendeth up for ever and
ever; and a fifth, to the open roof, over which the stars are seen
bending, and the far-off heavens are opening in glory; and of
these doors there is no end.   We saw, when lately in Copen-
hagen, the famous tower of the Trinity Church, remarkable for
the grand view commanded from the summit, and for the broad
spiral ascent winding within it almost to the top, up which it is
said Peter the Great, in 1716, used to drive himself and his
Empress in a coach-and-four.   It was curious to feel ourselves
ascending on a path nearly level, and without the slightest perspi-
ration or fatigue; and here, we thought, is the desiderated ' royal
road ' to difficulties fairly found.   Large poems should be con-
structed on the same principle; their quiet, broad interest should
beguile their readers alike to their length and their loftiness.   It
is exactly the reverse with ' Psyche.'   But if any reader is
wearied of some of the extracts we have given, such as his verses
on ' Eve,' on ' Paradise,' on ' End,' on ' The Death of his Wife,'
and on ' Imperial Rome,' we shall be very much disposed to
question his capacity for appreciating true poetry.

HELL.

1 Hell's court is built deep in a gloomy vale,
High walled with strong damnation, moated round
With flaming brimstone: full against the hall
Roars a burnt bridge of brass: the yards abound
   With all envenomed herbs and trees, more rank
   And fruitless than on Asphaltite's bank.

2 The gate, where Fire and Smoke the porters be,
Stands always ope with gaping greedy jaws.
Hither flocked all the states of misery;
As younger snakes, when their old serpent draws
   Them by a summoning hiss, haste down her throat
   Of patent poison their awed selves to shoot.

3 The hall was roofed with everlasting pride,
Deep paved with despair, checkered with spite,
And hanged round with torments far and wide:
The front displayed a goodly-dreadful sight,
   Great Satan's arms stamped on an iron shield,
   A crowned dragon, gules, in sable field.

4 There on 's immortal throne of death they see
Their mounted lord; whose left hand proudly held
His globe, (for all the world he claims to be
His proper realm,) whose bloody right did wield
   His mace, on which ten thousand serpents knit,
   With restless madness gnawed themselves and it.

5 His awful horns above his crown did rise,
And force his fiends to shrink in theirs: his face
Was triply-plated impudence: his eyes
Were hell reflected in a double glass,
   Two comets staring in their bloody stream,
   Two beacons boiling in their pitch and flame.

6 His mouth in breadth vied with his palace gate
  And conquered it in soot: his tawny teeth
  Were ragged grown, by endless gnashing at
  The dismal riddle of his living death:
      His grizzly beard a singed confession made
      What fiery breath through his black lips did trade.

7 Which as he oped, the centre, on whose back
  His chair of ever-fretting pain was set,
  Frighted beside itself, began to quake:
  Throughout all hell the barking hydras shut
      Their awed mouths: the silent peers, in fear,
      Hung down their tails, and on their lord did stare.

JOSEPH'S DREAM.

1 When this last night had sealed up mine eyes,
  And opened heaven's, whose countenance now was
          clear,
      And trimmed with every star; on his soft wing
      A nimble vision me did thither bring.

2 Quite through the storehouse of the air I passed
  Where choice of every weather treasured lies:
  Here, rain is bottled up; there, hail is cast
  In candied heaps: here, banks of snow do rise;
      There, furnaces of lightning burn, and those
      Long-bearded stars which light us to our woes.

3 Hence towered I to a dainty world: the air
  Was sweet and calm, and in my memory
  Waked my serener mother's looks: this fair
  Canaan now fled from my discerning eye;
      The earth was shrunk so small, methought I read,
      By that due prospect, what it was indeed.

312

4 But then, arriving at an orb whose flames,
  Like an unbounded ocean, flowed about,
  Fool as I was, I quaked; till its kind beams
  Gave me a harmless kiss.   I little thought
      Fire could have been so mild; but surely here
      It rageth, 'cause we keep it from its sphere.

5 There, reverend sire, it flamed, but with as sweet
  An ardency as in your noble heart
  That heavenly zeal doth burn, whose fostering heat
  Makes you Heaven's living holocaust : no part
      Of my dream's tender wing felt any harm;
      Our journey, not the fire, did keep us warm.

6 But here my guide, his wings' soft oars to spare,
  On the moon's lower horn clasped hold, and whirled
  Me up into a region as far,
  In splendid worth, surmounting this low world
      As in its place : for liquid crystal here
      Was the tralucid matter of each sphere.

7 The moon was kind, and, as we scoured by,
  Showed us the deed whereby the great Creator
  Instated her in that large monarchy
  She holdeth over all the ocean's water :
      To which a schedule was annexed, which o'er
      All other humid bodies gives her power.

8 Now complimental Mercury was come
  To the quaint margin of his courtly sphere,
  And bid us eloquent welcome to his home.
  Scarce could we pass, so great a crowd was there
      Of points and lines ; and nimble Wit beside
      Upon the back of thousand shapes did ride.

9 Next Venus' face, heaven's joy and sweetest pride,
(Which brought again my mother to my mind,)
Into her region lured my ravished guide.
This strewed with youth, and smiles, and love we find;
   And those all chaste : 'tis this foul world below
   Adulterates what from thence doth spotless flow.

10 Then rapt to Phœbus' orb, all paved with gold,
The rich reflection of his own aspect :
Most gladly there I would have stayed, and told
How many crowns and thorns his dwelling decked,
   What life, what verdure, what heroic might,
   What pearly spirits, what sons of active light.

11 But I was hurried into Mars his sphere,
Where Envy, (oh, how cursed was its grim face !)
And Jealousy, and Fear, and Wrath, and War
Quarrelled, although in heaven, about their place.
   Yea, engines there to vomit fire I saw,
   Whose flame and thunder earth at length must
     know.

12 Nay, in a corner, 'twas my hap to spy
Something which looked but frowardly on me :
And sure my watchful guide read in mine eye
My musing troubled sense ; for straightway he,
   Lest I should start and wake upon the fright,
   Speeded from thence his seasonable flight.

13 Welcome was Jupiter's dominion, where
Illustrious Mildness round about did flow ;
Religion had built her temple there,
And sacred honours on its walks did grow :
   No mitre ever priest's grave head shall crown,
   Which in those mystic gardens was not sown.

14 At length, we found old Saturn in his bed;
   And much I wondered how, and he so dull,
   Could climb thus high: his house was lumpish lead,
   Of dark and solitary corners full;
       Where Discontent and Sickness dwellers be,
       Damned Melancholy and dead Lethargy.

15 Hasting from hence into a boundless field,
   Innumerable stars we marshalled found
   In fair array: this earth did never yield
   Such choice of flowery pride, when she had crowned
       The plains of Shechem, where the gaudy Spring
       Smiles on the beauties of each verdant thing,

PARADISE.

1 Within, rose hills of spice and frankincense,
   Which smiled upon the flowery vales below,
   Where living crystal found a sweet pretence
   With musical impatience to flow,
       And delicately chide the gems beneath
       Because no smoother they had paved its path.

2 The nymphs which sported on this current's side
   Were milky Thoughts, tralucid, pure Desires,
   Soft turtles' Kisses, Looks of virgin brides,
   Sweet Coolness which nor needs nor feareth fires,
       Snowy Embraces, cheerly-sober Eyes,
       Gentleness, Mildness, Ingenuities.

3 The early gales knocked gently at the door
   Of every flower, to bid the odours wake;
   Which, catching in their softest arms, they bore
   From bed to bed, and so returned them back
       To their own lodgings, doubled by the blisses
       They sipped from their delicious brethren's kisses.

4 Upon the wings of those enamouring breaths
  Refreshment, vigour, nimbleness attended;
  Which, wheresoe'er they flew, cheered up their paths,
  And with fresh airs of life all things befriended:
      For Heaven's sweet Spirit deigned his breath to join
      And make the powers of these blasts divine.

5 The goodly trees' bent arms their nobler load
  Of fruit which blest oppression overbore:
  That orchard where the dragon warder stood,
  For all its golden boughs, to this was poor,
      To this, in which the greater serpent lay,
      Though not to guard the trees, but to betray.

6 Of fortitude there rose a stately row;
  Here, of munificence a thickset grove;
  There, of wise industry a quickset grew;
  Here, flourished a dainty copse of love;
      There, sprang up pleasant twigs of ready wit;
      Here, larger trees of gravity were set,

7 Here, temperance; and wide-spread justice there,
  Under whose sheltering shadow piety,
  Devotion, mildness, friendship planted were;
  Next stood renown with head exalted high;
      Then twined together plenty, fatness, peace.
      O blessed place, where grew such things as these!

EVE.

1 Her spacious, polished forehead was the fair
  And lovely plain where gentle majesty
  Walked in delicious state: her temples clear
  Pomegranate fragments, which rejoiced to lie
      In dainty ambush, and peep through their cover
      Of amber-locks whose volume curled over.

316

2 The fuller stream of her luxuriant hair
  Poured down itself upon her ivory back :
  In which soft flood ten thousand graces were
  Sporting and dallying with every lock ;
      The rival winds for kisses fell to fight,
      And raised a ruffling tempest of delight.

3 Two princely arches, of most equal measures,
  Held up the canopy above her eyes,
  And opened to the heavens far richer treasures,
  Than with their stars or sun e'er learn'd to rise :
      Those beams can ravish but the body's sight,
      These dazzle stoutest souls with mystic light.

4 Two garrisons were these of conquering love ;
  Two founts of life, of spirit, of joy, of grace ;
  Two easts in one fair heaven, no more above,
  But in the hemisphere of her own face ;
      Two thrones of gallantry ; two shops of miracles ;
      Two shrines of deities ; two silent oracles.

5 For silence here could eloquently plead ;
  Here might the unseen soul be clearly read :
  Though gentle humours their mild mixture made,
  They proved a double burning-glass which shed
      Those living flames which, with enlivening darts,
      Shoot deaths of love into spectators' hearts.

6 'Twixt these, an alabaster promontory
  Sloped gently down to part each cheek from other ;
  Where white and red strove for the fairer glory,
  Blending in sweet confusion together.
      The rose and lily never joined were
      In so divine a marriage as there.

7 Couchant upon these precious cushionets
  Were thousand beauties, and as many smiles,
  Chaste blandishments, and modest cooling heats,
  Harmless temptations, and honest guiles.
    For heaven, though up betimes the maid to deck,
    Ne'er made Aurora's cheeks so fair and sleek.

8 Enamouring neatness, softness, pleasure, at
  Her gracious mouth in full retinue stood;
  For, next the eyes' bright glass, the soul at that
  Takes most delight to look and walk abroad.
    But at her lips two threads of scarlet lay,
    Or two warm corals, to adorn the way,—

9 The precious way whereby her breath and tongue,
  Her odours and her honey, travelled,
  Which nicest critics would have judged among
  Arabian or Hyblæan mountains bred.
    Indeed, the richer Araby in her
    Dear mouth and sweeter Hybla dwelling were.

10 More gracefully its golden chapiter
  No column of white marble e'er sustained
  Than her round polished neck supported her
  Illustrious head, which there in triumph reigned.
    Yet neither would this pillar hardness know,
    Nor suffer cold to dwell amongst its snow.

11 Her blessed bosom moderately rose
  With two soft mounts of lilies, whose fair top
  A pair of pretty sister cherries chose,
  And there their living crimson lifted up.
    The milky countenance of the hills confessed
    What kind of springs within had made their nest.

12 So leggiadrous were her snowy hands
   That pleasure moved as any finger stirred :
   Her virgin waxen arms were precious bands
   And chains of love: her waist itself did gird
       With its own graceful slenderness, and tie
       Up delicacy's best epitome.

13 Fair politure walked all her body over,
   And symmetry rejoiced in every part;
   Soft and white sweetness was her native cover,
   From every member beauty shot a dart:
       From heaven to earth, from head to foot I mean,
       No blemish could by envy's self be seen.

14 This was the first-born queen of gallantry;
   All gems compounded into one rich stone,
   All sweets knit into one conspiracy;
   A constellation of all stars in one;
       Who, when she was presented to their view,
       Both paradise and nature dazzled grew.

15 Phœbus, who rode in glorious scorn's career
   About the world, no sooner spied her face,
   But fain he would have lingered, from his sphere
   On this, though less, yet sweeter, heaven, to gaze
       Till shame enforced him to lash on again,
       And clearer wash him in the western main.

16 The smiling air was tickled with his high
   Prerogative of uncontrolled bliss,
   Embracing with entirest liberty
   A body soft, and sweet, and chaste as his.
       All odorous gales that had but strength to stir
       Came flocking in to beg perfumes of her.

17 The marigold her garish love forgot,
   And turned her homage to these fairer eyes;
   All flowers looked up, and dutifully shot
   Their wonder hither, whence they saw arise
      Unparching courteous lustre, which instead
      Of fire, soft joy's irradiations spread.

18 The sturdiest trees, affected by her dear
   Delightful presence, could not choose but melt
   At their hard pith; whilst all the birds whose clear
   Pipes tossed mirth about the branches, felt
      The influence of her looks; for having let
      Their song fall down, their eyes on her they set.

TO THE MEMORY OF HIS WIFE.

1 Sweet soul, how goodly was the temple which
   Heaven pleased to make thy earthly habitation!
   Built all of graceful delicacy, rich
   In symmetry, and of a dangerous fashion
      For youthful eyes, had not the saint within
      Governed the charms of her enamouring shrine.

2 How happily compendious didst thou make
   My study when I was the lines to draw
   Of genuine beauty! never put to take
   Long journeys was my fancy; still I saw
      At home my copy, and I knew 'twould be
      But beauty's wrong further to seek than thee.

3 Full little knew the world (for I as yet
   In studied silence hugged my secret bliss)
   How facile was my Muse's task, when set
   Virtue's and grace's features to express!
      For whilst accomplished thou wert in my sight
      I nothing had to do, but look and write.

4 How sadly parted are those words; since I
  Must now be writing, but no more can look!
  Yet in my heart thy precious memory,
  So deep is graved, that from this faithful book,
    Truly transcribed, thy character shall shine;
    Nor shall thy death devour what was divine.

5 Hear then, O all soft-hearted turtles, hear
  What you alone profoundly will resent:
  A bird of your pure feather 'tis whom here
  Her desolate mate remaineth to lament,
    Whilst she is flown to meet her dearer love,
    And sing among the winged choir above.

6 Twelve times the glorious sovereign of day
  Had made his progress, and in every inn
  Whose golden signs through all his radiant way
  So high are hung, as often lodged been,
    Since in the sacred knot this noble she
    Deigned to be tied to (then how happy) me.

7 Tied, tied we were so intimately, that
  We straight were sweetly lost in one another.
  Thus when two notes in music's wedlock knit,
  They in one concord blended are together:
    For nothing now our life but music was;
    Her soul the treble made, and mine the base.

8 How at the needless question would she smile,
  When asked what she desired or counted fit?
  Still bidding me examine mine own will,
  And read the surest·answer ready writ.
    So centred was her heart in mine, that she
    Would own no wish, if first not wished by me.

9 Delight was no such thing to her, if I
  Relished it not: the palate of her pleasure
  Carefully watched what mine could taste, and by
  That standard her content resolved to measure.
      By this rare art of sweetness did she prove
      That though she joyed, yet all her joy was love.

10 So was her grief: for wronged herself she held
   If I were sad alone; her share, alas!
   And more than so, in all my sorrows' field
   She duly reaped: and here alone she was
       Unjust to me.   Ah! dear injustice, which
       Mak'st me complain that I was loved too much!
       *   *   *   *   *   *
11 She ne'er took post to keep an equal pace
   Still with the newest modes, which swiftly run:
   She never was perplexed to hear her lace
   Accused for six months' old, when first put on:
       She laid no watchful leaguers, costly vain,
       Intelligence with fashions to maintain.

12 On a pin's point she ne'er held consultation,
   Nor at her glass's strict tribunal brought
   Each plait to scrupulous examination:
   Ashamed she was that Titan's coach about
       Half heaven should sooner wheel, than she could
           pass
       Through all the petty stages of her dress.

13 No gadding itch e'er spurred her to delight
   In needless sallies; none but civil care
   Of friendly correspondence could invite
   Her out of doors; unless she·'pointed were
       By visitations from Heaven's hand, where she
       Might make her own in tender sympathy.
   322

14 Abroad, she counted but her prison: home,
  Home was the region of her liberty.
  Abroad diverson thronged, and left no room
  For zeal's set task, and virtue's business free :
      Home was her less encumbered scene, though there
      Angels and gods she knew spectators were.
  *   *   *   *   *   *

15 This weaned her heart from things below,
  And kindled it with strong desire to gain
  Her hope's high aim.   Life could no longer now
  Flatter her love, or make her prayers refrain
      From begging, yet with humble resignation,
      To be dismissed from her mortal station.

16 Oh, how she welcomed her courteous pain,
  And languished with most serene content !
  No paroxysms could make her once complain,
  Nor suffered she her patience to be spent
      Before her life ; contriving thus to yield
      To her disease, and yet not lose the field.

17 This trying furnace wasted day by day
  (What she herself had always counted dross)
  Her mortal mansion, which so ruined lay,
  That of the goodly fabric nothing was
      Remaining now, but skin and bone; refined
      Together were her body and her mind.

18 At length the fatal hour—sad hour to me !—
  Released the longing soul : no ejulation
  Tolled her knell ; no dying agony
  Frowned in her death ; but in that lamb-like fashion
      In which she lived ('O righteous heaven !' said I,
      Who closed her dear eyes,) she had leave to die.

19 O ever-precious soul! yet shall that flight
   Of thine not snatch thee from thy wonted nest:
   Here shalt thou dwell, here shalt thou live in spite
   Of any death—here in this faithful breast.
     Unworthy 'tis, I know, by being mine;
     Yet nothing less, since long it has been thine.

20 Accept thy dearer portraiture, which I
   Have on my other Psyche fixed here;
   Since her ideal beauties signify
   The truth of thine: as for her spots, they are
     Thy useful foil, and shall inservient be
     But to enhance and more illustrate thee.

IMPERIAL ROME PERSONIFIED.

1 Thus came the monster to his dearest place
   On earth, a palace wondrous large and high,
   Which on seven mountains' heads enthroned was;
     Thus, by its sevenfold tumour, copying
     The number of the horns which crowned its king.

2 Of dead men's bones were all the exterior walls,
   Raised to a fair but formidable height; ¡
   In answer to which strange materials,
   A graff of dreadful depth and breadth
     Upon the works, filled with a piteous flood
     Of innocently-pure and holy blood.

3 Those awful birds, whose joy is ravenous war,
   Strong-taloned eagles, perched upon the head
   Of every turret, took their prospect far
   And wide about the world; and questioned
     Each wind that travelled by, to know if they
     Could tell them news of any bloody prey.

4 The inner bulwarks, raised of shining brass,
 With firmitude and pride were buttressed.
 The gate of polished steel wide opened was
 To entertain those throngs, who offered
   Their slavish necks to take the yoke, and which
   That city's tyrant did the world bewitch.

5 For she had wisely ordered it to be
 Gilded with Liberty's enchanting name;
 Whence cheated nations, who before were free,
 Into her flattering chains for freedom came.
   Thus her strange conquests overtook the sun
   Who rose and set in her dominion.

6 But thick within the line erected were
 Innumerable prisons, plated round
 With massy iron and with jealous fear:
 And in those forts of barbarism, profound
   And miry dungeons, where contagious stink,
   Cold, anguish, horror, had their dismal sink.

7 In these, pressed down with chains of fretting brass,
 Ten thousand innocent lambs did bleating lie;
 Whose groans, reported by the hollow place,
 Summoned compassion from the passers by;
   Whom they, alas ! no less relentless found,
   Than was the brass which them to sorrow bound.

8 For they designed for the shambles were
 To feast the tyrant's greedy cruelty,
 Who could be gratified with no fare
 But such delight of savage luxury.

END.

1 Sweet End, thou sea of satisfaction, which
  The weary streams unto thy bosom tak'st;
  The springs unto the spring thou first doth reach,
  And, by thine inexhausted kindness, mak'st
    Them fall so deep in love with thee, that through
    All rocks and mountains to thy arms they flow.

2 Thou art the centre, in whose close embrace,
  From all the wild circumference, each line
  Directly runs to find its resting-place:
  Upon their swiftest wings, to perch on thine
    Ennobling breast, which is their only butt,
    The arrows of all high desires are shot.

3 All labours pant and languish after thee,
  Stretching their longest arms to catch their bliss;
  Which in the way, how sweet soe'er it be,
  They never find; and therefore on they press
    Further and further, till desired thou,
    Their only crown, meet'st their ambition's brow.

4 With smiles the ploughman to the smiling spring
  Returns not answer, but is jealous till
  His patient hopes thy happy season bring
  Unto their ripeness with his corn, and fill
    His barns with plenteous sheaves, with joy his
      heart;
    For thou, and none but thou, his harvest art.

5 The no less sweating and industrious lover
  Lays not his panting heart to rest upon

Kind looks and gracious promises, which hover
On love's outside, and may as soon be gone
   As easily they came ; but strives to see
   His hopes and nuptials ratified by thee.

6 The traveller suspecteth every way,
Though they thick traced and fairly beaten be ;
Nor is secure but that his leader may
Step into some mistake as well as he ;
   Or that his strength may fail him ; till he win
   Possession of thee, his wished inn.

7 Nobly besmeared with Olympic dust,
The hardy runner prosecutes his race
With obstinate celerity, in trust
That thou wilt wipe and glorify his face :
   His prize's soul art thou, whose precious sake
   Makes him those mighty pains with pleasure take.

8 The mariner will trust no winds, although
Upon his sails they blow fair flattery ;
No tides which, with all fawning smoothness, flow
Can charm his fears into security ;
   He credits none but thee, who art his bay,
   To which, through calms and storms, he hunts his
      way.

9 And so have I, cheered up with hopes at last
To double thee, endured a tedious sea ;
Through public foaming tempests have I passed ;
Through flattering calms of private suavity ;
   Through interrupting company's thick press ;
   And through the lake of mine own laziness :

10 Through many sirens' charms, which me invited
   To dance to ease's tunes, the tunes in fashion;
   Through many cross, misgiving thoughts, which
         frighted
   My jealous pen; and through the conjuration
     Of ignorant and envious censures, which
     Implacably against all poems itch:

11 But chiefly those which venture in a way
   That yet no Muse's feet have chose to trace;
   Which trust that Psyche and her Jesus may
   Adorn a verse with as becoming grace
     As Venus and her son; that truth may be
     A nobler theme than lies and vanity.

12 Which broach no Aganippe's streams, but those
   Where virgin souls without a blush may bathe;
   Which dare the boisterous multitude oppose
   With gentle numbers; which despise the wrath
     Of galled sin; which think not fit to trace
     Or Greek or Roman song with slavish pace.

13 And seeing now I am in ken of thee,
   The harbour which inflamed my desire,
   And with this steady patience ballas'd[1] me
   In my uneven road; I am on fire,
     Till into thy embrace myself I throw,
     And on the shore hang up my finished vow.

[1] 'Ballas'd:' ballasted.

MISCELLANEOUS PIECES.

FROM ROBERT HEATH.

WHAT IS LOVE?

1 'Tis a child of fancy's getting,
   Brought up between hope and fear,
Fed with smiles, grown by uniting
   Strong, and so kept by desire:
'Tis a perpetual vestal fire
     Never dying,
Whose smoke like incense doth aspire,
     Upwards flying.

2 It is a soft magnetic stone,
   Attracting hearts by sympathy,
Binding up close two souls in one,
   Both discoursing secretly:
'Tis the true Gordian knot, that ties
     Yet ne'er unbinds,
Fixing thus two lovers' eyes,
     As well as minds.

3 'Tis the spheres' heavenly harmony,
   Where two skilful hands do strike;
And every sound expressively
   Marries sweetly with the like:
'Tis the world's everlasting chain
     That all things tied,
And bid them, like the fixed wain,
     Unmoved to bide.

PROTEST OF LOVE.

When I thee all o'er do view
I all o'er must love thee too.

By that smooth forehead, where's expressed
The candour of thy peaceful breast,
By those fair twin-like stars that shine,
And by those apples of thine eyne:
By the lambkins and the kids
Playing 'bout thy fair eyelids:
By each peachy-blossomed cheek,
And thy satin skin, more sleek
And white than Flora's whitest lilies,
Or the maiden daffodillies:
By that ivory porch, thy nose:
By those double-blanched rows
Of teeth, as in pure coral set:
By each azure rivulet,
Running in thy temples, and
Those flowery meadows 'twixt them stand:
By each pearl-tipt ear by nature, as
On each a jewel pendent was:
By those lips all dewed with bliss,
Made happy in each other's kiss.

TO CLARASTELLA.

Oh, those smooth, soft, and ruby lips,
   *   *   *   *   *
Whose rosy and vermilion hue
Betrays the blushing thoughts in you:
Whose fragrant, aromatic breath
Would revive dying saints from death,
Whose siren-like, harmonious air
Speaks music and enchants the ear;
Who would not hang, and fixed there
Wish he might know no other sphere?
Oh for a charm to make the sun
Drunk, and forget his motion!

Oh that some palsy or lame gout
Would cramp old Time's diseased foot!
Or that I might or mould or clip
His speedy wings, whilst on her lip
I quench my thirsty appetite
With the life-honey dwells on it!

*   *   *   *

Then on his holy altar, I
Would sacrifice eternally,
Offering one long-continued mine
Of golden pleasures to thy shrine.

BY VARIOUS AUTHORS.

MY MIND TO ME A KINGDOM IS.

(FROM BYRD'S 'PSALMS, SONNETS,' ETC.   1588.)

1 My mind to me a kingdom is,
    Such perfect joy therein I find,
That it excels all other bliss
    That God or nature hath assigned:
Though much I want that most would have,
Yet still my mind forbids to crave.

2 No princely port, nor wealthy store,
    Nor force to win a victory;
No wily wit to salve a sore,
    No shape to win a loving eye;
To none of these I yield as thrall,
For why, my mind despise them all.

3 I see that plenty surfeits oft,
    And hasty climbers soonest fall;
I see that such as are aloft,
    Mishap doth threaten most of all;

These get with toil, and keep with fear:
Such cares my mind can never bear.

4 I press to bear no haughty sway;
   I wish no more than may suffice;
I do no more than well I may.
   Look what I want, my mind supplies;
Lo, thus I triumph like a king,
My mind's content with anything.

5 I laugh not at another's loss,
   Nor grudge not at another's gain;
No worldly waves my mind can toss;
   I brook that is another's bane;
I fear no foe, nor fawn on friend;
I loathe not life, nor dread mine end.

6 My wealth is health and perfect ease,
   And conscience clear my chief defence;
I never seek by bribes to please,
   Nor by desert to give offence;
Thus do I live, thus will I die;
Would all do so as well as I!

THE OLD AND YOUNG COURTIER.

1 An old song made by an aged old pate,
Of an old worshipful gentleman, who had a great
   estate,
That kept a brave old house at a bountiful rate,
And an old porter to relieve the poor at his gate:
     Like an old courtier of the queen's,
     And the queen's old courtier.

2 With an old lady, whose anger one word assuages;
They every quarter paid their old servants their wages,

And never knew what belonged to coachmen, foot-
    men, nor pages,
But kept twenty old fellows with blue coats and
    badges:
        Like an old courtier, &c.

3 With an old study filled full of learned old books,
With an old reverend chaplain, you might know him
    by his looks,
With an old buttery hatch worn quite off the hooks,
And an old kitchen, that maintained half-a-dozen old
    cooks:
        Like an old courtier, &c.

4 With an old hall, hung about with pikes, guns, and
    bows,
With old swords and bucklers, that had borne many
    shrewd blows,
And an old frieze coat, to cover his worship's trunk-
    hose,
And a cup of old sherry, to comfort his copper nose:
        Like an old courtier, &c.

5 With a good old fashion, when Christmas was come,
To call in all his old neighbours with bagpipe and
    drum,
With good cheer enough to furnish every old room,
And old liquor able to make a cat speak, and man
    dumb:
        Like an old courtier, &c.

6 With an old falconer, huntsmen, and a kennel of
    hounds,
That never hawked, nor hunted, but in his own
    grounds;

Who, like a wise man, kept himself within his own
    bounds,
And when he died, gave every child a thousand good
    pounds:
       Like an old courtier, &c.

7 But to his eldest son his house and lands he assigned,
Charging him in his will to keep the old bountiful
    mind,
To be good to his old tenants, and to his neighbours
    be kind:
But in the ensuing ditty you shall hear how he was
    inclined:
       Like a young courtier of the king's,
       And the king's young courtier.

8 Like a flourishing young gallant, newly come to his
    land,
Who keeps a brace of painted madams at his com-
    mand,
And takes up a thousand pounds upon his father's
    land,
And gets drunk in a tavern till he can neither go
    nor stand:
       Like a young courtier, &c.

9 With a newfangled lady, that is dainty, nice, and spare,
Who never knew what belonged to good housekeeping
    or care,
Who buys gaudy-coloured fans to play with wanton
    air,
And seven or eight different dressings of other women's
    hair:
       Like a young courtier, &c.

10 With a new-fashioned hall, built where the old one
    stood,
  Hung round with new pictures that do the poor no
    good,
  With a fine marble chimney, wherein burns neither
    coal nor wood,
  And a new smooth shovel-board, whereon no victuals
    ne'er stood:
      Like a young courtier, &c.

11 With a new study, stuffed full of pamphlets and plays,
  And a new chaplain, that swears faster than he prays,
  With a new buttery hatch, that opens once in four or
    five days,
  And a new French cook, to devise fine kickshaws and
    toys:
      Like a young courtier, &c.

12 With a new fashion, when Christmas is drawing on,
  On a new journey to London straight we all must be-
    gone,
  And leave none to keep house, but our new porter
    John,
  Who relieves the poor with a thump on the back with
    a stone:
      Like a young courtier, &c.

13 With a new gentleman usher, whose carriage is com-
    plete,
  With a new coachman, footmen, and pages to carry
    up the meat,
  With a waiting gentlewoman, whose dressing is very
    neat,
  Who, when her lady has dined, lets the servants not eat:
      Like a young courtier, &c.

14 With new titles of honour, bought with his father's
    old gold,
  For which sundry of his ancestors' old manors are
    sold;
  And this is the course most of our new gallants hold,
  Which makes that good housekeeping is now grown
    so cold
      Among the young courtiers of the king,
      Or the king's young courtiers.

THERE IS A GARDEN IN HER FACE.

(FROM 'AN HOUR'S RECREATION IN MUSIC,' BY RICH. ALISON.   1606.)

1 There is a garden in her face,
    Where roses and white lilies grow;
  A heavenly paradise is that place,
    Wherein all pleasant fruits do grow;
  There cherries grow that none may buy,
  Till cherry-ripe themselves do cry.

2 Those cherries fairly do enclose
    Of orient pearl a double row,
  Which when her lovely laughter shows,
    They look like rose-buds filled with snow:
  Yet them no peer nor prince may buy,
  Till cherry-ripe themselves do cry.

3 Her eyes like angels watch them still;
    Her brows like bended bows do stand,
  Threatening with piercing frowns to kill
    All that approach with eye or hand
  These sacred cherries to come nigh,
  Till cherry-ripe themselves do cry.

HALLO, MY FANCY.

1 In melancholic fancy,
   Out of myself,
In the vulcan dancy,
   All the world surveying,
   Nowhere staying,
Just like a fairy elf;
Out o'er the tops of highest mountains skipping,
Out o'er the hills, the trees, and valleys tripping,
Out o'er the ocean seas, without an oar or shipping.
   Hallo, my fancy, whither wilt thou go?

2 Amidst the misty vapours,
   Fain would I know
What doth cause the tapers;
   Why the clouds benight us
   And affright us,
While we travel here below.
Fain would I know what makes the roaring thunder,
And what these lightnings be that rend the clouds
   asunder,
And what these comets are on which we gaze and
   wonder.
   Hallo, my fancy, whither wilt thou go?

3 Fain would I know the reason
   Why the little ant,
All the summer season,
   Layeth up provision
   On condition
To know no winter's want:
And how housewives, that are so good and painful,

Do unto their husbands prove so good and gainful;
And why the lazy drones to them do prove disdainful.
        Hallo, my fancy, whither wilt thou go?

4 Ships, ships, I will descry you
        Amidst the main;
    I will come and try you
    What you are protecting,
        And projecting,
    What 's your end and aim.
One goes abroad for merchandise and trading,
Another stays to keep his country from invading,
A third is coming home with rich wealth of lading.
        Hallo, my fancy, whither wilt thou go?

5. When I look before me,
        There I do behold
    There 's none that sees or knows me;
    All the world 's a-gadding,
        Running madding;
    None doth his station hold.
He that is below envieth him that riseth,
And he that is above, him that 's below despiseth,
So every man his plot and counter-plot deviseth.
        Hallo, my fancy, whither wilt thou go?

6 Look, look, what bustling
        Here I do espy;
    Each another jostling,
    Every one turmoiling,
        The other spoiling,
    As I did pass them by.
One sitteth musing in a dumpish passion,

Another hangs his head, because he's out of fashion,
A third is fully bent on sport and recreation.
    Hallo, my fancy, whither wilt thou go?

    7 Amidst the foamy ocean,
        Fain would I know
    What doth cause the motion,
        And returning
        In its journeying,
    And doth so seldom swerve!
And how these little fishes that swim beneath salt water,
Do never blind their eye; methinks it is a matter
An inch above the reach of old Erra Pater!
    Hallo, my fancy, whither wilt thou go?

    8 Fain would I be resolved
        How things are done;
    And where the bull was calved
        Of bloody Phalaris,
    And where the tailor is
    That works to the man i' the moon!
Fain would I know how Cupid aims so rightly;
And how these little fairies do dance and leap so lightly;
And where fair Cynthia makes her ambles nightly.
    Hallo, my fancy, whither wilt thou go!

    9 In conceit like Phæton,
        I'll mount Phœbus' chair;
    Having ne'er a hat on,
        All my hair a-burning
        In my journeying,
    Hurrying through the air.
Fain would I hear his fiery horses neighing,

And see how they on foamy bits are playing;
All the stars and planets I will be surveying!
    Hallo, my fancy, whither wilt thou go?

  10 Oh, from what ground of nature
      Doth the pelican,
    That self-devouring creature,
      Prove so froward
      And untoward,
    Her vitals for to strain?
And why the subtle fox, while in death's wounds is lying,
Doth not lament his pangs by howling and by crying;
And why the milk-white swan doth sing when she's a-
  dying.
    Hallo, my fancy, whither wilt thou go?

  11 Fain would I conclude this,
      At least make essay,
    What similitude is;
      Why fowls of a feather
      Flock and fly together,
    And lambs know beasts of prey:
How Nature's alchemists, these small laborious creatures,
Acknowledge still a prince in ordering their matters,
And suffer none to live, who slothing lose their features.
    Hallo, my fancy, whither wilt thou go?

  12 I'm rapt with admiration,
      When I do ruminate,
    Men of an occupation,
      How each one calls him brother,
      Yet each envieth other,
      And yet still intimate!

Yea, I admire to see some natures further sundered,
Than antipodes to us.   Is it not to be wondered,
In myriads ye'll find, of one mind scarce a hundred!
    Hallo, my fancy, whither wilt thou go?

13 What multitude of notions
    Doth perturb my pate,
  Considering the motions,
  How the heavens are preserved,
    And this world served,
  In moisture, light, and heat!
If one spirit sits the outmost circle turning,
Or one turns another continuing in journeying,
If rapid circles' motion be that which they call burning!
    Hallo, my fancy, whither wilt thou go?

14 Fain also would I prove this,
    By considering
  What that which you call love is:
  Whether it be a folly
    Or a melancholy,
  Or some heroic thing!
Fain I'd have it proved, by one whom love hath wounded,
And fully upon one his desire hath founded,
Whom nothing else could please though the world were
    rounded.
    Hallo, my fancy, whither wilt thou go?

15 To know this world's centre,
    Height, depth, breadth, and length,
  Fain would I adventure
  To search the hid attractions
    Of magnetic actions,
  And adamantic strength.

Fain would I know, if in some lofty mountain,
Where the moon sojourns, if there be trees or fountain;
If there be beasts of prey, or yet be fields to hunt in.
     Hallo, my fancy, whither wilt thou go?

16 Fain would I have it tried
    By experiment,
By none can be denied;
If in this bulk of nature,
There be voids less or greater,
    Or all remains complete?
Fain would I know if beasts have any reason;
If falcons killing eagles do commit a treason;
If fear of winter's want makes swallows fly the season.
     Hallo, my fancy, whither wilt thou go;

17 Hallo, my fancy, hallo,
    Stay, stay at home with me,
I can thee no longer follow,
For thou hast betrayed me,
    And bewrayed me;
It is too much for thee.
Stay, stay at home with me; leave off thy lofty soaring;
Stay thou at home with me, and on thy books be poring;
For he that goes abroad, lays little up in storing:
Thou 'rt welcome home, my fancy, welcome home to me.

    ' Alas, poor scholar !
    Whither wilt thou go?'
       or
'Strange alterations which at this time be,
There's many did think they never should see.'

THE FAIRY QUEEN.

1   Come, follow, follow me,
You, fairy elves that be;
Which circle on the green,
Come, follow Mab, your queen.
Hand in hand let's dance around,
For this place is fairy ground.

2   When mortals are at rest,
And snoring in their nest;
Unheard and unespied,
Through keyholes we do glide;
Over tables, stools, and shelves,
We trip it with our fairy elves.

3   And if the house be foul
With platter, dish, or bowl,
Up-stairs we nimbly creep,
And find the sluts asleep:
There we pinch their arms and thighs;
None escapes, nor none espies.

4   But if the house be swept,
And from uncleanness kept,
We praise the household maid,
And duly she is paid;
For we use, before we go,
To drop a tester in her shoe.

5   Upon a mushroom's head
Our tablecloth we spread;
A grain of rye or wheat
Is manchet which we eat;
Pearly drops of dew we drink,
In acorn cups filled to the brink.

6 The brains of nightingales,
  With unctuous fat of snails,
  Between two cockles stewed,
  Is meat that's easily chewed;
 Tails of worms, and marrow of mice,
 Do make a dish that's wondrous nice.

7 The grasshopper, gnat, and fly,
  Serve us for our minstrelsy;
  Grace said, we dance a while,
  And so the time beguile;
 And if the moon doth hide her head,
 The glow-worm lights us home to bed.

8 On tops of dewy grass
  So nimbly do we pass,
  The young and tender stalk
  Ne'er bends when we do walk;
 Yet in the morning may be seen
 Where we the night before have been.

END OF VOL. II.

BALLANTYNE AND COMPANY, PRINTERS, EDINBURGH.